SYDNEY HARBOUR HOSPITAL: BELLA'S WISHLIST

BY
EMILY FORBES

DOCTOR'S MILE-HIGH FLING

BY
TINA BECKETT

MILLS & BOON

SYDNEY HARBOUR HOSPITAL: BELLA'S WISHLIST

BY
EMILY FORBES

To Marion, Alison, Amy, Fiona, Melanie, Fi and Carol.
Thank you for making this such a wonderful experience.
It was an absolute pleasure working with you all!
And to Lucy and Flo, thank you both for all your hard work
in making this series something we can all be proud of.

First published in Great Britain 2012
by Mills & Boon, an imprint of Harlequin (UK) Limited.
Harlequin (UK) Limited, Eton House, 18-24 Paradise Road,
Richmond, Surrey TW9 1SR

© Harlequin Books S.A. 2012

Special thanks and acknowledgment are given to Emily Forbes for her contribution to the *Sydney Harbour Hospital* series.

ISBN: 978 0 263 89176 8

Harlequin (UK) policy is to use papers that are natural, renewable and recyclable products and made from wood grown in sustainable forests. The logging and manufacturing process conform to the legal environmental regulations of the country of origin.

Printed and bound in Spain
by Blackprint CPI, Barcelona

**Welcome to the world
of Sydney Harbour Hospital
(or *SHH*… for short—
because secrets never stay hidden for long!)**

Looking out over cosmopolitan Sydney Harbour, Australia's premier teaching hospital is a hive of round-the-clock activity—with a *very* active hospital grapevine.

With the most renowned (and gorgeous!) doctors in Sydney working side by side, professional and sensual tensions run sky-high—there's *always* plenty of romantic rumours to gossip about…

Who's been kissing who in the on-call room? What's going on between legendary heart surgeon Finn Kennedy and tough-talking A&E doctor Evie Lockheart? And what's wrong with Finn?

Find out in this enthralling new eight-book continuity from Mills & Boon® Medical™ Romance—indulge yourself with eight helpings of romance, emotion and gripping medical drama!

Sydney Harbour Hospital
*From saving lives to sizzling seduction,
these doctors are the very best!*

Sydney Harbour Hospital

*Sexy surgeons, dedicated doctors,
scandalous secrets, on-call dramas…*

**Welcome to the world of Sydney Harbour Hospital
(or *SHH*… for short—because secrets never stay hidden for long!)**

In February new nurse Lily got caught up in
the hotbed of hospital gossip in
**SYDNEY HARBOUR HOSPITAL: LILY'S SCANDAL
by Marion Lennox**

And gorgeous paediatrician Teo came to single mum Zoe's rescue in
**SYDNEY HARBOUR HOSPITAL: ZOE'S BABY
by Alison Roberts**

In March sexy Sicilian playboy Luca finally met his match in
**SYDNEY HARBOUR HOSPITAL: LUCA'S BAD GIRL
by Amy Andrews**

Then in April Hayley opened Tom's eyes to love in
**SYDNEY HARBOUR HOSPITAL: TOM'S REDEMPTION
by Fiona Lowe**

Last month heiress Lexi learned to put the past behind her…
**SYDNEY HARBOUR HOSPITAL: LEXI'S SECRET
by Melanie Milburne**

This month adventurer Charlie helps shy Bella fulfil her dreams—
and find love on the way!
**SYDNEY HARBOUR HOSPITAL: BELLA'S WISHLIST
by Emily Forbes**

Single mum Emily gives no-strings-attached surgeon Marco
a reason to stay in July:
**SYDNEY HARBOUR HOSPITAL: MARCO'S TEMPTATION
by Fiona McArthur**

And finally join us in August as Ava and James
realise their marriage really is worth saving in
**SYDNEY HARBOUR HOSPITAL: AVA'S RE-AWAKENING
by Carol Marinelli**

And not forgetting *Sydney Harbour Hospital's* legendary heart surgeon
Finn Kennedy. This brooding maverick keeps his women on hospital
rotation… But can new doc Evie Lockheart unlock the secrets to his
guarded heart? Find out in this enthralling new eight-book continuity
from Mills & Boon® Medical™ Romance.

A collection impossible to resist!

**These books are also available in eBook format
from www.millsandboon.co.uk**

PROLOGUE

'LEXI, please, can't you do this for me?' Bella Lockheart begged her younger sister.

Bella was feeling dreadful. Her chest was hurting and every breath she took was a struggle. Her temperature was escalating with every passing minute and it felt as though her forehead was on fire. She wanted to be upstairs, in bed, not sitting at one end of her father's massive dining room table that comfortably seated eighteen people. She wanted to close her eyes and sleep. The only reason she'd agreed to meet with her sisters was because she wanted the chance to try to persuade Lexi to do this one thing for her.

Lexi was sitting at the head of the table with Bella on her left and their older sister Evie on her right. Evie had joined them at Lexi's invitation to begin planning what Lexi described as 'Sydney's society wedding of the decade' and, knowing Lexi and her talent for planning events, her wedding to cardiothoracic surgeon Sam Bailey would be one of the most spectacular events Sydney had witnessed for some time. That was unsurprising really—Lexi had plenty of experience as she was employed by her father's multi-million-dollar empire to run the events side of his company, and Lexi generally got what she wanted. Bella had some doubts about whether Sam was as keen on the idea of a huge wedding as Lexi was but if she'd learnt anything about Sam since he'd proposed to her sister it was that he wouldn't sweat the small stuff, and if an enormous wedding made Lexi happy, that's what she would get. Their father would never quibble either; nothing was ever too much trouble, expense or fuss for Lexi. Richard loved an extravaganza as much as Lexi did.

Bella knew the only way to get Lexi to move quickly on the wedding was to play the only card she had. 'I want to see you get married and the longer you wait the less chance I'll have of being there. Please.'

They all knew the odds of Bella seeing her next birthday weren't good but Bella had *never* played this card before. Not with her father, who had pretty much ignored her for her entire life, or with her mother, who couldn't cope and had replaced her family with bottles of gin, or with her sisters, who had always been there to support and protect her. But she figured if there ever was a time to play this card, it was now.

As Bella watched Lexi, waiting for her response, she was aware that Evie had stopped flicking through the pile of bridal magazines and was watching them both. The highly polished wood surface of the antique table reflected their images. The golden highlights in Evie's brown hair shone in the surface of the table and Lexi's platinum-blonde hair glowed in the reflection, while the dark auburn of Bella's curly locks was absorbed into the wood, making her seem dimmer in comparison. A sigh escaped Bella's lips. Seeing herself as a duller reflection of her sisters was nothing new. She'd had twenty-six years to get used to the idea that she wasn't as beautiful, intelligent or amusing as her two sisters, although she hoped that her kind heart went some way towards redeeming her character.

Not that it seemed to count for anything as far as her parents were concerned. She'd given up trying to mend those relationships, although she was blowed if she would give up on her sisters. They were the most important people in her world and she did not intend to miss out on seeing her younger sister get married. She *had* to convince Lexi to set a date for her wedding and make it soon. She'd missed out on an awful lot of things in her relatively short life and there was no way she was going to sit back and miss out on this. Lexi had to listen to her.

'You only need a month and a day to register. You could be married before Christmas,' she insisted.

'I need time,' Lexi replied.

Time. The one thing Bella didn't have. She knew that. Lexi knew it too, so why wouldn't she agree?

'Time for what?' Bella countered. 'I can't see why you'd want to wait. If I had the chance to get married, I'd grab it.'

All three of them knew what a romantic Bella was. Her favourite pastime was watching romantic movies, comedies, dramas, anything, as long as it had a happy ending. It was looking increasingly unlikely that she would get her own happy ending so she had to enjoy other people's. She adored weddings, she'd been glued to the television for the most recent British Royal wedding and avidly followed the lives of modern-day princesses in the magazines. But her own sister's happy ending was bound to be so much better than anything she could watch on television. Surely Lexi couldn't deny her this?

'I want time to find the perfect dress,' Lexi said.

'I'll design you the perfect dress.' Normally Bella would offer to make it too, but she knew she'd never have time to design and make a wedding dress, not if she wanted the wedding to take place this year. In a parallel universe her dream was to be a fashion designer and to see her sister walk down the aisle in something she'd created would be the icing on the cake for a romantic like her. But she'd have to settle for designing the dress and have someone else make it. Their father would probably fly Lexi to Hong Kong or even Paris to get it made. Money was no object. Richard Lockheart was phenomenally wealthy and Lexi was the apple of his eye. Everybody knew that.

'Look,' Bella said as she opened the sketch book that was lying on the table in front of her. Her sketch book was never far from her side. She turned some pages and then spun the book to face Lexi. 'I've already started.' The large page was covered with half a dozen wedding dresses—a halterneck, a strapless version, some with full skirts, some in figure-skimming satin. 'You just need to tell me which bits you like and I promise you'll be the most beautiful bride but, please, don't wait too long. You *know* time is running out for me, Sam told you that. If you won't listen to me, would you at least listen to him?' Bella paused to catch her breath. She could feel her chest tightening and could hear herself wheezing. 'What do you think, Evie? You agree with me, don't you?'

'I think you have a valid point but it is Lexi and Sam's decision. It's their wedding.' Bella would have argued if she'd had the breath to spare but the end of Evie's answer was partially drowned out by a coughing fit. Bella's slim frame shook with each spasm.

Lexi stood up. 'I'll get you a glass of water.'

'It's all right,' Bella replied as the coughs subsided and she caught her breath, 'I can get it.' She pushed her chair back from the table and stood. She looked at Evie and dipped her head slightly towards Lexi, silently imploring Evie to intercede on her behalf. She knew Evie would understand the signal. Having spent so much of their life relying on each other, all three sisters could read each other instinctively.

'Perhaps you should talk it over with Sam,' Bella heard

Evie suggest as she went to the kitchen to pour herself a glass of water and mix up her salt replacement solution. She was feeling quite feverish now and she knew she was in danger of dehydrating more rapidly than usual if she was running a temperature.

Evie waited until Bella had time to reach the kitchen and be out of earshot. As so often happened, her younger sisters deferred to her to solve any difference of opinion between them. At five years older than Bella and seven years older than Lexi she had taken over mothering duties at the tender age of nine when the girls' mother had walked out and left them with their father, to return only sporadically over the ensuing years. There had been a succession of nannies, with varying degrees of success, and Evie had adopted the role of mother and still maintained it twenty-two years later. Evie never minded the responsibility but she did wonder why she needed to act as referee in this case. Why was Lexi so resistant to Bella's request?

'What's the problem, Lex? You know Bella's right. She might not be around in six months. Why do you want to wait?'

Lexi's deep blue eyes shimmered with unshed tears. She fidgeted with Bella's sketch book, which lay on the table in front of her, absentmindedly doodling on the clean pages. 'I can't think like that. I can't stand the thought of Bella not being here.'

'That's why I think you should consider getting married sooner rather than later.'

'But what if we set a date that's soon and Bella gets sick again? She could be in hospital on the day of the wedding. Or what if she's in surgery? If I wait until Bella is okay, we'll all get a happy ending.'

'But Bella might not get her happy ending. You know

that, don't you?' Evie said gently. 'If you wait, Bella might not be there anyway. She's only asking you for one thing.'

Lexi was shaking her head. 'But if I give in then that's like admitting I think she's not going to make it. I don't want to think about her dying. I can't.'

Evie knew Lexi hated the idea of death. She'd been through one traumatic loss already in her life, when she'd terminated a pregnancy, and that made this situation more difficult for her. But she couldn't let her sister bury her head in the sand. Evie had to get her to face reality. 'Please, just agree to talk to Sam about it. If you set a date and you need to change it to accommodate Bella, is that such a big deal? It's certainly not impossible.' Sam knew what Bella's chances were better than anyone, Evie thought. As Bella's specialist and Lexi's fiancé, maybe he would have more success in persuading Lexi.

Before Lexi had a chance to agree or disagree, they were interrupted by the sound of breaking glass coming from the kitchen, followed by a loud thud as something heavy hit the floor. Then there was silence.

'Bella?' Evie and Lexi leapt from their chairs and ran to the kitchen. Broken glass was strewn over the marble bench tops but Bella was nowhere to be seen. Evie raced around the island bench and found Bella collapsed on the tiles surrounded by the remnants of the glass cupboard.

'Bella!' Evie knelt beside her sister, oblivious to the shards of glass that littered the floor. To her relief she could see that Bella was conscious and breathing. 'What happened? Are you hurt?'

Bella's grey eyes were enormous in her pale face. 'Dizzy.' Her words were laboured. 'Cramp.' She was obviously having difficulty with her breathing. 'I grabbed the shelf when I fell. Sorry.'

'Don't worry about the glasses,' Evie said as she brushed

Bella's auburn curls from her face. Her skin was flushed and her forehead was hot. Feverish.

Bella's powdered drink mixture that she used for salt replacement sat on the bench. Evie picked up Bella's wrist and took her pulse, counting the seconds. Her pulse was rapid and Bella's skin under her fingers was dry and lacking its normal elasticity.

Evie ran through Bella's symptoms in her head. A high temperature, dizziness, cramping, rapid pulse rate. 'You're dehydrated,' she said. 'Why didn't you tell us you weren't feeling well?'

Why hadn't she noticed something? Evie accused herself. *She was a doctor, for goodness' sake.*

She knew she'd been distracted by the tension between Lexi and Bella but she still should have known something was wrong. Bella's behaviour should have alerted her. She wasn't normally so insistent or stubborn.

But that didn't explain why she hadn't told them she was feeling unwell. Evie could only assume it was because she didn't want to make a fuss. That was typical of Bella. She'd been unwell more frequently than usual over the past few months and Evie knew she would be trying to pretend everything was normal. But they all knew it wasn't. They all knew Bella's health was going downhill and Evie was furious with herself for not noticing the signs tonight. But there was no time to berate herself now. They needed to get Bella treated, she needed to be in hospital.

'Lexi, ring Sam and tell him to meet us at the hospital,' Evie instructed. 'I'll call an ambulance and then see if you can get a drink into Bella. She needs fluids.'

CHAPTER ONE

BELLA lay on the stretcher in the rear of the ambulance. She was vaguely aware of her surroundings but the activity felt like it was going on around her, independent of her, even though she knew it all related to her. The emergency lights were flashing, it was dark outside and the lights were reflecting back into the interior of the ambulance, bouncing off the walls. The siren was silent, the traffic a constant background noise. Evie was with her in the ambulance, she could hear her talking with the paramedic. Bella could feel the pressure of the oxygen mask on her face, the grip of the oximeter on her finger, the sting of the IV drip in her elbow. She saw Evie take out her phone and heard her leaving a message for their father.

She was hot and sweaty, flushed with a fever and tired, so tired. She wondered what it would be like just to close her eyes and drift off. To never wake again. But she wasn't ready. There were still things she wanted to do and things she wanted to see.

She felt the ambulance come to a halt and the flashing red and blue lights were replaced by harsh fluorescent strip lighting. She knew where they were—in the emergency drop-off zone at Sydney Harbour Hospital. This was where she had spent countless days and nights over the past twenty-six years. It was the closest hospital to the Lockheart family home in the north shore suburb of Mosman and the cardiothoracic ward had become as familiar to Bella as her own bedroom.

But her connection to the hospital went beyond that of a patient. Her great-grandfather had been one of the original founders of the hospital and it was also where Evie worked. Bella couldn't fault the medical care she received here, she just wished she hadn't had to spend so much of her life within these walls.

The rear doors swung open and Bella felt the stretcher moving as she was pulled from the ambulance. A familiar face loomed over her. Sam Bailey, the hospital's newest cardiothoracic surgeon and next big thing, was smiling down at her.

'There you are,' he said. 'I've been stalking the ambulances, waiting for you.'

Sam was her new specialist, but again the connection didn't end there. He was engaged to Lexi, which also made him her future brother-in-law.

Bella tried to smile then realised it wasn't worth the effort as the oxygen mask was hiding her face and she was sure her smile would look more like a grimace. Sam squeezed her hand before he began talking to Evie and the paramedics, getting an update on her condition. Bella lay silently and concentrated on breathing in lungfuls of oxygen. She wasn't required to contribute. She wasn't required to do anything except keep breathing. 'I've notified Cardiothoracics, we'll take her straight up there,' Sam was saying, and Bella closed her eyes against the glare of the fluorescent lights as they began to wheel her inside.

'Evie? Is everything okay?'

Bella heard a familiar voice. She recognised it but her brain was sluggish and she was unable to put a face to the voice. If she opened her eyes she'd solve the mystery but that was too much effort.

'Charlie!'

Evie's reply jogged her memory and Bella was glad she'd kept her eyes closed.

Dr Charlie Maxwell was one of Evie's closest friends and definitely one of her cutest! Bella idolised him. But she kept her eyes closed, not wanting him to see her like this. She pretended that if she couldn't see him, he wouldn't be able to see her.

Charlie was too gorgeous for his own good and she knew she wasn't the only one who thought so. He had a reputation as a charmer and he'd cut a swathe through the female nurses and doctors at Sydney Harbour Hospital and most probably further afield too. Bella had long worshipped him from afar, knowing he'd never look twice at her, certain he saw her just as his friend's little sister. This wasn't a fairy-tale where the handsome prince would suddenly fall in love with the plain girl and sweep her off her feet. This was real life and the safest thing for her to do was to keep her eyes closed and wait for him to go away. That way there was less chance of her embarrassing herself.

'Is everything all right?' he repeated.

'No, not really. It's Bella.'

That was the last thing Bella heard before the paramedics pushed her into the hospital and Evie's voice faded.

Stay with me, Bella wanted to say. She didn't want to be alone even though she knew Evie wouldn't be far behind her.

Bella? Charlie took a second look at the figure on the stretcher. Her face was obscured by the oxygen mask but her hair was distinctive. It could only be Bella, but he hadn't recognised her at first. She had the same curly, dark auburn hair, the same pale, almost translucent skin, but she was thin, painfully thin. What had happened to her?

Charlie knew Bella had a rough time with her cystic fibrosis. She'd had a higher than average number of hospital admissions, but he'd never seen her looking as sick as she looked now.

'What's going on?'

'She's got a high temperature and she's badly dehydrated. I suspect she has another chest infection,' Evie replied.

'Is there anything I can do?' He knew it was unlikely but he wanted to at least offer his help.

Evie shook her head and he could see tears in her eyes. He and Evie had been friends for almost ten years and she was normally so strong, so resilient. Things must be grim.

'You'd better catch up with her but call me if there's anything I can do.' He leant down and gave Evie a quick kiss on the cheek. 'I'll drop into the ward in the morning.'

He watched Evie as she hurried after Bella's stretcher and wished he could offer more than just support. He viewed all three of the Lockheart sisters as his surrogate family. He knew they had a lack of family support and he knew how much of the burden of worry Evie carried on her slim shoulders. He would do what he could to help but he wished there was something more proactive that he could do for Bella too. But he was an orthopaedic surgeon. He was not what she needed.

Evie caught up to Sam and Bella as they waited for the lift. The next half-hour was frantic as Sam ordered a battery of tests and examined Bella. Lexi had driven to the hospital and she joined Evie on the cardiothoracic ward to wait. Together they tried to stay out of Sam's way. Evie had to remind herself she was Bella's sister now, not her doctor.

Sam appeared from Bella's room and motioned for them to join him. 'I'm admitting Bella. She has a temp of thirty-nine point five, which I suspect is the result of another chest infection, and she's lost three kilograms since her last admission. She was supposed to be putting on weight but her BMI is down to seventeen.'

Evie knew Bella was thin. Too thin. Her body mass index should be at least nineteen—although this would still only put her at the bottom end of normal. Evie knew it was difficult for Bella to put on weight, all cystic fibrosis sufferers had the same problem, but Bella should weigh five or six kilograms more than she currently did. Being underweight made it more difficult to fight infection and increased her chances of ending up back in hospital. Which was exactly what had happened.

'Is your father coming in?' Sam asked.

Evie shrugged. Sam's guess was as good as anyone's. 'I've just tried to get in touch with him again. I've left two messages but I don't know where he is.'

She kept one eye on Bella, wondering how she would react to the news that her father was uncontactable. Bella watched her, her grey eyes huge and pensive, but she didn't look surprised. Evie supposed the news didn't surprise any of them. 'Lexi, do you have any other way of contacting him?' Lexi worked with their father so it was possible she would know where to find him.

Lexi shook her head. 'No, he was going out to dinner but it was private, not business related, so I don't know any more details.'

Evie sighed. If Richard was out with one of his female 'acquaintances' it was highly unlikely that he'd answer his phone. It was also highly unlikely that he'd even make it home tonight, and if he did Evie wondered whether he'd even notice that Bella, and possibly Lexi, weren't in their beds.

'Do you think we need to try to find him?' she asked. Was Sam telling them it was important for Richard to get into the hospital tonight or did they have some time up their sleeves?

Sam was shaking his head and Evie breathed a sigh of relief. He couldn't think it was that urgent. 'I just want to try to get Bella stabilised tonight,' he said. 'I'll start a course of IV antibiotics and get her rehydrated. We'll have to see how that goes but this is now her third admission this year. To be honest, things are heading downhill, but she'll make it through the night. I'm sure your father will turn up eventually.'

Until then Evie would stay by Bella's side. Even when Richard decided to join them Evie knew that she and Lexi would be Bella's main support team. She wished things were different, for Bella's sake, but their father and Bella had always had a difficult relationship, he'd never coped very well with his second daughter or her illness.

Evie's own relationship with her father had been tainted by the departure of their mother. Something Evie held her father partially responsible for. She knew her mother had made her own choices but she felt that he could have been more supportive, offered more assistance, made more of an effort to convince her to stay. If he had, the bulk of the responsibility of raising her younger siblings wouldn't have fallen to Evie and she would have had a very different childhood.

But the Lockheart family dynamics weren't going to change overnight and once again Evie opted to set up a folding bed in Bella's room. She sent Lexi home with Sam but she wasn't going to leave Bella alone. She hoped Sam was right, she hoped Bella would make it through the night, but what if he was wrong? Doctors had been wrong before. She knew that better than anybody.

Bella had been awake since the crack of dawn, woken by the nurse who'd come in to take her six-o'clock obs, although in reality she felt as though she'd been awake most of the night. She always slept badly in hospital. Struggling for every breath ruined a good sleep, not to mention two-hourly obs and the fact she was always cold.

Evie had been by her side all night and she'd waited until Lexi arrived before disappearing in search of coffee while promising to be back in time for Sam's early-morning consult.

Evie and Lexi were the two constants in Bella's life. The two people she knew she would always be able to rely on. She knew she was lucky to have them and she'd given up waiting for her parents to give her the same support. But it didn't stop her wishing that things were different. She didn't like to be so dependent on her sisters but it was the way it had always been. She knew her illness was a strain on everybody but she also knew she wouldn't cope without the love and support of her siblings. She wondered sometimes how they managed, especially Evie, who traded looking after Bella for looking after all her other patients at the hospital. Bella knew Evie had a shift in Emergency today but she had no idea how her sister would carry out such a demanding job after spending the night in a chair by her bed. She hoped Evie didn't get any complicated cases.

'I brought something to brighten your day,' Evie said when she returned, carrying a tray of coffee and hot chocolate for her sisters. Bella felt her eyes widen in surprise; Evie wasn't talking about the drinks.

'Charlie Maxwell,' Lexi said in greeting. 'I'd recognise that bald head anywhere.'

Charlie Maxwell was in her room! Bella knew she was staring and she could hear the 'beep beep' of the heart-rate monitor attached to her chest escalate as her autonomic nervous system responded to his presence. Thank goodness he didn't seem to notice. He wasn't looking at her, his attention focussed on Lexi. Bella was used to that. People always noticed Lexi and Evie before they noticed her, and even though she wished, on the odd occasion, that someone would notice her first, today she was pleased to be ignored as it gave her time to try to get her nerves under control.

'Morning, Lexi,' Charlie said with a grin. 'And for your information, I'm not bald,' he protested. 'I do this on purpose. It stops the women from being jealous of my golden locks.'

'You'd have to be the only bloke I know who voluntarily shaves his head,' Lexi retorted, before Evie interrupted them.

'Bella, you remember Charlie, don't you?' she asked as she handed Bella a hot chocolate.

Who could forget him? Bella thought. She knew she never would, not in a million years. He looked as fit, healthy and fabulous as always. Charlie had been a professional surfer in a past life and he certainly had the body of an athlete. Muscular, tanned and perfectly proportioned, he was wearing a white shirt and Bella could see the definition of his biceps and pectoral muscles through the thin fabric. She swallowed hard as she tried to get her mouth to work but she was short of breath and her mouth was dry and parched. Unable to form any words, she nodded instead.

'*Ciao*, Bella,' Charlie said.

He always greeted her in the same way and it never failed to make her feel special, even though she didn't flatter herself that she was the only one on the receiving end of his charm. But therein lay even more of his appeal. He was one of the few people who didn't treat her any differently because of her medical condition. He was a serial flirt and he gave her the same attention he gave to every woman who crossed his path, and to Bella, who was used to either being shielded or ignored, Charlie's attention was a rare delight.

He winked at her and her heart rate jumped again. She felt herself blush and cursed her fair skin.

'How are you feeling?' he asked.

'I've had better days,' she said, finally managing to get some words out. But it wasn't the cystic fibrosis making her short of breath, it was Charlie. She was always shy around anyone other than family and even though Charlie behaved like family he was so damn sexy she'd never managed to overcome her self-consciousness around him, especially when other people were within earshot. One on one she was more comfortable but with other ears around she always worried about making a fool of herself.

He was gorgeous and she always felt so plain by comparison. His facial features combined so perfectly together she'd never really noticed that he shaved his head. Of course she'd noticed he was bald but she'd never wondered about the reality behind it, she was too busy being mesmerised by his other physical attributes—his chocolate-brown eyes that she felt she could melt into, his smooth, tanned skin, which provided the perfect foil for straight, white teeth, even his small, neat ears all combined into an appealing package. But his best feature was his mouth. She could visualise him with sun-bleached surfie hair but it was irrelevant really because her attention was constantly drawn to his lips. They were plump and delicious, full but not hard like a collagen-injected pout, they were juicy and soft, almost too soft for such a masculine face. He was smiling at her, a gorgeous smile, full and open and honest. You'd have to be dead not to be affected by his smile and while she wasn't feeling anywhere near one hundred per cent healthy, she wasn't dead yet.

'So Evie tells me,' Charlie replied, 'but if there's anything you need, just ask me. I know how to make things happen around here.'

He winked at her again and Bella didn't doubt for one minute that Charlie could get whatever he wanted both inside the hospital and out. She knew his reputation as a charmer, she'd heard the nurses talk about him during her numerous admissions, and she knew they competed for his affections and attentions. The combination of his wicked sense of humour, his infectious smile, his gentle nature and his hardened muscles had the female staff members regularly flustered, and Bella herself was no exception.

As far as she knew, only Evie seemed immune to Charlie's charm. Their ten-year friendship had only ever been platonic and for that Bella was grateful. It meant she was free to adore him without feeling as if she was invading her sister's territory. She knew that from the day Evie had first met Charlie she'd thought of him as the older brother she wished she'd had. But Bella's thoughts towards Charlie were far from familial—although she'd never be brave enough to flirt with him, she knew she wasn't experienced enough to handle Charlie Maxwell. So she just nodded dumbly in reply. She'd lost the capacity to speak again, completely tongue-tied at the thought of Charlie doing things for her. Fortunately Sam's arrival saved her from needing to answer. He was followed by a nurse and a couple of interns and suddenly her room was overflowing with people.

A ninth person came into the room and Bella saw Evie's double-take. It was their father.

Bella had assumed Evie had gotten in touch with him during the night, or vice versa, but looking at Evie's expression now it was obvious she'd heard nothing back and hadn't been expecting him.

He looked tired and drawn. Bella wished she could pretend he'd lost sleep worrying about her, his middle daughter, but she knew it was far more likely to be a result of a late night of a different kind. She waited for her father to push through the crowd gathered at the foot of her bed but of course he didn't. He remained standing just inside the doorway, separate and apart from his family. She sighed, wishing for the thousandth time that things were different. At least he was here, which was more than Bella could say for her mother. She nodded in greeting and then proceeded to ignore him as her sisters took up positions on the bed on either side of her. She was tired of always being the one who reached out to make a connection with her father.

Evie took her hand and Bella relaxed, knowing her sisters would try to protect her from harm. Bella saw Sam acknowledge Richard's arrival with a nod of his own before he began his consult. He checked Bella's vital signs, checked her obs, listened to her chest and generally prodded and poked while she tried to pretend she wasn't surrounded by people. The procedure was familiar to her but that didn't make it any less embarrassing. Once he'd finished he spoke to Bella as though they were the only two in the room.

'You've lost weight since I last examined you, that's not what we were hoping for, your admissions are getting more frequent and your lung function tests are down.' Sam was ticking things off on his fingers as he recited the list.

'Is there any good news?' Bella asked hopefully.

'One positive note is that you've made some improvement overnight. You've rehydrated and your temperature has come down but it's still higher than I'd like. You're showing some resistance to the antibiotics and I've had to increase the dosage to try to get your chest infection under control. Individually all these things are not so concerning but combined it means I need to reassess your management.' He paused briefly and Bella knew what he would say next. 'It's time for the next stage.'

Bella couldn't speak. This wasn't unexpected but she didn't know what to say. Sam was watching her, waiting for her to acknowledge his words, and she thought she nodded in response but she couldn't be sure.

Sam looked away from her now, turning to the members of her family, stopping briefly at each and every one as he spoke. 'I know we've talked about this before but the time has come. Bella needs a lung transplant now. She is already on the active transplant list but I have revised her status. This will move her up the list and means she will get the next pair of suitable lungs.'

Bella tightened her grip on Evie's hand. This was really happening. During her last hospital admission Sam had told her she would need a transplant eventually. That was the way things went with cystic fibrosis. But eventually had become now. Her lungs were officially failing.

Out of the corner of her eye she saw Richard collapse into a chair as though his legs would no longer support him. His response surprised her. Her father was a man of action, he always had a solution for everything, a way to deal with everything—except when it came to her and her mother—but he never normally showed any sign of weakness. Was he actually concerned for her? Bella knew there was nothing he could do for her now but she couldn't ever recall seeing him flummoxed. Was he concerned or was he confused?

'What do we do while we wait?' Lexi's voice was unexpectedly loud in her ear and Bella jumped.

'In the meantime, we start the pre-op processes. Physical tests, including blood work and organ function tests, as well as psych assessments,' Sam replied.

'What does the surgery involve?' Richard asked, and his question answered Bella's own. His tone said this was a question from a man who wanted information and clarification, not a question from a concerned father.

'Obviously it is major surgery. Bella will be several hours in Theatre. It can take up to twelve hours. She will be placed on a heart bypass machine while both lungs are transplanted via an incision across the bottom of the diaphragm, then she will be transferred to ICU for at least twenty-four hours and then back to the cardiothoracic surgical ward.'

'What are the survival rates?' As was his style her father was keeping any emotion out of the equation. He preferred to deal with the facts and figures.

'The figures are good. Currently eighty-five per cent of people undergoing bilateral, sequential lung transplants in Australia survive one year and sixty per cent are still alive after five years.'

Bella heard a sharp intake of breath. For a moment she thought she'd made the sound but then she realised it had come from Lexi.

Bella knew the odds. She'd lived and breathed them since her last admission. She knew the statistics were good, for the short term at least, but she also knew that to those who hadn't spent countless hours doing the research she'd done, the odds didn't sound that fantastic.

'These stats are not just for CF sufferers,' Sam clarified. 'They're for everybody and Bella has age on her side. Although she will still have cystic fibrosis, it won't be in her lungs.' Sam looked directly at Bella. 'If your lungs are functioning properly, you should notice a far improved quality of life. You'll have more energy, you should gain weight and you'll be able to be more active.'

'What do you mean, she'll still have CF?' Richard was frowning.

'Bella's lungs will be clear but she will still have CF in her pancreas, sweat glands and reproductive tract. She will still need her enzyme-replacement medication and she will start a course of anti-rejection medication. The transplant is not a cure for the disease, it just eliminates the disease from her lungs, and will hopefully extend her life.' Sam turned to face her. 'Bella, do you have any questions?'

She still hadn't uttered a word.

'How long do I have?'

'A month, maybe two.' Sam's voice was deep and soft but his words were clear and distinct in the absolute silence of the room.

It was already November. Would she see another Christmas?

'What choice do I have?'

Her question put an immediate and definite end to the silence. Lexi started to cry and Evie started to reason with Bella. They both knew her choices were limited.

Bella held up one hand, asking Evie to wait. 'It was just a question,' she said. 'I didn't say I won't have a transplant, I just wanted to hear if I have any other options.'

'Of course you have a choice,' Sam said, 'it's your body. You can choose to have a transplant if we find a suitable donor or you can choose not to. But you don't have any other options.' He spoke to her as though they were alone in the room. 'It's a big decision and I know how daunting this can be but ultimately I wouldn't expect you to find it a hard decision to make. The consequences of your decision are self-evident. You're free to talk to the psychologists and the transplant team in more detail, you can ask them anything you want or need to know, but you don't have a lot of time to decide. Your lungs are failing. Without a transplant you're on borrowed time.'

Borrowed time. She knew that but it made it more important than ever that she get things sorted. There were things she needed to do. She had to prioritise. She needed to think. She closed her eyes. As she'd hoped, Sam took that as a sign to usher everyone out of the room.

'Okay,' he said, 'I need to run a couple more tests and Bella needs to rest. You can come back later.'

Bella thought Lexi was going to argue but she saw her look at Sam before she said anything. Sam gave a slight shake of his head and Lexi stayed quiet. The medical team was leaving the room and Lexi and Evie kissed Bella before they followed. Charlie and Sam were the last ones remaining. Bella looked from one to the other. Charlie was wedged in next to the bathroom doorhandle, he would have to wait until everyone else had left before he'd be able to get out. She needed to ask a favour and if she was running out of time she needed to do it soon. It looked as if Charlie or Sam were her only options. Not that they were bad options. This was a topic she couldn't discuss with her sisters; she'd tried already and failed, but by the same token she didn't think it was something to discuss with Sam either.

Bella needed a sounding board. Charlie had offered his help and even though she knew this wasn't exactly what he'd pictured, perhaps he wouldn't mind. After all, this concerned Evie and he knew her better than most.

Bella hadn't seen Charlie for some time. He had been a frequent visitor to the Lockheart home but since Evie had moved out into an apartment there was no reason for Charlie to drop by. But she knew from experience that

Charlie was a good listener and he could be relied upon for level-headed advice. She and Charlie had a history of heart-to-hearts, albeit a very short one, and perhaps he could help her again.

Besides, she was running out of time and options. He would have to do.

'Charlie, could I talk to you for a second?' she asked. She knew he saw himself as family, maybe he could do this for her.

Bella saw Evie glance back over her shoulder as she left the room. She'd be wondering what on earth Bella needed to talk to Charlie about, wondering why she wasn't talking to her, but Bella knew this was one thing Evie couldn't help her with.

CHAPTER TWO

EVIE hesitated when she heard Bella ask Charlie to stay. She wondered what that was all about but she didn't stop. She had to catch her father before he disappeared again. There were things they needed to talk about.

'Richard,' she called out to him. She hadn't called him 'Dad' since she'd started working at the Harbour Hospital. Evie's paternal great-grandfather had been instrumental in establishing the hospital and Richard was one of its biggest benefactors. Evie hadn't wanted to be accused of nepotism when she'd joined the staff. Although the Lockheart surname was a clear indication that there was a relationship there, she hadn't wanted everyone to know just how close the relationship was.

He turned and waited for her to catch up.

'Where have you been?' Evie asked. She was furious that she'd heard nothing from him all morning. 'Why didn't you return my messages?' She must have left him half a dozen in total.

'I tried. Your mobile is switched off.'

Evie knew there would be no apology. She always switched her phone off at work and Richard knew that. He could have guessed she'd be at the hospital, he could have contacted her through other avenues. 'You could have paged me.'

Never one to back down he said, 'I spoke to Lexi and came straight here. Tell me, how do we fix this? What can I do?'

'You can't buy lungs,' she replied, knowing that Richard's preferred way of dealing with things was just to throw large sums of money at a problem until it went away. That wasn't going to work this time. 'We just have to wait.'

'What is Sam doing about this?'

'There's nothing he can do other than push Bella up the list, which he has done. It's all dependent on having a suitable donor and convincing Bella to go ahead with the surgery once compatible lungs are found. All we can do is support her through this.' Her little sister was in dire straits and while Evie had known this day was inevitable it didn't make it any less heartbreaking.

She hoped Richard was listening. She hoped, for once, he could be there to support his daughter. She hoped he re-alised he might never get another shot at this. But she and Lexi would be there for Bella even if her parents weren't. Which brought her to the next item on her mental checklist.

'Will you tell Miranda?' Evie asked.

Evie had started calling her mother by her first name when she was fifteen, when she had finally admitted that her mother preferred her bottle of gin to her daughters. Miranda's contact with her offspring was sporadic, associ-ated with brief periods of sobriety mostly, although there had been plenty of times when the girls had seen Miranda far from sober. But despite this Evie felt Miranda needed to know what was happening with her second daughter and she thought it was Richard's job to inform her.

Richard's expression told Evie all she needed to know but she was not going to let him out of this task. 'You need to tell her. Whether she can understand what's going on is not your problem, but she has to be told. I need to get back to work. I'll see you back here later.' Evie's final words were not a question. Someone needed to tell Richard what was required and she was happy to do that. But she'd have to wait and see if he listened.

Bella looked exhausted. She was waiflike, a pale shadow of a figure against the white hospital sheets. She was sitting up in bed and the only exception to her pallor was her auburn curls, which were vibrantly bright against the pillows that were plumped around her. Looking at her, Charlie thought she could pass for eighteen years old but he knew she was in her mid-twenties. She'd been seventeen when they'd first met, almost ten years ago, when he'd gone back to med school and found himself in Evie's class, and that would make her twenty-six now.

He waited until Bella's room had emptied itself of all the other occupants before he dragged a chair closer to the bed and sat. 'What can I do for you?' he asked. When he'd offered his help he hadn't expected there would be anything he could do, but his offer had been made in good faith and if Bella needed assistance he would do his best to give it to her.

'I need an unbiased pair of ears.'

Charlie frowned. Bella wasn't maintaining eye contact. Instead, she was fidgeting with the bed covers, repeatedly pleating them in her fingers before smoothing them out. He wondered what was bothering her. 'Is this about the transplant?'

'Sort of,' she replied.

'You *are* planning on going ahead with it?'

'Yes.' Bella nodded and her auburn curls bounced. 'But I don't want to talk to you about the actual operation or anything medical. I'm worried about Evie.' She looked up at him then but her fingers continued to fiddle with the bed sheets.

'Evie?' He'd expected that she wanted to discuss the transplant. He had expected to advise her to talk to Sam. Charlie was an orthopaedic surgeon. Lung transplants were Sam's area of expertise, not his. 'I don't understand.'

'You heard Sam, I'm on borrowed time. I'm not ready to give up yet but there's no guarantee that a suitable donor will be found in time.'

Her breathing was laboured and when she paused to catch her breath he could hear a faint wheeze. She had an oxygen tube resting on her top lip and out of habit he checked the flow and her oxygen sats on the monitor to make sure she was getting an adequate supply. The flow was fine so he returned his attention to Bella.

'If I'm running out of time,' she was saying, 'I want to make sure my sisters are okay.'

His frowned deepened. 'Sam has just told you that your last hope is to find a suitable donor for new lungs and you're worried about your sisters?' Charlie was amazed. If he were in the same situation he doubted he'd be able to think about anything except whether he was going to live or die.

Bella shrugged. 'There's nothing I can do about finding a donor but making sure Evie is okay might be something I can have some influence over.'

'What's wrong with her?' He hadn't noticed anything amiss but, to be honest, he hadn't seen a lot of Evie lately.

'I know this whole donor thing is stressing Evie out. She feels responsible for me. She always has ever since our mother walked out on us. But, really, this situation isn't unexpected, we all knew this day would come. But Evie doesn't seem to be coping as well as I would have thought.'

Bella stopped, interrupted by a coughing fit, and

Charlie could only watch as her slight frame shuddered with each spasm. She had asked him to stay behind. There must be something she needed. 'What did you want me to do?' he asked as he poured some water into a glass for her and waited while she sipped it.

'Thanks,' she said as she moistened her throat before she continued to speak in a voice that was just louder than a whisper. 'She seems on edge, which isn't like her, and she's been like that for a little while. Something is bothering her but she won't tell me what it is. Have you noticed anything?'

'I haven't seen that much of her lately,' he admitted. But if Bella was right and Evie was troubled, he was pretty sure he knew what the problem was. The sisters were extraordinarily close and he could just imagine how much this situation was tearing Evie apart. 'I imagine she's just worried about you and doesn't want to burden you with her concerns.' He wished he felt like he was doing a better job of comforting Bella but he didn't think he'd be improving her spirits with this clumsy attempt at reassurance.

'I think it's something unrelated to me,' Bella admitted.

'Like what?'

'I don't know. Sometimes it's as though she has the weight of the world on her shoulders and you know what she's like, she doesn't like to burden people with her troubles. A couple of the nurses were talking about Evie and they mentioned Finn Kennedy. I wondered if something had happened between them, something that would upset her. Have you heard anything?'

Bella's earlier nervousness had disappeared. She'd stopped fidgeting and Charlie wondered whether he'd only imagined her to be on edge. He shook his head. 'I've heard nothing. There's been the usual gossip about the staff and usual complaints about the doctors' egos, but I've heard nothing about Evie specifically.'

'Will you promise me that if anything happens to me, you'll look out for her?' Bella asked. 'She needs somebody to take care of her and she's so independent, which makes it tough. At least she might let you close.'

Charlie nodded. 'I promise I'll make sure she's okay.' He could do that. He wished he could tell Bella that she'd be able to keep an eye on Evie herself but they both knew that might not be the case. They both knew what the reality was.

He could hear Bella wheezing as she breathed and he knew she needed to rest. He should leave and let her recover but he needed to know that everything was under control first. 'Is anything else bothering you?' he asked.

'Well, I also want to see Lexi happily married to Sam but I don't think you can help me there.' Bella smiled and Charlie caught a glimpse of humour despite her circumstances.

'Why wouldn't they get married?' he asked.

Bella shook her head. 'I'm sure they will but I want to be there when they do. Lexi wants time to organise a huge circus, and I know it's her wedding...' She smiled. 'Their wedding,' she corrected, 'but I wish she'd agree to hurry things up. I don't want to miss out.'

Her smile had gone and the tension had returned to her shoulders. She had the bed sheet bunched up tight in her right hand and her knuckles were white with the effort. Maybe it had been stress he'd been witnessing all along.

Charlie wished again that there was something he could do to reassure her. 'You need to be positive. You have to believe you will get a second chance.' He knew his words were hopelessly inadequate but he was out of his depth.

'All right, I'll go along with your fairy-tale for now,'

Bella replied. 'Let's say a donor is found in time, before Lexi and Sam have a chance to get married. What if something happens to me during the surgery? That's a risk too. Sam is my surgeon. How do you think that will affect their relationship? I know the idea of me dying terrifies Lexi but if they're already married they'll have to get past it, but if they're not...' Bella paused and shrugged her bony shoulders. 'I don't want to be responsible for something happening and coming between them.'

'How can what happens in surgery be your responsibility?'

'It's my decision to have the surgery and the other alternative if something goes wrong is for it to be Sam's responsibility. If I don't have the surgery then that pressure is removed.'

'If you don't have the surgery, you'll die.' Charlie knew he was being blunt but he also knew Bella understood the facts. 'It's Sam's job to make sure nothing happens to you. He's a surgeon, that goes with the territory.'

'Don't get me wrong. If a donor is found, I will have the transplant, but I'd just prefer it if Lexi and Sam were married first. Does that make sense?'

Charlie nodded. In some strange roundabout way it did make perfect sense. He could understand her logic. 'I assume you've spoken to Lexi about this?'

She nodded. 'But Lexi has a tendency to get her own way and she wants it all to be perfect. In Lexi's mind the wedding will happen when I've had a transplant and life is going on for everyone just as it should. She won't consider the possibility that I might not make it. She won't admit that waiting might mean she doesn't get perfection. She thinks if she ignores the facts, it'll all go away. She thinks wishing it will make it so. I don't want to make a fuss but it's a big deal to me.'

'What about having someone else perform the surgery? Someone other than Sam?'

'Like who?' Bella asked. 'Evie told me Sam is one of the best. If I'm going to have a lung transplant, I want the best odds I can get.'

Charlie thought about Bella's options. Finn Kennedy, Head of Surgery at Sydney Harbour Hospital, was one of the best cardiac surgeons in Australia but he wasn't a heart-lung specialist. If Charlie had needed heart surgery, he'd happily choose Finn to operate on him, but if he needed a lung transplant his money would be on Sam.

'I guess Sam is your man,' he agreed. 'But if Lexi isn't listening, why don't you talk to Sam? See if you can get him to persuade Lexi to speed things up. Get him to explain the urgency to her.'

Bella nodded. 'That makes sense. I wanted Lexi to talk to Sam about it but I don't think she will. Maybe I should approach it from the other angle, from Sam's side.'

Charlie watched as Bella's fist relaxed and her fingers uncurled, releasing the bed sheet. Perhaps his advice had been more effective than he'd anticipated. Could he leave her to rest? 'So you'll talk to Sam?'

'I guess.'

'Shall I come back tomorrow, check up on you?'

'You don't need to do that.'

'Why not? I can be your conscience, make sure you've spoken to Sam. And once you've got your sisters' lives sorted out, I'm interested to know what you want for you.'

'Me?' Her tone suggested she hadn't given any thought to herself and Charlie was astonished by her undemanding, unselfish attitude.

'Yes. What do *you* want?'

She frowned as if she'd never given any consideration to her own desires and her grey eyes darkened. 'Nothing.'

* * *

How could she want nothing? Charlie wondered as he left the cardiothoracic ward. Everyone wanted something. But he supposed the only thing she wanted might be unattainable. Bella's life was in someone else's hands. Actually, it was in someone else's body. Bella's chance at life would come at the expense of someone else's. Was it better then *not* to think about it? Was it better not to put that longing into words?

And what was he doing, offering to come back tomorrow? Offering to be her conscience? Why was he getting involved?

Normally he would steer clear of any sort of involvement. He'd learnt that lesson a long time ago. He yearned for freedom and in his experience that didn't come from involvement with others. But the Lockheart sisters were different. He'd learnt *that* a long time ago too. Almost ten years ago.

Besides, it was too late to ask himself whether he should get involved. He already was. Ever since he'd first met Evie and she'd dragged him into her world and rescued him from the depths of darkness, the Lockheart sisters had become part of his life. They'd been good for him at a time when he'd been disheartened about life and his future. Evie had helped him through that period, and her situation with her parents and with Bella's illness had made his troubles seem less significant.

Now it was his turn to repay that debt. It was his turn to support the girls and he would do what he could to make sure all three of them got through this time with their spirits and hearts intact.

Bella was Evie's little sister. He would help in any way he could. He would be involved but in a practical sense only. This was one woman who was safe from his advances. Not because she was unattractive, far from it, her auburn hair, pale skin and grey eyes were a mesmerising combination, but Bella was Evie's little sister, which meant she was practically family and she was definitely off limits. But he could offer support, he knew they would need it, and that would be the extent of his involvement. She was Evie's little sister and he would be wise to remember that.

With his involvement sorted in his mind, he headed for the bank of elevators to take him up to the orthopaedic wards and was surprised to find Evie waiting in the corridor. He thought everyone would have been long gone.

'Were you waiting for me?' he asked.

Evie shook her head. 'No. I just finished talking to Richard.'

Charlie waited. He knew Evie and her father had a volatile relationship. Sometimes things went smoothly, other times not so much. He wondered how things were at the moment. 'How did that go?'

'No different from the usual,' Evie sighed. 'Bella needs his support, she needs support from all of us right now, and I don't know if any of them understand how serious this is. Richard certainly doesn't seem to grasp just how difficult it is to find suitable donors, Lexi doesn't want to think about the consequences if there is no donor, and don't get me started on my mother.'

'So that leaves you to try to hold it all together?'

'I guess so.'

The burden of Bella's illness had always fallen on Evie and it looked as though that was still the case. Sam was obviously some support but Evie's immediate family sounded as though they were all still in denial, assuming her mother even knew what was going on. He wondered if he'd been right. Was the stress upsetting Evie? Even so, Charlie knew Evie would always be there to support Bella. Maybe Bella was right—if something was bothering Evie, perhaps it was another issue.

'Walk with me?' he invited. 'I need another coffee.'

She was silent as they walked back to the doctors' lounge. He kept quiet too, thinking that if he waited she might tell him what else was on her mind, but she didn't break the silence. He shrugged as he spooned coffee into the machine. He'd never pretended to understand women. Perhaps there wasn't anything else bothering her.

Evie watched as Charlie fiddled with the coffee machine. The doctors' lounge in this ward had a proper coffee machine and the hospital's best coffee. Technically neither of them should be using it as it had been purchased by the cardiothoracic unit for their doctors, but Evie knew Charlie would get away with it, just like he got away with most things, and she wasn't about to argue.

She was silent as the machine gurgled to life. She knew Charlie was watching her, waiting for her to say something, but she didn't know what else to say. She didn't know what she could do.

'It'll be okay, Evie.'

Did he know what she was thinking?

'You don't know that,' she retorted.

'You're right, I don't, but it's all we can hope for. We have to stay positive. Bella needs that from all of us,' he said as the coffee dripped into the cups.

'What did she want to speak to you about?'

'She needed to get some things off her chest.'

'Why didn't she talk to me?' she asked, hating the petulant tone she heard in her voice, but she couldn't help it. For as long as she could remember she'd been Bella's confidante and protector. What made Bella think she couldn't come to her now?

'I think she just needed to talk to someone who isn't quite as invested emotionally in her as you are.'

'But she's always confided in me.'

Not always, he thought. But Evie didn't need to hear that now.

'Don't worry, she's okay.' Charlie's deep brown eyes were sombre as he stepped towards her and wrapped his arms around her, hugging her against his chest. 'The best thing you can do for her right now is just be there. Just like you've always been. She needs you.'

Evie closed her eyes and leant against Charlie's solid chest as she let out a long breath. It felt good to have a hug with no hidden agenda, a straightforward, comforting hug from a friend. It felt good to let someone else worry about her for a change.

'I'm consulting today. Call me if there's anything you need,' he said. 'Anything. I'm here for you, okay?'

His words vibrated in his chest and into Evie but she was also aware of the air in the room moving and she knew someone else had entered the lounge. She opened her eyes and her gaze settled on the last person she expected to see. The last person she wanted to see.

Finn Kennedy.

The last time she'd been in somebody's arms they'd been his. He stood in the doorway, rigid and forbidding, with his usual unfathomable expression on his face. His gaze was locked on her as she was held in Charlie's embrace. He didn't speak and he didn't move. Heat flooded through her, unbidden, unwanted, unplanned, as he watched her with his piercing blue eyes.

Evie stepped back, breaking Charlie's hold on her. 'I'd better go. I need to hit the showers and get downstairs.' She picked up her coffee and stirred milk and sugar into it, resolutely keeping her gaze focussed on her drink.

'I'll see you later,' Charlie said.

She looked up at him as he spoke. The doorway was empty. She and Charlie were alone again.

It was probably just as well, she thought with a sigh. She didn't have the time or the energy to deal with Finn Kennedy, esteemed cardiac surgeon, Head of Surgery and her most recent lover. Although that term was probably too generous. They'd shared one fiery sexual interlude but she couldn't call it lovemaking. It had been steamy, fierce and passionate but without tenderness. It had been raw, impulsive and gratifying but it could not be repeated.

She did *not* have time to think about Finn Kennedy. She needed to stay in control and, where Finn was concerned, she'd already demonstrated an extreme lack of self-control.

She thanked Charlie and kissed his cheek before she left to get on with her day, hoping and praying for it to improve. She showered in Bella's bathroom and changed into surgical scrubs. She hadn't thought to ask Lexi to lend her some clean clothes and there was no way she'd fit into any of Bella's things, even if Lexi had packed some choices other than pyjamas. At five feet nine inches, Evie was four inches taller than Bella and about two dress sizes bigger. While no one would call Evie plump, Bella was as thin as a whippet because of the cystic fibrosis.

She kissed Bella goodbye and headed for the lift to go to A and E. She yawned as she waited. She was halfway through the yawn when the lift doors slid open to reveal one occupant.

Finn.

Obviously she hadn't been wishing hard enough for her day to improve.

All it took was one glance, no more than a second long, before her heart was racing in her chest. Her lips were dry and her face burned under the scrutiny of his gaze. She couldn't let him see how he affected her.

She turned her back to push the button for the ground floor only to find it had already been pressed. No other buttons were lit. Which meant Finn was riding all the way down with her.

'Late night?' Finn's deep, husky voice made her jump. She hadn't expected him to speak to her. The way he'd looked at her earlier with his disapproving, ice-cold blue eyes she would have bet he'd ignore her. What was it about him? When she wanted him to talk he refused to open up to her yet when she wanted to be left in peace and quiet he had to engage her in conversation. He was so infuriating.

'Yes.' She turned to face him as she answered and saw him look her up and down. She knew he would notice what she was wearing.

'I take it you couldn't make it home?'

Yep, he'd noticed, and she knew what he was implying. She was tempted to let him think he was right but she was too tired to play games.

She glared at him. She was tired and worried. She'd let him take the brunt of her bad mood.

'I spent the night in the cardiothoracic ward. Bella is in hospital again. She was admitted last night.' She was happy if her comment made him feel bad. Why should she be the only one who worried about other people's feelings?

He reached out a hand and took half a step towards her before he thought better of it. She could literally see him change his mind. His hand dropped to his side and his tone softened. 'Evie, I'm sorry, I didn't know. Is there anything I can do?'

Don't be nice to me. I don't know how to handle it if you're nice. She was terrified she'd burst into tears in the lift. In front of Finn. 'There's nothing you can do unless

you're a miracle worker. She needs a pair of new lungs.'
She was snappy and defensive. It was the only way to ensure she didn't crumble.

'I doubt even the Lockheart name can get lungs to
order.' His tone was cool now, his blue eyes appraising. 'I
meant, is there anything I can do for you?'

'What could you possibly do?'

'I could organise for someone to cover your shift so you
could be with Bella.'

*Great, Finn hands you an olive branch and you set
it on fire before you give it back. That's just great. Well
done, Evie.*

She would love to take him up on his offer but she
couldn't back down now. It wasn't in her nature and she
certainly wasn't about to give Finn the satisfaction of having the last word. 'There's nothing I can do for her,' she
said. Evie expected Bella to sleep for most of the day and
Lexi was going to stay with her. 'I'd rather be busy down
here,' she added as the lift doors opened and she stepped
out into the emergency department. Work would ensure
her mind was occupied. Staying busy was the best way to
keep her mind off Bella's situation. And off Finn.

CHAPTER THREE

It was amazing what a difference twenty-four hours and a hefty dose of no-nonsense antibiotics made. After a full day and two nights in hospital Bella was feeling a lot more positive and Sam was pleased with her progress too. She'd broached the topic of hurrying the wedding along with him and he'd seemed amenable to the idea. Now Bella just had her fingers crossed that he could convince Lexi it was a good idea.

Thinking of weddings, Bella's fingers itched to continue sketching. If her plan was to succeed she needed to build Lexi's excitement and feed her imagination about how beautiful this wedding could be. She needed Lexi to be so excited she couldn't wait to get married and would agree to do it soon. She needed to get some more ideas down on paper but her sketch book wasn't there. Lexi hadn't considered it a priority when she'd thrown belongings together the other night and Bella had been too concerned about other things yesterday to miss it. Lexi was bringing it into the hospital this morning but until she arrived Bella would have to make do with scraps of paper.

She was halfway through sketching a sleeveless figure-hugging satin gown with a plunging back when Lexi appeared, carrying a large tote bag.

'Morning,' she said as she dumped the bag onto Bella's

bed before kissing her cheek. 'Sam says things are looking up?'

Bella nodded. 'I'm definitely feeling better today.'

Lexi unzipped the tote bag and began to haul things out of it. 'I've brought the things you asked for. There's plenty to keep you occupied if you get bored,' she said as she deposited Bella's laptop and a stack of DVDs on the bedside cupboard.

'Did you bring my big sketch book and coloured pencils?'

'Yes,' Lexi said as she retrieved the items and put them on the table over the bed. 'Is Charlie coming in to see you today?'

Bella frowned. 'I think so,' she said cautiously. 'Why?' He'd told her he would call in but why was Lexi asking?

'I thought you might need this,' Lexi said as she pulled a wisp of red fabric from the bag. She shook it out and Bella recognised the skimpy red negligee Lexi had bought for her the last time she'd been in hospital. 'It took me ages to find it. Why was it in the back of your wardrobe? You're supposed to wear it.'

Bella looked at the minuscule slip. It was so not her style and she had no intention of wearing it, which was why she'd shoved it to the back of her cupboard.

'I'm not going to wear it in hospital,' she protested. She had no plans to wear it at all, not in hospital or anywhere else. 'You know how cold I always feel in here.' She floated her old excuse past Lexi. Because she was so thin she did feel the cold and she used that as a reason to wear thick winter pyjamas that hid her figure. She couldn't imagine why Lexi would ever think she'd wear something as tiny as that red negligee.

'I knew you'd say that so I brought you this to wear over the top.' Lexi pulled out a little black, cropped bed jacket.

Or something Bella assumed was a bed jacket. It wasn't much bigger than the negligee but it did have sleeves and a fluffy, furry collar, but even so Bella knew it still wouldn't leave much to the imagination. She'd feel like a model in a lingerie catalogue. Lexi might be comfortable in that situation but she certainly wouldn't be.

'I'm in hospital, Lex, not in an adult movie!'

'Come on, Bella,' Lexi pleaded. 'One of the hottest doctors in the hospital is coming to visit and you're in daggy old flannelette PJs. If ever there's a time for some glamour, it's now. You can't wear what you had on yesterday.'

Bella felt her eyebrows shoot up and almost disappear into her hairline. Lexi expected her to wear this in front of Charlie!

She wished she had the confidence to wear something like that. Just once. She knew Lexi had a dozen items just like this one in her own wardrobe. She'd bought herself one too when she'd purchased this for Bella, and Lexi made sure she wore them. But Bella wasn't Lexi. She didn't have her confidence, or her figure, and she couldn't imagine she'd ever feel comfortable in something that revealing.

Bella was shaking her head in protest but Lexi was used to getting her own way and she hadn't given up yet. 'Won't you at least try it on? Look how cute this jacket is.' She held it up against her. The black was a dramatic contrast to her platinum blonde hair and Bella knew the colour would work well against her own auburn curls. Lexi held the negligee and jacket out to her. 'Why don't you go into the bathroom and try it on?'

Bella could tell from Lexi's expression that she wasn't going to let this rest. The quickest way to get some peace and quiet was to give in. She'd try it on and then change straight back into her pyjamas.

She slipped the oxygen tubing over her head and unhooked the IV drip to carry it with her. She sighed. Getting changed wasn't simply a matter of swapping clothes. All the paraphernalia attached to her made the task that much more complicated. She grabbed the clothes and stepped into the bathroom, wondering why she always gave in and Lexi never did. Once again she was letting Lexi get her way while Lexi refused to budge an inch over the wedding date. Bella knew it wasn't quite the same thing but, still, it wouldn't kill Lexi to give in for once.

She hung her pyjamas on a hook behind the door and wriggled into the negligee. The bodice was firm and she had to tug it down over her head. It had built-in support that pushed her breasts together and created the illusion of a cleavage before the silk skimmed her ribs and flared out slightly over her hips. The silk was cool against her skin and as she turned around to try to see the view from the rear the silk swished around her hips and the sound of it made her feel like an actress in one of the 1950s movies she loved so much. But the negligee left very little to the imagination. She felt extremely exposed. She slid her arms into the jacket and tied it together at her throat. It gave her a little bit of cover but not nearly enough. She stuck her head out of the bathroom to catch Lexi's attention. She had no intention of stepping back into her room dressed like this. She waited until she'd caught Lexi's eye before opening the door a little wider.

Her sister looked her up and down. 'It looks gorgeous. Do you like it?'

'It feels fantastic,' Bella admitted. She loved the feel of the silk against her skin but it was far too revealing an outfit for her. 'But I couldn't possibly wear it in here.'

'Not even the jacket?' Lexi asked.

The jacket was rather fun but Bella knew it would look ridiculous over her pyjamas. Maybe she could wear it over a singlet top but she'd still have old pyjama pants on. She shook her head, she had nothing to wear it with, and then she closed the door and swapped glamour for comfort.

She handed the garments to Lexi as she emerged from the bathroom.

'I'm not taking them home,' Lexi said, 'I'll just leave them on the bed in case you change your mind.' Slightly mollified, Lexi laid them across the foot of Bella's bed before she left, promising to come back later in the afternoon.

Bella's morning tea had been delivered but as she ate she couldn't stop thinking about the red negligee. And about how different she was from her sister. Although perhaps their taste in men wasn't so dissimilar, she thought. She had to agree with Lexi, Charlie was hot. But that was where the similarities ended. Bella would be mortified if anyone saw her in that outfit whereas Lexi would lap up the attention. Lexi would have worn the negligee and flicked her platinum locks and flirted up a storm with an attractive man, while Bella would retreat into the safety of her androgynous pyjamas. She reached for the negligee and picked it up, letting the silky fabric run through her fingers before she stroked the soft collar of the jacket. Perhaps she could redesign this into something she might wear. Something a little less flamboyant, a little less show-girl, a little more restrained.

She had one last mouthful of chocolate ice cream and a final bite of the chocolate muffin before she pushed the morning tea tray to one side to start drawing. She looked at the wedding-dress sketch she'd begun on the scrap of paper and ideas based around the little jacket began popping into her mind. She started sketching another wedding dress, pretending it was something she might one day wear but knowing she was kidding herself. It would never be her. She'd spent so much time in and out of hospital in her short life that she'd never even had a proper boyfriend. When she'd been well enough to go to school she'd always been so far behind in her work that her time had been spent trying to catch up. Making matters more complicated was her mild dyslexia, which had made schoolwork even harder. She could have decided not to bother and concentrated on boys and having a good time instead but it wasn't in her nature to give up so she'd struggled on. Besides, it wasn't like the boys had ever been interested in her anyway, not when her gorgeous younger sister had always been nearby.

The only time Bella had ever come close to having a romantic experience had been on a camp run by the cystic fibrosis foundation. That was where she'd had her first, and only, kiss and she didn't kid herself it had been because the boy hadn't been able to resist her. It had happened because it was a teenage camp and most of them had been in the same boat, looking for normal teenage experiences. With her history, walking down the aisle as a bride wasn't something that was likely to happen in her future. She was resigned to being the spinster sister. Lexi was already engaged and even though Evie wasn't showing any signs of settling down yet, Bella knew it would only be a matter of time. Whereas, for her… She sighed, but, she supposed, being unmarried was probably better than being dead. Probably.

She needed to be positive. That's what Charlie had told her. She looked again at the red negligee as she thought about Charlie. She wondered what he would make of it. He'd probably seen more than his fair share of gorgeous, scantily clad women and she wondered how she would compare. Unfavourably, she imagined.

She thought back to their conversation yesterday. She'd amazed herself that she'd actually been able to get the words out, she'd been terribly nervous and had had difficulty stopping herself from fidgeting obsessively, but in the end she'd managed to have a one-on-one conversation with Charlie. It was no small coincidence that the last time she'd had a personal conversation with someone who wasn't related to her or who wasn't her doctor had also been with Charlie. She doubted he even remembered that night, the night of her high-school graduation ball, or more accurately the night she'd missed her high-school ball, but Charlie had made her night considerably better and even if he might have forgotten all about it, she knew she never would. She didn't find it easy to open up to people but Charlie was a good listener. He was always so relaxed and that seemed to relax her. Still not enough to completely eradicate her nerves, but it was a start.

Charlie had wanted to know what she'd wanted. 'Nothing,' she'd said. But that wasn't quite true. There were a lot of things she wanted. Well, not things exactly, experiences would be a better term for it. Because of the cystic fibrosis she'd missed out on so many things her sisters had done and if she could, she'd love a chance to try some of those things for herself.

She wanted to go on a proper date.

She wanted to be held in the arms of a gorgeous man and twirled around the dance floor.

She wanted to wear a fabulous dress with a full skirt that floated around her and a plunging neckline before she had terrible scars.

She wanted to stand under a starry sky and be kissed senseless.

She wanted to stay up all night and watch the sun rise over the ocean.

She wanted to lie on a picnic rug with her head in her boyfriend's lap and eat strawberries and drink champagne.

She wanted to be able to say, 'They're playing our song.'

She wanted someone to look at her as though she was the most desirable woman he'd ever seen.

She wanted to fall in love.

Bella laughed at herself. She couldn't go back in time and she was so unaccustomed to looking forward that she couldn't imagine getting a chance to do any of those things. There were way too many variables.

First she'd have to have the opportunity to meet someone, then she'd have to be brave enough to engage them in conversation, then she'd have to wait and hope for them to ask her out. She wished she could be a bit more like Lexi. Lexi wouldn't wait to be asked out. Lexi never needed to wait.

Bella wished she was confident enough to flirt and chat but even if she was, who would she flirt with? Who was she going to meet in here? Charlie was coming but there was no way she could flirt with him. Even assuming she knew how to flirt, he would wonder what on earth had gotten into her. It was all she could do to have a normal conversation, she'd have to be crazy to push herself any further. She wished she didn't find Charlie quite so attractive. She might be able to flirt with someone she didn't have a crush on, but what was the point in that? She wouldn't want to date anyone she didn't fancy. But did that mean she would date Charlie? She knew she would in a flash and just thinking about it made her blush. It was a ridiculous idea. She couldn't imagine him asking her out any more than she could imagine flirting with him.

'*Ciao*, Bella, you're looking brighter today.'

The sound of his voice made her jump. She'd been a million miles away and for a moment she wondered if she'd imagined him and his familiar greeting, but when she looked up she found him smiling at her and her heart skipped a beat.

He was wearing short-sleeved blue scrubs and had obviously just come from Theatre. His forearms were tanned and muscular but tapered nicely into narrower wrists and the long, slender fingers she always associated with surgeon's hands.

Bella took a deep breath as she willed herself to stay calm. *You've known him for years, he's just a man.*

But he was so gorgeous, was it any wonder she got all flustered? He was standing in front of her, looking hot and sexy, while she was in bed, looking frumpy and pale. They were at opposite ends of the spectrum as far as sex appeal went. Perhaps she should have left the negligee on. It might have been better than her ancient pyjama pants.

The two of them were such a contrast it almost made her laugh out loud. It was ridiculous to even imagine he'd ever ask her out.

Somehow she found her voice. 'I'm feeling much better,' she answered. 'Whatever cocktail Sam has put me on seems to be working.' She knew she had more colour in her cheeks but it wasn't because she was feeling better, it was because she'd been daydreaming about Charlie, and now that he was standing in front of her she felt her cheeks redden further.

Charlie stepped closer and brought the smell of sunshine with him, which overpowered the antiseptic smell of the hospital. Bella took a deep breath and savoured his scent as she tried to commit it to memory.

'Have you had a chance to speak to Sam about the wedding?' he asked.

She nodded.

His brown eyes watched her intently. 'How did that go?'

She smiled, remembering how nervous Sam had seemed. 'He said he'd do his best but I could tell he didn't like his chances. You'd think someone who's feted as being a top-class surgeon would be afraid of nothing, but I think Lexi is calling the shots.'

Charlie burst out laughing. The sound of happiness filled the room and made Bella smile even wider.

'He did say he'll file their notice of intent to marry. They need to have that lodged a month and one day before they can legally tie the knot.'

'That's a start at least,' Charlie said as he reached out his hand and ran a finger lazily around the edge of her almost empty bowl. He slid his finger into his mouth and Bella's eyes were riveted to the sight of it disappearing between his delicious lips as he licked it clean. He raised one eyebrow. 'Chocolate ice cream for morning tea? That's an interesting diet.'

'Don't you know? A high-fat diet is recommended for cystic fibrosis sufferers.'

'Is that right?' His brown eyes caught the light and the tiny flecks of gold in his irises reflected the light back at her.

She nodded. 'There has to be an upside every now and again, and eating dessert at any time of the day or night is one of them.' Never mind the assortment of tablets lined up on her shelf. Pancreatic enzyme replacement tablets, vitamin capsules and salt replacement tablets marched along the wall in an orderly row, ready and waiting to be taken regularly, but fortunately Charlie hadn't noticed them. His attention had moved on from the ice cream to her sketch book, which was lying open on the table.

'What have you been up to?' he asked.

She glanced down at her sketch book, surprised to see the pages covered with drawings.

A full-skirted wedding dress with a fur-trimmed fitted jacket took up most of one page and beside it she'd drawn a pair of intertwined rings. She remembered starting the dress but she didn't recall filling in the rest of the pages. Luckily she could pass the dress off as Lexi's wedding dress but the other sketches had nothing to do with Lexi. While she'd been daydreaming her hand had been transferring her thoughts to the paper. There was a sunrise warming an ocean and casting light onto a sandy beach. She could see footprints in the sand and in the corner of the page, where the footprints stopped, she could see the tasselled fringing of a picnic rug.

In the centre of the other page she'd drawn a pale green silk dress, its neckline similar to that of the negligee but with a full skirt. She'd drawn the skirt so that it was billowing out as if it was spinning to the music made by the notes she'd surrounded it with. She must have continued doodling absent-mindedly and stars, strawberries and music notes were scattered over the page, surrounding the green dress.

Around the edge of this page, framing it in a border, were lips—plump, juicy, soft lips, coloured in shades of pink and red. She blushed as she saw the frame she'd made, a frame of Charlie's lips. But it was too late to close the book, too late to hide her thoughts. Charlie had spun the book around, looking more closely at the pictures.

'Your drawings are really good.'

Please, please, don't let him recognise the lips.

'Is this for Lexi?' he asked, pointing to the wedding dress.

'Mmm,' Bella replied.

'And is this the bridesmaid's dress?'

She shook her head. 'No.'

Could she tell him? Talking about other people was easy, that came much more naturally to her; talking about herself was harder, much harder. But she'd managed to talk to him yesterday. It was silly to be so nervous.

She looked at her sketches. If she wanted any of those things to happen she would have to force herself to bury the introvert within her. Shy, retiring wallflowers didn't get any of those things she wanted, experience had taught her that already. She was twenty-six years old, she'd known Charlie for ever, it was time to start being a little more extroverted.

She took a deep mental breath. 'That's the dress I want to wear to go dancing.'

'Who are you going dancing with?'

She could hear the note of surprise in his voice.

'No one,' she replied. 'I was daydreaming. These are things I'd like to do when I get out of here.'

'You've drawn a "to do" list?' he asked.

Bella shrugged. 'I think in pictures, not words,' she explained. Even before she'd been diagnosed with dyslexia she'd always thought in pictures and found drawing a much easier way of expressing herself. 'And it's not exactly a "to do" list, more a wishlist.'

'So, dancing?'

Bella nodded and Charlie pointed to the next picture.

'I want to stand on the beach and see the sun rise,' she told him. She held her breath as she waited for him to point to the next picture. *Please don't ask about the stars in the sky.* She didn't have the words to explain that she wanted to be properly and thoroughly kissed by someone who knew what they were doing. She relaxed when he pointed to the footprints in the sand that led from the sunrise to the picnic blanket.

'I want to go on a picnic.'

'A picnic?' He was frowning. 'Surely you've been on a picnic?'

'A proper picnic,' she said.

'What on earth is a "proper picnic"?' he asked with a smile which made Bella's heart rate kick up a notch.

'You know, like the ones in movies where there is such an enormous amount of food you wonder how they've managed to fit it all into the basket let alone carry it across the field. Just two people, in a world of their own, no one else around, just peace and quiet.'

'Let me guess.' Charlie laughed. 'The champagne has stayed cold, the salad isn't soggy and the ants aren't trying to share your meal.'

'Laugh if you must, but someday I am going to enjoy a proper, perfect picnic.'

'So you're going to be at Lexi's wedding, watch the sunrise, go on a perfect picnic and dance under the stars?' he said as he turned the page, obviously looking for more pictures. 'Where're the rest?'

'That's it.'

'That's not much. You could knock that all over in one weekend.'

'You might be able to. I'm not sure if I'd have the stamina.'

'So what's this for?' Charlie treated her to a wicked grin as his hand dipped down towards the end of her bed and disappeared behind the table holding the remnants of morning tea. When he lifted his hand back up the red negligee dangled from his index finger. The table positioned across her bed had hidden the negligee from sight and Bella had forgotten it was lying in full view.

Bella blushed furiously. 'Nothing. Lexi was supposed to take it home for me.'

'Pity. I was hoping it had something to do with your list.' The negligee looked particularly minuscule and flimsy hanging from Charlie's finger and Bella couldn't help but recall that this was the same finger that had sampled her ice cream and been licked clean by those luscious lips.

'Like what?' Bella asked, half terrified and half excited to hear what his answer might be.

'It looks like something you might wear for a long lazy weekend in bed...' he paused ever so slightly '...with company. Drinking champagne by moonlight and getting up only to cook scrambled eggs at midday before getting back between the sheets.'

The picture Charlie painted was enough to make her blush. She'd never had a weekend like that, although it sounded as though Charlie was speaking from experience. He was folding the negligee as he waited for her answer and his hands looked strong and masculine tangled up in the flimsy fabric. The sight took any words right out of Bella's head. All she could do was shake her head in reply.

'So that's really it, that's your entire wishlist? What about something more challenging?' Charlie asked.

'Like what?'

'I don't know. Learning a musical instrument, running a marathon, learning another language, all those things other people always talk about doing one day.'

'I'm not sure I'm going to have time to do those sorts of things.'

Charlie frowned. 'Why not?'

'They're all long-term goals,' Bella said.

'What's wrong with that?'

'Nothing.' There was nothing at all wrong with it for other people. 'It's just I've never really thought long-term.'

'Oh.' She could see him connecting the dots.

'I've never got into the habit of long-term goals,' she explained. While things had improved considerably in the past twenty years, cystic fibrosis sufferers still didn't have a long life expectancy.

'But if you're going to have a transplant, surely now's the time to set some long-term goals. There must be something big you want to do?'

'I've learnt not to set unrealistic goals,' she told him. 'Every time I started something that was going to require a large investment of time the wheels would fall off and I'd get sick and never finish anything. I barely even finished high school because I missed so much time. I haven't expanded the list for after surgery because I've never thought long term, I wouldn't know where to start. My goals have always had to be achievable in the short term.' She looked up at him. 'Do *you* have a plan for your future?'

'Most definitely,' he replied.

'So how did you work it out?'

'Trial and error mainly. It's a work in progress.'

'If you thought you only had a few years left, would you be doing anything differently?'

That was an interesting question but not one he wanted to examine too closely. His current goals centred around his medical career. Medicine had served him well, it had given him another option when his life had gone pear-shaped, but if he hadn't had to plan for a long life, if he'd been living on limited time, would he have tried harder to recover a lost passion? A lost love?

Who was he kidding? He could have tried to resurrect those dreams but he never would have succeeded. He shook his head. Those dreams hadn't died, they'd been killed off and he hadn't had a chance to resurrect them.

'I guess I wish some things could have been different,' he answered, 'but they were out of my control. Things happen for a reason. One door closes, another one opens.'

'I'm just worried about doors closing at the moment,' Bella said. 'If I get through the surgery I can make a new list but I thought I'd start with the ones I've missed.'

'Fair enough, but I still think you should put a couple down for post-surgery. Something to look forward to, instead of back. There must be something.'

She didn't answer immediately and Charlie wondered if perhaps she had really never dared to dream of a future. Was there really nothing she wanted? He didn't think he'd ever met anyone as selfless as Bella. She had her head down again, drawing more pictures on her sketch pad. He watched as her hand flew across the page covering it with tiny high-heeled shoes that reminded him of Cinderella. Then, as suddenly as she had started sketching, she stopped and looked up at him.

'Fashion design,' she said, her voice whisper quiet.

'Fashion design?'

She nodded. 'That's my dream. To study fashion design.'

'Why aren't you already doing it?'

'I have to submit a written application.' She also had to submit six examples of her work but that part was easy. She had hundreds of sketches and finished designs to choose from.

'And?'

'I haven't been able to get the written part done.' Because of her dyslexia she'd never been a competent reader or writer and she'd gravitated towards the practical courses like art and design where she could rely on her drawing skills. The idea of writing a submission to a college, one that would determine whether or not she secured a place in their course, terrified her.

'What does the written part involve?'

'I have to explain why I want to do the course, what I hope to get out of it and why I should be accepted.'

'That doesn't sound too bad.'

She couldn't begin to imagine where to start. 'I can draw anything but I'm not good with words.' She wasn't about to admit her struggles to Charlie. She wasn't ready to have that conversation with him.

'I'll help you but you'll have to add it to your wishlist. It's already November—applications for next year will close soon if they haven't already.'

'Next year?'

Charlie was nodding. 'This is perfect. It'll give you something to look forward to. You tell me what this course means to you and I'll write the application letter for you,' he said as his pager began beeping. He took it from his pocket and checked it before adding, 'I'll come back tomorrow and we'll get started.'

He gave her a quick wink and was gone before she could protest. Before she could tell him she couldn't possibly go to college. It wasn't just the submission—how would she manage the written aspect of a serious course?

She picked up the negligee from where he'd dropped it on her bed. She stroked it while she imagined wearing it, imagined wearing it while Charlie's finger slid underneath the strap and pulled it from her shoulder. She imagined him bending his head and pressing his lips to the bare skin over her collarbone. She could almost feel the heat of his soft lips searing her skin.

She opened her eyes and shoved the negligee into one of the drawers beside her bed. That could stay buried along with her fantasies about studying fashion design and her fantasies about Charlie. None of those things needed to see the light of day again.

CHAPTER FOUR

BELLA felt as though she spent the best part of the next day with one eye on the door, waiting for Charlie. Lexi visited, Evie visited, Sam came on his rounds and pronounced her almost ready for discharge again, but Charlie didn't appear.

She didn't want to think about how much she'd been looking forward to seeing him. How often she'd checked the time during the day and as the hours advanced thought he must have forgotten about her. How she'd deliberately changed out of her daggy pyjamas into a slightly more re-spectable T-shirt and leggings. How she'd made sure the red negligee was still safely stowed out of sight in one of the bedside drawers.

It was late in the afternoon and Evie was visiting for a second time when Bella heard a new set of footsteps approaching. For a moment she let herself hope it was Charlie but she could hear that the steps were slightly un-even and whoever was walking towards her room was wearing high-heeled shoes.

An older version of Lexi tottered into her room. This woman had the same platinum blonde hair and the same bright blue eyes but Bella knew the similarities were only skin deep. This was her mother.

As usual she was immaculately dressed all in black. She had tucked her skinny black pants into high-heeled black patent leather boots and she wore a long black cardigan over a black top. A stranger could be forgiven for thinking Miranda was on her way to a funeral but this was her colour of choice broken up only by her blonde hair and masses of silver jewellery. Her make-up had also been perfectly applied. But underneath the make-up Bella could see the tell-tale redness of Miranda's nose. It wasn't red from crying, it was red from alcohol, and her eyes had a familiar glazed appearance. But otherwise her presentation was flawless.

Even when she's been drinking she's better groomed than I am, Bella thought. She and Evie exchanged a glance. *What is she doing here?* But before either of them had a chance to speak, Miranda broke the silence.

'Bella! My baby!' She leant over to kiss Bella and almost lost her balance. She reached out one hand and steadied herself on the bed. Bella's nose wrinkled under the smell of gin.

'Mum. What are you doing here?'

'I came to see you, of course.'

'I've been in hospital for three days and you're only coming in now?' As usual it was plainly obvious to Bella that she was not high on the list of her mother's priorities.

'Three days! I only just found out. Why didn't someone tell me sooner?'

'Richard has been trying to contact you,' Evie told her.

'Well, he didn't try very hard.' Miranda pouted.

'He's left several messages.'

'Why didn't *you* ring me?' Miranda asked Evie. 'Do you know how much it hurts to think that my own daughters wouldn't contact me?'

Typical, Bella thought. It was always about what was happening in Miranda's world. She had no great regard for anything other than her appearance and her alcohol supply.

Her daughters came a poor third behind her wardrobe and her alcohol addiction. Bella wanted to ask her if she knew how much she'd hurt her daughters. How much her abandonment of them as young children had hurt, how much her selfishness and drinking continued to hurt. But Bella didn't want to create a scene, she always did her utmost to avoid scenes, although that was hard to manage whenever her mother was around.

'We agreed that Richard would contact you,' Evie replied. 'Don't tell me you haven't got his messages. If you've been in no state to answer the phone or listen to your messages, that's no one's fault but your own. There's no need for all of us to be running around after you. Bella needs us now. We've been here for her as much as possible.'

Bella didn't know how Evie stayed strong. Bella wanted to stand up for herself but she wanted her mother to love her even more, and because of that she very rarely took a stand.

Miranda did her best to appear affronted. She drew herself up to her full height of five feet six inches but her heels gave her the extra two inches, which brought her almost up to Evie's height. 'I beg your pardon. I had one pre-dinner drink, you know how much I hate hospitals.'

Bella knew that even if her mother did detest hospitals, which she thought was unlikely, one pre-dinner dinner drink would still have preceded several more and dinner would be forgotten in favour of another glass of gin.

Did their mother have any idea how much her daughters wished she loved them enough to fight her demons? Bella knew Evie had long ago given up praying for that day but Bella hadn't. But there was no point in arguing about it. She wasn't going to change the facts. But she was exhausted and her mother's visit was making her emotional. She wondered if she had the strength to ask her mother to leave. Before one of them said something they might regret.

'Perhaps you should go, then, if hospitals disagree with you so much,' Evie said, coming to Bella's rescue once more.

'I have as much right as you to be here.'

'Actually, you don't,' Evie said. 'Bella needs to rest and as a doctor at this hospital I can ask you to leave. This is not about you. Bella needs positive support. If you can't give her that then you should leave. You need to take responsibility for your actions. Bella doesn't need to listen to your complaints. She doesn't need you to try to make her feel guilty about being in hospital. It's not as if she wants to be here. I'll walk downstairs with you and organise a taxi to take you home.' Evie turned to Bella. 'Will you be all right on your own for a bit?'

Bella nodded. 'I am tired. Perhaps you could come back one morning,' she said to her mother, unable not to make a peace offering, as Evie took a slightly bewildered Miranda gently but firmly by the elbow and steered her towards the door.

Evie kept hold of Miranda partly to make sure she came with her but also partly to prevent her from stumbling. While Miranda was so neatly presented Evie could pretend everything was fine. The girls knew that their mother's fastidiousness with regard to her appearance was all part of her deception but they held onto the hope that while she retained her sense of vanity maybe there was a chance she would one day seek the help she desperately needed. While she knew Miranda's disease wasn't something she could control or be responsible for, Evie wasn't sure that everyone else would see it from her point of view and she didn't want the hospital staff to see her mother in this state. Did that make her complicit in Miranda's problem? Did that make her an accessory to Miranda's addiction? She knew it probably did but she wasn't going to stop and think about it. Not now. She didn't want to be mean but she didn't have the energy to deal with her mother's issues today and she knew Bella didn't need the drama either. She would make sure her mother got safely out of there.

As she reached the doorway she saw Charlie approaching and saw him rapidly assess the situation. But she didn't worry. Other than her immediate family Charlie knew Miranda's history better than anyone. Evie and Charlie had shared many confidences during their final university years but Evie knew Charlie would be discreet, just as she always was with his personal history.

'Is everything okay?'

'Yes,' Evie answered, but she kept walking. She didn't want to stop and give Miranda an opportunity to create a scene. She knew very well just how likely that was. 'Are you on your way to see Bella?' She waited for Charlie to nod. 'Can you stay for a bit?' she asked. She didn't want Bella to be alone. Miranda's impromptu visits were always disturbing and she knew Bella would replay the conversation and stress over it. She needed company and Charlie would be a good distraction.

'Sure.' He knew what was needed.

Charlie continued walking and knocked briefly on Bella's door as he entered her room. She was sitting up in bed. She was still pale but the oxygen tubing had been removed from under her nose and for the first time since she'd been admitted Charlie could see her whole face without obstruction.

'*Ciao*, Bella. Is this a bad time?' he asked. 'I brought chocolate,' he said as he showed her the paper carry bag he held.

Bella's smile lit up her face. 'As far as I'm concerned, there's never a bad time for chocolate.'

Suddenly Charlie didn't notice how pale she was, or how thin—all he noticed was how her grey eyes sparkled and how the shape of her face changed. For someone of such a slight build she had a round face, but when she smiled her face became heart shaped and she looked less like a teenager and more like a woman. She was beautiful.

He'd always thought of Bella as the quiet one, the unobtrusive one. He'd never thought of her as being the pretty one. Tall, slim, glamorous Lexi with her platinum blonde hair and extroverted personality was hard to miss and Evie with her positive, confident attitude and easy smile was always in the midst of whatever was going on. Thinking of them like that, he supposed it wasn't surprising that Bella could slip through the cracks between her sisters and go unnoticed, that she would become lost amongst the dominant characters of her siblings.

But when he looked at her now it was as though he was seeing her properly for the first time. Her grey eyes were luminous, an unusual cool contrast to the fiery colour of her hair, and her skin was slightly flushed now, giving her a healthy glow. Her unusual colouring had always made her interesting to look at but he couldn't believe he'd never noticed her classic beauty.

He shook his head, trying to clear his mind as he handed her the bag of sweet things and pulled a chair up to the bed. Her bed was covered with pencils and sketch books but the red negligee was nowhere to be seen.

Her laptop was on the overbed table and she pushed it to one side before she emptied the contents of the bag, depositing them beside the computer. Chocolate muffins, chocolate cheesecake, caramel slice and chocolate bars covered the surface. 'What would you like?' Bella asked.

'You choose first, it's your treat,' he replied as he searched in the bag for spoons for the cheesecake. Bella was still smiling and he realised that for the first time she didn't seem self-conscious around him. Her smile seemed natural today; perhaps that was why she looked so different. He was amazed she didn't seem more rattled by her mother's visit considering the state she was in but he supposed she was used to it. 'So things haven't improved for Miranda?' he asked.

'No. But I've learnt there's nothing I can do that will change things there,' she said.

He saw her straighten her skinny shoulders, preparing herself. He was finding her more and more admirable. For someone who looked so frail and young and delicate she was showing a remarkable amount of spirit. He liked that about her. The fact she wasn't going to give up.

'My mother has never made any secret of the fact that I have been nothing but a problem. I spent years trying to atone for it but nothing I do has ever made any difference so now I try to ignore her barbs. Although at times I admit it's difficult. But I certainly don't want to dwell on her tonight. She doesn't spend any time worrying about me. I'm going to return the favour.'

The Lockheart sisters were lucky to have each other, he thought; they certainly didn't get a lot of love and attention from their parents. No wonder they were so close. He may not have had the same privileged lifestyle that the girls had had, in fact his family had struggled financially, but he'd never suffered from a lack of love and attention. His family was close, and even though more money would have made a difference to their daily lives, it wouldn't have changed their relationships. Money could never replace love.

Bella reached out and took one of the spoons from his hand as he sat mutely contemplating their differences. 'I suggest we eat chocolate and talk about something else,' she said as she reached for the bottles of tablets, shaking some enzyme-replacement pills into her hand before selecting several, which she swallowed with a mouthful of water.

He tried to stop staring but he was finding it difficult. He didn't want to freak her out but he couldn't think of anything to say and it took him a moment to even remember why he was there. 'Let's talk about your course application. I came to help you submit it.'

Bella looked startled, her grey eyes wide. 'I appreciate your offer but you don't have to help me, you know.'

'Are you going to do it without my help?'

Bella shook her head and her auburn curls bounced around her shoulders. 'No.'

'Did you want me to come back tomorrow instead?'

'Sam thinks I'll be able to go home tomorrow. I'll get Lexi to help me then.'

'No, you won't,' he argued.

'How do you know?'

'If you were going to let Lexi help you, you would have done this ages ago. I've done all the research, we have chocolate, let's get to work.' He'd promised Evie he'd keep an eye on Bella. She needed distracting. Otherwise, despite her protests, he knew she'd dwell on her mother's issues. Working on her application would provide a perfect distraction.

'You've done all the research?'

He nodded. He liked to be prepared in everything he did. He didn't like surprises. In his experience surprises were never a good thing. 'I had a look at it in some more detail last night. It shouldn't take too long to get it together.'

'You looked at it last night?' Bella raised an eyebrow. 'Didn't you have a date?'

Last night had been Wednesday, traditionally a big night with half-price drinks at Pete's Bar, the local watering hole for hospital staff. Normally Charlie would have been at Pete's. It was always a good place to hook up with an attractive woman, there were plenty of them at the hospital and plenty of them frequented Pete's for drinks at the end of a shift. But he had promised to help Bella and he'd been keen to see her reaction when he arrived prepared. Besides, pretty nurses would be at Pete's again the next time he called in.

'Not officially.' He changed the subject, bringing them back to the reason he was there. 'Did you know the cut-off for applications is next week? Have you got samples of your work to send in?'

Bella nodded. 'The practical aspect of things I'm prepared for, it's just the written application that terrifies me. Words aren't my thing.'

Charlie grinned. It felt good to be doing something like this. He enjoyed finding solutions to problems and that was something he loved about medicine too. 'That's why I'm here. Can you log onto the college website?'

Bella opened her laptop and ran her finger over the mouse pad, bringing the computer back to life. She'd forgotten she'd been watching a DVD earlier and before she could minimise the screen the movie reappeared and Charlie immediately recognised it. Normally she'd be embarrassed if someone discovered her watching the romantic comedies she adored but she'd decided that after the episode with the red negligee she wouldn't waste time being embarrassed. Besides, he already knew her deepest, darkest secrets and if he could accept her alcoholic mother, surely he'd accept her penchant for light cinema.

'Good movie,' he said as he sat down.

Bella felt absurdly pleased that he hadn't criticised her taste in movies. She smiled. 'You've seen it?'

'*Pretty Woman*? Of course. Hasn't everyone?' he said. 'If I remember correctly, it's a modern version of the classic fairy-tale. The rich, handsome hero arrives in his chauffeured limousine, climbs the fire escape to the heroine's tower with a rose between his teeth and rescues her from her tortured life. That sounds suspiciously like Snow White, or maybe Sleeping Beauty, don't you think?'

'Careful. You're having a go at one of my favourite movies,' Bella retorted as she closed the program and logged onto the internet. 'I like to think there's more to it than that. Vivienne wants someone who can see past her outer shell, someone who can see the woman underneath.' Bella knew she identified with the character of Vivienne, probably more than was good for her. 'Edward needs someone to make him see the joy in the little things, to make him see that there's more to life than making money. They need each other. That's what I love. There's nothing wrong with a happy ending, is there?'

'No, not at all. I'm only teasing. I meant it when I said it was good, I just didn't know people still watched it.'

'Go ahead, make fun of my taste in movies, but I'm not the only one who loves it.'

He laughed at the expression on her face and the sound of his laugh and the way his brown eyes crinkled at the corners made her forget all about being cross. She could sit there all day and watch him laughing. He looked so comfortable, completely at ease, happy and relaxed. She couldn't remember feeling like that for a long time. Perhaps if she could spend more time in his company some of his joie de vivre would rub off on her.

'Has that website loaded yet?' he asked once he'd finished laughing at her expense.

She turned her attention back to her laptop, pleased to have something to focus on, something to distract herself from those fanciful thoughts.

'Why are you doing this for me?' she asked as she waited for the website to load. Once she was in she followed the links to the page she needed. She knew how to navigate her way around the site; she visited it regularly. She'd just never been brave enough to take the next step of applying online.

'You'll thank me when you've recovered from your op and you've got all those years stretching ahead of you.' He was still grinning at her and she forced herself to concentrate on what he was saying. She knew she was too easily mesmerised by his smile, by his perfect pink lips. 'You'll need something to do. Even Vivienne in *Pretty Woman* has a job. Not that I'm recommending you follow in her footsteps, I think fashion design is a better fit for you.'

There he went again, making jokes at her expense. 'I never realised you were such a comedian,' she said.

'I'm doing this because I want to help. You asked me to keep an eye on Evie and she asked me to do the same for you,' he admitted. 'This is a way I can be useful at the same time.'

That made sense. Charlie was here because Evie had asked him to come.

Bella wanted to be upset that he hadn't come for her sake but if this was the only way of getting him to visit, she wasn't going to complain. She was used to people doing things for Evie, just like she was used to Lexi always getting her own way. It was just how things worked around her sisters.

'But I don't mind, I can think of worse things to be than the Lockheart sisters' unofficial guardian,' Charlie added, and he sounded so sincere that, once again, Bella found her irritation disappearing immediately. She couldn't have stayed annoyed with him even if she'd wanted to.

He lifted the laptop off the table and set it on the edge of the bed. 'Now, you need to tell me all the reasons why you're desperate to do this course, what your goals are and why you should be considered as an applicant. Then I'll make you sound so fantastic they won't be able to refuse you entry.'

And, over the course of the next hour, that's exactly what he did. By the end of it Bella didn't recognise herself as the girl who'd barely graduated from high school and struggled to read. Instead she sounded accomplished and talented and Charlie had made it sound as though the college would be lucky to have her. 'Okay, that box is ticked,' he said as he saved the file. 'Once you get home you'll need to choose which examples of your work you want to submit and get everything into the college by the end of next week. What else do we need to organise?'

'I think you've done more than enough,' Bella said gratefully. 'I really appreciate your help but I'm okay. I'll be home tomorrow and then I just have to wait and hope that things don't deteriorate too much more before I get new lungs.'

'What about your wishlist?'

'That was just me being silly. It's not important.' She tried to stifle a yawn, knowing that Charlie would leave if he thought she was tired, but she was unsuccessful.

'Okay,' he said, 'we'll save that discussion for another day.' He stood and gathered up the remnants of their chocolate feast. 'Get some rest. I'll see you again soon.'

Bella didn't know when. She wanted to remind him she'd be going home tomorrow but she didn't want it to sound as though she was begging him to come and see her before she left. Why was it so hard to know what the right thing to say or do was? She'd made good progress over the past couple of days, she could actually talk to Charlie without blushing furiously or stammering, but she still continued to second-guess herself. Why couldn't she be more confident? Why couldn't she be more exuberant? Why couldn't she be more like her sisters?

CHAPTER FIVE

IT WAS late afternoon and Bella had not long woken up from an afternoon nap when she heard the intercom at the front gate buzzing. She wandered into the kitchen, wondering where Rosa was. The succession of nannies the girls had grown up with had long ago been replaced by a succession of housekeepers, but the kitchen was empty, Rosa was nowhere to be seen. The buzzing continued. Bella crossed the room to the intercom. Rosa had left a note on the bench, letting Bella know she'd popped out to the shops, and on the intercom screen Bella could see a courier waiting at the bottom of the driveway. She pressed the button to open the gates and met him at the front door.

'I have a registered letter for Miss Lockheart.'

'Alexis Lockheart?' Bella asked, assuming it was for Lexi, who, as far as she knew, was out of the house. 'Does she have to sign for it?'

The courier checked his records. 'Miss Arabella Lockheart, it says, but anyone can sign.'

Registered mail for *her*? Bella frowned and signed the digital receipt, wondering what it could possibly be. The courier handed her a small envelope. It was thick, glossy cream; it could only be an invitation. The only things Bella ever got invited to were Lockheart Foundation events and she'd never received a formal invitation for those. Her hands were shaking as she closed the front door and slit open the envelope and pulled out the contents.

> *Dr Charles Maxwell*
> *Requests the pleasure of the company of*
> *Miss Arabella Lockheart*
> *On Saturday 17 November*
> *For dinner and dancing*
> *On board the* MV Endeavour 2000
> *Please be ready to depart at 6 p.m.*
> *Dress: After Five*
> *RSVP: None required. Dr Maxwell will not accept*
> *any excuses!*

The invitation *was* for her.

Bella sank onto a chair in the front hallway and read it again just to make sure. Charlie was inviting her out. *Her*.

She couldn't possibly go. Could she? A list of excuses ran through her head. She could think of plenty.

She read the invitation a third time. Then re-read the RSVP. Charlie would not accept any excuses. What was she going to do?

At a few minutes after six on Saturday evening Bella eased herself into the soft, puffy comfort of the leather seats and tried to think of something clever or witty to say. *Quick, think of something, anything, before Charlie gets into the car. Before he realises I'm a dud date.*

But Charlie was already getting into the limousine. His subtle, spicy scent combined with the smell of leather and wood polish and made it impossible for her to think.

She was ridiculously nervous. Her heart was racing in her chest and her palms were clammy. She had thought about trying to get out of the date, not because she didn't want to go but because she didn't want to be disappointed. She knew her expectations of the evening would far surpass anything Charlie could have imagined. But when Lexi had arrived home the other day to find her still sitting by the front door, clutching the invitation in her hand, she had quickly put her 'event coordinator' hat on and organised Bella. Lexi wouldn't hear of her passing up this invitation and Bella had let herself be carried away by Lexi's excitement. To be honest, she'd been glad to let Lexi make the decision for her but now here she was, in a limousine, with Charlie, and no matter how many times she tried to tell herself that this wasn't a real date, that Charlie was just being nice, it didn't work. She still held out the hope that this would be the date she'd always dreamed of.

It was almost a fantasy come to life except for the fact that Charlie hadn't greeted her with a kiss. That should have reminded her this wasn't a real date. At least, not in a romantic sense. That should have settled her nerves but as she looked across to where Charlie sat in his dark navy suit, looking more handsome than she'd ever thought possible, her nervousness kicked up a notch. The cut of his suit was perfect, the back was double-vented, which accommodated Charlie's muscular frame and gave him room to move, and his plain white shirt had French cuffs which he'd fastened with silver cufflinks. She knew most people wouldn't notice little details like that but fashion had been her obsession for as long as she could remember. As she looked at Charlie sitting alongside her, she wondered whether she was becoming just a little bit more obsessed with him than was healthy. He was truly gorgeous.

'Can I pour you a glass of champagne?' His question broke into her thoughts.

She wasn't accustomed to drinking, after seeing its effect on her mother she tended to avoid it, but surely a taste of champagne couldn't hurt? Perhaps it would take the edge off her nervousness. She needed to relax if she was going to fully enjoy the evening.

'Are you still taking antibiotics?' Charlie asked when she didn't reply immediately. 'Would you rather something soft to drink?'

Bella hadn't even considered the medication she was taking. Perhaps it wasn't a good idea? But she felt like celebrating, tonight was a big deal for her. 'Would a small glass be all right, do you think?'

'I think so. I promise to keep a close eye on you and administer first aid if necessary,' he replied with a grin as he rotated the champagne bottle and removed the cork with a satisfying 'pop'.

Bella watched as he poured champagne into flutes. He handed her one before gently clinking their glasses together in a toast.

'Here's to a fun evening. And to you. You look beautiful.'

Had he just told her she was beautiful? She couldn't believe her ears. 'I do?' She swallowed hard, trying to dislodge the lump in her throat so she could speak clearly. If she sipped her champagne now, she knew she'd choke on it.

Charlie nodded. 'It's a big improvement on flannel pyjamas.' He laughed.

Bella's cheeks reddened. Once again he'd managed to make her blush. Being embarrassed seemed to be becoming a permanent state around Charlie. 'It's bad manners to laugh at your own jokes,' she managed to mutter.

'My apologies,' he said, looking anything but apologetic. 'But what happened to the green dress?'

She sipped her champagne and felt the tiny bubbles fizz in the back of her throat. For the life of her Bella couldn't remember what she was wearing. She looked down at her dress and saw silver sequins and white chiffon. Not a trace of green in sight. That's right, she'd borrowed a dress of Lexi's. 'The green dress?'

'The one in your sketch book.'

'That was just a design, I didn't have time to make it!' She'd only just had enough time to take Lexi's dress in at the seams and it was still a little big in the bust, but Lexi had fixed that with a padded bra. It was a beautiful dress, a bodice of silver sequins that would shimmer in the lights and a skirt of white chiffon that was made for dancing, but it definitely wasn't green. 'I need a bit more notice if you expect me to whip something up,' she added as the champagne loosened her tongue.

'I'll remember that next time.' Charlie smiled at her and Bella's heart did a funny flip and collided with her stomach.

She had no idea whether it was the effect of his smile or the champagne or his words that caused her insides to take up gymnastics. *Next time?* She didn't even understand what was happening this time.

'Where are we going tonight?' she asked, barely managing to get another sentence out.

'We will be cruising Sydney Harbour in style,' he replied. 'Dinner and dancing under the stars. I'm sorry it's not a picnic on the beach but I wasn't sure if that was wise given you've just come out of hospital. I thought we could save that for another time.'

There he went again, talking about the next time almost as though he really did have plans to see her again. She couldn't let it go again. 'Why would there be another time?'

'Bella! I'm gravely offended,' he joked, clutching a hand to his chest. 'Most girls wait till the end of the date before deciding they don't want to see me again.'

Bella laughed at his expression and she could feel herself relax. She knew it was his intention to put her at ease. 'Sorry, that's not what I meant. I'm just not sure why you're taking me out tonight, let alone why you might want to do it again.'

'I promised to help you with your wishlist and this cruise had all the things I know you love. Music, dancing, a starry sky and plenty of food.'

It's a pity she suffered from seasickness but she didn't tell Charlie that. She didn't want to hurt his feelings. He was being so sweet. 'You're right, it does sound perfect,' she replied.

She'd had the perfect excuse to get out of the evening, she did get terribly seasick, but he'd said on the invitation he wouldn't accept excuses and she wasn't about to give up what might be her only chance to have a night like this.

'Have you been on this cruise before?' she asked, hoping his answer would be no. She wanted the experience to be a first for both of them. But he was already nodding. It had been a silly question. She knew his reputation. He'd probably done this trip a dozen times, each with a different girl. She felt deflated but his next words cheered her up.

'Once before. The ortho department's Christmas party was on board last year.'

That wasn't so bad, that would have been a totally different experience to tonight. He wouldn't have been dining at a table for two that night, she assumed. Although with Charlie she suspected anything was possible.

The limousine came to a stop and through the glass partition Bella saw the driver get out of his seat. Charlie let himself out and came around the vehicle and waited for her as the driver held her door open. She climbed out as elegantly as she could in her unfamiliar high heels, and when her legs felt a little unsteady she blamed her strappy, silver stilettos and not the champagne.

The driver had delivered them straight to the gangplank of the MV *Endeavour* and Bella looked up at it amazed. It was sleek and white and ultra-modern. She wasn't sure what she'd been expecting but this was very slick. And enormous. It towered above them—she could count three decks rising above the water, and dozens of passengers were making their way on board.

Charlie took her hand as they joined the queue. His hand was warm and strong and secure and she was grateful not only for the emotional support but for the physical support as well. She could just see herself stumbling up the gangplank and making a spectacle of herself.

They made their way to the second deck where a waiter led them to a table beside the window on the starboard side. The dining room stretched the width of the yacht and the windows wrapped right around it. They would get glorious views of the harbour through sunset and into the evening, Bella realised as she sat down while the waiter held her chair for her.

Even seated she still felt a little light-headed and it wasn't until her entrée had been served and she had some food in her stomach that she was able to think clearly. At least, she blamed her hunger for her poor concentration, although it had as much to do with Charlie sitting opposite her. She couldn't quite get used to the sight and she was finding it hard to tear her eyes away from him long enough to look down at her plate or to enjoy the view of the harbour that was passing before them. She had no idea what they spoke about as she ate her prawn dumplings but she knew most of the conversation revolved around her. When their main courses arrived she tried to distract Charlie from the multitude of tablets she needed to take by asking him about himself.

'I think it's time you told me something about you. I've

known you for years through Evie but I don't actually know anything about your life, whereas I feel you know everything about me.'

'Even what you wear to bed,' he teased in reply.

Bella felt herself blushing again. 'See, it's only fair that you tell me something about yourself now.'

'Okay, but if I bore you, you only have yourself to blame.' He paused momentarily as he took some vegetables from a bowl in the centre of the table and added them to the beef fillet on his plate. 'Let's see, I'm the youngest of three siblings, an older brother and an older sister. We grew up in Wollongong, south of Sydney, my dad was a professional fisherman, mum is a nurse. I was a little bit wild as a kid. The Gong has some of the best surf beaches in the country and my mates and I spent just about every afternoon after school in the ocean. That's where I learnt to surf.'

Bella closed her eyes and imagined spending lazy afternoons lying on a warm beach or diving through the waves.

'Am I boring you already?' Charlie laughed.

She opened her eyes and smiled at him. She was happy in his company and happy to listen to him share some of his past with her. It made her feel special. 'No, I'm just imagining what it would have been like to be so lucky. I would have loved to have had that freedom.'

'I was given a long leash partly because of the community we lived in and partly by circumstances,' he told her.

'What do you mean?'

'My father had an accident at work when I was fifteen. He was out at sea, chasing a large school of fish, when a big storm hit. The crane on the fishing boat was damaged and fell onto Dad, fracturing his spine. That was the end of his days as a fisherman. He's in a wheelchair now. You might say I didn't cope very well at the time,' he said with a wry smile. 'Mum was understandably caught up in Dad's needs and I was angry, thinking I'd lost the father I knew. That's when I went a little bit wild. As long as I was home before dark no one minded where I was. I think it was easier if they didn't have to worry about me too. I had always surfed, most of the local kids did, and after Dad's accident I spent more time in the water than out of it. It was an escape. I went looking for freedom. I couldn't stand being cooped up in the house. I think seeing my father confined to a wheelchair, seeing him lose his freedom, made me hungry to make sure I had my own and I found that in surfing.'

'And later did they start to worry about where you were or did you run wild for the rest of your teenage years?' Bella wondered if she and Charlie had something in common after all. Were they both products of emotionally absent parents?

'Eventually things settled down at home, the dad I knew was still there, just physically different. We repaired our relationship. Dad accepted his situation more quickly than I did, he was amazing really. Mum too. Once I learnt to deal with the changes we were okay. Mum got a routine established and I was still allowed a lot of freedom but mum and dad needed to know where I was. By then I was quite a good surfer and I loved it. I think Mum was happy for me to be down at the beach as it meant I burnt off a lot of energy, although I'm not sure they were quite so happy when I won the junior world title and announced I was deferring university to join the professional surfing tour.' He gave her a half-smile and a slight shrug. 'But they didn't try to talk me out of it, just persuaded me to keep my options open. Dad had never had a chance to go to uni, fishing was the only thing he knew, and when that was taken away from him he really pushed the value of getting a good education. He saw it as a form of insurance.'

'So you had your parents' blessing to goof off and travel the world with your surfboard?'

'I did.' He grinned at her then, his smile open and honest. She couldn't see a trace of hurt or disappointment in his dark brown eyes, he looked as though he didn't have a care in the world. But Bella couldn't help but wonder what he'd gone through when his own accident had ended his surfing career, ended the freedom he obviously craved. But their heart-to-heart conversations had always been about her life and she felt it would be too intrusive on her part to ask him how he coped without surfing.

She chose to stay on safer, neutral ground. 'I'm still jealous. I've never travelled anywhere. I feel as though I spent my childhood indoors.'

Charlie was frowning. 'You've never been anywhere? I know Evie went on ski trips and didn't she have a trip to Europe when she finished school? Didn't you do those things too?'

She shook her head, sending her auburn curls dancing around her shoulders. 'Evie and Lexi got to do a lot of things that I never did. Not that I blame them. It wasn't as if it was their fault but it would have been nice to have been at my high-school graduation ball instead of in hospital or to have been sent to Paris when I finished school, but some things are just not meant to be.'

'Didn't I come and see you on the night of your grad ball?

Bella nodded and a warm glow suffused her, spreading from her heart through her body. *He remembered.* That had been the first time she'd ever spoken to Charlie alone. The first time she'd opened up to him, but she couldn't believe he remembered. That was the night she had become infatuated by Charlie.

She had been eighteen at the time and Charlie, at twenty-five, had seemed so mature. He'd travelled the world and was studying medicine. Because she'd taken two years longer than most to finish school, the boys she'd known had all been younger than her and in comparison to Charlie they'd seemed immature and silly. Charlie had entertained her with stories about his fellow students and their university pranks and Bella had thought how wonderful it all sounded compared to the drudgery of school. For the first time she'd found herself comfortable talking to someone who wasn't family. In Charlie's company she was able to relax and he'd managed to make her forget all about the graduation ball. Her adoration of him had started that evening and it had never stopped.

'You brought me flowers and chocolate,' she said. She didn't admit she still had the chocolate wrappers and the pressed flowers in a box in her wardrobe. In a box that contained very few keepsakes from her youth but ones that were precious nonetheless.

He grinned. 'I knew the way to a woman's heart even back then.'

Especially this one, she thought.

'You've earned your reputation as a charmer, that's for sure, but I still don't know how you happened to be there that night.'

'Evie and I were meant to be studying for our end-of-year exams but Evie was stressing because while you and Lexi should have been going to the ball together, Lexi was going and you were in hospital. Evie wanted to be in two places at once. She wanted to be with you both but that was clearly impossible. I figured we weren't going to get any studying done so I might as well come to the rescue. I couldn't help Lexi get ready so I volunteered to keep you company instead.'

'That doesn't seem fair.'

'On whom?'

'On you. Getting stuck with the hospital visit instead of the fun.'

'It was fine,' he said with a smile that took the sting out of his words. She wanted it to be better than fine. 'According to you, it wasn't fair that you were missing out on your high-school grad ball so keeping you company seemed like a small sacrifice.'

Bella winced. 'Did I complain an awful lot?'

'Actually, you didn't, even though, in my opinion, you would have been entitled to. You seemed to accept it as par for the course. You couldn't have behaved too terribly. I'm still here, eight years later.'

Yes, he was, but once again it had nothing to do with her and everything to do with his relationship with Evie. He'd promised Evie he'd look after her and Bella knew that was the real reason he'd agreed to help her with her list. That was the real reason they were here tonight.

'But I didn't realise,' he was saying, 'that along with missing your high-school graduation ball you never went on a ski trip or a school camp either.'

'I did get to go on one camp when I was about fifteen,' she admitted, 'but only because it was run by the cystic fibrosis association and Dad felt it would be okay. A whole bunch of us went away for a weekend and it wasn't too bad. Actually, it was quite good to be with other kids who were all going through the same issues but then the camps were stopped because there seemed to be an increase in the number of hospitalisations after the camps and the medicos were worried about cross-infection between the kids.'

'I can imagine what it was like, a camp full of teenag-

ers with raging hormones. It's no wonder kids got sick!'
Charlie laughed.

'I know.' Bella knew exactly why kids caught infections. After experiencing her first, and only, proper kiss
on that camp she was one of the ones who had ended up in
hospital. 'The trouble was we couldn't afford to be sharing
germs around so that was the end of that.'

'Well, that's why I'm here. I'm going to make sure you
get to try all those things you missed out on.'

'I think it's a bit late for school ski trips and my high-
school graduation,' she said.

'Maybe,' he agreed. 'But will you invite me to your
college graduation ceremony when you finish fashion design?'

Bella didn't imagine for a minute that Charlie was serious but she was touched that he asked. She smiled, 'Yes.
I will.'

'Great. Now finish your dessert so I can take you dancing.'

Bella realised then that the band was moving from dinner music into dance music. 'Aren't you going to finish
yours?'

When Charlie shook his head Bella finished her dark
chocolate mousse, minus a spoonful which she gave to
Charlie to taste, and then polished off most of his Eton
mess before she let him take her from the table.

He took her hand and led her past the dance floor and
out onto the large open-air deck on the bow of the yacht.
The music followed them.

'Why are we out here?'

'Wasn't dancing under the stars one of the things on
your wishlist?' Charlie asked.

Actually, she wanted to be thoroughly and properly
kissed under the stars but no way was she going to tell

him that! 'Yes, yes, it was,' she said as she stepped into his arms. She closed her eyes and let the music flow over her as she blocked out the thought of other people on the deck watching them. She didn't care, she wasn't going to think about them, she was going to savour the moment, the feel of Charlie's hand on her back, his breath on her skin. This was nearly as good as being kissed and she was determined to enjoy every second and commit the sensation to memory.

Charlie's embrace was warm and solid, making her feel as light as air on her high heels. The skirt of her dress swirled around her calves, just as she'd pictured it, the evening air was warm and the music was the perfect tempo. Bella closed her eyes and relaxed and pretended the night was never-ending as Charlie guided her around the deck. He was a graceful dancer. He danced like he walked, fluid of movement and light of foot. Bella supposed his graceful movement was a legacy of his surfing days—he would have needed good balance and smooth changes of direction—and she gave herself over to his lead as the songs blurred into one another.

'Look, the Opera House.' His voice was soft in her ear.

She opened her eyes as the yacht cruised past the Opera House. The white sails, backlit by the city lights, glowed against the evening sky. Even though she could see the Opera House from her own bedroom window, seeing the famous roof from within Charlie's arms made her feel as though she was seeing its beauty for the first time.

'It's magnificent, isn't it?' he said.

And it was. But it was poignant too because it reminded her they were now on their way back to Darling Harbour, and the night was almost over.

As if the band was in sync with her thoughts the music ended and the guests inside applauded. 'It sounds as though that's the end of our dancing,' Charlie said. 'Come.' He kept hold of her hand as they made their way back to the table. 'We have time for one last drink before our evening ends.'

The champagne was on ice and Charlie poured the last of it into their glasses as the dance floor cleared. 'So,' he asked, 'as far as dates go, did tonight meet with your approval or is now the point in time when you tell me you never want to see me again?'

She looked across the table at him. 'It was one of the best dates I've ever had,' she said honestly. She couldn't possibly tell him this was her first proper date. Not unless she wanted to confirm she was a total failure in the romance stakes. 'But to be honest, I haven't a lot to compare it to.'

Charlie laughed. 'Careful, woman, you're doing serious damage to my ego tonight. I was hoping to take home the prize for best night ever because it was fabulous, not because of a lack of competition.'

'We haven't all got as many notches in the bedpost as you reportedly have.'

'None of them serious, though,' Charlie told her.

'How come? What's been wrong with them?' She was genuinely curious and she knew a small part of her wanted to know in case the pitfalls were easily avoided.

'Some of them have been lovely but I've always measured my relationships against my passion for surfing.'

'What does that mean?'

'When I was surfing, if I wouldn't choose to spend time with a girl instead of hitting the waves, I decided I wasn't serious about her and that relationship never lasted long. I didn't see the point. If she wasn't special enough to make me give up an early-morning surf then she wasn't for me. Even when I couldn't surf, I still had that mindset. If I'm being honest, I probably thought even more about it. Surfing was a passion, the sense of freedom, the danger, the escape. A girl had to be something special to rival surfing. And when I couldn't surf any more I had to find a new passion and I found it in medicine, not relationships.'

'I can see how you could have a passion for medicine but it can't be similar to surfing in terms of freedom, surely?'

'You'd be surprised. Being in the operating theatre is a lot like being in the zone when you're surfing. I have to be in control because, if I lose it, things go wrong. But at least I am in control. I had to make split-second decisions while I was surfing and I have to do that when I'm operating too, but they are my choices. Everything that happens is up to me and that's a kind of freedom.'

'Does the same apply to your relationships—do you like to have total control, a sense you can get out of it whenever you choose?' It didn't take a rocket scientist to deduce that Charlie still craved freedom and making sure he didn't restrict himself by getting tied down in a serious relationship would ensure that. Even so, Bella was surprised to hear herself actually ask the question. The champagne must have loosened her tongue, she thought, she'd never normally be so forthright. Did she imagine a very slight hesitation before Charlie shook his head?

'Don't get me wrong. I haven't always been the one to end relationships. Sometimes the girl has done it first.'

That surprised her too. 'Why?' she asked.

'Usually because of my hours. Some of them have felt as though they haven't been my priority. They've been right, but...' he shrugged '...I never promised them my undivided attention. I still haven't found a girl whom I'd choose before surfing or my work.'

* * *

She raised her glass to her lips and looked over the rim at him. Her eyes were huge and it seemed to take her a second or two to focus on him. He wondered briefly if she'd had too much to drink before he dismissed the notion as ridiculous. She'd only had two glasses of champagne over four hours and even though she was taking antibiotics it wasn't as though she'd been drinking on an empty stomach.

She sipped her champagne and smiled at him and her grey eyes shone silver. Charlie relaxed. Perhaps she was just tired. Even though it was relatively early, she hadn't long been out of hospital. But he'd have her home, in bed, very shortly. Looking at her creamy skin, her warm hair and her flushed cheeks, he thought it was a pity she'd be in bed alone.

Where did that thought spring from? he wondered. That wasn't what the evening had been about.

He'd arranged tonight as a way of repaying a debt of gratitude he felt he owed the Lockheart family and also because he'd wanted to do something nice for Bella. It hadn't been about feathering his own nest. But old habits died hard and he couldn't pretend he didn't find her attractive. Couldn't pretend he hadn't noticed Evie's little sister had grown up. But that was the problem. She was Evie's little sister. She was off limits.

Tonight was about helping make some of Bella's dreams come true but now it was time to get her home.

She was a little unsteady on her feet as they left the yacht and, as he put his arm around her, keeping her upright, he wondered again about the wisdom of mixing antibiotics with even a small amount of alcohol. He was a doctor, he'd promised to keep her safe. He hoped he hadn't failed to keep his word.

Their limousine was waiting and Charlie bundled Bella into the warm interior. There was another bottle of champagne on ice but he ignored that and poured them both a glass of water instead. Bella drained hers in a few seconds and Charlie could feel her staring at him while he refilled her glass.

'Why did you shave your head?' she asked.

Yep. He'd definitely let her down. That didn't sound like something a sober Bella would ask. It was far too personal.

'It was time for a change.' That was partially true but the whole truth was far more complicated than that and tonight was about Bella. It wasn't the time to tell her about Pippa.

'You've had a shaved head for as long as I've known you and how long's that? Nine years? You don't change things very often, do you?'

'I guess not.'

'So what was the calatyst? I mean the cat-a-lyst,' she repeated, enunciating the word very slowly.

This was a story he normally avoided telling but he figured she was going through something much worse than the drama he'd experienced. She would probably understand—if she even remembered this conversation in the morning.

'I was on holiday in Bali, on my way home from a surfing tournament, and I was getting around the island on a scooter. The Balinese are not known for their good road safety record and I was young with a foolish sense of invincibility so I guess I was an accident waiting to happen. I got cleaned up by a truck on a mountain road and ended up in hospital with a collapsed lung and a shattered knee. That and torn cruciate ligaments put an end to my career as a professional surfer.' He spoke as though it hadn't been an extremely dark period in his life. It had taken him over a year to accept the fact his surfing days were over. The only thing that had stopped him from losing hope altogether had been going back to uni and meeting Evie. 'When I eventually got back to Australia and went back to uni I didn't want to be reminded of what I'd lost every time I looked in the mirror.' He'd lost more than his surfing career in the accident. It had also cost him his relationship with the first woman he'd ever loved. 'My hair reminded me of surfing and Bali and the accident. So I shaved it off.'

Bella reached out and ran her hand over his head. 'I think it suits you.'

Her hand was cool and soft against his skull and her touch sent a shiver of desire through him. 'You've got lovely lips too. They look sho shoft.' She was slurring her words ever so slightly and Charlie was mortified. Was she drunk? He couldn't believe he'd got her drunk. She lifted her hand again and Charlie waited, certain she was going to put her fingers on his lips, but her hand fell to her side as though she had no control over it any more.

'Didyouknow...' she was mumbling now and her words were running together and Charlie had to concentrate to work out what she was saying '...I've only been kished oncebefore. I'd like to be kished properly.'

Charlie felt Bella lean her head on his shoulder as she finished speaking. Had she just said she'd like to be kissed? He peered down at her, waiting, listening for more. But there was no more. Her eyes were closed and her breathing was slow and deep. Was she asleep?

He shifted in his seat and turned to face her, moving his arm to wrap it around her so she settled against his chest, telling himself he was doing it because it would be more comfortable for her than bouncing around on his hard shoulder. He hoped she was sleeping because she was exhausted, not because she'd passed out. Out of habit and concern he counted her respirations and took her pulse. Both were normal and Charlie breathed a sigh of relief.

Bella's handbag was lying on the seat between them

and feeling only slightly guilty he opened it, looking for her phone. He scrolled through her contacts list, looking for Lexi's number, hoping and praying she was home as he called.

Lexi was waiting at the front door when the limousine pulled to a stop. She raced over and yanked open the door. 'What happened? Is she all right?'

'She's okay, she's asleep. I'm hoping she's just tired but…' he winced as he finished the sentence '…she might be drunk.'

'Drunk!'

A wave of guilt and embarrassment swept over Charlie. 'I'm so sorry, she only had two glasses of champagne and she had plenty to eat.'

'She's not used to drinking—'

'I know,' Charlie interrupted. He knew this was his fault. 'And I know she's on antibiotics but I really thought she'd be okay.'

'That wasn't a criticism,' Lexi said. 'I was just going to say that the motion-sickness tablets she took tonight probably didn't help.'

Charlie frowned. 'What?'

'She gets seasick,' Lexi explained, 'and she took a couple of pills for that before you picked her up.'

This was going from bad to worse. 'Seasick? Why didn't she tell me? I would have cancelled.'

'That's exactly why she didn't tell you. She was so excited about tonight. It would have killed her if you'd pulled the pin.'

At least the extra medication explained why she'd been so affected by the champagne. The motion-sickness tablets would have dehydrated her more than normal and made her more susceptible to the alcohol. Perhaps he wasn't as negligent as he'd feared. 'We'll need to get plenty of water into her to counteract the dehydration from those tablets. Do you want me to organise a drip?'

'No. I'll keep an eye on her,' Lexi said, and Charlie wasn't sure if she was implying he was incapable or irresponsible or whether she thought she couldn't rely on him. He couldn't blame her, he hadn't given her a reason to think otherwise. 'Can you bring her inside?' she asked.

He scooped Bella up in his arms, surprised at how light she was, and followed Lexi up the stairs to Bella's room. Even carrying her upstairs was no problem.

'I'm really sorry, Lexi, are you sure there's nothing else I can do?'

'We'll be fine.'

'Her heart rate and respiration rate are normal but please ring me if you're worried at all,' he said as he scribbled his number on one of Bella's sketch books, which was lying beside her bed.

There wasn't anything else he could do. He let himself out of the house and climbed back into the limo for the trip home. He couldn't believe he'd let this happen; he couldn't believe he hadn't taken better care of her.

CHAPTER SIX

CHARLIE woke frequently through the night, constantly checking his mobile phone to see if Lexi had called him, but there was nothing. As soon as the sun rose the next morning he was out of bed, too restless and remorseful to sleep. He wanted to check on Bella but, if she was sleeping, which he hoped she was, it was far too early for a house call. He needed to clear his head, he needed to get into the water.

Even though his knee injury had cut short his professional surfing career he was still able to bodysurf for fun, but the surf this morning was flat and not at all appealing so he hit the Kirribilli pool. At this early hour only the keen swimmers were in the water and he joined their ranks, slipping into the fast lane and swimming hard for close to an hour. Swimming normally gave him a chance to clear his mind but it wasn't working today. Thoughts kept swirling around in his head. How could he have been so irresponsible?

There he was telling her an edited version of his life story while she was trying to combat seasickness. The tablets had certainly done their job, she hadn't shown any signs of queasiness. He smiled as he finished another lap, thinking about how much Bella had managed to eat. With everything she'd eaten he couldn't understand how the two glasses of champagne had affected her so badly. Perhaps she'd taken more tablets than she needed to?

But that didn't exonerate him from his responsibilities. He should have taken better care of her. But he'd been both distracted by her and absorbed in her and he hadn't been able to think clearly. She was virtually a stranger to him yet he felt as though he already knew her intimately through Evie. He was comfortable with Bella, he could be himself, just as he was in Evie's company, and that was a novelty for him. He was able to let his defences down. He climbed out of the pool and towelled himself dry as he wondered what it was about the Lockheart sisters that struck a chord with him.

Out of habit he scanned the other swimmers, looking for familiar faces. Finn Kennedy was just getting into the pool and Charlie nodded in greeting as he headed for the change rooms. He saw Finn fairly regularly at the pool but they rarely stopped and chatted, Finn always seemed so intent on his exercise that Charlie didn't like to delay him.

Charlie showered and changed quickly before leaving the pool. Sunday-morning traffic over the Harbour Bridge was just starting to increase as he walked out into the street and he looked up at the bridge as it stretched away overhead, spanning the water, before he turned away and headed back towards Mosman. To Bella.

The sun was high in the sky before Bella felt well enough to open her eyes properly and keep them open. Her tongue felt swollen and her lips were dry. She could remember Lexi forcing her to drink a glass of water every time she'd stirred in the night but still it felt as though her tongue was sticking to the roof of her mouth. She sat up, and she could see the indentation from Lexi's head in the pillow next to her. She knew Lexi had slept there but she was alone now.

She reached for the glass beside her bed as she tried to piece together what had happened last night.

She remembered dancing with Charlie, the feeling of his strong arms encircling her, making her feel as though her feet weren't touching the floor, as though she was floating across the deck. She remembered having a half a glass of champagne as the yacht came into dock. She remembered stroking Charlie's head.

Oh, my God, I didn't really do that, did I? But she knew the answer. She could still recall just how his head had felt, the short regrowth soft and fuzzy under her hand.

She slid down in the bed, burying herself under her quilt. How would she ever face him again?

She supposed she wouldn't have to. After last night he probably wanted nothing more to do with her.

She heard her door open. She couldn't face anyone right now. Maybe she could just stay under the covers and never come out again.

'Bella? Are you awake?' Lexi's voice was quiet. 'Charlie sent you flowers.'

That got her attention. She pushed the quilt away from her face and peered out. Lexi was half-hidden behind a mass of sunny, happy sunflowers. Just seeing their cheery, yellow petals made Bella feel brighter.

'He sent flowers?'

'He brought them around this morning, while you were asleep.'

'I thought he'd never want to speak to me again,' Bella said. 'I must have looked like a complete fool, passing out like I did.'

'I think he thought it was his fault. He felt terrible because he'd been plying you with champagne.'

'Hardly plying. I only had two glasses.'

'I know. I told him about the motion-sickness tablets

but I guess he still feels terrible,' Lexi said as she put the vase of flowers on Bella's chest of drawers. 'There's a card here,' she said as she removed the card and passed it to Bella. 'What does it say?'

Bella opened the little envelope and slid the card out to read the inscription. *'Ciao, Bella, I'm sorry I didn't take better care of you. Can I make it up to you on dry land? Charlie.'*

Suddenly she felt a whole lot better. He hadn't written her off, he was going to give her another chance.

'Charlie! I'm glad I found you.'

Charlie turned around at the sound of Evie's voice. She didn't look pleased to see him, she looked mad. He'd been keeping a low profile until he could organise to make up for his faux pas with Bella but he had been expecting Evie to track him down and haul him over the coals for leading her baby sister astray. He'd spoken to Bella, he'd apologised, she'd blamed herself and they'd agreed to forget about it and try a second 'date'. It would be something else from her wishlist but this time Charlie intended to keep to dry land.

Evie did not look happy. Not that he blamed her for wanting to tear strips off him. As far as he was concerned, he deserved it, but he still thought he'd try to minimise the fallout by apologising quickly. He held his hands up in surrender. 'I know, I'm sorry, it won't happen again.'

He watched as her expression changed from cross to puzzled. 'What are you talking about?' she asked.

'I assume you want to give me a bollocking over what happened with Bella?'

'No. She's fine. She's a bit embarrassed but she hasn't stopped talking about what a great night she had, right up until she fell asleep. There's something else I wanted to talk to you about. How well do you know Finn?'

'Finn Kennedy?'

'Of course,' she replied in a voice that suggested he'd lost his mind.

Charlie shrugged. 'As well as anyone can know him, I suppose. I see him at the pool a bit but we really only exchange greetings. He's never been one to socialise much, not even with the surgeons. Why?'

'I wanted to ask his opinion about Bella but he seems rather moody, more so than usual, as though he's angry with the world and everyone in it. I didn't know whether it would be wise, especially after what's happened today. And I just wanted to get your take on things, see if you knew about anything that might be going on that could have put him in a bad mood. See if you think I'm going to get my head bitten off for even going near him.'

'What happened today?'

'He went missing in action.'

'Finn did?'

She was nodding and she looked cross again but now it was obvious she was mad with Finn, not him. 'I had a patient who came in with a penetrating chest wound and I was trying to find Finn. I thought being an ex-army surgeon he'd be the one to call in for a consult, but no one knew where he was.'

'How's the patient?'

'We managed to keep him alive and he's gone to Theatre but it's very out of character and I'm a bit concerned. I need him to be on top of his game.'

'Why?'

'Because I need to ask him about Bella,' she replied, giving him a look that very clearly said, *Keep up!* 'And if he's got problems of his own, I don't want to risk it.'

'Risk what?' Now Charlie even felt like he was missing the bigger picture.

'Would you let him operate on you?'

'I thought Sam would do Bella's transplant...' He let his sentence tail off. He didn't want to state the obvious, which meant assuming compatible lungs were found in time.

'I was going to ask him if he'd assist,' Evie explained, finally allowing Charlie to catch up with her train of thought. 'Do you think there's anything to worry about, given that he's gone missing today and generally seems to be out of sorts, or would you let him operate on you?'

'I haven't noticed anything off. He might not be the most personable of people but he's a damn good doctor. You don't get to be Head of Surgery without being something a bit special.'

'That's what I thought but that was before he vanished in the middle of the day.'

'If you want my advice, it would be to stay out of Finn Kennedy's personal life. He may have had a perfectly good reason to take off in the middle of the day.'

'Don't you think he should have told someone where he was going? No one knew where he was.'

'And I imagine that's how he wants it to stay. You said yourself he doesn't confide in anyone. He's a loner and I think he likes it that way. I'm sure he's fine and I'm sure that even if there is something going on with him, he wouldn't let it affect his surgical skills.'

Charlie couldn't understand her concerns. In his mind they were unfounded. As far as he knew, Finn had never disappeared from the hospital before and just because Evie hadn't been able to track him down it didn't mean Finn had gone missing. He could have told someone where he was, and perhaps Evie didn't ask the right people in time.

But while he couldn't understand her concerns, he could

understand her logic in asking Finn to assist with the operation. While Charlie thought Sam was perfectly capable of performing Bella's surgery without Finn's help, Sam would need assistance and he guessed having two experts operating together was better than one. Whether or not Sam and Finn saw it the same way was something Evie would have to sort out, but until lungs were found it was all hypothetical and, in the meantime, Charlie had some plans of his own to arrange.

He had three days to organise his apology.

Bella hung her car keys on the hook and mixed herself a salt-replacement drink before wandering through to the conservatory. She'd had a long day at the hospital with several appointments all related to her transplant work-up and she couldn't afford to get dehydrated. She was exhausted and her chest felt tight but she put it all down to a long and tiring day. Rosa had pots simmering on the stove and Bella could see trays in the ovens and the kitchen benches were groaning under the weight of several other dishes covered with foil or teatowels. She lifted one corner of a teatowel. This platter held smoked salmon, pâté and other antipasto assortments. Her stomach growled with hunger but she needed to rest for a bit. She'd kick her shoes off and sit down for a few minutes and then she'd come back and see if she could sample whatever yummy things Rosa was making.

The conservatory overlooked the garden and the harbour. As Bella entered the room her attention was caught by the sight of a white marquee sitting in the centre of the lawn. That hadn't been there when she'd left the house this morning. It was the smallest of several her father had, and this one was sometimes used for garden parties. Bella wondered why it had been put up in the middle of the week. Initially all her attention was focussed on the tent and it wasn't until Lexi spoke that she noticed she was in the room.

'Good, you're back.'

Lexi was sitting on one of the day lounges, feet curled up underneath her, flicking through a bridal magazine.

'What's going on?' Bella inclined her head towards the garden and the marquee.

Lexi stood and tossed the magazine onto the table. 'Where have you been?' she said, ignoring Bella's question.

'At the hospital.'

'I expected you ages ago. You'll have to hurry now if you're going to be ready in time.'

'Ready in time for what?' Bella had no idea what was happening. Was there a function she was supposed to know about that had slipped her mind? That would explain the quantity of food in the kitchen.

'Charlie will be here in half an hour. He's organised another date. That's what the marquee is for.'

'What do you mean, "he's organised another date"?' Bella was frowning as she was looking out of the conservatory windows. The marquee was for Charlie? 'How did he do this?' she asked, waving one hand in the general direction of the garden. 'And how do you know so much about it—did you help him?'

Lexi was nodding. 'Rosa and I agreed to help.'

'You should be spending your time organising your wedding,' Bella argued. Lexi was constantly telling her how much time it was going to take to organise the wedding so she should be spending every spare minute on that, then the wedding might actually happen sooner rather than later.

'Charlie can be very charming and persuasive when

he wants to be,' Lexi replied. 'I thought this was more important.'

Bella knew she should argue but she couldn't think straight. Charlie had organised another date for them? She was getting a second chance? She forgot all about being tired as she ran upstairs to get changed. Lexi had said he'd be there soon. Bella had to get it right this time.

When she emerged from the shower she found that Lexi had selected an outfit for her. She assumed Lexi knew what the date entailed so she dressed in the clothes that were laid out on her bed. She'd chosen white cotton trousers, a white camisole and a lightweight caftan to wear over the top. The caftan was made from sheer cotton that had been printed with a pale green and white pattern with a scattering of beads hand sewn onto it. She teamed the outfit with flat sandals and put her medications into a small silver purse. She left her freshly washed hair loose, the curls cascading around her shoulders, and applied the bare minimum of make-up, mascara, lip gloss and a touch of blush.

'*Ciao*, Bella.' Charlie was waiting for her in the conservatory when she came back downstairs and hearing his familiar greeting made her catch her breath. He stood and came to meet her and she watched as his plump, juicy lips spread into a wide smile. He was casually dressed in denim jeans and a T-shirt that moulded nicely to his chest and his chocolate-brown eyes shone with good humour.

He kissed her on the cheek, pressing his delicious lips against her skin, and a tingle of desire shot through her, warming her from the inside. 'Thank you for giving me another chance. I promise to take better care of you this time,' he said.

Not for one moment had she blamed Charlie for her

condition the other night. It hadn't been his fault at all but she couldn't formulate the words to tell him so.

He cocked one elbow and waited for her to slide her arm through the gap before he covered her hand with his. She trembled under his touch.

'Shall we?' he asked.

She took a deep breath and nodded, eager to find out what lay in store for her tonight. With arms linked, they stepped into the garden and walked across the lawn towards the marquee. The grass sloped gently away from the house towards the harbour and the expanse was large enough for the water to still be visible past the marquee. Ferries criss-crossed the water, leaving a trail of white behind in their wakes, and a very slight breeze carried the sound of ferries tooting as they docked and departed from the Mosman Bay wharf to the west of the Lockheart home. The breeze also carried the perfume from the frangipani trees that hugged the boundary fence and had just started flowering. Across the water Bella could see the city lights and the shining white sails of the Opera House. The tent was enclosed on three sides and had been positioned with the open side facing the harbour. Bella knew they would have views of the city from within but the views paled into insignificance as Charlie led her around to the front of the marquee and took her inside.

'Oh, it looks beautiful,' she sighed.

The interior of the marquee had been set up to resemble a picnic. The space inside the small marquee was intimate but dominated by a massive Persian rug which had been laid out in the centre of the tent. The carpet was scattered with brightly patterned, oversize cushions and cashmere blankets, and fat candles and hurricane lamps were grouped in the corners of the marquee, casting a warm glow around the space. Fairy-lights had been strung up against the ceiling, giving the illusion they would be dining under the stars. Music was playing softly in the background and picnic baskets were lined up along one wall beside a large metal tub filled with ice that held an assortment of drinks.

'I thought we'd stay on dry land this time,' Charlie said as Bella stood, fixed to the spot, mesmerised by the colour and light and amazed by the effort Charlie had gone to. Somehow he'd managed to create a little oasis in the middle of a suburban garden in the centre of the city. 'Make yourself comfortable,' he said as he guided her towards the pile of cushions. 'I'm going to mix us a couple of baby Bellinis.'

Bella was about to protest, she wasn't planning on touching a drop of alcohol tonight, but Charlie interrupted her. 'It's okay, I'm using non-alcoholic cider, not champagne,' he said as he retrieved the peach nectar from the tub of ice. 'These will be perfect for our picnic.'

From the middle of the tent Bella could still see across the harbour but she had the sense they had the world to themselves, everything and everyone else seemed so far away.

'How on earth did you manage to organise all this?' she asked as he handed her a champagne glass.

'I can't take all the credit. I had some inside help. Evie told me you'd be out most of the day, Lexi got the marquee set up and Rosa has spent the day cooking your favourite things. I just told them what I had in mind. My only concern was that you'd be wiped out after your day of appointments.'

Her earlier fatigue had vanished in the excitement of the evening. 'I'm good, just starving,' she said as she slipped her sandals off and sat cross-legged on a cushion. Charlie stretched out beside her and his hand rested inches from her thigh. She wanted to pick his hand up and put it on her leg but before she had a chance he was on the move again.

'I haven't known you to be anything but hungry,' he said as he jumped up and searched through the picnic baskets, returning with two platters of appetisers, one warm and one cold. Pâté, smoked salmon and grapes on one, filo pastries and spring rolls on the other. Rosa must have transferred the food from the kitchen to the marquee while she had been in the shower. But surely all that food couldn't have been for them?

'How was your day?' he asked as he put the platters on the carpet between them.

'Interesting,' she replied.

'Who did you see?'

'I had a few tests, blood work, lung function, the usual, and saw Marco D'Avello and John Allen. At least John didn't tell me I'm crazy,' she said as she spread pâté onto a biscuit.

Charlie smiled. 'That would be a psychiatrist's job, John's a psychologist.'

'I know, but it always makes me nervous when someone starts delving into my psyche. It's only a matter of time before someone decides I'm a bit loopy. But he was more interested in whether I've got a good support network—although that could potentially open a whole other can of worms if he expects my parents to come to the party. Luckily I've got Lexi and Evie.'

'You're not expecting your parents to step up?'

Bella shook her head as she swallowed the pâté and biscuit. 'I've learnt it's better not to expect anything, particularly where my mother is concerned. She has very little to do with any of us. It's been that way for years. And she certainly hasn't wanted anything to do with me. I'm not glamorous enough—'

'You can't be serious,' Charlie interrupted. 'That can't be right?'

Bella shrugged. She appreciated his vote of confidence, even though she thought he was wrong. 'I'm sure it's part of it but I also think she can't handle having a sick child. Anything less than perfection isn't allowed in her world. If she could have removed me from her world, I think she would have. Instead, she removed herself from us.'

Charlie couldn't begin to imagine what Bella's life had been like. He knew she'd never wanted for material things but he could hear in her tone how much she longed just to be loved. He wondered how different her life would have been if she'd been healthy, if she hadn't been born with a defective gene. But he guessed they'd never know the answer to that question.

A fierce protectiveness rose up in him, stemming from anger towards Miranda Lockheart. Did she have any idea how her behaviour and her choices had hurt her daughters? Did she have any remorse? He knew Miranda's alcoholism was an illness but it was treatable. Unlike Bella's cystic fibrosis, Miranda could be controlled if treated if only she sought help. But as far as he knew, she hadn't tried and if she wasn't willing to do that then it was obvious her daughters were not her priority. 'What about your father? Have you been able to depend on him?'

'Financially I have, but while he's been in the picture more than Mum he's never really spent any time with me, not like he has with Lexi.' She shrugged again. 'I don't think he knew what to do with me. You heard him in hospital last week, he's used to throwing money at problems to solve them or make them go away, and if something can't be fixed with money, he doesn't know what else to do. With me, he paid for nurses and made me their responsibility so he could ignore the issue, ignore me.'

Charlie may not have had Bella's privileged background but he had a solid, tight-knit family and that included parents who had helped him find his place in the world. Even in his darkest days, when his surfing career had prematurely ended, no one could have taken his family away from him. Bella had her sisters but she deserved more, all three of the girls did.

'My life is what it is,' she said as she selected a slice of smoked salmon. 'Let's talk about something else.'

He was constantly amazed by her selfless nature. Even now she wasn't going to condemn her parents over her upbringing.

She stood up gracefully, unfolding herself from her cross-legged position on the cushion, and wandered over to the picnic baskets. 'What else did Rosa make me to eat?' she asked as she peered into the baskets.

Charlie followed Bella to the picnic baskets. Rosa had left crusty bread, sliced roast meats, mustards, salads, boiled eggs, mini savoury pastries, cheeses, fruit and a whole basket full of chocolate desserts. Looking at the amount of food, he was pleased he'd managed to organise the picnic in Bella's back garden. He knew she'd envisaged a private picnic but he hoped it was more about the company and less about the location—he certainly didn't fancy carrying these heavily laden baskets across a field to set up next to a meandering creek. This was far more civilised; he just hoped it satisfied Bella's expectations. He opened a third basket and handed her a china plate, silver cutlery and a linen napkin, and once she'd made her selection he followed suit before resuming his position on the Persian carpet.

'I put my college application in yesterday,' Bella told him as she sat beside him.

'Good girl.' He was thrilled she'd actually done something for herself for a change. 'How did it feel?'

'Terrifying,' she admitted. 'It's been years since I studied and even then I wasn't very good at it. I was eighteen when I finished school, two years later than I should have. You know Lexi and I did year twelve together and I wouldn't have got through without her help. That's why I was so reluctant to apply for fashion design, I didn't think I'd be able to do it. I still don't. But I'll give it a go.'

He was inexplicably proud of her. Tackling a tertiary degree was obviously a major hurdle for her to overcome. 'Studying a topic you love will be totally different from what you did at school.' He just hoped, having pushed her to apply, that she wouldn't be disappointed. He hoped she'd love it.

'That's what I'm praying for.'

'You're so passionate about design, I'm sure you'll enjoy every minute of it.'

'I hope so. I'm excited as well as terrified, if that makes sense, but you were right, it will be good to have something to look forward to. If I do have this transplant I can't sit around doing nothing for the rest of my life.'

'I'm sure you haven't been doing nothing,' he said as he realised she could have been doing just that for eight years. But that didn't gel with the woman he thought she was or with the woman he wanted her to be.

'I suppose not, but I can't say I've been doing anything terribly worthwhile either, although I do enjoy doing some interior decorating on behalf of the Lockheart Foundation.'

'Interior decorating?'

'Yes. Dad quite regularly buys flats around the hospital. He donates them to the hospital and they use them as short-term accommodation for country families who need somewhere to stay. I get to decorate the ones that need it and furnish them before they're handed over to the hospital. I enjoy doing that.'

'How can you say that's not worthwhile? Think of all the families who benefit from what you've done.'

'I guess, but it's not like your job. You do so much good.'

'Don't be so hard on yourself. You give people somewhere nice to stay when they're going through a tough time and once you've got your fashion design degree you'll be able to help people's self-esteem.'

'That's a lovely thing to say but it's hardly in your league.'

'Don't underestimate the power of self-confidence,' he told her. 'Your designs could give people that.'

She smiled at him. 'You have a knack of making me feel better about myself. Thank you.'

'You're welcome,' he said, as he fetched a bowl of strawberries and a bowl of dipping chocolate. He didn't know about making Bella feel better but her smile made him feel invincible. She groaned and stretched her arms over her head as he returned to the rug. 'Are you all right?'

'Yes. I think I just need to rest before I tackle dessert,' she said as she lay back on the cushion. 'Thank you for organising tonight. No one has ever done anything like this for me before.'

It broke his heart to think of how much Bella had missed out on, how little attention she'd been given. 'I'm glad I could surprise you,' he said as he vowed to do more to help her realise the dreams she had on her wishlist.

'I feel like I've been let loose on the world. No one asking how I feel, or getting me to breathe in and out, no one taking blood samples or poking and prodding. I can pretend I'm just like everyone else,' she said as she shuffled over to make room for him on the rug.

He placed the two bowls by her knees and lay on his side, facing her. They were inches apart. He could see the faint, individual freckles that were scattered across the bridge of her nose and her grey eyes shone silver in the candlelight. She wanted to be like everyone else but she was so different from anyone he knew. And it wasn't because of her illness, although perhaps that had contributed. She had a vulnerability about her but he knew that was deceptive because he'd seen her strength of character time and again; and she had a generosity that was uncommon. She was a selfless person and she made him want to be more selfless too.

He took a strawberry from the bowl and dipped it into the chocolate. 'Can I tempt you?' he asked as he held the strawberry above her lips. She reached up and brought his hand down towards her. She parted her lips and bit into the berry with tiny white teeth.

She rolled onto her side towards him as she swallowed the strawberry. His hand dropped to her hip and then he was motionless. His other hand was supporting his head and he could feel his biceps tighten with the effort. He watched as Bella slowly, hesitantly, stretched out her hand and traced the bulge of his biceps.

In the distance a ferry tooted but the two of them were silent.

Charlie lifted his hand from her hip and threaded his fingers through her auburn curls. They were soft and springy under his touch. He shouldn't be doing this, he shouldn't be touching her like this, she was supposed to be off limits, but he couldn't resist. The movement of his arm made the hem of his T-shirt ride up, exposing his abdominals. He saw Bella's silvery grey eyes drop to his waist and follow the movement of his shirt. She removed her hand from his arm, slid her fingers under his T-shirt and traced the ridge of his abdominal muscles. Her fingers blazed a trail of fire across his skin and made him catch his breath.

He released her curls and caught her hand in his, stilling her movement as he entwined his fingers with hers. Bella held his hand and ran her thumb along his fingers. He tried to fight the attraction that was building in him. He tried to do the right thing but then Bella lifted his hand to her mouth and kissed the tips of his fingers then placed his hand over her heart, holding it against her chest. He could feel the swell of her breast under his palm. Her eyes were enormous. Her lips were parted and he could feel her warm breath on his face.

He knew he should resist but he also knew he was powerless to do so.

They were frozen in time and space. Their gazes locked as they held onto each other, as he tried to fight temptation and tried to resist desire.

He wasn't sure who moved first but suddenly the space between them, which was infinitesimal to begin with, had disappeared. Nothing separated them. Bella's eyes were closed, her lashes dark against her pale cheeks, and then his lips were on hers. Her lips were on his.

Desire and temptation had won.

It was a gentle kiss, a soft exploration, a beginning. He shouldn't be doing this but her lips were so warm, pliable and tender and now that he'd started he didn't want to stop. But he had to stop, he needed to stop. She was Evie's little sister, she wasn't his to conquer. He pulled back, releasing her, and watched as she opened her eyes. They were dark grey now, her pupils had grown so large the silvery grey was barely visible around the edges, and he knew she'd come back for more.

Would that make it all right? If she came to him, would that make it okay?

This time he watched and waited. It had to be Bella's choice.

She closed the gap. He waited until her lips covered his and then he took over. She tasted so sweet. His tongue teased her lips open and she didn't resist. She opened her mouth to him and their tongues met. She tasted like chocolate and strawberries. Warm chocolate.

Her breasts nudged against him and he could feel her nipples, hard against his chest. Her hips pushed into his groin as she slid both her hands under his T-shirt. He felt his own nipples harden as her fingers brushed over them.

Had she really told him she'd only been kissed once before? Maybe he'd misheard her the other night. He was finding it hard to believe right now as she certainly wasn't behaving like a novice. Her fingers were trailing over his abdominals again and then all thoughts of prior conversation fled his mind as he felt her fingers at the waistband of his jeans. She broke the kiss. He could hear her panting and at first he thought she was having difficulty with her breathing but when he looked into her eyes he knew it was simply arousal.

Bella sat up and pulled her shirt over her head. She was wearing a white cotton camisole underneath but no bra. Charlie could see the peaks of her nipples pushing against the fabric and he felt his own arousal stirring in response. She licked her lips. Her pink tongue traced the outline of her mouth and Charlie forced himself not to claim her mouth with his.

She cast her shirt aside and picked up the hem of his T-shirt, pulling it up to expose his stomach. She bent her head and kissed the warm skin on his hip bone, just above the waistband of his jeans. Charlie bit back a groan of desire. He felt her fingers slide behind the button of his jeans as her nails lightly scratched his skin.

'What are you doing?' he asked, and his voice was thick and heavy.

She poised, her fingers on his waistband, and fixed her gaze on him. 'Would you make love to me?'

He could feel her cool fingernails where they rested inside his waistband, against his stomach. He knew she was ready to flick his button undone, ready to make the decision for him, and he nearly didn't need to be asked twice. But then he remembered this was Bella, the girl he'd always thought of as shy, quiet, younger than her years. Had he got her wrong? Did she know what she was doing?

'You want me to make love to you?' he asked. His voice was thick in his throat, his words accompanied only by the sound of Bella's breathing. 'Now?'

She nodded.

'Are you sure?' He had to make certain she knew what she was asking.

'Yes.' Her voice was a whisper. 'I want you to be the first.'

CHAPTER SEVEN

HER first.

He hadn't misunderstood. She wasn't naïve but she was inexperienced.

Did he want to be responsible for this momentous event in Bella's life?

He couldn't do it. There was no way he could make love to her.

Not here, not tonight.

He knew he'd already broken the first rule. She should have been off limits entirely. But he could stop before he made things worse.

He should stop.

He held her hands in his, stilling her, and lifted them from the waistband of his jeans.

He would stop.

He shook his head. 'No.'

'No?' Bella's voice wobbled. 'Why not? Am I not your type? Am I not pretty enough?'

'Oh, Bella.' He shook his head again. 'You're beautiful. So beautiful.' He reached out and slid his fingers into her auburn curls. His suntanned hand was dark against the paleness of her cheek as his fingers rested lightly against her scalp. Her grey eyes watched him, unblinking. 'But I can't.'

'Can't, or won't?'

'Won't.'

'Why not?'

Because I'm not ready for this. He'd never thought that before but he knew this time it was true. Sex was usually about fulfilling a need, a desire. It wasn't something he thought too deeply about. But he wasn't prepared mentally or practically to make love to Bella. She had such a romantic view of the world and she would have expectations that went beyond simply fulfilling a need. This couldn't be a spur-of-the-moment decision.

She'd given up waiting for his reply. 'I know what I want. I want to experience this and I want it to be with you,' she said.

'Why?' Why on earth had she chosen him?

'Because I trust you.'

He almost groaned aloud. That made it ten times worse. It meant he had a duty of care to do it right. Still he hesitated.

'I won't regret this,' she said as he shook his head again.

'It's not because I think you'll regret this.' He'd make certain she didn't. 'But you're Evie's little sister.'

Perhaps saying it out loud would remind him to think of her only in a platonic sense. That was exactly how he used to think of her, but somewhere along the way his feelings had changed, grown and developed, and now he was having difficulty separating his conscience from his desire. He needed to remember that she was Evie's little sister. She was not his for the taking. No matter how nicely she asked.

'So? I'm twenty-six years old. I make my own decisions. Please,' she begged, 'I can't bear the thought that I won't ever know what it's like and I'm not brave enough to go looking for someone else who doesn't know me or care about my reasons.'

He couldn't imagine that either. He couldn't imagine her in bed with someone who didn't care about her or her reasons for wanting this. She was right. Why shouldn't she experience it? And why shouldn't she experience it with someone of her choosing? Half his brain said he should tread carefully but the other half agreed with Bella. Why shouldn't she have this experience while she still could? He knew he could give her pleasure. He knew he'd be able to give her what she wanted, at least physically, but he wasn't going to rush into it. He had to have time to make it special.

He felt an incredible obligation to make it perfect. To fulfil her dreams. It was immensely important that Bella got the experience she dreamed of. Perhaps because there was always a chance that this would be her only experience, it needed to be perfect.

She was looking at him hopefully.

He nodded. 'All right,' he said as his conscience gave up the fight, 'but you have to let me do it my way.'

'What does that mean?'

'It means yes, but not tonight. I want to make it perfect for you. Will you let me arrange it?'

She smiled at him. A glorious, bright smile that turned her grey eyes silver and made him forget about all the reasons he should be letting her down gently instead of agreeing to her crazy request.

'I'm going to Brisbane tomorrow for a weekend conference,' he said. 'You could meet me there? I'll book us a suite in a five-star hotel and we'll have a weekend to remember. You can pack your red negligee,' he suggested.

It had taken all her courage to ask him to make love to her but she was determined not to die a virgin and she couldn't think of anyone better to gift her innocence to than Charlie. She adored him but, better than that, she trusted him too. She knew she might only get one chance at this and she knew Charlie was capable of giving her something to remember. Something to cherish.

But she hadn't expected him not to take advantage of the present opportunity and her emotions felt as though they were on a roller-coaster ride. She'd gone from the high of their kiss to plummeting down the slippery slope when she'd heard 'No' but then he'd lifted her up again to a peak of expectation. She wondered where it would stop.

Brisbane sounded perfect but she couldn't do it. Her heart took another dive, colliding with her stomach, as she realised it wasn't going to happen. Not tonight. And not this weekend. Maybe not ever.

'I can't come with you.' Reality intervened and her euphoria vanished. She hoped it didn't mean she was going to miss her opportunity. 'I need to stay in Sydney in case a donor is found for me.'

'When I get back, then. The anticipation will make it even better, I guarantee it.' He smiled and his brown eyes held all sorts of promises.

He was going to grant her wish! Her emotions rocketed towards the heavens again as she felt her stomach do a lazy somersault when she thought about the things that lay in store for her. She was so close she could almost taste it. She could envisage in glorious detail how she would feel in his arms. How his skin would feel against hers, warm and silky with a firm layer of muscle underneath.

'But if a donor is found for me I'll be in hospital when you get back.'

'Then I'll let you out of our deal. If you have the surgery before we do this, you'll have plenty of time to choose someone else.'

Bella didn't want to choose anyone else but it was pretty obvious she couldn't tell Charlie that. He didn't want to hear how she'd fancied him for ever and that this was a way of making her fantasies a reality. So she had to be content with his promise for now.

'Come on, it's getting late. You should get inside before it gets too cold out here.' Charlie stood and held out his hand, pulling her to her feet. He scooped a cashmere rug up from the carpet and wrapped it around her shoulders before he walked her back to the house. He stopped at the conservatory doors and turned her to face him. He reached out one hand and cupped her chin, tilting it up until his lips met hers. Her mouth opened under his pressure and she felt herself float under his caress. A slow-burning fire was glowing in her belly, awakening every nerve ending in her body. The kiss was full of promise and expectation. It was a kiss that could change her world.

'I'll see you soon,' he said as he broke their contact. Her lips were cold without his touch. 'Wait for me.'

It had been the perfect kiss. And he was promising more. In a few days she would be in Charlie's bed.

Wait for me, he'd said.

She could wait. But only just.

Charlie watched Bella as she slept. Her auburn curls were bright against the white sheets, her lashes dark against her cheeks. He could see the rise and fall of her chest as she breathed in and out and he could see her fingers move as one hand twitched involuntarily. He wondered if she was dreaming.

Her lips were pale pink and he recalled how they'd tasted of strawberries and warm chocolate. He watched as her lips moved and he wondered what she was dreaming about. He wondered if she was making any sound at all but he couldn't tell from where he stood, separated, distant and apart from her.

It had only been three days since he'd seen her but it seemed like a lifetime. So much had changed. So much had slipped away. Would things ever be the same? Would they ever recover what had been lost, the chances they'd had? The chances they hadn't taken. The chances *he* hadn't taken.

He'd left for the conference in Brisbane full of hope. He'd told Bella that anticipation would make the experience even better and that was something he firmly believed. It was one of the things he loved about beginnings. One thing he loved about the start of a new relationship. The build-up of anticipation and expectation that culminated in a crescendo of pleasure. Once that died away he knew he struggled to maintain interest. Once the excitement of new experiences and new challenges had been tasted he had a habit of losing interest, but with Bella things felt different.

He'd spent the last nine years deliberately doing his own thing. Avoiding relationships, avoiding commitment, making sure he always had an escape route, making sure he always had freedom, but when he was with Bella he forgot about running away. Instead, he was thinking about what he could do for her. He wanted to show her things, teach her things, he wanted to see her face light up when she tried something new or made a discovery, he wanted to see her smile when someone did something nice for her.

He was entranced by her. He felt like a different person when he was with her. He was calmer. More content. He wanted to have a connection with her. A connection that went beyond sex, and it felt good to be thinking about someone else for a change. It felt good to be looking forward.

He'd expected to come home from Brisbane to find

Bella eagerly awaiting his arrival. But he hadn't expected to find her here.

He'd called her while he'd been away only to be told she was back in hospital with another chest infection. He couldn't get back soon enough.

And now he stood, watching her from the other side of a glass window. It was fair to say things hadn't turned out quite as he'd planned.

At Sam's insistence Bella had been put into an isolation room. Her immune system had taken a hammering and she couldn't afford to get any other infections, something that was always a risk in hospital.

He watched her as she slept, although he could barely see her for all the leads and tubes she was connected to. He tried to ignore the oxygen tube, the nasogastric tube, the drip, the cardiac monitors and the oximeter. He knew she'd gone downhill rapidly over the past forty-eight hours. He knew it was critical that a donor was found for her; her lungs weren't going to last much longer.

He tried to focus on her hands, her eyes, her hair, her lips, on the parts of her that looked familiar. He wanted to go in to see her, he wanted to tell her he was back, but he wasn't sure if he should. She might not be quite as keen to see him as he was to see her.

He couldn't go into her room without scrubbing. He had to gown and glove first. He turned away from the window as he tried to decide what to do and saw Evie coming towards him.

'Hi,' she said. 'Have you just been in to see Bella?'

Charlie shook his head. 'She's asleep and I'm not sure if I should go in.'

'Why not?'

'I think I've caused enough trouble. I'm probably the last person she'd want to see.'

Evie frowned. 'What are you talking about?'

'I think I might have made her sick.' Logically he knew it was unlikely but he hadn't been able to get the idea out of his head.

'She's got another chest infection,' Evie replied. 'How is that your fault?'

'I kissed her.'

'You did what?'

Charlie cringed inwardly at Evie's tone. 'I kissed her,' he repeated.

'Why? What on earth for?' Evie sounded furious and she hadn't finished yet. 'I thought you were keeping her company, keeping her occupied so she didn't have time to dwell on things. I didn't think you had ulterior motives.'

'It wasn't like that.'

'No? She's not someone you can play with. She's vulnerable, innocent. Don't think of making her one of your conquests.'

He'd thought she was innocent too, until the other night. Now he knew she was just inexperienced and that had put a whole different perspective on things. But he couldn't tell Evie that any more than he could tell Evie how he felt about her little sister. He still wasn't sure himself.

'You'd better have a damn good reason for kissing her.'

'Bella has a list of things she wants to do,' he explained. 'A wishlist she calls it. A kiss was one of the things on her list.'

'So you were doing her a favour?'

Evie sounded sceptical and he couldn't blame her. It was a pretty lame excuse and one he didn't believe himself.

'In a way.'

'Well, don't do her any more favours. She's not worldly enough to handle you. You'll break her heart.'

'It was just a kiss. A consensual one. She asked me to

kiss her and I did,' he said with a shrug as he tried to pretend it hadn't turned his world upside down. 'I have no intention of breaking her heart.'

'No one ever intends to do that but it happens anyway,' Evie argued.

'I don't think her heart's in any danger but if it makes you feel better, I'm sorry. I didn't mean to make her sick.'

'When did you kiss her?'

'Why? What difference does that make?'

'Just answer me.'

'It was Thursday night.'

Evie was shaking her head now. 'Bella was back in hospital on Friday. It would be unusual for her to get sick that quickly, she must have already had the infection. You can't blame yourself for that, but promise me you'll keep your lips to yourself from now on.'

Charlie didn't want to make that promise. He didn't trust himself to keep it. He tried a compromise and hoped Evie wouldn't notice he hadn't agreed to her request. 'Believe me, I have no intention of hurting Bella. If there was anything I could do to help I would. I want to keep her safe. I want to make her better but it's not up to me. Do you know how that feels?'

Evie looked through the window at Bella's inert form. 'I know exactly how that feels,' she said quietly, her earlier anger replaced with a hint of regret.

Of course she would. After all, Bella was her sister. Charlie wrapped one arm around Evie's shoulders and hugged her tightly. 'I'm sorry.' He was sorry she was going through this and sorry there was nothing he could do for Evie or Bella. He hated feeling so powerless.

Evie sighed. 'I'm sorry too,' she said.

* * *

Evie was sorry for a lot of things but she wasn't sorry that Bella had Charlie in her life. Not really. But she hadn't counted on a romantic involvement between them. In her opinion that complicated matters.

Physically Bella was a mess and Evie didn't want to have to worry about her emotional state as well. With their mother's medical history there was always a chance that the girls could have issues as well. Who knew what it might take to push one of them over the edge and into the abyss if they weren't coping? Who knew if Bella was susceptible?

Evie didn't want to find out.

In Evie's mind it didn't matter what was on Bella's wishlist, Charlie should have known better. What had he been thinking? Bella didn't have the emotional strength or experience to handle Charlie.

Evie had to protect her little sister. She couldn't do anything about Bella's lungs but she'd make certain no one trampled on her heart. Not that she thought Charlie would intentionally do that but she knew how Bella worshipped Charlie. Anyone who knew Bella as well as she did would see that. And she also knew Charlie's reputation. He didn't set out to hurt women, he just wasn't prepared to invest in a relationship emotionally. He wasn't prepared for anything serious, and Bella wouldn't handle a casual fling well, not as her first experience. Evie needed to do whatever she could to protect Bella. She acknowledged that Bella's physical state was more serious at the moment than her emotional state but Bella certainly didn't need Charlie, or anyone else, throwing spanners in the works at present. She had enough to deal with.

But no matter what she thought about Charlie kissing Bella she knew he couldn't have made her sick. She'd got sick much too soon afterwards for that. Evie didn't blame

Charlie for giving Bella an infection but she would certainly blame him if he broke Bella's heart.

Although he'd seemed sincere when he'd said he wished there was something he could do for Bella, and Evie knew he meant it, it was just that there wasn't anything practical either of them could do. They were both in the same situation, both useless.

Or was she? she wondered, as the lift doors opened, delivering her to the emergency department, and she saw Finn going into the doctors' lounge. Was she useless or was there something she could do?

She'd been avoiding Finn as much as possible. She was still irritated with him over the disappearing trick he'd pulled, but now she needed to speak to him. Here was her chance.

She followed him into the lounge, hoping he was alone.

As she pushed open the door she saw Finn turn away and shove something into his pocket before he turned back to face her. She glanced around and noted there was no one else besides them in the room. 'Do you have a moment?' she asked.

'What is it?' he barked at her, but Evie chose to ignore his tone. She needed to speak to him and if he was going to bite her head off, that was a chance she was prepared to take.

'I have a favour to ask, a professional favour,' she added before he had a second to object. 'Bella is back in hospital, she has another lung infection and she's deteriorated badly. She's in a critical condition and desperately needs a transplant.' As quickly as she could she explained why she was there—she didn't want Finn to have an opportunity to interrupt. She didn't want him to have time to think of a reason to say no. 'The other day you asked if there was anything you could do. I need to know if your offer still stands.'

'What do you need?'

He was rubbing the outside of his right upper arm while he was speaking to her. His movement was distracting but he didn't seem to be aware of it. She'd noticed this habit on a few occasions, usually when he was in a bad mood, and although his tone wasn't quite as angry as before it was still hardly what she'd call pleasant. But she wasn't going to let him dissuade her and she pushed ahead with her request.

'If—when,' she corrected herself, 'a donor becomes available for Bella, would you assist Sam with the surgery?'

'Why? Sam is more than capable.'

'I know, but I'd feel better if you were both in the theatre. I couldn't think of two better people to have operating.'

'Joe Minnillo would normally assist,' Finn argued. 'What do you plan on telling him? That he's not required?'

Evie shook her head. 'No. He could be there as well. I'd just prefer it if you were there too.'

'It's not all about you, princess.'

She hated it when he called her that but she wasn't about to have that discussion with him now. There were far more important things on her agenda. 'I know that,' she retorted. She felt like stamping her foot or shaking him. Why did he have to be so pig-headed? 'It's about my little sister. Organ transplant is a massive undertaking. You and Sam together are the best in the business. Wouldn't you want to give your sibling every chance if you were in my situation?'

Finn's heart had been so badly damaged a long time ago that he was amazed it could still beat, let alone still be wounded by old memories, but Evie's words were like a knife through his heart and he could feel the air being knocked from his chest. Evie knew he'd lost his brother. How dare she use that against him like this?

The memories flooded back into his consciousness, accompanied by the sensations of a time he'd rather forget. He could almost feel the hot desert wind on his face and taste the gritty sand in his mouth, the sand that had managed to make its way into every crevice, making life uncomfortable, making working conditions even more difficult. But the heat, the noise and the sand had been the least of his problems.

Isaac's face erupted from his subconscious. He closed his eyes but that just made the memories more vivid.

He could hear the whistling of the bombs raining down onto the army base. The deafening explosions as they thudded into the buildings and the ground and the people unlucky enough to be in their way. He could feel the sensation of the earth shuddering as bombs detonated. The screams of the injured, the moans of the dying.

He could smell the scent of death, the sweet, distinctive smell of blood, the putrid, foul scent of torn intestines. He could feel the warm stickiness of fresh blood, his own blood mingling with the blood of others. He could see devastation everywhere he looked. Buildings were reduced to rubble and protruding from that rubble were the limbs of the dead and the dying.

He remembered how it felt to hold someone he loved in his arms and watch as they died. He could recall his final words, begging, pleading, for Isaac to hang on just a little bit longer, until help was at hand.

But it had all been in vain. He'd had to watch as Isaac breathed his final breath, watch as his eyes stared vacantly, seeing nothing. He remembered the awful feeling

of helplessness and hopelessness, knowing there was noth-
ing he could do.

At the time his anguish had been so all-consuming it
had obliterated his physical pain. He hadn't even regis-
tered until much later that he too had been injured.

And even though his injuries had been extensive, his
physical pain severe, it had been nothing compared to the
pain of losing his brother.

'Finn? Are you okay?'

CHAPTER EIGHT

HE OPENED his eyes to find Evie watching him closely. She was staring at him, a worried expression in her hazel eyes, a narrow crease between her eyebrows as she frowned. She was probably wondering what on earth had got into him. Isaac had died a long time ago but Finn still felt his loss just as keenly today.

A sharp, hot pain burned into his right biceps, shooting from his neck down his arm. This pain was a daily reminder of everything he'd lost. He could feel his thumb going numb and he opened and closed his hand rapidly, trying to encourage his circulation, even though he knew it was a wasted exercise. The numbness wasn't caused by poor circulation—it was all related to a damaged cervical disc—but although the physical pain was coming from his neck, the emotional pain was coming from deep inside him. Rubbing his arm and clenching his fist would do nothing for his discomfort.

'I'm fine,' he lied.

He thought he'd done such a good job of burying his grief. He was surprised to feel the pain of events from years ago resurfacing and shocked by its intensity. He knew he would react just as Evie had in the same situation. He knew he'd try his hardest, try anything, to save his sibling.

He'd been there too. He couldn't blame her for wanting the best.

'There's no point discussing this now, not until a suitable donor is found. I'll talk to Sam then,' he said. He would speak to Sam about assisting him for Bella's operation and, if Sam was agreeable, he would help, but he couldn't see the point in making arrangements until there were lungs for Bella. The pain in his arm—and in his heart—was starting to overwhelm him.

He knew his tone was dismissive but he wanted Evie out of the room. His painkilling tablets were burning a hole in the pocket of his white coat and he needed to take them soon, before his pain worsened, before he developed a headache, but he wasn't about to take them in front of anyone. Especially not Evie. She was bound to ask questions. She didn't seem to know when to leave well enough alone.

Charlie's day had been long and exhausting. He'd had a complicated hip replacement op, which had required total concentration, but he'd found his mind had kept drifting to Bella and fighting to keep his attention focussed in Theatre had only added to his exhaustion. He was looking forward to calling into Pete's Bar for a beer before heading home but he wasn't leaving the hospital without seeing Bella first. If he had to sit beside her and wait for her to wake up, he would. Being with her gave him some respite from the madness of his days. She was always so calm and composed and he found that refreshing. He had a habit of being constantly on the go and Bella made him stop.

Usually he got his downtime in the water. Swimming laps gave him a chance to clear his head. He loved that solitary sensation, the fact that no one could talk to him or expect a conversation as he swam lengths of a pool or dived through the waves, but recently he'd found that Bella's company gave him that sense of peace as well.

He made his way to her room. Through the window he could see Evie sitting with her. A surgical mask covered the lower half of Evie's face but her eyes were puffy and her cheeks, what he could see of them, were tear-stained. She was holding Bella's hand but Bella was very still and very pale and for a moment Charlie thought the worst before he realised all the monitors were still attached and he could see her pulse and blood pressure registering on the screen.

Evie looked up and saw him standing on the other side of the glass. She stood and came to meet him, pulling the mask from her face as she came out of Bella's room.

'What's going on? Why are you crying?' he asked as the worry he'd been battling with all day came flooding back.

'She's gone downhill, I don't know what the matter is, it's almost like she's giving up.' Evie's voice caught in her throat and Charlie knew she was holding back tears.

'Why would she do that?'

'I have no idea.'

'Has Sam been to see her?'

Evie nodded. 'But he didn't have any answers. Physically he says her condition is unchanged.'

'What else has happened today? Has anything happened to upset her?'

'Miranda came to see her.'

'Your mother? Why?' Charlie knew Miranda's presence was always enough to upset any of the Lockheart sisters.

'Apparently Bella asked her to come.'

'What on earth for?'

'I don't know, she wouldn't tell me. She hasn't said anything else. The nurses told me Bella asked them to call Miranda. And now Bella's just lying there. Not speaking.'

'She's awake?'

Evie nodded. 'Would you talk to her, see if you can find out what's going on? She can't give up, she has to keep fighting.'

Charlie agreed with Evie. Bella couldn't give up. 'Bella seems to think your mother left because of her. Because she isn't perfect enough. Is she right?' he asked.

'She told you that?' Evie's voice was incredulous.

Charlie nodded.

'We've never had an explanation as to why she left so I couldn't say if Bella's illness contributed to Miranda's problems, none of us can say, but Bella has always felt it was tied to her. I'm not so sure.' Evie was frowning. 'I can remember, even when I was small, being told she was lying down with a headache and I wasn't to disturb her. That probably started when I was five, around the time Bella was born, and I have wondered whether that was when she started drinking, but I couldn't say for certain because I don't remember anything from a younger age. I do know things escalated when I was nine. That's when Miranda left for the first time. Bella was four, Lexi was two and I was nine.

'I'm really not sure who even made the decision that Miranda would move out,' she continued. 'It could have been our father. He bought her an apartment and he still makes sure she's okay but from then on we were never allowed to spend any time alone with her, not while we were little. Any time she spent with us was always super-vised by nannies. Sometimes I wonder whether that was the right decision—children need a mother—but I guess Miranda wasn't the sort of mother Richard wanted for us. Whether it was him or her who decided she'd move out, I know it was Richard who organised the supervision and none of us has an easy or normal relationship with our mother.' Evie shrugged. 'Miranda suffers from depression and an addiction to alcohol. If you want my opinion, I think Miranda would have had problems even without Bella's illness. I think she's one of those people who just finds life itself hard to cope with. Her behaviour has affected us all but in time you learn to ignore it or accept it.'

Charlie didn't think any of the sisters had accepted it and he wasn't sure how successfully they ignored it either. Particularly Bella. 'Bella's made a few references to your mother and I think it's something she hasn't learnt to ignore or accept yet. You and Lexi might have been able to do that but I don't think Bella has. I'll talk to her but there's no guarantee she'll tell me anything.'

'I know, but she's told you a lot of things lately that have surprised me and I don't have any other ideas,' Evie said as she stripped off her gown and threw it into the linen basket as Charlie started to scrub.

Scrubbed and gowned, he hesitated in the doorway of Bella's room. The room looked wrong but it took him a second or two to work out why. There was none of Bella's personality on display. There was no sketch book, no laptop, no DVDs.

Bella's eyes were still closed but some sixth sense must have alerted her to his presence because she opened her eyes as he crossed the room. The expression in them made his heart shrink in his chest. He felt it shrivel with fear. She looked crushed, exhausted, and he realised he'd hoped Evie had been wrong. But she knew Bella better than anyone so of course she'd pick up on her sister's emotions.

Bella looked defeated and his immediate thought was that he had to find a way to restore her spirit. He'd come to rely on her strength and courage and to see this expression of resignation in her eyes was frightening. He was *not* going to watch her give up. Not without a fight.

He mustered up his courage, striving to sound positive as he picked up her hand and brought it to his lips. '*Ciao*, Bella.'

She had so many leads coming off her it was impossible to get near her, and her hand was the only part of her he could get to. He kissed her fingers through his mask. As far as kisses went it was rather unsatisfactory but it was better than nothing.

He got a faint smile in response to his greeting. Her usual warmth was lacking and her smile didn't reach her eyes but he refused to give up. He sat beside her in the chair Evie had recently vacated. He didn't let go of her hand. It was silly but he felt by holding onto her he could anchor her to his world.

'I missed you while I was in Brisbane.'

'You did?' Her voice was hoarse. It sounded like her throat was hurting, which wasn't surprising given the nasogastric tube she had running into her stomach.

'You would have loved it. There was more food than even you would have known what to do with; the drug companies are very generous with their sponsorship of those conferences. I'll take you with me next time.'

'Next time?'

'Unless you've changed your mind. Is all this…' he gestured around the room '…an elaborate ruse to get out of our deal?'

She was shaking her head but even that slight movement seemed like an effort. 'I don't think there's going to be a next time.'

'What do you mean?'

There was a cup filled with ice chips on the table over her bed and she reached out and picked up the spoon, slipping an ice cube into her mouth. Sucking on it, moistening her throat before she answered. Charlie waited, still holding her hand.

'I'm tired. I've had enough.'

His heart, which was already sitting in his chest like a lump of stone, sank to his stomach. 'What? Why? What about all the things you wanted to do?'

'It's too late.'

'No, it's not. You were going to fight. What's happened? Why would you give up now?'

Bella turned her head away from Charlie but not before he saw tears in her eyes. First Evie, now Bella. What was going on? Miranda. It had to be.

He wasn't going to let her ignore him. He wasn't going to let her keep her problems bottled up inside her. That wouldn't do her any good. He needed to know what had happened. He needed to understand what was going on if he was going to be able to help. And there was no other option. He knew that keeping things bottled up allowed the hurt to fester, allowed it to feed on itself until it could take over a person's soul until you couldn't see a way out.

'Evie told me Miranda came to see you today. How did that go?'

She turned her head to face him. 'It was good.'

Charlie felt his eyebrows lift. That wasn't the answer he'd expected. 'Good?'

'I asked my mother to come,' Bella explained. 'There were questions I wanted answered, questions I've never been brave enough to ask. I told her I wanted to know some things before I die.'

'You're not—'

'Don't.' She lifted a hand as she interrupted him. 'I'm struggling, Charlie. I don't want to keep fighting for every breath.'

Charlie couldn't find the words he needed. Why couldn't

he think of something to say? He should have some words of inspiration, words of encouragement, but he had nothing. Bella continued speaking as Charlie sat, mute and confused. 'I got the answers I'd been looking for. It's not my mother's fault they weren't the answers I wanted. I've only got myself to blame.'

'What was it you wanted to know?' he asked, even though he was pretty sure he knew the answer.

'I asked her why she left us.'

Bella pulled her hand from his hold to pick up the cup of ice chips. He thought she was using the cup as an excuse to break the contact but there wasn't much he could do about it.

'And?' Surely she was going to tell him the rest of the story? He could understand why she might not have shared this with Evie, particularly if the tale was unpleasant, but she couldn't leave it here. He had to know more.

'Apparently she had postnatal depression after my birth but it was undiagnosed until after Lexi was born. She says she couldn't cope with any of us, she found motherhood totally overwhelming.'

Charlie breathed a sigh of relief. PND made perfect sense and it meant Miranda's issues couldn't be attributed to Bella. 'There you go. It wasn't your fault. Postnatal depression is not the baby's fault. You are not responsible for your mother's mental health issues.'

But Bella continued as though he hadn't spoken.

'She said she felt guilty because I was sick. She started drinking after I was born. At first it was a gin and tonic when Dad got home from work, to keep him company, but then it became one late in the afternoon while she waited for him and then one after she'd picked Evie up from school. She said she tried to stop when she fell pregnant with Lexi but after a while she started again. She drank gin with lemon and soda, though, because of the side effects of tonic water.' Bella laughed, but her laugh was devoid of humour. 'Ironic, isn't it? She gave up the soft drink because of the side effects but she couldn't give up the alcohol. She would have been worried that Lexi was going to be born with CF too. I don't think she would have cared if she'd suffered a miscarriage. I think that's probably why she kept drinking. So, you see, it all started with me,' she said as she slid another ice chip onto her tongue.

Was Bella right? Had she been the catalyst? Maybe she had but he wasn't about to agree with her.

'Your mother needs to take ownership of her problems.'

'I don't blame myself for my mother's addiction but I do blame myself for her abandonment.'

'How can it be your fault? You were four when she left.'

'There's plenty more to the story. Are you sure you want to hear this?' Bella paused and didn't continue until Charlie nodded. He wasn't certain he wanted to hear what she had to say but he knew he had no choice. 'Apparently she fell pregnant again when Lexi was eighteen months old. The pregnancy was unplanned and she freaked out, worried she couldn't cope with another baby, but especially worried about coping with another child with cystic fibrosis. Genetic testing for CF was very new but she was offered the test and she had it done. The test came back positive. She was going to have another child with CF. She terminated the pregnancy. She didn't want to bring another CF baby into the world. Her depression got worse after that, she says it was the guilt. She couldn't cope with life at all without alcohol to prop her up. And then she left. She abandoned us.'

'But you weren't the trigger for her abandonment.' Charlie tried to get Bella to see reason. Tried and failed.

'Don't you see, if genetic testing had been available

when she was pregnant with me, she would have aborted me. I know she would. But it was too late, she couldn't get rid of me, so she left. I always thought I was the reason she left. Now I know I was right.'

'But she wouldn't have even *known* to be tested for CF with you. She wouldn't have been expecting it.'

'Either way, she wouldn't have wanted me. Doesn't want me. Everything started with me. It would have been better for everyone if I was never born.'

Bella was normally so upbeat, so ridiculously positive despite everything she faced, that he found it quite disturbing to hear her being so negative. Was she depressed? He couldn't blame her if she was, she was critically ill, but he couldn't understand why she was so fixated on her mother. Surely she had more important things to worry about, like whether compatible lungs would be found in time to save her life. He wondered if he should speak to Sam about getting John Allen to assess Bella again but he'd hate to find that a potential transplant was cancelled because of Bella's state of mind. He couldn't instigate something that might put her in that situation. 'How do you figure that?' he asked.

'Life would have been very different for Evie and Lexi if Mum hadn't had me. She might never have got postnatal depression. She might never have left.'

'That's a lot of "mights",' he said. 'She might have got it after Lexi anyway and from where I sit your mother clearly has a lot of issues. You can't blame yourself.'

'I've been waiting to die all my life. I never expected to live to an old age. Having my suspicions confirmed, knowing I wasn't wanted, kind of makes it all seem so pointless.'

'Hang on, your mother never actually said she didn't want you, did she?'

'She said motherhood was overwhelming.'

'I don't think she's alone in that sentiment but it doesn't mean she didn't want you. It just means she couldn't cope and unfortunately her depression wasn't diagnosed early. It's not your fault.'

'I don't care. I'm too tired to care. Lexi and Sam can get married in one week, I just want to last that long.' She'd had enough. She wasn't going to get the happy ending she'd always wanted. No one could give that to her. Not Sam, not her sisters, not her parents and not Charlie.

Her mother would be relieved she didn't have to visit hospitals any more, her father wouldn't even notice she was gone. Her sisters would miss her but Lexi would settle down to her new life with Sam and Evie would be able to lead her own life once the burden of worrying about Bella had been lifted from her slim shoulders. And Charlie, well, Charlie would continue to live his life completely oblivious to the fact that Bella had been in love with him.

She was tired of fighting and she was tired of wishing for things that weren't going to happen.

But Charlie was distraught. Bella had to fight. If she stopped fighting, if she gave up now, she'd be lost. He knew it was only willpower that would keep her going, keep her alive. Lexi's wedding might be enough incentive to get through the next week, but then what? He had to find another reason for her to keep fighting.

'What about your wishlist? What about us? You and I have unfinished business.'

She smiled at him and his heart lifted as he caught a glimpse of the old Bella, the one who had a desire to go out and live her life. She shrugged her skinny shoulders. 'It doesn't matter any more. It'll just be something else on my wishlist that isn't done. It was a stupid list and a stupid idea. There's only one thing I want now and that's to see Lexi and Sam married. That's my last wish. My dying wish.'

CHAPTER NINE

'BELLA, no! Please, you can't give up. You have to find something worth fighting for.'

'It's my time, Charlie, I can feel it.'

'But you're not the type to give up. You just need to hold on for a little bit longer. You'll get new lungs, you have to.'

She gave the tiniest shake of her head. 'I'm so tired.' Her voice caught in her throat. 'I'm tired of fighting to stay out of hospital, I'm tired of fighting to put on weight, I'm tired of taking a thousand tablets, I'm tired of fighting to breathe, I'm tired of wanting my parents to love me.'

So that's what this was all about. He should have known. Bella just wanted to be loved. She needed to be loved.

'I know what it's like to want to give up but you can't, you have to keep fighting. Do it for the people who love you. Do it for Evie and Lexi.'

A reflex almost made him say 'Do it for me' but he hesitated and Bella picked up on his hesitation.

'Yes?'

He shook his head.

'What were you about to say?' she asked.

You're a coward, Charlie Maxwell, his conscience told him, but he couldn't talk about things he didn't understand. He couldn't tell her he couldn't imagine his life without her in it because he wasn't exactly sure what that meant and, if his words could be misconstrued, if he upset Bella, Evie would have him hung, drawn and quartered.

He'd promised Evie he wouldn't break Bella's heart so he swallowed his words and delivered some different ones. Safer ones. 'I was about to tell you a story.'

'Go on.'

He wasn't sure if she was really interested but he had one last chance to convince her to keep fighting. 'I understand what you're going through,' he said. 'I know what it feels like to want to give up but you've got to believe that this is not the end. You've got to believe things will get better. After I had my scooter accident in Bali I struggled to deal with it. I couldn't see what the point in living was once I lost everything that was important to me. At the age of twenty-three I thought my world was over. For some time I wished I'd died in that accident. It ended my surfing career but it also took away the woman I loved.'

He could tell from her expression that he'd shocked her. That was good. It meant she was listening. Maybe he'd get through to her after all.

'Was she killed in the accident?'

'No.' He shook his head. 'I'd fallen in love and fallen hard. We dreamt of travelling the world together, following the surfing tour, living in perpetual sunshine and good times. But after the accident it turned out that Pippa preferred the life of sunshine and good times to a life with me. She followed the tour and left me behind. I'd lost everything. I went home to lick my wounds, wallowing in my misery. Eventually Dad got sick of me and what he saw as my unhealthy, obsessive behaviour and convinced me to find a new interest. He talked me into going back to uni, back to medical school. He told me in no uncertain terms that I had to find a new obsession and a new way of making a living, just as he'd done. I didn't dare argue.

If Dad hadn't given up after his accident, I couldn't. I let him talk me into it and I'm glad I did. Initially it gave me something else to focus on but it soon became my passion. My family pulled me back to living and once I got to uni Evie's friendship pulled me through that first year. It was tough but between my family and Evie I got back on track. Now it's your turn to look to the future.'

'But my family doesn't need me.'

'If you truly believe that then you need to find another reason to keep going. What about going to college? What about your dream?'

'There's no guarantee I'll even be accepted. It all seems so pointless.'

'Let me help you through this,' he offered.

But that wasn't enough to convince her and why should it be? He wasn't offering her what she wanted. He couldn't. He couldn't imagine his life without her in it but that wasn't the same as being in love with her. It couldn't be. People didn't fall in love that quickly.

Charlie turned and started another lap. He'd been swimming for close to an hour but his head had only just started to clear. When he'd left Bella last night he'd been upset and frustrated and he'd stopped at Pete's Bar, where he'd had one too many beers in an attempt to escape the fact there was nothing he could do for Bella. He was paying the price this morning.

He'd tried his best but it wasn't enough. He hadn't been able to get through to her, hadn't known how to, so he'd tried to forget. She was looking for unconditional love. He couldn't help her.

When he eventually climbed out of the pool and towelled himself dry, he saw a message waiting for him on his phone. A message from Evie.

His thoughts immediately turned to Bella. Had something happened?

His hand shook. He didn't want to read the message, he was terrified it would be bad news, but then his brain slowly kicked into gear and he realised she wouldn't text with bad news. But his hand was still shaking as he pushed 'open'.

'We have lungs. Sam prepping Bella now.'

Charlie started pulling on his clothes, not bothering to get properly dry, shoved his things into his bag and ran to his car. Evie had left the message a little over half an hour ago. Bella would be in Theatre now but he needed to be at the hospital. He wasn't working today but he'd wait there. He might as well pace those corridors, it was better than being home alone.

Bella was getting new lungs. It wasn't over yet.

Lexi and Richard were already in the family lounge attached to the cardiothoracic unit when Evie arrived.

'Have I missed Sam?' she asked. She hoped not, she had some urgent questions for him.

Lexi shook her head. 'He should be back soon.'

Three heads swivelled expectantly as a fourth person entered the room. But this person was wearing two-inch heels, was dressed all in black and had platinum blonde hair.

Evie froze. Miranda looked sober, but it was only early.

Richard stepped forward, and for a brief moment Evie wondered if he was going to stop Miranda from coming any further, but then she realised he was positioning himself between her mother and her as if he expected Evie to react badly. He lifted a hand and ushered Miranda into the room, settling her in a chair. 'Hello, Miranda.' His voice was tender as he greeted his wife. As far as Evie knew, neither of her parents had ever contemplated a divorce and it was obvious Richard still cared for Miranda, making Evie wonder again why he hadn't tried harder to help her. Perhaps he'd done all he could.

Miranda sat, clutching her handbag on her lap, holding it in front of her like a protective shield, but it wasn't enough to stop her hands from shaking. But Evie wasn't going to criticise her today, her own hands were shaking too.

Richard spoke to them all next. 'Do you think we could all put our differences aside, just for today at least, and focus on getting through this day? Forget the past and look to the future, one, I hope, will include Bella.' He looked at each of the women in turn but Evie felt his message was directed at her.

Three heads nodded in reply as they all contemplated what this day might bring.

Sam walked into the lounge and if he was surprised by how quiet everyone was, he didn't show it. 'All right, I'm just about to go and see Bella before we start. Is everyone okay here?' he asked. 'Any last-minute questions?'

'Are you sure Bella is strong enough for the surgery? She's not too sick, is she?' Miranda asked, astounding Evie, who'd thought Miranda was too self-involved to even realise how sick Bella was. Had she misjudged her mother?

'This is her best chance,' Sam replied. 'What's making her so sick at present is the infection in her lungs. The transplant will get rid of that, along with her diseased lungs, and I expect she'll feel better almost from the moment she comes out of the anaesthetic.'

'Is Finn going to assist?' Evie asked. That was her urgent question. She needed to know if Finn had kept his word.

'No.' Sam gave her a puzzled look.

'Didn't he speak to you?'

Sam shook his head.

'I asked him if he'd speak to you about assisting. I wanted you both to be there.'

'I haven't heard from him,' Sam said, but he didn't dismiss her query lightly. He put his hands on her shoulders and made her focus on him. 'We don't have time to organise it anyway. I don't need Finn. Bella will be fine.'

Evie knew Sam couldn't guarantee that, she knew he was saying that because it was what they all needed to hear. At the moment she wasn't a doctor, she was Bella's sister. She too needed to believe that modern medicine could work miracles. And she knew miracles did happen. But she also knew they didn't always happen when you wanted them to.

But all she could do was wait and pray and hope Sam was right. But if anything went wrong, if anything happened to Bella, she was going to track Finn Kennedy down and flay him alive. She didn't care if he was the Head of Surgery, all that meant was that if anything did go awry the buck stopped with him and she'd make sure he knew all about it.

'What do you mean, you can't take her off the ventilator?'

After close to nine hours, Bella's surgery was over. It had gone like clockwork, according to Sam, except for one thing.

'Her new lungs are viable, they're inflating perfectly, but Bella isn't breathing independently. I'm positive it's only a temporary measure but obviously we have to keep her breathing. She's ventilated but we have her on the lowest oxygen setting so when she's ready to breathe on her own, we'll know. She's sedated now but we'll wake her for short periods each day to assess her condition.'

Charlie was stunned and judging by the expressions he could see around him the Lockheart family was just as bewildered. This wasn't how the day was supposed to turn out. Bella's life was supposed to be improving. She wasn't supposed to be in ICU on a ventilator, and to make matters worse he knew he wouldn't be able to see her today. It would be family only and even they would only be allowed in one at a time for a few minutes. He was just a family friend. He was a long way down the list.

He didn't want to be at the bottom of that list, he realised, but he couldn't do anything about it at present. He would have to be patient.

Evie visited Bella very briefly, staying just long enough to see for herself that everything was as Sam had said. Bella was fine, if you counted being ventilated fine, and at least her new lungs worked. As long as she didn't reject them, everything would probably be okay. But probably wasn't good enough for Evie. She was angry and upset and looking for someone to take her frustrations out on. She went looking for Finn. He was Head of Surgery, she'd asked him to help, and he'd been nowhere to be seen. He'd better have a very good reason for ignoring her. She could accept it if he'd said he wasn't going to help but he'd told her he would talk to Sam if lungs became available. Yet, when the time had come, when it had mattered, he'd been nowhere to be found. In Evie's opinion that wasn't good enough. Not from any surgeon and especially not from the Head of Surgery.

Finding out that Finn wasn't in the hospital, had in fact not been seen all day, didn't deter her. If the mountain wasn't coming to Mohammed, she'd have to go to him.

Her heart was racing in her chest as she knocked on

his penthouse door. Visions of what had happened the last time she'd knocked on his door came flooding back. She felt a rush of heat to her cheeks as she remembered what had transpired between them then—raw, impulsive, take-no-prisoners sex. The best sex she'd ever had. She still wasn't sure how that was possible. Wasn't sex supposed to be better if there was an emotional connection? Wasn't that why it was called making love? But there had certainly been no love between them. It had simply been sex, down and dirty, and incredible.

'Princess, what a pleasant surprise.' Finn opened his door and greeted her with a voice heavily laden with sarcasm.

Once again she didn't wait to be invited in when the door swung open. 'You think,' she said as she stormed past him into his lounge, resolutely keeping her back turned to the wall where she'd let him claim her the last time she was here.

She didn't give Finn an opportunity to say any more, she didn't want to give him a chance to tell her to leave. 'Bella got new lungs today,' she told him.

'I heard.'

That took the wind out of her sails momentarily.

She frowned. 'How did you hear that?'

He raised one eyebrow in a habit she found intensely irritating but it was only one of his many habits that annoyed her.

'I *am* the Head of Surgery,' he said. 'People tend to keep me in the loop.'

Being told he'd known Bella was having surgery today and he still hadn't bothered keeping his word sent Evie over the edge. 'You said you would speak to Sam. I asked you for help.' She tried desperately to rein in her temper but she knew she could either yell at Finn or burst into tears, and she wasn't going to give him the satisfaction of seeing her cry.

'Sleeping with the head of a department doesn't grant you the right to ask favours.'

Evie clenched her fists, willing herself not to hit something. God, he was infuriating. 'You arrogant bastard, is that why you think I slept with you?'

'I don't know,' he replied. 'Is it?'

'No!' She couldn't stop herself from yelling that time. 'That was an impulsive mistake and I'm sorry it ever happened,' she lied. 'I don't have a good reason for what we did but wanting the liberty of asking favours wasn't it.'

Finn didn't react to her rising temper. In contrast to her heated tone his voice was cool, calm and measured. 'How's Bella doing?'

'You tell me,' Evie snapped. 'I thought you were "in the loop".'

'I've been out of contact a bit today. I haven't caught up on everything I should have.'

'Her new lungs are working, she's in ICU, as expected, but she's on a ventilator. This was supposed to be the start of her new life but she can't even breathe by herself.' Evie could hear her voice wobbling with emotion and she fought to keep things under control.

'That will only be temporary.'

'I know that. But somehow I think if you'd been there it might have turned out differently. If things had gone according to plan.'

'Whose plan?' he asked.

'Mine.'

Finn was shaking his head. 'I'm sorry it hasn't gone as

smoothly as you hoped but I'm sure she'll be fine. Trust me when I tell you it was better for Bella that I wasn't there.'

'Trust you!' Evie retorted. 'I don't think I'll ever trust you.'

Finn sighed. 'Before you get carried away as judge, jury and executioner, there's something you need to hear.' He gestured to his sofa. 'I think you should sit down.'

Evie stomped over to Finn's leather couch. On the coffee table was a tumbler filled with an inch of amber fluid. It looked like whisky. Finn remained standing in front of her. His back was ramrod straight and his hands were thrust deep into the pockets of his jeans. Even in her irritated state she was aware of how the denim of his jeans strained across his thighs, emphasising his long, lean physique, and she was aware too of her own reaction to his maleness. It seemed that being annoyed with him wasn't enough to prevent herself from finding him attractive. Not that she planned to go anywhere near him ever again. Especially not after today.

'There's a reason I wasn't at the hospital today,' he said, and Evie had to drag her eyes away from his hips and back up to his face as he spoke to her. 'Look.' He took his hands out of his pockets and held them out to her. His right hand was shaking badly. 'I didn't avoid surgery today because I didn't want to do it. I avoided it because I didn't want to be a liability. There was no way I could have operated today. You wouldn't want me near Bella like this, would you?'

'Oh, my God!' She tore her eyes away from his hands and looked up at him. She realised the shadow in his blue eyes that she'd thought was anger was, in fact, pain. She'd marched into his home and accused him of all sorts of terrible things when he'd been suffering. She felt dreadful and for a moment she forgot the nasty things he'd said to her in reply. 'What's wrong with you?'

'I have a ruptured cervical disc at five/six.'

'When? How?'

'It happened years ago, ten years ago, when I was in the army.'

'Ten years?'

He nodded. 'But the disc has deteriorated further.'

'Tell me you've been to see someone.'

He nodded. 'I saw Rupert today.'

'Rupert Davidson, the neurosurgeon?'

Finn sat on the couch opposite her but he didn't collapse into the couch as she had. His posture remained stiff, upright and he held his head still as if even the slightest movement was painful. 'He thinks a fragment of the nucleus has broken off and is causing more C-six nerve root impingement.'

'He thinks? Have you seen anyone else, had a second opinion?' she asked, but who else would he see? Like Finn and Sam, Rupert was another one of the Harbour's surgeons who was the best in his field. 'Have you had an MRI scan?'

Finn gave her a wry smile. 'I've had about a dozen opinions. I trust Rupert. And, no, I haven't had an MRI. Remember the scar on my left shoulder?'

Did she remember? She didn't think she'd ever forget how that puckered scar had felt under her fingers or the fact that when she'd felt it they'd just made love. No, they'd just had sex, she corrected herself.

She nodded.

'I still have shrapnel in that shoulder. I can't have MRI scans.'

He had shrapnel in his shoulder and a destroyed cervical disc. No wonder he was always so grumpy. 'What are you going to do?'

'Rupert wants to operate.'

'What does he want to do?'

'He has to remove that fragment but the disc has lost its height so he's talking about trying an artificial disc.'

Evie frowned. 'Isn't that a bit experimental?'

Finn nodded.

'What does he think the odds are of it being successful?' Her earlier antagonism was forgotten as she tried to process what she was hearing.

'He has no idea. He reckons fifty-fifty that I'll even pull through the surgery and no guarantees that it will work, but I can't continue like this. If my condition deteriorates any further, I may never operate again. I don't think I have much choice. So, that's why I wasn't there for Bella today. I'm sorry.'

He was sorry? Evie felt like a complete bitch. She'd known something was wrong with Finn. She'd seen it in the way he rubbed his arm, she'd seen it in his eyes when a shadow crossed them, darkening his piercing blue irises, she'd known he suffered from migraines but she'd done nothing except badger him about her own needs.

Finn stood and Evie watched as he unfolded his limbs and rose from the couch. It seemed their little heart to heart was over. 'Don't let me keep you any longer. I'm sure you want to check on Bella.'

Evie stood too but that brought them standing within a few inches of each other. She was tempted to reach out, to try to wipe the look of pain from his face. It was etched deep into the furrows of his forehead but as if he sensed what she was about to do he took a step backwards, putting some distance between them.

'I'll see you out,' he said, effectively dismissing her.

He led her to the door but paused as he reached for the doorhandle. 'Can I ask you not to mention this to anyone? They'll all find out soon enough if I need to have time off.'

Evie nodded.

'Thank you.'

She thought that was the most sincere she'd ever heard him sound. Perhaps they could be friends after all.

'Don't mention it. I'm glad you told me,' she replied, then impulsively raised herself up on tiptoe to kiss his cheek. She didn't care if her attention was unwanted. He needed to know she would keep his confidence. He needed to know she was in his corner. 'If you need someone to talk to, I think I'm a pretty good listener.'

Finn didn't respond to her invitation but he didn't refuse it either. He held the door for her and Evie pressed the button to call the lift, before deciding to take the fire escape stairs back down to her apartment. She didn't want to share the lift with anyone, she needed to think.

Finn had been carrying this injury for ten years. She understood that it had obviously not always been as incapacitating as it was now but how had he managed not only to keep it quiet but to continue to do the job he did? Bending over an operating table would be hell with a ruptured cervical disc, particularly at the C five/six level.

The pain would account for his bad temper and she wondered what he'd be like if he was pain free. But there was no guarantee that the surgery would be successful. And if it didn't work, what would that mean for Finn? He might lose more upper-limb function and then he wouldn't be able to operate. What would that do to a man like him? One who obviously prided himself on his skills and no doubt measured his worth by his performance as a surgeon? And that wasn't even considering the complications associated with the surgery itself.

She could see the stubborn set of his jaw and recognised in him the same traits of independence and stubbornness she saw in her mother. She knew her mother's issues stemmed from low self-confidence and self-worth. Finn couldn't possibly have some of those same issues, could he? Not someone who seemed so sure of himself.

Whatever his issues, he needed someone to be there for him and Evie would have bet her last dollar that he had no one. Could she do it? Would he let her?

CHAPTER TEN

CHARLIE sat and watched Bella as she slept. He'd been beside her every chance he'd had for the past two days but he felt he could sit there for ever. He'd be there for as long as she needed him.

'*Ciao*, Bella.'

He picked up her hand. It was cool to his touch. He rested his thumb over her wrist, over the pulse that flickered under her skin, and let the beat of her heart vibrate through him.

Her dark eyelashes fluttered against her pale cheeks but her eyes remained closed. She was still sedated. Still ventilated.

He threaded his fingers between hers and gently squeezed her hand. 'Can you hear me?' he asked as he willed her to return his pressure. Just the smallest of movements would have done but there was nothing.

He could have kicked himself for not telling her how he felt when he'd had the chance. He couldn't believe he hadn't told her he needed her in his life. Wanted her in his life.

He couldn't bear the thought of not seeing her smile. Not hearing her laugh. Not seeing her grey eyes turn silver when she asked him to kiss her, asked him to make love to her. He couldn't bear to think he might not have the chance to introduce her to the delights of lovemaking, might not get to have her naked in his arms or take her to the heights of pleasure. That he might not get to hear her cry out in ecstasy as he tasted, teased and thrilled her.

But he didn't regret not seizing the opportunity the other night. Even if it meant he'd missed his chance, he knew the timing had been wrong. He'd wanted to give Bella the attention she deserved and he couldn't have done that. It would have been hurried and hasty, not the languorous experience that he wanted her to have. Even one night wouldn't be enough. Not for her and not for him. He wanted more than that.

If only she'd wake up he could tell her how he felt.

But he could still tell her now. He could accept the theory that comatose or heavily sedated patients were still aware of conversations, sounds and smells around them, even if they were unable to respond. He could tell her how he felt now and he could tell her again later.

He was convinced her depression was due to her mental state prior to the surgery. If she'd wanted to give up then this was a way to let go. But he couldn't let that happen. He needed to get her to fight.

He wound his fingers through her auburn curls and bent his head, burying his face in her curls and breathing in her scent. Even among the hospital odours he could smell her, fresh and sweet.

'Bella?' he whispered. 'Please wake up. I miss you.' He wanted to talk to her, wanted to hear her laugh. He could talk, he could tell her about his day, but it wasn't what she needed to hear. It wasn't going to get her breathing on her own.

He kept his back to the ICU, blocking out the rest of the world as he concentrated on Bella. His words were for Bella alone.

'I'm sorry I didn't make love to you when you asked me to. I don't want to think we've missed our chance. Believe me when I say I was tempted, very tempted, but I wanted to make it perfect for you. You deserve that. You deserve more than a quick tumble on the grass. Not that it wouldn't have been fun,' he said with a smile, 'but I want to spend an entire night with you. More. I want you to wake up in my arms and decide to do it over again. And again. Not to end up cold and sore in the back garden, having to sneak inside like a recalcitrant teenager. I'll make it up to you. I promise you an experience to remember, but first you have to wake up.' He held her hand, connecting them. 'I want to do it properly.

'Did you know I promised Evie I wouldn't break your heart?' he continued. 'She scares me, your big sister. You didn't know I was a coward, did you?' He was only half joking. He wasn't looking forward to the lecture he was expecting from Evie but he would let her have her say, as long as she didn't try to stop him from seeing Bella.

'If you get through this, I promise I'll make it up to you.' He lifted her hand to his lips and kissed her fingertips. 'I'll be waiting for you when you wake up.'

Bella was dozing, trying to piece together the past few days. It was still so hard to believe she'd had a lung transplant, everything felt so vague and distant. When she'd woken she'd been disoriented and she'd had to ask the nurses where she was and what day it was. Apparently it was her third day in the ICU and she'd only been taken off the ventilator that morning.

Her memory was hazy and she kept her eyes closed as she tested out her new lungs. It hurt to breathe in but it was external pain, muscular pain, not her usual tight, blocked, breathless feeling. She put her hand over the base of her ribcage where the pain was worst and felt the dressing. She followed it as it ran across the lower part of her chest and felt where the drain emerged from the dressing and dropped away over the edge of the bed.

Above the dressing, between her breasts, she could feel ECG leads stuck to her chest but there were no bandages higher up. The scar from the surgery was a horizontal one, down low, just as Sam had told her it would be. But she hadn't believed him. She'd been convinced the scar would be between her breasts, visible to everyone any time she wore a V-neck top. Sam told her that was the case for heart surgery, not lung surgery, but she'd been terrified of waking up and finding out he'd been wrong.

She took another deep breath, in, out, in, almost scared to think her new lungs actually worked. She breathed out as she heard two nurses talking as they came towards her bed. She opened her eyes, thinking they were coming to her, but they stopped at the bed beside hers, ready to turn that patient. They continued talking as they worked.

'Has Dr Maxwell been in yet?'

'No. I haven't seen him since he was at Pete's the other night.'

'I told you you should have talked to him then when you had the chance.'

They were talking about Charlie! Did he have a patient in ICU or had he been in to see her? She racked her brain, struggling to see if she had any recollection of a visit from him, but the past few days were nothing but a fuzzy jumble of images and she had no idea which ones were real and which ones were her imagination.

'I was going to but then he disappeared,' the nurse replied.

Bella couldn't believe how much the nurses in this hospital gossiped in front of the patients. They talked about their lives as though all the patients were deaf. Maybe they've forgotten I'm awake, she thought. She opened her eyes, just a fraction. She had to see who this nurse was but she didn't want them to know she was listening. She squinted through her lashes. She could just make out the name on the nurse's nametag. Philippa.

Philippa? Why did that sound familiar?

No, it wasn't Philippa that was familiar. It was Pippa. The ex-girlfriend Charlie had been talking about before Bella had gone in for surgery. She remembered Charlie talking about how he'd given his heart away and lost everything. The girl, his career, his surfing dreams. No wonder he avoided relationships.

Charlie had obviously thought he'd been helping her, telling her he knew how she felt. But all she could think about was how he'd given his heart away once and would probably never do it again.

In Bella's mind Pippa morphed into Philippa—brunette, big busted, long legs—the complete opposite from her. A woman who knew what she wanted and went after it. Not someone who'd have to beg a man to make love to her.

Bella couldn't believe she'd been such a fool. What on earth would Charlie see in someone like her? He'd even told her, more than once, that the reason he spent time with her was because Evie asked him to. He obviously thought of her as Evie's little sister, nothing more. She felt tears welling in her eyes. He'd probably had no intention of making love to her, poor, tragic, inexperienced Bella, not at any time. He'd probably just been trying to let her down gently.

She wanted to fall in love but she couldn't give her heart to Charlie. Not now. Not now she knew about Pippa. Not now she knew why he avoided relationships. That would be asking for trouble. Trusting him with her heart yet knowing he would only break it. She wanted to fall in love but she'd have to make sure it wasn't with Charlie. He'd given his heart away once before, she couldn't expect him to do it again.

Well, she decided, she'd find a way to let him out of their deal. She didn't think she could bear to hear him say no to her again.

'*Ciao,* Bella.'

By the time Charlie arrived in the ICU Bella had planned her strategy, but as soon as she heard his usual greeting she felt her resolve start to crumble.

'You're a sight for sore eyes. You're looking a million dollars,' he said.

She knew he was exaggerating hugely but his effortless charm still made her feel better. His voice was bright and cheery, he sounded happy to see her; she needed to stay strong.

He placed his hand over hers and squeezed her fingers. His hand was warm and Bella drew comfort from his strength. 'You had us all so worried.'

'I did?'

'Of course.' Charlie looked at her as if she'd gone a little mad and Bella mentally rolled her eyes. Of course people would have been concerned. 'This was supposed to be the answer for you but knowing how you were feeling before the surgery I was worried you were going to give in. But I shouldn't have doubted you—you're a fighter, a survivor.'

But she'd come close to giving up. She knew it. She normally made such an effort to be strong and to fight but she'd been so tired, she'd been almost ready to call it quits. Almost. Charlie had been right, she'd needed a reason to get through the surgery and she'd found it. She didn't need

Charlie's assistance and attention any more, she was a survivor and she'd get through this too.

'I have you to thank for getting me past this,' she told him.

'Me?'

She nodded and reached for an envelope that was beside her bed. She grimaced slightly with the stretch and Charlie picked the envelope up and handed it to her. She held it up. 'In here is a letter from the college.' She couldn't stop the grin that spread across her face. 'I've been accepted into fashion design.'

She was about to let Charlie go, to let him out of their deal and possibly out of her life, but she couldn't let him go without telling him the good news. After all, she did have him to thank for it.

'That's fantastic! Congratulations.'

He leant over and kissed her cheek and Bella felt her resolve slipping through her fingers and sliding to the floor. She closed her eyes to block out the sight of him, his gorgeous brown eyes, his smooth olive skin, his perfect ears and his divine lips. But his image was just as clear with her eyes closed and his lips were soft and warm on her cheek. She felt her heart flip-flop in her chest and she forced herself to remember what he'd said about Pippa. How he'd given her his heart and she'd thrown it away. Forced herself to remember he'd said that medicine was his new passion and he didn't need relationships.

'I knew they'd love you. When do you start?'

She opened her eyes as Charlie's lips left her cheek.

'Not until March.'

'You'll be fighting fit by then?'

'I plan to be. I've got a more pressing engagement before then.' She paused and took a deep breath, still surprised at the feeling of freedom, and told him another one of her reasons for living. 'Lexi and Sam have set a date for their wedding.'

'They have? When is it?'

'In three weeks, the Saturday before Christmas.'

'That's not a lot of time. Will you be okay for that?'

'I'm going to make sure I am. Sam seems to think I have a good chance if I focus on my exercises and eating properly and being vigilant with my medication. Studying in March should be a piece of cake if I can get through the next three weeks.'

'Have you got time pencilled in for me some time after you get out of here? I seem to recall we have unfinished business.' His brown eyes were shining and Bella's insides melted as she imagined letting him take her to bed. Just once.

Was he still planning on honouring their deal? He was grinning at her and Bella was very tempted to let their arrangement stand but she knew she couldn't do it. She wanted to be special and Charlie didn't do special, at least not for more than one night at a time. She wanted to be different and the only way to be different was to make sure she wasn't just another notch in his bedpost.

She steeled herself to stick to her plan. Now was her chance to let him off the hook before he could seduce her. Before he could reject her.

She took a deep breath, still amazed that she could actually fill her lungs, even though the wound gave her some discomfort. 'That's not a priority any more. I have three weeks to get well enough for Lexi's wedding, that's my goal.'

'And after the wedding? Are you going to keep working your way through your wishlist?'

'I have a new list now.'

Charlie frowned. 'A new list. What about staying up all night to see the sun rise? Being kissed under the stars?'

'My list wasn't set in stone. I can change it if I like, it's my list.'

'But why would you change it?'

'I've got more time now. I can look further ahead. Do you know how amazing that feels?'

Charlie was grinning at her, his eyes shining. She could tell he knew exactly how she felt. She'd bet he'd got the same thrill of excitement when he'd been surfing. 'What's on your new list?' he asked.

'I'm going to college and I'm going to travel. Halfway through next year I'm taking myself to Paris.'

'Paris?'

'I've always wanted to go to Paris but I thought it was an impossible dream.'

'You're going on your own?'

'Evie will come with me. She doesn't know it yet but she will.'

'You have everything planned but no time for me?' He actually sounded disappointed but Bella knew he'd get over it. There'd be plenty of women eager to take her place, plenty of women eager to be charmed and bedded by Charlie Maxwell.

'I don't want a quick roll in the hay,' she explained. 'I don't want to be just another notch in someone's bedpost. Not that I don't appreciate your offer,' she added, 'it's just that I want more now. I have my life back. I have time to find the things I want and I want a proper relationship. I want to be in love. I want it to be special.' Bella knew she couldn't expect Charlie to choose her over all the other women out there but she wasn't going to agree to a fling.

Movement to her left distracted her. Busty, long-legged Philippa was coming towards them.

'Hello, Dr Maxwell. I didn't realise you knew Bella,' she said as she checked Bella's monitor. She looked back over her shoulder at Charlie as she added, 'My shift is just about finished and I'm heading to Pete's. Will you be there tonight?'

Bella held her breath, waiting for Charlie's answer, as she watched Philippa making cow eyes at him. She wished she could get out of that stupid bed, out of the ICU, as far away as possible from Charlie and all the silly nurses who threw themselves at his feet. But she was stuck, literally tied to the bed by the tubes and leads and drains that Philippa had come to check, and she had no option but to lie there and listen to her flirt with Charlie.

She didn't want Charlie to choose someone else but she especially didn't want to see him do it right in front of her.

'No, I won't be at Pete's,' he said, as he stood up, and Bella let out the breath she'd been holding. He leant over and squeezed Bella's hand, 'I'll see you later,' he said before he left the ICU.

Bella and Philippa both watched him go. Charlie left and took their dreams with him. Philippa sighed in admiration but Bella felt like crying. She could only assume her dreams were very different from Philippa's.

Charlie didn't think he could do special. He'd been prepared to offer Bella amazing, incredible and delightful but only on a temporary basis. But he knew that wasn't what she had in mind. She wanted to fall in love and he couldn't do that. Love meant giving up too much of himself.

He needed to walk away. He needed to make sure he didn't hurt her. She didn't deserve that. And Evie would kill him if he hurt Bella. For everyone's sake he needed to walk away.

He'd made himself take those steps, he'd made himself

leave Bella behind, and he'd kept away because he wasn't what she needed. He wasn't even what she wanted.

But it was a lot harder than he'd expected.

He sat on the beach and let the sand trickle through his fingers as he watched the waves. The sun was warm on his back and the breeze coming off the ocean left the taste of salt water on his lips. He closed his eyes as he let his memories wash over him. Images of him on a scooter in Bali collided with images of Bella. It wasn't Pippa he pictured on the scooter with him, it was Bella. Images of Bella in hospital, her auburn curls bright against the white sheets, her skin pale, overlapped with memories of the two of them dancing under the stars, of her asking him to make love to her, her grey eyes dark like a stormy sea, her skin the colour of pearls, her lips the pink of a perfect sunset.

He'd driven down to Wollongong to try to clear his head. There were only so many laps of the Kirribilli pool he could do before he went completely stir-crazy. The surf was good and he felt the usual pang of regret that he couldn't be out there, but this time that feeling of regret was overshadowed by thoughts of Bella. If he really wanted to, he could body-surf, but that wasn't what he needed either. That wouldn't make things right. He glanced to his left, at the empty sand around him. He knew if Bella was sitting beside him everything would be okay with the world. With his world.

He missed her. He missed the touch of her hand, her laugh, her smile when he said her name.

He wished he could teach her to surf. He wished he could share with her the feeling of freedom and exhilaration surfing could produce. He knew she would love it. But knowing he couldn't surf again was different from accepting that he couldn't teach Bella. For once he wasn't sorry for his sake, he could remember how it felt to be flying down the face of a wave, to feel nothing but the rush of wind and salt spray in his face, to feel the ocean moving under his feet, alternately lifting him up before it did its best to discard him to its watery depths, the feeling of euphoria when he bested a wave, and he was sorry he wouldn't get the chance to share that with Bella.

But there were other things he could share with her. Other things he could show her. He could take her to the ski fields. They could make love in front of a fire and drink hot chocolate while the snow fell outside. He could go with her to Paris and watch the sunset from the Eiffel Tower. They could take an early morning trip to Bondi and watch the sunrise over the ocean. They had a whole world to explore and he knew then he'd rather have that adventure with Bella than surf one more wave.

When he was with her he stopped searching for the next adrenalin rush, the next hit, the rush he used to get from taking on a monster wave and coming out of it unscathed, victorious. The rush he got from performing a difficult operation and doing it successfully. Bella gave him that same rush of excitement but she also made him feel grounded, content, happy. When he was with her he felt comfortable. He felt free.

And that was when he knew. He missed surfing but not as much as he missed Bella.

He'd offered her an experience to remember but he'd been thinking along the lines of a weekend, maybe two. But that wasn't what she wanted and he realised it wasn't what he wanted either. Could he be the man she wanted?

He wasn't sure but he was prepared to try. He wanted Bella more than anything else and he was going to make sure he got her. He stood up from the sand. He had one

week until Lexi and Sam's wedding. One week until he
knew he'd be seeing Bella again. There were things he
needed to do.

CHAPTER ELEVEN

THE wedding was perfect, Bella thought as she watched couples moving to the music on the dance floor. Even though it had been pulled together in a hurry, every tiny element had been attended to. For the past three weeks, in between her exercise and rehab sessions, Bella had been absolutely frantic, helping Lexi with myriad details for the wedding, coordinating dresses, tuxedos, caterers, musicians, florists and the cake, but to see how happy Lexi was made it all worthwhile.

Lexi looked stunning in the dress Bella had designed for her and she watched as Sam guided Lexi expertly around the dance floor. Their eyes hadn't strayed from each other, they were caught up in their own little world, and Bella envied them.

The pale green of Evie's bridesmaid's dress caught her eye as she glided past in the arms of Marco D'Avello. Marco was an obstetrician at the Harbour and one of several doctors Bella had seen in her pre-op work-up, but she was fairly certain he and Evie were nothing but friends.

While Lexi hadn't danced with anyone but Sam, Evie had had a stream of admiring partners. But Bella had seen her constantly stealing glances at Finn—though she could tell Evie was trying desperately to look as if she hadn't noticed him. Bella wondered what was going on between

Evie and Finn. Evie was passionate in her dislike of him yet Bella could sense something else.

Finn was nursing what looked like a glass of whisky and Bella hadn't seen him on the dance floor. He looked like a man who needed a friend and for a moment she thought about going to speak to him before she realised she'd have nothing to say. The song ended and Bella saw Evie cross the dance floor and head towards Finn. She wondered if Evie was planning on rescuing him from his demons. Watching Finn with the whisky in his hand and the 'keep your distance' expression on his face, Bella hoped his weren't the same demons that her mother faced. Evie needed a new project now that Bella was on the mend; she always needed to be helping someone, but none of them had been able to help Miranda, and Bella didn't want Evie to be disappointed all over again by Finn.

She turned back to the dance floor as another song began. The wedding had been perfect and there was nothing she could do now for Evie and Finn so she might as well enjoy the evening. Charlie was in the middle of the floor. She recognised his graceful movements even before she saw his broad shoulders and bald head. His movement was fluid and rhythmical and she could picture him in his surfing days gliding down the face of a wave, at one with the power of the ocean. He looked sensational in a crisp tuxedo and she devoured him with her eyes as he moved past her.

The wedding had been perfect, everything had been perfect, including Charlie.

Especially Charlie.

She'd expected that she'd have been too busy over the past three weeks to even think about him but he'd filled her dreams every night and he'd been the first person she'd seen today as she'd entered the ballroom where the wedding ceremony was going to take place. She hadn't seen him for three weeks but she'd picked him out the moment she'd stood in the doorway waiting to walk down the aisle in front of Lexi. He'd been sitting on the left of the aisle, on the bride's side, and Bella's heart had done its funny little flip-flop thing when she'd seen the back of his bald head. He'd turned as the 'Wedding March' had started and met her gaze. He'd winked at her and grinned as if nothing had changed. As if they'd seen each other only yesterday. How was it that he could behave as if everything was the same? How was it that he could seem so calm and composed and yet her hands had started to shake and her stomach was in knots with just one look?

But if nothing had changed, why had he still not asked her to dance? She'd begun to think he was avoiding her.

Well, she only had herself to blame for that, she thought as she saw him dance past her again. After telling him about her new wishlist, there was no reason for him to seek out her company any more. At least he'd been dancing with lots of different women, at least she hadn't had to watch him pick up one particular woman at Lexi's wedding. She didn't think she could bear to sit through that.

She forced herself to look away from Charlie. No matter how tempting it was to imagine having a quick fling with him, she knew she couldn't do it. Her heart wouldn't survive. She'd made her decision and she needed to stick to it. But now that the wedding was almost over she needed something else to focus her attention on, something else to keep her mind off Charlie. Her fashion design course didn't start for another three months so she had to find something to keep her occupied.

She turned away from the dance floor knowing the only possible way to keep her mind off Charlie was to keep him out of sight.

* * *

Charlie watched Bella as she hovered on the edge of the dance floor, chatting to her father. He felt as though he'd been watching her all evening, waiting for her to be free from her official bridesmaid's duties. Waiting for her to be free for him. Her auburn curls shone under the soft lights and she seemed to float against the background of the other guests. She looked divine in a dress that hugged her chest and then flared out into a full skirt that looked as light as air and floated about her legs as she moved. He recognised the outfit, he'd seen it in her sketch book.

Richard was moving away, leaving Bella alone. He excused himself from his dance partner as politely as possible and went over to her.

'*Ciao*, Bella.' He bent down and kissed her cheek, savouring the softness of her skin under his lips, the slight brush of her curls against his jaw, the lightness of her dress fabric as his hand grazed her hip. 'You're wearing the green dress.'

She smiled at him and his heart soared. 'I told you I just needed time.'

'It's perfect on you.' The pale green was a perfect foil for her colouring and she reminded him of a butterfly—delicate, ethereal and exquisite. 'Would you dance with me?'

She nodded and stepped into his embrace. She felt slight and fragile but he knew she wasn't. She had a strength of character that belied her petite size. He held her in his arms and revelled in the sensation of having her pressed against him. They talked about everything that had happened in her life for the past three weeks—about the wedding preparations, her recovery from the surgery, her rehabilitation. He'd thought there might be awkwardness between them but they slipped easily back into their relationship as though it had only been one day, not twenty, since they'd seen each other.

Everything they discussed was important but it didn't get Charlie any closer to knowing what he needed to know. He felt they talked about everything but nothing because they didn't talk about them. And he needed to know if there could be a 'them'.

'Have you finished your official duties?' he asked as the song ended. 'Do you think anyone would notice if you sneaked outside with me?'

Her eyes sparkled silver and her pink lips broke into a wide smile. 'You're not going to drag me down to the frangipani bushes and take advantage of me, are you?'

'Not unless you want me to,' he teased. 'I have a proposition for you,' he added, 'but I'd like some privacy.'

Bella nodded silently, and then surprised him when she took control, keeping hold of his hand and leading him out into the garden, guiding him along the path. The air was heavy with the scent of frangipani flowers but Bella walked past the bushes and headed for the Moreton Bay fig tree that stood sentinel over the lawn. An old wooden swing hung from its branches, the seat big enough for two, and Bella pulled him down beside her under the canopy of the old tree.

'I'm listening.'

He wondered what was going through her mind. What she was expecting him to say? She seemed so calm. He was a bundle of nerves. It mattered so much to him to get this right. This was the most important conversation he ever expected to have.

He stood up from the swing, too keyed up to sit still, and paced backwards and forwards, working up the courage to start. What if she said no?

He took a deep breath and began. 'This new list of

yours, I was wondering if you'd share it with me, tell me what's on it?'

'What do you mean?'

'The wedding is almost over and you must have close to three months until college starts. What's next on your list?'

She'd been wondering the same thing herself just moments before. She needed to find something to occupy her time until college started otherwise she'd waste it day-dreaming about things that were never going to happen.

'I'm going to go out in the world and experience life,' she told him. Being deliberately vague allowed her to keep her options open but also suited her because she really had no idea what she was going to do. 'I've been given the second chance I've always wanted. Now I can do anything, so I'm going to search out as many new experiences as I can.'

'Do you think I could persuade you to share some of those experiences with me? I want to ask you for another chance.'

She hesitated. She wasn't sure what she'd been expecting but this declaration wasn't it. Or to be more accurate, it wasn't what she'd hoped for. She hadn't hesitated to join him outside but she knew it was because she was eager to have just one more moment with him. It didn't mean she would be okay with a casual relationship. She still wanted Charlie but unless she could have all of him, emotionally and physically, she was better off alone.

She shook her head. 'I don't think you can give me what I'm after. I don't want a casual relationship, I want something deeper. Not that I expect to find that in a hurry but I want my heart intact so that when the time is right I'm ready. I don't think I can risk my heart with you.'

Charlie sat down beside her and his weight made the swing sway on its ropes. 'Don't give up on me.' His brown eyes were unreadable in the darkness but his voice was thick with emotion. 'I promise I won't hurt you. I've already promised Evie I wouldn't break your heart.'

'I'm okay by myself,' she told him. 'I don't want you to ask me out because of my list or because you feel sorry for me or out of some sense of misguided loyalty to me because I'm Evie's little sister. I'll be fine.'

Charlie reached for her hand. 'This has nothing to do with your list and definitely nothing to do with Evie. Just because I see Evie as my little sister it doesn't mean I see you the same way. I'm asking you to let me date you. Give me a chance. Please.'

He hadn't let go of her and her fingers trembled under his touch. She yearned to give in to him but somehow she managed to shake her head again. 'I'm going to use the next few months as a chance to find out where I belong and I don't think I'll be able to do that unless I spend some time by myself. I need to learn to be independent. I need to learn to stand on my own two feet.'

'I get that, but what if I stood beside you? I want to be with you. I want to be the man you're looking for.'

'Why?'

'I've missed you.'

The way he said it, so simply, as though that explained everything, made her want to believe him and almost made her want to give in, but it wasn't enough.

'I've missed your courage and your spirit,' he continued. 'I've missed our conversations. I've missed everything about you. I've missed hearing your name on my lips, I've missed seeing you smile when I walk into a room. I've missed the taste of your mouth, the touch of your hand.' He lifted her hand to his lips and kissed her fingertips. 'I've had plenty of time to think over the past weeks and to work out what's important in my life. And I know now that it's you. I can't imagine my life without you and I want to be a part of your life. I want to be beside you when you see the Eiffel Tower for the first time, I want to be the man you kiss standing on the banks of the Seine under a starry sky, I want to drink champagne with you at midnight and stay up and watch the sun rise.'

'You want to do all that with me?'

He nodded. 'When you were in hospital after your operation I realised if I had to choose between being able to surf for one more day or seeing you, I would choose you. I'm not talking about a casual relationship. I'm ready to make a commitment to you. Not for the next week or the next month but for ever.'

He reached into the pocket of his tuxedo and pulled out a thin envelope. He opened it and removed two sheets of paper, which he handed to Bella.

'What's this?' she asked.

'Two tickets to Paris.'

'Paris? I don't understand.'

'I want to take you to Paris. In July.' He got off the swing and knelt in front of her, holding her hands in his. 'I want to take you to Paris for our honeymoon. I love you, Bella, and I want you to be my wife.'

Bella's heart was racing in her chest and her mouth was dry. He what?

'You don't need to answer me now,' he said. 'I'm prepared to wait, as long as you agree to go on another date with me. Just agree to let me love you.'

'You love me?'

'I do. And I want to be the best man I can be. For you.'

'Are you sure I'm who you want?'

'I've never been more certain of anything in my life. You have made my world a better place and you have given me the freedom to be myself. That's something I've been searching for ever since I had to give up surfing. When you thought I couldn't give you what you wanted you didn't judge me, you left me to be my own person, but I found out I didn't want to be my own man, I wanted to be your man. If I could still surf I would give it up for you, I would give up everything for you, but the only thing I can offer you is my love. I thought I wanted freedom but I don't. I want you.'

The tickets to Paris were resting on Bella's lap. She folded them up and slid them back into their envelope. 'I don't need Paris.'

'But—'

She reached out and put her fingers on Charlie's perfect, plump lips, quietening him.

'I don't *need* Paris but I would love to go and I would love to go with you. I also don't need time to think about us. I don't need anything except you. I used to feel like a fairy-tale princess, locked away watching the world pass by, kept separate and apart from everyone else, restricted by my illness, but you have never treated me as a fragile invalid who needed protection. You are the only person who treats me as if I'm the same as everyone else.'

'I don't want you to feel as though you're just like everyone else. I want you to feel special.'

'I do feel special when I'm with you,' she told him. 'It's funny, I envied you your freedom but you've set me free. You're my very own Prince Charming. I've been waiting for you all my life. I love you and I know where I belong in the world. I belong with you.'

Charlie stood and lifted her off the swing, pulling her to her feet, and kissed her long and hard, and Bella knew that with Charlie by her side, loving her, all her dreams would come true.

'So you'll marry me?' he asked.

Her heart flip-flopped in her chest. 'Yes, I will marry you,' she replied.

'And we can honeymoon in Paris?'

'Definitely.'

'Then I just have one more request,' he said.

'Anything.'

'You have to throw away all your old pyjamas. You're too beautiful to be wearing them. They're not coming to Paris, they're not allowed anywhere near you. From now on it's red negligees only. Agreed?'

'Agreed,' Bella replied, as she sealed her promise with a kiss.

* * * * *

DOCTOR'S
MILE-HIGH FLING

BY
TINA BECKETT

First published in Great Britain 2012
by Mills & Boon, an imprint of Harlequin (UK) Limited.
Harlequin (UK) Limited, Eton House, 18-24 Paradise Road,
Richmond, Surrey TW9 1SR

© Tina Beckett 2012

ISBN: 978 0 263 89176 8

Harlequin (UK) policy is to use papers that are natural, renewable and recyclable products and made from wood grown in sustainable forests. The logging and manufacturing process conform to the legal environmental regulations of the country of origin.

Printed and bound in Spain
by Blackprint CPI, Barcelona

Dear Reader

One would expect a seasoned traveller to love the adventure of flying from place to place, living in lands far from home, learning about new cultures and different types of food. That's me! All except for the very first point: flying from place to place. During my adult years I've lived outside my home country more than I've lived within its borders. That means I have to fly. A lot. And you know what? I tremble every time I step foot on a plane.

My father—a man I look up to—spent his life around planes. He served with the Hurricane Hunters, a group of brave souls who fly into hurricanes gathering information. And later, during his time with the Navy, he worked as a flight mechanic aboard an aircraft carrier. He still loves planes. I should have inherited a little of that love, right? Nope. My husband still has to grip my hand during each and every take-off. What would I do if I were *married* to a pilot? That simple thought led to DOCTOR'S MILE-HIGH FLING—the story of a rescue pilot and the doctor who works with him.

Thank you for joining Blake and Molly as they experience the joy and heartbreak of working under very difficult conditions. Their dedication to their patients helps Molly overcome her fear and rise to meet each new challenge. Best of all, this special couple finds love along the way. I hope you enjoy reading about their journey as much as I enjoyed writing it!

Sincerely

Tina Beckett

To my two greatest heroes: my father and my husband.
I love you both.

CHAPTER ONE

A FINE line existed between taking a dare and actually going through with it.

Molly McKinna was about to cross that line. Belted in and ready to take off, she glanced out of the window at her partner in crime, who simply made a rolling motion with his hand: get on with it.

Easy for Doug to say. His clammy fingers weren't the ones glued to the sides of the copilot seat of the small Cessna.

Flying. Why did it have to involve flying?

"Are you ready?" The flash of a hard dimple signaled the rescue pilot's amusement, but he could laugh his head off for all she cared. As long as he brought her back from Dutch Harbor alive.

She agreed with Doug, really she did. She had to decide if she could hack the flight from Anchorage to the Aleutian islands before accepting the job. But why did she have to choose a location where the only mode of transportation involved whizzing across the ocean as if shot from a giant slingshot?

You'd think being born to a bush pilot would give her an innate love for flying. But since her father, a man with thirty years of experience, had died in a plane crash on this very same route while she'd been in medical school, she no longer had much confidence in the whole flying scene. In fact, she'd avoided it ever since.

And yet here she was. Desperation sometimes bred stupidity.

Realizing the man at the controls was awaiting her reply, she mumbled, "Do I look ready?"

Either he didn't hear her, or figured that was as close to an affirmative answer as he was likely to get, because his mouth quirked once again before he revved the engines to a howling fury and raced toward the end of the tarmac.

Oh, God, oh, God, oh, God...

Then they were off the ground and climbing fast.

She only realized her eyes were screwed shut when her traveling companion's deep voice broke through the whine of the engine. "You can let go now."

Cracking open one eyelid, she glanced sideways and encountered the pilot's strong tanned jaw, the lightest dusting of dark stubble making him look more human somehow. When she'd first arrived at the airport, he'd seemed a little annoyed at being recruited to fly her to check out the medical facilities on the islands. Moments later, she'd decided she'd either imagined his reaction or he hid his emotions all too well.

Even so, she couldn't blame him for being irritated, since he'd wound up having to watch and wait while Doug had given her a pep talk about cars being more dangerous than planes. Not that his speech had helped calm her racing heart!

No way could she run now, though. She was strapped in and hanging high above the sea. And she still had the return trip to look forward to.

"So the flight takes three hours?" Molly forced her hands off the seat and into her lap, linking her fingers in what she hoped was a reasonable facsimile of casual indifference.

"Depending on weather conditions, yes."

"And today's conditions are...?"

"For this time of year?" He slid a sideway glance at her and raised his brows. "About normal."

Normal.

Molly gave an inward eye roll. Well, that certainly gave her a lot to go on. Why did every pilot she'd ever met speak in that deep soothing baritone that only made her want to scramble for the nearest life vest? Did their final exam include an "octave" test or something? Were the pilots with high squeaky voices ejected in mid-flight?

Her teeth came down on her lip. Okay, the words *ejected* and *mid-flight* were officially banned from her vocabulary.

"I'm sorry about your father." He looked straight ahead. "He was a good man."

"You knew him?" That surprised her—enough to let her push aside some of her fear. She'd seen the hunky pilot around the hospital from time to time. She even knew his name was Blake Taylor, but her father had never mentioned him when he'd been alive.

Maybe someone had seen fit to enlighten him. The accident had happened four years ago, but the people in charge had laid the blame squarely in her dad's lap. They felt he'd been reckless to attempt to fly during that storm. As did her mother. It infuriated her to no end. Most of her friends knew better than to bring up his name in her company. Then again, this man wasn't a friend, neither was he likely to become one. And if he said one ugly word about her father, she was going to—

"Wayne helped train me. In my opinion." His voice trailed off.

Molly's backbone stiffened further. Was Blake aware of the circumstances of the accident?

A hand came off the yoke—how had she even remembered that word?—and touched her arm. "I think he made the right call to fly that day, for the record."

"Y-you do?" It was chilly inside the cockpit, and the heater struggled to keep up, kicking out a lukewarm stream of air. But the touch of the pilot's hand heated her instantly. "That's not the prevailing opinion, from what I've heard."

Not even her mother had cut her dad any slack, nagging him relentlessly to give up flying—to get a job closer to home. Her bitterness at his refusal had aged her, tilting her mouth permanently down at the corners. Once Molly had returned from medical school, her mom had focused that vast reservoir of neediness on her only daughter, urging her to live at home. Between her mother and her ex-boyfriend, those two years in Anchorage had sucked the life from her, left her feeling suffocated and alone.

Then a job had opened up in the Aleutians, and she'd leapt at it, flying or no flying. Her mother's reaction to the news still rang in her ears: *Go on and get yourself killed. Leave me all alone. You're just like your father!*

Was she?

Heavens, she hoped so. Maybe that was another reason she'd needed this job so very badly. It was not only a means of escape but a way to hang on to a little piece of her father.

She glanced out the window. The more altitude they gained, though, the more she rued her decision as an impulsive lapse in judgment. But the alternative was untenable. Staying at the hospital had been awkward at best, disastrous at worst. Besides, her father had loved his job, had said he couldn't imagine doing anything else. Maybe she just needed to make peace with that—to try to understand what had motivated him to keep making these trips.

Blake smiled at her, breaking into her thoughts. "Don't listen to them. They're all too happy to shift the blame to someone other than themselves."

She had to blink a few times to realize he wasn't talking about her mother but about those who blamed her father for the accident. "So not everyone thought my father was at fault?"

"Ask a few of the local pilots. I think you'll be surprised at their answers." He paused. "The weather over the islands can be unpredictable even during the summer. One minute it's clear blue skies, and the next..."

"So why do it?" Maybe she should be asking herself that very same question. "Surely you could have been an EMT or chosen something safer than this? Alaska Regional could always use a few more paramedics."

And not one of the single nurses—or any of the married ones, for that matter—would complain if he hung around the hospital a little more. Blake was something of a legend around that place. But from the whispered comments she'd overheard, none of the women in question had managed to worm their way past that charming smile and into his bed.

He shrugged. "As a kid, I loved watching old videos of Evel Knievel. Since I can't rocket across Snake River Canyon, I figure I can fly from Anchorage to Dutch Harbor. All I lack is the cool jumpsuit."

"Evel Knievel never successfully jumped that river."

"But he tried."

Molly shuddered. She hoped he wasn't drawing an analogy between the famous daredevil's doomed flight and the one she was now on. Did she really want to work with a man who seemed to be hooked on adrenaline? She didn't have a choice, since he was considered the best of the best now that her father was gone. Accepting this position meant she'd fly with him from time to time as

they medevaced patients from the islands to the hospital
in Anchorage.

If she took the job.

Nothing was set in stone. In fact, she couldn't risk jeop-
ardizing the project, if she couldn't get past her fear. She'd
have to let someone else take her place. Except none of the
other doctors had stepped up and volunteered—they all
had families, and no one was anxious to leave a thriving
hospital to work in a government-funded clinic.

And part of her father's heart was still on those islands.
A part she wanted desperately to understand.

She blinked, realizing the stabbing terror that had frozen her on takeoff was trickling away. She was still afraid,
but the more Blake talked the more her nerves settled.

It had to be his voice. Maybe flight instructors gave les-
sons in hypnotism as well as voice modulation.

"What about you?" he asked. "Are you seriously thinking about taking the position? Forgive me for pointing out
the obvious, but you don't seem to be in love with the idea
of flying."

Was that his way of calling her chicken? The urge to
flap her wings and cluck had only happened once so far,
during takeoff. "Maybe I need to understand why my dad
traveled back and forth between the mainland and the islands. To make peace with where his journey led him."

No need to tell him she was a coward in more ways than
one. That sometimes it was easier to run than to stand your
ground and fight.

He was silent for a minute, before he answered softly.
"You can't always make peace with it. Sometimes all you
can do is accept what life dishes up and then move past it."

Or you could always fly away from it as fast as you
could.

The plane dipped for a second and so did Molly's heart. "What was that?"

"Just a pothole."

"Sorry?" The fear was back, stronger than ever. She licked her lips, trying not to focus on the vibrations of the plane around her but noticing every tiny shiver just the same.

"Turbulence. It's like bumps in a road. You wouldn't expect to have glassy-smooth highways forever, would you?"

"No, of course not." She relaxed her grip on the shoulder harness.

He was right. It was just a pothole. Not even a very big one.

Somehow thinking of it like that made it easier. "My mom hated flying. She never went to the islands with my dad, no matter how many times he asked her to. Not even to take a vacation. She wouldn't let me go either. And after his plane went down, she became even more…" Demanding? What exactly was she planning to say? "I just don't want to be like that, you know?"

"Understandable. But if your mom didn't let you fly with him, then when did you…?" He frowned. "This isn't your first time up, is it?"

"No!" She bit her lip. "Well, not exactly. I mean, I've been on a plane before."

He scrubbed a hand through his hair, the dark silky locks falling neatly back into place. "Really? When was the last time you were on one?"

"A few weeks ago." She tossed her head as if it had been nothing special.

He seemed to relax in his seat. "Where'd you go?"

"Go?"

"On your flight."

"We, uh, didn't exactly go anywhere." The mumbled words sounded weird even to her.

"I don't follow."

She hesitated. If she didn't tell him, he'd just ask Doug why she'd acted so whacked out during the flight once they got back to Anchorage. "The plane was part of a desensitization course."

Something she'd needed to make sure she could survive this trip.

"A what?" His head jerked to stare at her. "You mean you've never flown before in your life?"

Indignation washed over her. She had, but why should it matter? It was ridiculous to expect everyone to have flown all over the world from the time they could crawl. "I have flown. Just not recently. I—I couldn't."

Not since her father's accident.

"Oh, hell."

She shifted in her seat to face him. "What's that supposed to mean?"

"It means if you're looking for a pilot to help you get past your fear, you'd better keep looking. A desensitization expert I'm not." He laughed and the sound was no longer low and mellow. "I know of at least one person who'd testify to that fact. Only she's no longer speaking to me."

The anger behind that last comment made her hackles rise. Had he purposely scared someone during a flight? If so, he was right. She didn't want him flying her anywhere. "Fine. Once we get back to Anchorage, I'll make sure you never have to—"

"Wrong. Those 'bumps in the road' I mentioned? They're going to get worse the closer we get to the islands. And the landing strip at Dutch Harbor is barely up to FAA standards." He glanced up as if sending a distress

call to some higher power. "Listen, I signed on to take a
doctor to Unalaska to scope out the work at the clinic. I'm
not here to be the next rung on your twelve-step ladder. If
you expect me to sweet-talk you into getting back on the
plane tomorrow, you're out of luck."

Her chin went up. "I guarantee that's not going to happen."

"You're right. It's not." His dark eyes swept over her
face and the expression in them chilled her to the bone. "If
you're not on the plane, strapped into your seat, by eight
o'clock in the morning, you can find yourself a new pilot."

Okay, so he could have handled that better. A lot better.

But from the moment Blake had noticed her clutching her seat, a warning siren had gone off in his brain.
He'd quickly dismissed it, chalking up her reaction to
takeoff jitters. A lot of people got nervous, especially on
flights to the Aleutians, where landings could be very
hairy. Transitioning from a jet engine to a turboprop seven
years ago had given him a few gray hairs of his own, so
who could blame her?

Besides, her dad—a man Blake had looked up to and
respected—was famous in these parts, so he'd had some
ridiculous notion that Wayne McKinna's daughter would
have logged some serious flight hours. Her physical appearance had only added to that impression. Brown,
choppy locks were cut in a way that gave her delicate face
a fearless impudent look. And the bold, take-charge style
drew immediate attention to her eyes. Green. Intelligent.
Framed by incredibly thick lashes.

She looked ready to take on any challenge that came
her way.

Desensitization classes. *Great.*

What the hell was she doing, taking a job that involved medevacing patients to Anchorage?

Even Sharon hadn't been that afraid of flying. And yet her constant nagging to move back to the mainland and to switch to flying passenger jets had proved to be the final straw in an already disintegrating marriage. Wayne had understood exactly where he was coming from, said he'd fought the same battles with his own wife.

Blake loved the island where he'd grown up. Loved the challenge of landing on that tiny airstrip in Dutch Harbor.

Sharon hated both.

After the divorce, he'd decided no one would take those things away from him. Not again.

He glanced over at Molly. She was furiously staring out the front window, her arms folded across her chest, her full bottom lip thinned.

You can find yourself a new pilot.

The fact that she'd answered his outrageous declaration with silence told him everything he needed to know.

He'd blown whatever chance he might have had with her.

If he'd even had one. The woman probably had men doing penance laps until their knees bled, hoping for a chance to go out with her.

He'd noticed Molly bustling around the ER over the past year as he'd checked on some critical-care patients he'd flown in from the islands. Her cheery attitude and gorgeous smile had attracted his attention immediately. When someone had told him she was the daughter of the late, great Wayne McKinna, what had started as a tiny spark of attraction had caught and held. She'd been away at medical school when her father had shown him the ropes, so they'd never been officially introduced. By the time he'd realized who she was, she was already spoken for. Besides, he was from the islands, and Molly appeared to be very much a city girl at heart.

As he'd found out the hard way, oil and water might flirt with each other for a while, but they eventually separated.

He should have reminded himself of that fact and kept his distance.

Then she'd broken off her relationship and signed up for the new health-care position the government had opened up in the Aleutians. The temptation had been too much. He'd juggled his schedule so *he'd* be the one flying her to the islands. Hoping he was wrong and that they might not be so different after all. Surely Wayne's daughter had vestigial wings hidden somewhere under that lab coat— the love of flying must be bred into her.

Wrong.

His jaw tightened. When would he learn? He should swear off marriage forever.

But he eventually wanted a wife. A family. Just not with someone who wanted to crush who he was and remake him into someone completely different.

That need went both ways, however. If he expected a woman to love him as he was, she had a right to expect the same.

Could he love a woman who was afraid of flying, who might end up hating the islands as much as his ex-wife?

Not a chance—he'd already tested that theory once. But that didn't mean he had to be an ass about it.

"Hey, listen. About what I said—"

"Don't worry. As soon as we land, I'll be out of your hair."

"Let me hook you up with someone I know who can fly you back. He's totally safe. Doesn't take any unnecessary chances."

"I'm a big girl. I can take care of myself."

She might be all grown up, but the quiet joy that had caught his attention at the hospital was gone.

Reaching over, he touched her hand, marveling at the softness of her skin. "Molly, we haven't got off to the best start here."

"You think?"

"I just didn't expect Wayne's daughter to be…"

Was there any good way to finish that phrase? He didn't think so.

"You didn't expect her to be what? A wimp?"

"I wasn't going to say that." Well, not those exact words, but the meaning was still there. "Knowing how your father died, it can't be easy for you to get back on a plane."

"Good thing you won't have to deal with *that* problem any more, then, isn't it?"

He waited for her to finish chopping him to bits, but Molly was evidently done, and rightly so.

Before he could figure out a way to smooth over the situation, the plane bucked, then settled back into place. He glanced out the cockpit window, realizing their heated words had diverted his attention for the past several minutes. Not good, because they were heading right into a long line of clouds stretching from side to side.

A front.

And an ugly one, from the look of it.

Molly threw him a panicked look, and Blake tensed.

There'd been nothing in the weather reports to indicate rough conditions today. But he knew things could blow up out of nowhere in this part of the world. This wasn't exactly the way he'd hoped the day would go.

But then again, when did his plans ever fall smoothly into place?

"Make sure your harness is tight."

"Why? What's happening?"

"See those clouds?"

"Yes."

"The little bumps in the road we've experienced are nothing compared to what's coming up." He glanced at her, adrenaline already beginning to spike through his system. "It looks like our smooth highway is about to turn into one oversize construction zone."

CHAPTER TWO

A SIREN sounded somewhere inside the plane, but Molly was too busy trying not to throw up to open her eyes and look around her.

They'd been bouncing around for what seemed like forever. How much more could the tiny aircraft take without coming apart at the seams?

Her fingers gripped her shoulder strap, the nausea from the turbulence almost overwhelming her. She breathed through her mouth, but didn't try to talk, too afraid she'd distract Blake and cause him to make some kind of fatal error.

Like her sniping and complaining might have already done.

Why hadn't she just sat back and pretended she was heading for the warm sands of the Caribbean with a handsome man? Because she was done pretending. Done going along with what others wanted her to be and do.

Maybe he'd report her.

To whom? The Brotherhood of Wronged Pilots?

Pilots probably had to deal with frightened passengers on a regular basis. Molly had just never dreamed she'd end up as a prime example of one.

He could report her to anyone he wanted, as long as

he got them through this storm in one piece. And if he couldn't...

She swallowed the bile that rose higher in her throat. Her mother would have one more loved one to bury. Just like she'd predicted in that last rant before Molly had left the house for good.

Scratch that. They'd never found the bodies of her father or the nurse he'd been travelling with.

If Molly and Blake crashed into the ocean, theirs probably wouldn't be found either.

The siren cut off. Chancing a glance to the side, she noted the way Blake's hands fought with the controls, and she hurriedly shifted her attention to his face. The sight there wasn't any better. The muscles in his jaw stood out in stark relief to the rest of his features, his eyes narrowed in fierce concentration.

That had to be a bad sign. The man who worshipped Evel Knievel was worried.

Are we going to crash?

She kept the words to herself, but they repeated over and over inside her head.

The plane plummeted for several gut-wrenching seconds, before righting itself and climbing back to its previous position. Her stomach didn't follow suit, though. It was still dangling somewhere beneath the aircraft.

A mass of multihued gray bands seemed to scrape along her window as the plane plowed through the middle of the clouds. She flinched at each new bump and shimmy, expecting to be sent tumbling headlong into the sea at any moment. The fact that they were even high enough to be swallowed by clouds surprised her. For some reason she'd thought they'd be cruising well below them. "Don't worry. I've flown through worse." The tight words swirled around the cabin as if they too were caught up in the boiling turbulence outside.

Her hand went to her stomach and pressed hard. He'd flown through worse? An alarm had sounded, for heaven's sake. How much worse could it get?

A gust of wind shoved the plane to the right before releasing its grip. She couldn't hold back the question any longer. "How much farther?"

"We're about a half hour out. We can't land until the weather clears a little."

"Can't we climb above the storm?"

Another blast of air kept Blake from answering her for a minute or so. "Cessnas can't fly as high as commercial jets."

"Oh." Molly decided it was in her own best interests to let him concentrate on flying rather than having to field a constant stream of questions. Besides, there was always the not so off chance that her voice could transform into a high-pitched scream that would end up killing them both.

Better to maintain silence.

Between stutters and bumps, she studied him, finding that concentrating on something other than the conditions outside the plane helped keep the nausea and fear at bay. At least, partially.

Blake's hands were strong, his long tanned fingers gripping the controls. He'd shoved the sleeves of his black sweater halfway up his forearms, exposing lean muscles that bunched and released as he worked to steady the aircraft. Her eyes followed his arm up, curving over substantial biceps before she reached his shoulder. Broad. Taking up his space and some of hers in the tiny cockpit.

Reliable. Competent.

She couldn't see his eyes at the moment, but knew they were deep blue. She'd watched them go from warm and balmy to icy cold in a matter of seconds. Much like the weather outside had done.

Unfortunately, just as she was about to move her attention to that thick head of dark hair, he turned, catching her in mid-stare. "You okay?"

"Oh, uh…yeah." She scrambled for an excuse. "Just seeing if the view from the side is as horrible as it is from the front."

Ack! That hadn't come out right. "I meant the view outside the plane. I wasn't talking about you."

Maybe trying to explain herself wasn't the way to go.

She caught the flash of white teeth as he turned to face the weather again. "Well, that's a relief."

Forcing her attention back to the front windshield, she noted that the wind was calming a bit, along with her stomach.

Thank God. Maybe it was almost…

Suddenly, like a bullet exiting the barrel of a gun, they shot through the clouds and came out on the other side. The fierce turbulence vanished as quickly as it had started.

The contrast between dark and light was so startling, she was forced to squint as the sun peeked in at her and glinted off the nose of the plane. Once she regained her equilibrium, she sat up and drew a slow, careful breath, making sure she was still in one piece. Still alive.

She exhaled just as slowly. The second breath she took, however, was in reaction to the beauty surrounding her.

"It's gorgeous," she whispered. "I've never seen skies so crisp and blue."

"It's pretty amazing, isn't it?" Blake's voice had gone soft as well.

She glanced to the side and caught him looking at her. Her stomach tightened. Why had she ever thought his eyes were cold? Right now they were warm and alive, and looking at her like…

She shook herself. He was glad they'd broken through the clouds. Just like she was.

That shivery look he'd thrown her meant nothing more than that.

She leaned forward as several land masses came into view. Some of them stretched toward the sky like the volcanoes she knew them to be. "The Aleutians."

"Yes." The reverence behind the single word made her take a closer look below. Her father had loved the islands, despite the treacherous conditions she constantly heard about in the news reports. She'd never understood why someone would willingly live in a place where fog, wind and icy conditions were almost constant companions.

Until now.

One of the distant island peaks wore a thick covering of clouds like a top hat. It brought a smile to her face.

"My father loved it here."

"I know." Blake's hands loosened on the wheel. "He told me."

Molly's mother had often complained he loved the islands more than his own family. Why else would he take a job most pilots chose to avoid? He could have had a nice cushy job as an airline pilot, and been better paid for his trouble. He'd turned a deaf ear to his wife's protests and as the years had gone by, her clinginess and grumbling had taken a toll on their relationship. If he hadn't been killed, Molly doubted their marriage would have survived another year.

It was one of the reasons she'd wanted to take the job, to try to see the islands through eyes that weren't tainted by bitterness.

The turbulence of the last half hour had made her rethink that decision. But the second they exited that storm, well, she'd been blown away.

The experience had been breathtaking. Magical.

She'd never seen anything like it in her life.

The plane banked slightly, heading toward the islands. She listened as Blake called in their position and requested permission to land.

As they descended, she craned her neck but couldn't see anything that looked like a landing strip. The mountains seemed to take up every inch of surface space. "Where's the airport? Is it on the other side of the island?"

"Nope, we're heading right for it."

All she saw was a short road bisecting a narrow pinch of land. The pavement went nowhere, both ends dumping into the...

Ocean.

"You're kidding me. That?" She wedged herself into her seat as Blake pushed the yoke farther in, increasing their rate of descent. *Oh, Lord.* "You've landed this before, right?"

"Many times. Relax."

Easy for him to say. If they set down too early or too late, they'd be swimming instead of flying.

Or worse.

As the plane continued to descend, the turbulence picked up again. Molly tried to remain calm, but ended up back in her original takeoff position, both hands gripping her seat, fervently praying she'd live to see another day.

Down, down, down they went. Just when she was sure the wheels were going to trail through the whitecaps below, the landing strip reached for them, grabbing them to safety.

Or so she thought.

Nothing could have prepared her for the bone-jarring

conditions of the asphalt as they hurtled down the strip and toward what looked like the end of the world.

Her fingers tightened with each yard they gained, the brakes of the plane throwing her against her shoulder harness. She pressed down with both feet, hoping the plane would intuitively figure out that she wanted it to S-T-O-P. Now!

What seemed to take forever was, in all probability, over in a matter of seconds. They slowed to taxi speed, with several yards of runway to spare. Okay, so it was more than that, but when you were landing on something the size of a small driveway, any extra room between you and disaster was a welcome sight.

"Are you all right over there?" Blake turned the controls, and they powered toward a building that stood at right angles to the landing strip.

"Yeah. Fine." She hoped he didn't notice the way her voice cracked from one word to the next.

"See? We made it all in one piece." He squeezed her wrist and, as if he'd pressed a switch, her hands released their hold of the seat. "You did great, by the way. The first time is always the hardest. But, believe me, once you get used to it, you'll find yourself wanting to do it every chance you get."

CHAPTER THREE

HAD he really just said that?

Blake jerked his hand from hers. Any hope that she'd missed his unfortunate choice of words flew out the window when color flared along her cheekbones.

Serve him right if she took off to find a new pilot, especially after the way he'd acted on the flight. He'd been angry when he'd realized how afraid she was of flying. Leave it to him to be attracted to women who were the worst possible match for someone like him. First Sharon and then Molly.

He'd always thought Sharon would come around, but she hadn't.

And now he'd unintentionally compared flying to sex with the next girl who came within range of his radar. Two for two. Yeah, he was in rare form.

Shutting off his internal critic, he went about his after-flight check. Molly unhooked her restraint harness and turned toward him.

"Thanks for getting us down in one piece. I know I probably haven't been your easiest passenger." She paused as if expecting him to heartily agree. "But I appreciate you not turning around and hauling my butt back to Anchorage."

"Would that have been before we entered the storm, or after we came out?"

She tried on a smile. "Just so you know I didn't set out to deceive you. I never claimed to be a seasoned traveler."

"I know. Your reaction on takeoff just took me by surprise. Sorry for being rude." He stood to unlock the door, then followed her down the steps as they exited the plane. Once they hit the tarmac, the ground crew met them, asking about their bags. He squared everything away then crossed to where she stood.

"I don't blame you for not wanting to fly with me again, but…" She paused as if gathering her thoughts. "I'd appreciate it if you'd give me a lift home tomorrow. I promise you won't have to sweet-talk me onto the plane."

Despite the sun shining down on them, super-chilled air quickly found its way into the collar and sleeves of his leather jacket. He could do without the constant wind on the islands. Or the reminder of how his marriage had crashed and burned. Against his better judgment, he asked, "You sure?"

"Sure you won't have to sweet-talk me?"

He shifted his weight, trying not to think about how he might like to do just that. "No, I meant are you sure you want *me* to fly you home? I was serious about hooking you up with an experienced pilot."

Glancing at his face, she bumped him with her shoulder and wrinkled her nose. "You've seen how I handle rough weather. Do you really want to foist that on some other unsuspecting soul?"

So she could laugh at herself. His shoulders lost some of their tension.

Actually, now that they were on the ground, she was charming and funny. "Well, since you put it that way, maybe it would be better for everyone if we stuck to our original arrangement. For this trip, anyway."

"My thoughts exactly." She wrapped the flapping ends of her jacket around herself and zipped it tight. The stiff breeze played with her hair, lifting the short strands up and away from her face, before allowing them to fall in delightful disarray. "Now, if you could point me in the direction of the nearest diner, I have two urgent needs."

"Food?"

"That's second on my list. The first is to find a heater that actually works. No offense, but my toes are still frozen from the flight." She pursed her lips. "But I *could* go for a nice hot meal, now that my stomach's starting to settle down. The cold is good for something, anyway."

"I know where they make a mean crab cake. I could show you around the island afterward." He shoved his hands into the pockets of his leather coat, trying to keep the cold from encroaching any further. It was evidently disrupting his thought processes. "You've seriously never been here before?"

"Nope. First time, remember?"

Just like that flight out. Hard to believe she'd lived in Alaska all her life and had never visited the islands.

Sharon had called Unalaska "quaint" on her first visit. Until she'd realized there was no mall. No fashion boutiques. Just simple, hard-working folks. She'd quickly felt trapped—had run back home before six months had been up. He'd do well to keep that in mind before he went and did something stupid.

Like offer to eat lunch with Molly and show her the sights? Who knew how long she'd even stick around?

She was terrified of flying. Her *mother* was afraid of flying. If she had a dog, a cat, or a chipmunk, it would probably be petrified as well. It didn't bode well for some-

one who'd be medevacing patients on a regular basis. Even
as he told himself distance was his friend in a situation
like this, he'd already committed himself as tour guide
for a day.

Damn. No backing out now. But after lunch and a quick
trip around the island, he'd put his pro-distance plan into
motion.

Over a basket of crab cakes and fries, Molly grilled him
about the islands. She already knew the obvious stuff, like
the reality show dealing with the perils of deep-sea fishing that was filmed here, and that the island chain separated the Bering Sea from the Northern Pacific. But she
seemed fascinated by some of the quirkier details. Dutch
Harbor and Unalaska were essentially the same community separated by a short bridge, but the arguments about
which name was correct continued unabated. Both names
had stuck. Dutch Harbor was used for the port and business sections, while Unalaska was where everyone lived
when the workday was through.

"So, if *Aleutians* comes from a native word for island,
doesn't that make it redundant to call them the Aleutian
Islands?"

He took a sip of his soda, then leaned back in his seat.
"I guess it does."

"How long have you been flying this route?"

"Seven years, but I grew up here."

"And you said my father helped train you?"

Setting his drink back on the table, he nodded. "Yes. I
already had my pilot's license, but decided I wanted something with a little more oomph."

"Like Evel Knievel. I remember." Her brows went up.
"My mom never understood why my dad wanted to leave
a relatively safe job as a commercial pilot in order to be
a bush pilot."

He tensed, hoping she wasn't going to ask him if Wayne had talked about his family. Because, while Wayne had loved his wife and daughter, he'd given serious thought to ending his marriage and moving away. His mentor's misgivings had echoed his own. It had taken Blake two years from the time of Wayne's death to realize Sharon's attitude wasn't going to change. After forcing him to leave one job, she'd ended up hating its replacement just as much, more so once they'd moved to his old house on the islands.

The home where he'd been born and raised—given to him when his parents had retired and moved to Florida—had gone from a place of happy memories to a battle zone where no one had ever won. The happiness his parents had found with each other seemed to elude him. When Sharon had finally filed for divorce, he'd been secretly relieved.

"The weather's not always as bad as it was today." No. Not always. Sometimes it was much worse.

He motioned at her empty plate, ready to be done with this particular conversation. "If you're finished, I can show you where the clinics—the two that are currently functioning, anyway—and the hotel are. Are you staying at the Grand Aleutian?"

"No, I'm at the UniSea."

He'd expected her to spring for the pricier accommodations, although he wasn't sure why. Maybe because it was what Sharon would have done. "I have a house here, but I can drop you off at the hotel."

"If I take the job, I may end up renting something."

If I take the job.

Blake motioned for their check. "That flight didn't scare you off?"

"Maybe. We'll see. A lot of it depends on whether or not there are enough patients to make it a wise use of funds. Alaska Regional agreed to partner with the clinic for a year. After that…who knows? There's plenty of need in Anchorage, if not." Her lips tightened. "Or in one of the other big cities in the lower forty-eight."

Big cities. Was that a prerequisite?

When the waitress came with the bill, he waved off Molly's attempt to pay. "I'll turn it in for reimbursement. No sense in each of us filling out an expense report."

"Thanks. My turn next time."

Next time.

Right. Like that was ever going to happen. He needed to bow out of this gig as soon as possible.

But as she moved from the booth and stretched her slender frame, his resolve seemed to dry up—along with his mouth.

The heavy jacket she'd shrugged out of while they were eating had done a thorough job of hiding her figure, as did the white lab coat she normally wore in the ER. But the creamy white sweater had no such problem. Soft and clingy, it skimmed over each and every curve all the way to the middle of her thighs, where dark jeans bridged the gap between the sweater and her knee-high leather boots.

Hell, she was gorgeous.

Maybe he should rethink this.

Crazy. Allowing a flicker of attraction to dictate his actions could never end well.

They moved outside, and Blake clicked the lock on the car he'd left at the airport.

Molly hesitated before getting in. "I should have rented a car. I don't expect you to be my taxi service while I'm here."

"The island's not that big, so it's no trouble. Once I drop you off at the hotel, though, I'll need to head home and get some rest before the flight tomorrow. So if you're looking to take in some of the night life, you're on your own."

At least his mouth had finally got with the program.

The last thing he wanted was to see another woman's lip curl at what the island had to offer in that regard.

"I'm an early riser, actually, so I think I'll turn in after dinner." She tilted her head back to glance at him. "Besides, I want to make sure I don't miss my flight. The pilot didn't seem all that inclined to wait around."

Several strands of hair slid across her cheek as she looked at him, exposing a delicate earlobe. It took more effort than he expected not to reach out and sift his fingers through the shiny locks to see if they were as soft and silky as they looked.

"I'll be there." The temptation to touch her washed through him again. But before he could, she opened the car door and got inside.

He climbed in as well, irritated by the repeated tugs of attraction. Being trapped inside the closed vehicle just made the situation worse. He'd been too busy during their flight to notice the delicate mixture of vanilla and clean sea spray that clung to her skin. Now the scent drifted toward him, making its way inside his head.

Damn. Erasing that fragrance from his memory was going to be impossible. The image of sliding his nose along the naked length of her neck and inhaling deeply rose unbidden, and he gritted his teeth.

The sooner he dropped her off the better.

This whole trip carried a surreal element he struggled to understand. Some of the nurses at the hospital had thrown him looks that held veiled invitations, but he'd never been tempted to return the flirtation or even ask for a phone number. He valued his hard-won freedom far too much to risk messing things up. And he had no intention of moving back to Anchorage to be with another woman.

But his reaction to Molly made him wonder if he was really as immune to the opposite sex as he liked to think. He started the car and tried to put the thought out of his mind. Unfortunately the very thing he'd decided *not* to think about ended up being the one subject he couldn't banish.

Go home. Take a shower. Go to sleep.

If he could do those things, in that order, this whole crazy day would soon be behind him. Before he knew it, Molly McKinna would be out of his life forever. Unless she actually decided to stay on the island, in which case they were bound to run into each other on a regular basis. And there was the fact that he was one of the few medevac pilots who flew these islands. But that didn't mean he and Molly had to be anything more than casual acquaintances or professional colleagues. She would still be tied to the hospital in Anchorage and would probably return there eventually.

He gave himself a mental thump.

Thick skull, meet harsh reality. You two are about to become really good friends.

Molly stood in the white-tiled waiting room of the clinic as Blake made the introductions. Sammi Trenton, the community health aide, tossed her thick dark braid over her shoulder. Tall and slender with high cheekbones that spoke of an island heritage, the young woman smiled in welcome. CHAs played a huge role in healthcare in Alaska, especially in the Aleutians, where population density was low and funding dollars were scarce. Learning about the medical problems the island faced on a regular basis would give Molly a head start for when she actually came to work in a few weeks. Besides, she could do with a few friends right about now.

"Glad to have you." Sammi shook her hand. "We could

sure use the help. Hope you plan on sticking around longer than…"

The woman's eyes cut to Blake, a playful smirk on her face. "Oops. Sorry. Don't know where that came from."

"Still kicking me in the shins after all these years, I see."

Sammi's brows lifted. "I didn't have a choice back then. That was the only thing I could reach." She glanced at Molly. "I was the runt who always got picked on."

"You were the runt who always did the picking on," Blake returned, with an easy smile that carved out a deep groove in his cheek.

Molly's heart rolled over for a second before righting itself.

Okay. No staring. She forced her gaze back to Sammi.

"How was the flight in?" Sammi tilted her head at Blake, her thumb rubbing at a tiny spot on her monkey-stamped smock.

Great. Here it came. The perfect opportunity for Blake to get in a shot at Molly's expense. She tensed in preparation.

"We hit a stormy patch on the way in, but once we got through it, it was smooth sailing."

A sardonic brow lifted in her direction made her wonder if he was referring to the actual weather or to the clash of tempers that had gone on between them. As for *smooth sailing*, that was yet to be seen.

"Well, now that you're here, let me give you the grand tour. Besides, that'll give us girls a chance to get to know each other better."

Blake's brow furrowed. "Be nice."

"*Moi*? I'm always nice." She motioned for Molly to follow her through the door that led to the back of the clinic, wiggling her fingers at Blake as a goodbye.

Although these two were obviously friends from way back, nothing seemed to suggest there was anything more between them than that. Even if there was, it was none of her business. She had to admit, though, they'd make a gorgeous couple, with Blake's rugged good looks and Sammi's dark hair and striking features. And the other woman was tall enough to almost look Blake in the eye, whereas Molly barely reached his chin. Talk about runts.

Sammi took her to one of the exam rooms which, along with the familiar scent of disinfectant, was clean, airy and well appointed. The soft green walls and creamy Formica countertops gave the space a cool, calm atmosphere, a definite plus when working with worried parents or frightened youngsters. "We have three exam areas, but there's normally only one of us on duty at any given time. Having the Anchorage hospital sponsor you will make our jobs a lot easier."

"You said, 'our.' What's the staffing like?"

"We have two receptionists, a nurse and a PA, who can also write prescriptions. During medevacs, things get hectic because someone has to accompany the patient." She gave an innocent blink. "That's where you come in, right? You'll be taking over that part of the job, unless we have more than one emergency."

Molly was tempted to plead ignorance and say she was strictly part of the ground crew, but the hospital had specifically wanted one of their own doing the medical transports. So that line of reasoning wasn't going to fly. "That's what they tell me."

"Blake's great. You'll like working with him."

This was her chance. "You've known each other a long time?"

Sammi led her back out into the hallway and pushed open a door to the restroom, so Molly could see it. "We grew up together, so I guess you could say that." She hesitated. "His ex put him through the wringer a couple of years back. He can be a bit touchy about the subject."

"Understandable." Molly was a little raw from her own experience with her ex, Gary, so she'd be happy to swing clear of that particular subject.

The door at the end of the hallway opened to a tiny break room, complete with refrigerator and microwave. There was also a cot along one wall. "You spend the night?"

"Every once in a while, if we're waiting on a birth or need to transport a patient to the airport to be medevaced. But we all carry cellphones. If there's an emergency, most folks know how to reach us after hours. Are you okay with going on the phone list?"

"Of course. Anything I can do to help."

"Now for the all important question: when do you want to start?"

Molly swallowed. If she wanted to back out, now was the time. But Sammi was so nice, seemed eager for her to take some of the load off the other workers. And she really, *really* didn't want to go back to Anchorage and face Gary day in and day out or field his constant calls. He refused to believe it was really over, even after six months. As did her mother. Was it really fair to allow them both to keep holding out hope?

No. It wasn't. "I have to go back to Anchorage to finish packing. I could probably start in two weeks. Oh, and I'll need to find a place to rent. Do you know of anything?"

"Let me check and give you a call in the morning. Blake says you'll be over at the hotel? We'll find you something. Any preferences?"

"Not really. Just a place to sleep. Nothing fancy."

"Good, because nothing fancy is what Unalaska does

best." She squeezed Molly's hand. "Just leave it to me. Now I'd better get you back to Blake before he has a hissy fit. See you in two weeks?"

"Definitely."

And if Blake didn't want to fly her back in two weeks, well, like he'd said, there were plenty of pilots where he came from.

Molly awoke to the sound of something pinging against the windowpane of her hotel room. Squinting, she tried to see the clock.

Too blurry.

Ugh, her contacts were still on the nightstand. She reached over and felt around for the glasses she'd left next to her contacts case. Slipping them on, she glanced again at the clock.

Her heart stalled in her chest.

Seven-thirty! She was supposed to be at the plane in a half hour.

Blake hadn't asked about her breakfast plans or mentioned picking her up and taking her to the airport. In fact, by the time he'd shown her around the island and dropped her off at the hotel yesterday afternoon, he'd seemed all too anxious to be rid of her. He'd said goodbye with a wave of his hand, before getting back in his car and driving away to wherever he lived.

He'd probably been exhausted from their flight and from schlepping around with her all day. Molly loved the clinic, and Sammi had seemed especially nice, not a hint that she or anyone else viewed her as a threat.

Except maybe Blake, who'd said she needed to be strapped into her seat by eight o'clock.

Or else. Leaping out of bed, she scrambled for her

clothes, thankful she'd taken a shower the previous night to banish the chill that had burrowed deep into her bones.

The pinging noise outside was still going strong, like someone throwing pebbles repeatedly against the glass. Well, she could think of at least one person she could rule out, if that was the case.

She tiptoed to the window, clothes in hand, and parted the curtains several inches. Still dark. Then she caught the glitter of stones on the sidewalk.

No, not stones. Hail. The size of gumballs.

And it wasn't just hailing. Now that she was awake, she realized the gloom was caused by heavy gray clouds that covered the sky. The wind was also howling, kicking up leaves and sending some of the scattered ice drops skittering down the walkway. Her fingers tightened around the clothing she held. Even if she made it to the airport on time, could they take off in these conditions?

Please, no. She'd already flown through one storm. The last thing she wanted to do was make a bigger fool out of herself than she had yesterday.

With her luck, no pilot in his right mind would agree to fly with her after that.

And by the end of the day Blake had seemed so...

Impatient.

He was probably dreading the return trip as much as she was. Maybe she'd be better off not even taking the job.

Except she'd promised Sammi she would, and the hospital was counting on her to follow through. And this job was a lifeline, appearing just when she'd really needed it.

Apart from the flying, which she wondered if she could do—especially while dealing with critically ill patients— she found she liked the island and its inhabitants. She knew the biggest industry was fishing, but was surprised to learn the port itself did quite a bit of business. As they'd driven around yesterday, Blake had pointed out a huge vessel stacked high with various-colored shipping containers getting ready to dock.

She continued to stare out the window, wondering what she should do, when a dark familiar shadow stopped in front of her door. With one hand shoved deep into his pocket, Blake braced himself against the wind, preparing to knock. Just as she got ready to slam the curtains back together, their eyes met.

Argh! Too late.

She still had on the sweatpants and threadbare white tank top she'd worn to bed. And if she could see him, he could see...

His lips quirked, and a rush of heat poured into her face. She held up a finger, hoping he'd catch her meaning. Maybe she could get dressed really fast and...

Poor guy. It was freezing out there. She glanced down. It wasn't like she was in a negligee or anything. She could at least let him into the room while she ducked into the bathroom to get dressed.

Padding over to the door, she made sure her clean clothes were draped to conceal key areas of her chest before opening it. "Come in. I'm running a little late—sorry."

"I tried to call, but they're having trouble with the phones evidently, because I couldn't get through." He glanced at her as if seeing her for the first time. "Uh, I can wait out here until you get ready."

"Don't be ridiculous. It's hailing. Besides, I'm freezing standing here."

That worked. He slid through the opening and let her shut the door behind him.

Heading for the bathroom, she called behind her, "I'll just be a minute."

Once she made it safely inside, she leaned against the wall. Did she even want to look in the mirror?

She opened her eyes and peered into the reflective surface.

Glasses. Great. They weren't even her good pair. And she'd left her contact case on the nightstand.

Leaning closer, she moaned at the sight that met her eyes. Tangled hair, sticking out every which way. Waistband of her sweatpants skewed way to one side, creating a series of unflattering wrinkles that slanted from right to left. And was that a piece of sleep?

Yep. Right in the corner of her eye.

She dropped her head in her hands and moaned. Maybe if she stayed in the bathroom long enough, he'd go away and let her die in peace. He looked clean, rested and, most of all, well groomed.

He smelled good, too, like he'd just hopped out of the shower.

Well, all she could do was work with what she had. He'd just seen her at her worst, so even dragging her fingers through her hair would be an improvement.

She worked as fast as she could, dressing in jeans and a heavy turtleneck, scrubbing her teeth and face then sweeping a coat of clear gloss over her lips. Once she'd finished, there was a moment or two when she entertained the thought of hiding out for a while, before deciding to be a big girl and face him. One deep breath later, she'd opened the door.

Camped out in a chair, Blake sat next to the bed, which was a wreck from all the tossing and turning she'd done during the night. His elbows were propped on his knees as he stared at the images flickering across the weather channel. He glanced up, his eyes sweeping over her as she came into the room. He sat up straighter.

"I like your...er, glasses. I didn't notice them yesterday."

"That's because I wore contacts." That he'd had to scrounge around for something nice to say couldn't be good. She gave an internal shrug. So what if she'd noticed every incredible inch of him from the moment he'd climbed aboard that plane, while he barely even remembered what she looked like?

She squared her shoulders. The last thing she was trying to do was impress him. "How's it looking out there?"

"Not good. I think we might end up staying another—"

A knock at the door interrupted whatever he'd been about to say. Molly frowned at him in question before hurrying over to fling it open.

"Dr. McKinna?" A man, shrouded in a drab green raincoat, stood in the doorway, his head covered by the jacket's hood. Even shadowed, and with water sluicing down his face, she thought she saw worry in his eyes.

"Yes. Is something wrong?"

"Sammi said she tried to reach you by phone and couldn't get through, so she asked me to drive over and see if you were still here. There's a man down over at the dockyard." He braced himself against a gust of wind, and Molly had to hold the door to prevent it from being ripped from her hands. Blake came up behind her, the heat from his body warming her back.

"Hi, Mark," he said, confirming his presence. "What's going on?"

"The damn wind knocked a container sideways and it caught one of the workers in the leg. I was checking on a shipment for a customer and saw it happen. It's bad, there's bone showing through. I came to see if the doc here could take a look." He glanced at her just as a growl of thunder rumbled through the atmosphere, bringing with it another blast of wind. Her fingers scrabbled to retain their hold of the door just as the man's next words chilled her to the bone. "If there's any way you can get the plane up, he needs to be transported out. The sooner, the better."

CHAPTER FOUR

"Have you moved him?"

Yanking on her jacket, Molly's mind ran through various scenarios. Compound fractures could be tricky. When a bone ripped through skin and muscle and was left open to the elements, infection could easily follow. The less sanitary the accident location, the worse it was for the patient, especially if anything outside the body had contaminated the exposed bone.

The man who Blake called Mark dragged a hand through his hair. "No, the bone is... Hell, it looked so bad, no one dared. The men threw a couple blankets over him and were rigging some plastic to keep him dry until I could find you. I'd medevac him myself, but Blake's plane is basically a flying ambulance. Mine just doesn't have that kind of equipment."

"You made the right decision." Although she hated to think of an injured man out in this weather, she didn't want that exposed bone receiving additional damage from attempts to drag him to another site. And she hoped to God those blankets were clean. "How much bleeding is there?"

"Some. But nothing's gushing."

Thank God. No severed arteries.

"Is he conscious?"

Mark shook his head. "As soon as he hit the ground, he was out cold."

Blake had gone out to warm up the car without being asked, for which she was grateful.

She and Mark hurried outside, and Molly slammed the hotel room door behind them. "We'll follow you, okay?"

"You bet. The crate fell across the aisle, so we'll have to circle around a bit to reach him, but at least it'll block the worst of the wind."

After she jumped into the car, Blake accelerated, following the taillights in front of them. "Put your hands over the vent. It'll help keep them warm until we get there."

She yanked off her gloves and held them over the heated flow of air. Not because it felt good, but because the warmer her hands stayed now, the more nimble they would be once they arrived. For a pilot, Blake knew a thing or two about medicine. But then again he flew rescue missions all the time. It gave her another insight into her father. By the time of his death he must have known almost as much as the EMTs and nurses he'd worked with.

"How far to the dockyard?" she asked.

"With the weather, fifteen minutes or so. It's in Dutch Harbor, so we won't have to cross the bridge into Unalaska." He clicked the wipers into high gear to keep up with the sleety rain as they followed Mark's taillights.

She peered into the sky. Heavy gray clouds. No sign of the rain letting up any time soon. "Why would anyone work in weather like this?"

"Sometimes you don't have a choice." He slid a glance at her, his lips tight. "*You're* working."

"Yes, but this is an emergency. And it's my job."

"Mine, too. The dockyard folks have to work as well, even if it's just to secure the area."

He had a point. And in a place famous for its rough

weather, it probably came down to working or going hungry.

This was what her father must have faced time and time again. And yet he'd claimed to love it.

Why?

By the time they got to the container area, her thoughts had shifted to the job at hand. Blake followed Mark as he cruised between aisles of stacked containers.

So big.

She swallowed. "Can you imagine if one of these fell on somebody?"

"Yeah. I can."

He'd not only imagined it, he'd seen it up close, if his tense jaw was anything to go by.

"Did he live?"

"Who?"

"The person you're thinking about."

A quick shake of his head conveyed his meaning all too well. Crush injuries were among the worst. And if the crate landed directly on top of someone…

The truck in front of them pulled to a stop, and Molly immediately spied a huge blue tarp stretched between two shipping containers.

She pulled the hood of her coat into place since it was still sleeting, grabbed her medical bag, then exited the vehicle. She was vaguely aware that Blake had also gotten out. Hurrying around Mark's parked car, she found four men standing under the plastic, with a fifth man kneeling next to the victim, who appeared to be unconscious at the moment. The patient's pale face and the slightly blue cast to his lips signaled shock. Her eyes quickly scanned the body through the blanket.

Crouching next to him, she felt for a pulse—which seemed strong enough—before pulling back the layers of blankets from his bottom half, noting the fabric of his work pants had been slit up the middle, laying bare his leg from ankle to groin. Good thinking.

The fracture was in the left femur, the jagged edge of the exposed bone pointing to the left as if thumbing a lift out of there.

Soon. I promise.

The other half of the break was nowhere to be seen, hidden somewhere deep inside his leg. But if it looked anything like the bone she *could* see… Her stomach knotted. Move him the wrong way and the sharp edges could indeed slice through an artery and kill him.

"How long's he been unconscious?"

One of the men behind her answered. "About a half hour, maybe a little longer. I saw the whole thing. He was out as soon as his head hit the ground."

"How hard did he hit?" She made a mental note to check for signs of a concussion or skull fracture.

"Pretty hard. And once we saw the angle of the leg, we knew it was broken. We just cut his pant leg to see how bad it was." The man swallowed hard. They hadn't expected to find what they had.

She slipped on a pair of latex gloves then used her thumb to pull back the wounded man's right eyelid. Flicking the beam from her penlight across the pupil, she then repeated the action with the other eye.

Equal and reactive. Good. No evidence of brain trauma at the moment.

Working quickly, she again took his pulse, then ran her hands down his unaffected limbs, making sure she wasn't missing another obvious fracture. Everything felt solid.

Blake knelt beside her. "What can I do?"

"I want to get an IV into him, but we can do that once we get to the plane. Right now, I need to stabilize his leg.

Can you find me some heavy sticks or a couple pieces of lumber? Not too long, maybe—"

She held her hands apart, approximating the size she wanted.

"I'm on it."

He hadn't balked at the task, neither had he batted an eyelash at the sight of the man's open wound. Evel Knievel or not, he was evidently good at his job.

While he was gone, she grabbed a small bottle of saline and sponged away the blood so she could see the area better. She then wet several pieces of sterile gauze and laid them over the wound, one on top of the other, to keep the bone moist and avoid further contamination. Those layers were topped with a few dry ones, in case the bleeding continued. Blake was back by the time she was done, holding a couple of clean-looking one-by-fours.

"These okay?"

"Perfect." She nodded toward her bag. "I've got some hand sanitizer and some surgical gloves in there. I'll need you to help me splint him, if you're up to it."

As soon as she said it, she glanced up to make sure he was in agreement, but he'd already handed off the wood to someone else and was squirting the sanitizer onto his hands.

"Does anyone have a truck or a van we can use to transport him to the airport? Something with a large covered area?"

Neither of the local clinics were equipped to do surgery like this, and Anchorage had a great orthopedic surgeon who was willing to come in at a moment's notice. She'd radio it in once they were in the air.

"I do." The man who'd been kneeling next to the patient spoke up. "It's in the parking lot."

She noticed his hesitation and wondered if he was

worried about liability issues. "I'll take responsibility," she said.

"It's not that. He's going to be okay, isn't he? He's… he's my…"

When the man's voice cracked, Mark spoke up. "They're brothers. Jed—your patient—lost his wife to cancer a few months ago. He's got two young kids at home."

Oh, boy.

She turned to the man who couldn't have been older than his early twenties. No need for him to see what she was about to do. "We're going to take good care of him, I promise. Do you think you could bring your truck as close as you can? Once we splint his leg, we'll be ready to go."

"Sure." He glanced one last time at his brother as keys exchanged hands, then got to his feet and strode away.

"Do we need to contact someone?" she asked Mark.

"I'll call his sister. She can watch the kids when they get out of school." He took a step closer, his eyes narrowing in on hers. "Listen, I appreciate you coming down here with me."

"Hey, it's what I'm here for. No need to thank me."

He smiled, his mouth opening as if to say something else, when a sharp snap sounded next to her yanking her attention back to Blake, who rubbed the area where his surgical glove met bare skin. A glimmer of irritation shone in his blue eyes.

At what? They weren't even in the air yet.

She gave a mental shrug. Men!

"I'm going to have you hold the wood on either side of his leg, from upper thigh down to midcalf. I'll wrap gauze around the whole thing to immobilize it." She raised her brows. "You sure you're going to be okay?"

"I usually am."

The annoyance she'd thought she'd seen in his eyes was in his voice as well.

What the hell was wrong with him?

Without another word she positioned the pieces of wood and motioned for Blake to hold them in place. She then made a coil of about twenty loops of gauze, so she wouldn't have to repeatedly lift his leg, then slid Jed's foot carefully through the center of the bundle, easing it past his knee until it was draped around the makeshift splint. Separating the loops, she positioned them, making sure the moist pieces of gauze she'd placed a few minutes ago were still covering the wound and that the bone hadn't shifted. Satisfied, she tugged the slack out of the bindings, her stomach tightening when the man suddenly groaned and shifted on the ground, his eyes rolling back in his head.

Please don't regain consciousness. Not yet.

The pain would be agonizing if he woke up before she finished. She tied the upper portion of the bandage so it wouldn't unravel. She repeated the process on the bottom half of his leg, working as fast as she could. He didn't cry out again, however, and she breathed a sigh of relief when she fastened the last knot.

"Can you give him some morphine?" A sheen of moisture had appeared on Blake's upper lip, despite the cold. He wasn't as unaffected as he seemed.

"Not until we get to the plane. I don't want to risk it without having an IV hooked up."

The sound of wheels crunching on loose gravel signaled the vehicle's arrival. She eyed a nearby piece of plywood. "I want to use that as a back brace. I'll need three men to stabilize his neck and back and to turn him while I slide that wood underneath him. Volunteers?"

Mark immediately moved to her left side, two others kneeling next to him. "Tell us what to do."

Beside her, Blake stiffened before climbing to his feet and stripping off his gloves. "I'll get the wood."

"Thanks."

On her signal, they rolled Jed onto his side, while she and Blake maneuvered the plywood into place. "Okay, lay him back, gently."

Blake and the men carried the injured man to the truck and slid him inside. Freezing rain pelted her once again as she ducked from beneath the plastic tarp and climbed into the back of the vehicle. She had to bend over at an awkward angle to keep from hitting the roof of the pick-up shell. Away from the shelter of the fallen shipping crate, the wind caught the truck, jostling it back and forth.

Another long and terrible flight to look forward to. Great.

Leaning down to peer inside the truck, Mark reached in and squeezed her hand for a long moment, before releasing it to pull a card out of his wallet. He handed it to her. "If you ever need a charter pilot, I'm available."

Wow, this place was just brimming with flyboys. What was it with this island?

"Thanks." Good to know, if Blake kept his word and abandoned her.

Mark hesitated, and a thread of irritation ran through her. They needed to get a move on. Before she could voice the words, he said, "Can you call and let me know how Jed's doing once you get to Anchorage?"

"Sure thing." She glanced around for Blake, who stood off to the right, arms folded across his chest, water streaming down his face. When Mark took a step back and nodded at him, he didn't move a muscle. He could have been made out of stone. Motioning him over, she asked, "Can you drive ahead and get the back of the plane set up for us?"

One brow went up as he glanced at the card in her hand.

She had no idea what she'd done, but this was ridiculous. Shoving Mark's card into the pocket of her jacket, she stared right back at him. If he had something to say to her, he could do it right now.

Instead, he turned and stalked toward his car, shoulders stiff, moving through the punishing rain and wind as if it were a spring shower. She watched him until he was out of sight. "Okay, Mark. Tell Jed's brother to head for the airport."

The ride there was almost as rough as the flight to Dutch Harbor had been. She braced her back against the side of the truck to maintain her balance. She also had to anchor her patient the best she could to keep his pallet from scooting from one side of the truck bed to the other—no easy feat, since the man probably weighed close to two hundred twenty pounds—most of which was solidly packed muscle.

She really needed to work out more.

The vehicle slowed to a stop, and before she had time to wonder whether they'd just stopped at a red light or reached their destination, the glass at the back of the topper opened, and Blake peered in. "Everyone okay?"

He'd made an ass of himself back at the dockyard, but he'd seen that look in Mark's eye often enough to know what it meant. His buddy had seen something he liked—Molly—and he was about to take aim with his thousand-watt charm. He'd seen that stuff work on one too many women.

He and Mark had been friends since elementary school. They'd both grown up in Unalaska—had both graduated from high school together. And both had served in the military as pilots before Blake had turned to civilian pursuits. While he knew Mark had endured some hard knocks since leaving the service, that was no excuse for going through women like squares of cheese on a gourmet sampler tray.

Although, to be fair, it had never really bothered Blake. Before now.

Molly slid from the back of the truck, again pulling her hood over her head to protect herself from the rain. The soft, furry edge framed her face and brought her deep green eyes into sharp focus. "I should have asked Mark to come and help us load our patient. He's heavy. Even for you two guys." Jed's brother had joined them at the back of the truck.

Mark? Not a chance. Not even if Blake had to drag the patient, travois-style, across the tarmac all by himself. *Where had that come from?* If he were smart, he'd tell Molly to call the number on that business card and let his buddy ferry her back and forth across the ocean.

Why was he even hesitating when it was the perfect solution for everyone? Molly would get the handholding she evidently needed during flights, and he could put the memories of his ruined marriage out of his mind. The only time they'd ever have to deal with each other would be during medevacs, like this one. "I've got a wheeled stretcher on the plane. We'll use that."

Between the three of them they got the man into the back of the plane without letting him get soaked in the process. He still hadn't regained consciousness, though. Molly turned to the patient's brother. "I'd ask you to come along, but there's nothing you can do. Maybe you can make sure Jed's kids are taken care of. I'll call as soon as I know something." She fished a card out of her pocket—Mark's—and turned it over. "If you'll give me a number where I can reach you—"

"Sure, sure. It's..." He scrubbed his palm across his

jaw as if struggling to remember what it was, then he appeared to get a grip, reciting the digits.

Molly scribbled it down. "Got it." She glanced up. "I promise I'll call as soon as we arrive."

"Thanks. I appreciate everything you've done, Doc."

"My pleasure. Take care."

Blake waved goodbye and climbed into the cargo area beside her, closing the door.

"What are you doing?"

"I thought you could use an extra pair of hands." The fact that the man still hadn't woken up worried him, especially with the weather conditions the way they were. According to the weather channel, it was going to stay this way until late this afternoon. He figured he could at least see if he could take some of the load off Molly's shoulders. Although why she'd wanted to come to the plane rather than ride out the weather at one of the clinics was beyond him.

Her brows came together as she worked to set up an IV. "Don't you have a plane to fly?"

The question hit him right between the eyes, and he suddenly realized why she'd chosen to head for the plane.

She thought he was going to take off in this weather? He'd have thought she, of all people, would be happy sitting on the ground for the next couple of hours. If she thought their trip to Dutch Harbor had been bad… "Have you looked at the sky recently?"

"Of course I have. But we need to get him to a hospital remember? The sooner the better." She'd repeated Mark's earlier words almost verbatim. Reaching out for the card she'd tossed onto a nearby table, she glanced down at it. As subtle a threat as he'd ever seen: if he wouldn't take her, she knew someone who would.

Anger churned through him. So she was suddenly the

Fearless Flyer? No way. He was not about to be bullied into anything. Not by her. Not by Mark. Especially not into something that could get them all killed.

"I hate to disappoint you, Doctor. But you might want to take advantage of my help while you can. Because until this weather clears, we aren't going anywhere." He paused, then decided to drive his meaning home. "*No one* is."

CHAPTER FIVE

BLAKE was right.

The skies had magically cleared later that morning, allowing them to finally get off the ground. And the return flight had been a whole lot better sitting in the back with her patient, rather than up front where she could see how short that runway actually was as they careened toward the end.

She checked her watch. They'd been in the air for almost two hours. Her patient had come to soon after they'd got airborne, for which she was relieved. Not only did it keep her from dwelling on where she was—no easy feat—but she could assess his condition a little better as well. He was stable, the pulses in his injured leg strong and steady. No compartmental syndrome setting in. And she'd finally been able to give him a little pain medication to make him more comfortable.

"My kids?" He'd already asked that question a couple of times, making her heart ache.

"Mark promised to check with your sister, but I'll ask Blake if he's been able to speak with anyone. I'm sure they're fine."

Giving his shoulder a quick squeeze, she made her way to the front of the plane, holding on to one of the seats as she went. She'd ask him to check with the hospital while she was at it and make sure the orthopedic surgeon was standing by. At least it had been a relatively smooth flight so far, although by facing forward she could now see nothing but the air in front of them. Her stomach kicked up a protest as it had the two previous times she'd gone forward to ask Blake something.

She stood behind him and leaned close so he could hear her. "Hey. Everything okay?"

"Fine." Tension radiated off him as he threw a quick glance over his shoulder then faced forward again. "Jed hanging in there?"

"Yes, but he's asking about his kids again. Any luck raising his brother or Mark?" Molly tried to ignore the clean masculine scent coming off him. Tried to ignore the urge to scrape her cheek along the tiny grains of stubble that lined his firm jaw.

Knock it off, Moll.

"I reached his brother a few minutes ago. The kids will stay with him for the night. His sister's there as well. They're fine."

"Oh, good. I'll tell him." She turned to go back to her patient, but Blake stopped her.

"Molly?"

"Yes."

He hesitated. "You did a hell of a job back at the dockyard."

She blinked. "Uh, thanks. Working beats sitting up here worrying about how high we are."

"Feeling any better this time around?" The words were light enough, but there was an edge to them that put her on alert. Was he still mad?

"Anything's better than that storm we came through yesterday." If she wanted to apologize, now was the time to do it. "Sorry about demanding we take off. You were obviously right. I was just worried about Jed reaching the hospital quickly."

"It's okay." He glanced back again and his shoulders relaxed a bit. "Just for the record, I would have taken off if I was sure I'd make it. Evel Knievel and all."

She shivered. That's right. He'd have probably relished the challenge if she and Jed hadn't been on board.

And what happened to those he left behind, if it all went bad?

She shook off the morbid thought. "Well, anyway, he's doing fine."

When she turned around to head back, a hand on her wrist stopped her. His skin was warm against hers. "Can you sit for a minute?"

"I—I guess so. Just for a minute."

What was this all about?

Perching on the seat, she turned her body to face him. He scrubbed his knuckles along his jaw line in the exact spot she'd imagined sliding her cheek. A wave of heat swept over her. Focusing on the steady chill in the cockpit had no effect whatsoever.

She waited for him to say something, but when he remained silent, she spoke up. "Did you want to talk to me?"

He nodded. "About Mark. Well, he… What I mean is that…" His voice trailed away as the hand worrying the edge of his face moved to the back of his neck, the palm kneading the muscles.

"What about him?" Her heart dropped. "Is there something wrong with Jed's children after all?"

"No, no. Nothing like that." Again he stopped. "Mark is kind of a…"

What on earth was he trying to say?

"Kind of a what?"

"A ladies' man. He gets around."

She frowned. "And I need to know this because…?"

"Well, because…" one shoulder gave a quick shrug "…I think he might be interested in asking you out. Just wanted you to know he doesn't tend to stick around for the long haul."

She didn't know if she should be pleased or angry that Blake had taken it on himself to warn her off someone she barely knew. "And what gave you the idea he might ask me out?"

"He asked if I thought you'd say yes."

"I see." Except she didn't. Not at all. "And what did you tell him?"

Another shrug. "That he'd have to ask you himself."

She let that roll around her head for a few seconds. "Do you think he will?"

Molly hadn't even decided to take the job yet. The last thing she needed to be thinking about was getting involved with someone on the islands. Although, if Mark liked to keep things light with no commitments, getting too involved shouldn't be an issue. In fact, that kind of arrangement might even be ideal for someone like her. She'd never have to worry about disappointing him—he'd never start demanding more and more of her. And if Gary heard she was going out with someone else… Her brain grabbed onto that thought.

"He might. Which is why I decided to say something. We're friends and all, but I'd hate you to get the wrong idea about him."

The wrong idea. As if she couldn't figure things out on her own. Or as if she received so few offers from men that she'd be in danger of dragging him to the nearest jewelry store to shop for rings. After Gary? Not likely!

"Well, thanks for your concern, but I think I can take care of myself." She stood. "Speaking of which, I have someone else I should be caring for right now, so if you'll excuse me…"

"Sure."

He didn't even give her a sideways look as she headed toward the back.

Huh! Poor little Molly can't tell the difference between casual interest and a proposal of marriage. So we'll just explain how these things work.

Ooooh!

If he really *were* Evel Knievel, she wouldn't mind dumping him over the side of Snake River Canyon right now and daring him to make it to the other side. The nerve of the man!

Somewhere inside her, a little voice whispered that it wasn't Mark she should be worried about but—

Shut up.

Wiping his words from her mind, she knelt by her patient and dabbed a few beads of sweat from his brow with a dry cloth. The chill in the plane was numbing, yet Jed was dotted with perspiration. She'd given him a low dose of pain meds, but she didn't dare let him have any more. Not until they reached the hospital. Although his pupils still seemed fine, that crack on the head worried her a bit. He had quite a lump on the back of his skull. She'd probably order an MRI just to be safe.

His eyes opened. "Kids?"

"They're fine. They will be staying with your brother tonight. Mark's going to fly them all to Anchorage tomorrow, if you're still in the hospital."

Which he would be.

He sucked down a deep breath. "Good." He touched her arm. "Thanks."

Whereas the warmth of Blake's fingers had raised alarming little frissons of awareness along her skin, Jed's touch did absolutely nothing. All she felt was the invasive cold of the plane.

He's your patient. *You're not supposed to be attracted to him!*

She got up and plopped into a nearby seat, settling in for the rest of the flight.

One thing was certain, however. Flying had now become the least of her worries.

He wasn't looking for her.

Right. That's why he'd offered to give Mark, along with Jed's two kids, a lift from the airport this morning. Jed had been whisked away almost as soon as they'd arrived at the airport yesterday afternoon. Since the hospital had a length of runway almost butting up to one of its entrances, Molly, still holding the IV bag, had accompanied the stretcher from the plane to the double doors. A quick "Thanks" was all he'd got before they'd disappeared into the hospital.

What did you expect? You were her ride. Nothing else.

But that didn't stop his eyes from scouring every inch of the emergency room, wondering if she was working today.

Mark had charge of Jed's daughters so, when the girls were ushered in to see their father, Mark went with them. Where, even now, Molly was probably leaning against a nearby wall, tucking strands of her short dark hair behind her ears as she talked to him. Smiled at him.

Accepted his offer of dinner and a movie.

As she had every right to do.

From what he'd heard, the surgery on Jed's leg had been a success. He'd remain on heavy doses of IV antibiotics for the next day or so to make sure no infection took hold.

And Blake, smart guy that he was, had raised his hand

and offered to take them all back to Dutch Harbor as soon as Jed was released from care, which meant he'd have to stick around Anchorage—his least favorite place—for a day or so, if he didn't get any other emergency calls. Yay, him.

He huffed out a breath. Well, he might as well pick up some supplies while he was here. He'd call Sammi and see if the clinic needed anything.

He also needed to get a hold of Molly as he still had her suitcase in his car. Mark had gone to the hotel room and packed all her stuff—Blake's gut tightened at that thought—since neither he nor Molly had given a thought to her belongings in their mad dash to the dockyard. The knot of resentment grew even more, which was ridiculous. His friend had done nothing wrong.

Yeah, but I saw her first.

One hand tightened into a fist. What the hell was he, a little kid?

Funny how all that worry about flying with Molly— about how she'd react to the island once she saw it—hadn't stomped out the instant attraction he'd felt for her. In fact, her insistence on going up in that storm had been damned sexy. He'd seen a little bit of himself in her in that moment.

And now Mark was probably back there with her.

He dragged a hand through his hair and swore under his breath. He didn't even know if Molly was at the hospital.

Enough was enough.

Stepping outside, he made his way to the concrete "Emergency Room" sign a few yards away and leaned his elbows on it while he punched in a number on his cellphone.

"Hello?"

"Hey, Tony, Blake here." His boss ever since Wayne had died, Tony was as easygoing as they came.

"You back already? I thought you flew that new doctor to the islands."

"Yep, an emergency came up, and we had to come back in."

"What did she think?"

"I have no idea." He hesitated. If he was going to do this, he'd better do it now. Otherwise he was going to chicken out like a dumbass. He knew they'd have to fly together during medevacs, but she'd be in the back while he rode up front. Better to keep it to that as much as possible. "She's supposed to head back there in about two weeks. Any chance you can find another pilot to take her? How about Ronny?"

Silence reigned for half a minute. "Ronny? What gives? You asked for this gig in the first place. Is she that hard to work with?"

"No, it's just..." He forced the words out. "I think she'd do better with another pilot for the return trip. That's all."

Tony paused again. "You sure?"

"Yep, I am." Saying the words out loud might just trick his brain into believing them.

"Okay. I'll let you know what Ronny says. If he says no, you're stuck picking her up."

He wouldn't. Ronny never turned down the chance to fly. "Thanks. I owe you."

He clicked the phone shut, wishing he could walk away right now and never look back. But he had Mark and the kids to shuttle to a hotel, and then he'd have to fly everyone back to Unalaska while Mark's plane was being serviced here in Anchorage.

He'd be flying everyone except Molly.

And that's the way it was going to stay.

Before he could move away from the sign, she appeared

out of nowhere. "Hey, there. I thought I saw you a few minutes ago. I was afraid I'd missed you."

"I'm giving Jed's kids and Mark a ride back to the hotel." He straightened, leaning his hip against the sign as he faced her. "How's Jed doing, by the way?"

"He's good. The surgeon had to put a pin in his femur. He'll be out of commission for a couple of months, but he should make a complete recovery." She smiled up at him. "Good thing you were part of his medical team, because these HIPPA laws mean I have to…" She made a zipping motion across her mouth that made him smile.

Something in his chest gave a weird *ka-thunk* at her including him as part of the team, no matter what the reason. Maybe he should let her know he was no longer a part of it.

As soon as he figured out how.

"I appreciate the update, in any event. I bet his girls were glad to see him."

She laughed. "They're quite…active. But you should have seen Jed's face light up when they appeared in his doorway and tried to swarm his bed. It was really nice of Mark to take on flying them here, since Jed's brother had to work. Not many men would be up to the task."

The *ka-thunk* became a rock that dropped right to the pit of his stomach. "Yeah, he's a real…" *Tool. Nope. Wrong word. Try again.* "He's good with kids."

He cleared his throat, wanting to change the subject. "I meant to let you know that I've got your suitcase in my car. From the hotel?"

"Ah, yes. Thanks." Her fingers came up and flicked her hair behind her left ear—much as he'd imagined her doing earlier—revealing a delicate, perfect ear, which sported a simple pink bauble at the lobe.

The effect it had on him was exactly as he'd feared. He hardened instantly. Forcing himself to look away into the parking lot, he tried to take charge of his body. In the process, he spied a man and a very pregnant woman making their way toward the entrance. They stopped halfway to the door, and she pulled in a deep breath, blowing it out slowly, her cheeks puffing as she did. She was in labor—her husband supporting her as she breathed.

Lucky man. He'd have given anything to be the guy in that picture. To have the happy marriage his parents still shared. But he didn't, and the possibility of that changing any time soon was slim to none.

His jaw hardened. "I'm just out in the lot. Where are you parked? Maybe we could transfer the case now."

"Sounds good. I'm just getting off duty. How about if I bring my car around, and I'll meet you out there?"

"I'll be standing about halfway down that third row."

"Great."

Blake tried not to notice the slight swing of her hips as she walked away with easy grace, but it was impossible. She was a beautiful woman. Confident. Kind.

And about to exit his life forever.

He headed toward his rental car, reaching in his pocket for the key. By the time he got her bag out of the car, she'd pulled up beside him. Climbing out of her car, she pushed a button on her keyring, unlocking the trunk of the compact. "I'll just throw it in the back. How did you manage to...?"

"Mark cleared out the room."

"Ah, that makes sense. Remind me to thank him."

He wouldn't be around to remind her of anything. If ever he was going to tell her about her new pilot, now was the time. He lifted the bag and put it into her trunk, rehearsing the sentence in his head. "Listen, about your next flight—"

"Hey, you two! I wondered where you went." Mark came up beside Molly, a little girl's hand in each of his own. He grinned at Blake, causing every muscle in his body to tighten. He recognized his friend's Cheshire-cat smile.

Mark was on the prowl, and he evidently wasn't above using Jed's two daughters to bait his trap.

"Did you get a chance to meet Jed's kids, Molly?"

"I did." She knelt down. "Hi, girls. Did you have a good visit with Daddy?"

"Yeah!" the one on the right said. "And Uncle Mark promised us ice cream on the way to the hotel."

"Lucky you." Molly kissed each of them on the cheek.

"Care to join us?" Mark's invitation grated across his last nerve, causing his hands to tighten.

"I wish I could, but my mother's expecting me." She sighed. "And I need to start packing."

"I guess we'll be seeing a lot more of you once you move to the island."

"I guess you will."

Well, he wasn't wasting much time! Nothing like having to stand there and watch the scene unfold in slow motion.

Molly gave the two girls another quick squeeze. "I'll see you both tomorrow at the hospital?"

Mark's smile widened. "I'll be there as well."

Climbing to her feet, she smiled back at him. There was silence for a couple of seconds, but before Blake could put a boot to the seat of Mark's jeans, his friend seemed to snap out of it.

"Well, it's getting late, and I need to get the girls to the hotel." He glanced at Blake. "You ready, old man?"

Since Blake was Mark's transportation, he didn't have much choice but to play along. So much for explaining to Molly about the change in plans.

Then again, it got him off the hook. She'd find out soon enough when she arrived at the airport and found another pilot waiting for her. It might be the coward's way out. But at this point that's exactly what he was.

A coward.

CHAPTER SIX

"WHY are you still in Unalaska? You're due back in Anchorage ASAP. Command performance—compliments of the top brass."

What the hell?

Blake sat up in bed, gripping his phone with one hand while fumbling to turn his clock to face him with the other.

Seven o'clock on Sunday morning—it was his first day off in ages, for crying out loud. "Is there an emergency?"

"You might say that. Seems your doctor friend is raising quite a stink about the pilot switch trick you played on her. She's having none of it. It's either you or she's out the door as far as the Unalaska job goes. And the hospital isn't any too happy about the prospect of those government dollars landing somewhere else, if she backs out."

"Slow down there, Tony. I have no idea what you're talking about."

"You're being tapped as Molly McKinna's official escort tomorrow morning. She's moving out to the island, right on schedule. I'm told that refusing is not an option at this point."

"You've got to be kidding me!" Anger shot up his spine as the last remnants of sleep deserted him. "What about Ronny?"

"Ronny's a tourist pilot. You and the doc will be working together on medevacs, so the bigwigs think you need to be more of a team player."

"Since when have they ever worried about that?"

His boss chuckled. "Since the doc got wind of the change in plans."

"What?"

"Someone told her you'd rather not take her, and she evidently took it personally." A sigh came over the line. "Maybe she's right, Blake. I don't know what happened between you two, but you're going to have to work together, so you might as well get used to it."

Really? He'd just got used to the idea of seeing her as little as possible. His skyrocketing heart rate told him he'd been right to draw a firm line in the sand and stay on the professional side of it. Hell, if he believed that being with someone like her wouldn't pop all the rivets he'd used to patch up his sorry life he'd have flown her without a qualm. Seven days a week, if that was what it took. But one last shred of sanity had stepped in and demanded to be heard. Besides, if Mark was interested...

Well, his friend was everything he wasn't.

Hell!

He kicked his way out from under the covers, half stumbling over them as he got out of bed. Hopping on one foot to regain his balance, he cursed under his breath and headed for the bathroom. What a way to start the day. "Okay, I'll meet her at the airport in the morning."

"Don't screw this up, Blake. That clinic needs her. You piss her off, and your job could be on the line."

"Yeah, well good luck finding someone to take my place."

The last thing Blake wanted was to get to the airport and hear about some date she and Mark had gone out on—without kids this time. Or fly through another storm with her. *Or* hear she'd decided she didn't like island life after all.

He hardly knew Molly, so why was he letting her get to him?

Because she was Wayne McKinna's daughter?

Maybe. But seeing her standing in the window of that hotel room, hair all mussed from sleep, a picture had formed in his head. Sleepy eyes blinking up at him. A whispered plea to come back to bed. Her soft, warm body welcoming his home.

The mental image had lit a fire within his chest that still burned.

Impossible. He'd barely got his life back on track. Which meant he had to face the possibility that Mark—and not him—might be the one who lived out that fantasy. A scenario he didn't want to watch unfold. Switching pilots was the best option. For everyone.

He gritted his teeth.

The silence on the other end of the phone line made him realize Tony had said something and was waiting for a reply. "I didn't catch that."

"I said don't let me down on this one."

"Right." He shook his head to clear it. "I'm on my way."

Signing off, he made short work of showering and shaving, then pulled on a pair of khaki slacks and a brown polo shirt. He slung his leather jacket over his shoulder with one hand and used the other to scoop up his keys, making a fist that pressed the sharp metal edges into his palm.

He and the doc needed to get a few things straight.

Molly shifted from foot to foot, the thin stream of heat drifting from the overhead vents in the hangar doing little to warm the icy apprehension in her chest. She'd heard about the uproar she'd caused. But she'd had no idea a few stray words to Doug would come back to bite her.

She wouldn't have said anything if she hadn't been so hurt that Blake didn't want her back on his plane. He'd actually *asked* to be replaced. Had she been *that* terrible during the flight?

Yes.

She'd been nursing her bruised ego when Doug had come up behind her at the hospital and asked if she was looking forward to the flight. The hurt and anger had somehow poured out before she'd had a chance to think about what she was saying. Her friend had been furious on her behalf. But she'd had no idea he'd done anything crazy.

Then again, this was Doug Porter. Crazy was his middle name.

Oh, no, Blake had to be furious.

He had every right to be. Despite the chill lingering deep in her bones, her back-and-forth pacing—along with a bad case of the jitters—had caused a fine sheen of sweat to break out over her body. Shrugging out of her down jacket but leaving on the sweater beneath it, she reached down to unzip her overnight bag, stuffing the garment inside.

Blake had offered to set her up with someone else, but the thought of yet another pilot watching her go into a panic as they took off made her cringe. And what if they ran into another storm? She distinctly remembered a high-pitched keening noise ricocheting around the interior of the cabin.

Yes. Hadn't *that* been lovely?

No wonder he wanted to be rid of her. But it still hurt. And he probably hated her even more now that he was once again stuck with babysitter duty. Why, oh, why hadn't Doug kept his big mouth shut?

Except, deep inside, she had to admit she was glad

Blake was taking her and not another pilot. She trusted him. He might have daredevil blood flowing through his veins, but he'd proved there was a limit to the number of risks he was willing to take. He'd refused to take off during the storm that had caused Jed's injury, despite her urging to the contrary—*what had she been thinking?*—which meant he didn't take his job lightly. He wasn't just in it for the thrills, despite his cocky words to the contrary. He wanted to come back from each flight alive.

That made him very attractive in her eyes.

Anyone else was just a big question mark. She knew herself well enough to realize the less she left to chance, the better equipped she'd be to handle future flights and to kick her fear in the teeth and send it skidding down the road.

The door across the room opened and Blake strode in. Without a hint of hesitation he headed straight for her. The only thing in his hand was a jacket, which was slung over his shoulder. And a big frown between his brows.

Uh-oh.

Her elbows pressed close to her body—hands clasped in front—as she tried to prepare herself for the inevitable explosion.

He stopped in front of her. Every inch of his six-foot-three frame vibrated with anger. "Why?"

The word was deadly soft.

His dark shirt hugged his muscular frame, the color bringing out chocolate highlights in his hair. It might have been a warm and comforting combination—if not for his eyes. They held a chill that made her want to take a step backward. She resisted the temptation.

"I know you're upset, but believe me—"

"Why me?" he repeated.

"It was a misunderstanding."

"Oh, I think I understood everything quite well. I was told to get my ass back to Anchorage, and here I am."

"I swear it wasn't me who made that call. It was a friend of mine. But…" How could she explain this without sounding like some kind of loon? "I was hoping you'd reconsider and agree to fly me."

"Why?"

They were back to his initial question. One she wasn't sure she had the answer to. "Because I know you, maybe?"

His brows went up.

"Okay, so I don't *know* you, know you. But I've been on your plane. I've seen you in action. The thought of having a different pilot so soon in the game…" She paused. "I need time to adjust to being in the air before tossing another variable into the mix."

"Another variable?"

"Like a new pilot." She took a deep breath of courage and forced herself to continue. "Someone who might spread stuff around the clinic. I have to be able to get on that plane every time we medevac someone off the island. I need patients to trust that I'll do my very best to care for them while we're in the air. And I will. I *can* set my fear aside, I know I can. Please. Just give my nerves a chance to settle down."

His eyes softened a fraction. "How do you know I won't say anything to anyone?"

"You were at the hospital for several hours the other night when we brought Jed in. After you left, I waited for the whispering or wisecracks to start up. They never did. Even your friend Mark didn't seem to know what happened during that storm. And if you didn't tell him…"

He stiffened. "I didn't talk about the flight, if that's what you mean. I figure it's your business, unless you put someone at risk." He paused. "If that happens, I won't hesitate."

"I wouldn't expect anything less." She unclasped her hands and touched his arm for a second, hoping against hope he'd agree to be her pilot. "So what do you say? Will you take me to Dutch Harbor? Maybe I can earn my first set of wings this time."

She shivered, the chill in the hangar hitting her all at once. Blake's leather jacket somehow wound up draped over her shoulders. The warmth and scent of his body embraced her in a rush. She swallowed, glancing up at him in question.

"You looked cold." A few more slivers of ice melted from his eyes. "And I've got to get my bag out of the car and turn in a flight plan."

She grabbed the edges of his jacket and burrowed deeper into it, trying to make it appear nonchalant.

He had his bag in the car. Which meant he was going to take her!

Doing a happy dance right in front of him would probably not endear her to him. Instead she stood very still. "Thank you."

"You might want to wait until we get there to say that." He stared at the far side of the hangar before glancing back at her. "And in case you're worried about someone at the clinic finding out, don't be. You'll find I'm good at keeping secrets."

Molly breathed a sigh of relief once her feet were back on solid ground. The flight to the Aleutians had been less traumatic this time. At least she hadn't cried or screamed. That had to count for something. She'd still gripped her seat and closed her eyes during takeoff, and her heart had threatened to claw its way out of her chest during landing, but there'd been no storms. No wind. No big "construction zones." Just clear skies.

And Blake.

Two weeks without seeing him should have dampened the attraction. And if that hadn't worked, the reality of passing Gary in the hospital parking lot two days before she was supposed to leave should have snapped her back to her senses. His glower had told her in no uncertain terms that going back to a professional relationship—ever— would be impossible. Getting involved with a medevac pilot would be a very, very bad move on her part. Gary's I'll-get-even attitude had played a big part in her decision to move to the Aleutians. How much worse would it have been if he'd been a pilot—one she had to work with on a regular basis?

Molly shuddered. She really didn't want to go through that again.

Standing on the tarmac beside Blake, she looked out over the water in the distance, trying to compose herself. "Sammi got a line on a rental place for me. She said the outside could use a little work—it doubled as a private business, evidently—but it's nice enough inside and the landlord has promised to paint over the sign out front."

He put his arms behind his head and stretched. A couple of ligaments popped along his back in the process, bringing a smile to her face despite her best efforts. "A sign? Did she tell you where the place is?"

"Nope, she's supposed to go over with me at lunchtime." She took a deep breath. The mixture of chilly air and briny tang burned along her sinuses, but it wasn't unpleasant. Far from it. She wrapped her arms around her waist, as a sense of freedom swept over her.

"Did you bring a coat?"

"I stuffed it in my overnight case while I was waiting at the airport. I didn't have a chance to pull it out before you gave me yours."

"You might need it later. It's pretty mild for Dutch Harbor this time of year. Autumn can be brutal, as you saw on our last trip."

"I remember." His remark brought Mark and the accident at the dockyard to mind. "Did Jed and the girls make it home?"

"I flew them back last week."

"Is he doing okay?"

"I went by on Friday, he seems to be hanging in there. I was planning to check on him again today."

"Do you mind if I go with you? It'll give me a chance to see how his leg is doing. I'm not due to start at the clinic until tomorrow."

"Not a problem."

There'd been a quick hesitation before he'd answered that made her blink. "Are you sure?"

"Absolutely." No pause this time.

"Thanks. How about Mark? Did he get back as well?"

Blake's eyes shifted to her face. "He did."

His voice held some kind of weird tension, but she forced herself to ignore it. Instead, she let the calmness of the ocean act as a soothing balm. After the frenetic couple of weeks she'd spent tying up loose ends in her personal life and at the hospital, she needed some peace and quiet. Scratch that. She'd gotten plenty of quiet at her mother's house as she'd packed her things and got them ready for the movers, but it had been the kind of silence you dreaded.

She didn't have to worry about that any more. "It'll feel good to get settled in. Hopefully we won't have any medevacs for the next couple of days." A sudden thought hit her when she remembered his irritation at the airport this morning and the strange way he was acting now. "Did I pull you away from something? From someone? I never thought to ask."

Her stomach squirmed. She knew from the grapevine he wasn't dating anyone at the hospital, but Anchorage was a big city. And there was always Unalaska. The thought of him kissing someone goodbye cast a pall over her day.

"Nope. Just my bed."

Her heart took a little swan dive, giving her a happy wave as it did.

Get a hold of yourself, Molly. That doesn't mean he's unattached. For all you know, there might have been someone lying in that bed.

"Sorry about that," she said.

Of course, maybe he really was single.

Forget it. Hadn't she just finished ticking off all the reasons why dating a coworker would not be a smart idea?

Besides, her mother would have a stroke if she got involved with a pilot. She was already upset that Molly's job involved flying of any sort. *Isn't it enough that I've already lost one person to that profession?*

Although if her mother could see the way Blake's tight hindquarters filled out those khakis...

Ack! Steam filtered into her face. She had *not* just noticed his butt.

Her eyes snuck another quick peek. Okay, so maybe she'd glanced a time or two. But that was what girls did. They looked at men's behinds.

Enough was enough. Clearing her throat, she said, "Mind if we swing by the clinic on the way to Jed's? I want to let Sammi know we made it and double-check with her about the rental place. I'm hoping the landlord is willing to do a twelve-month lease with an option to increase it, if I stay."

Blake shoved his hands into his pockets. "If you stay. When will you know?"

"I signed a one-year contract with the clinic, so I need

to honor that. If I decide it's not for me, I'm hoping Alaska Regional will send another doctor in my place."

Yeah. She could always dream. What doctor would want to come to a public clinic for what the government wanted to pay? Her advantage was she didn't have a family to support. Just herself.

"Right." He turned away from the water. "You ready to head out?"

"Whenever you are."

The trip to the clinic took just a minute or two, which was a good thing because Blake didn't seem all that inclined to talk. Maybe he was tired after his flight.

Or maybe he was thinking about how long a year would be if she continued to be chicken about flying.

Going through the doors, she caught Sammi just as she was picking up a chart from the receptionist.

The other woman smiled. "Good, you made it." She glanced at the folder in her hand. "Listen, I know I said I'd run you over to the property today, but I have a lunch appointment. One of my prenatal patients, Mindy Starling, is experiencing some Braxton-Hicks contractions, and I want to run over to make sure nothing else is going on."

"Don't worry about—"

Sammi interrupted her with a wave of her hand, glancing at Blake. "Do you mind showing her where it is? I have the keys and the address. The landlord needs a decision by tomorrow morning. He evidently has someone else who's interested if Molly doesn't want it. But don't worry—he's been threatened with bodily harm if he lets the place go before she sees it."

"I need to see what's on the schedule for today."

Sammi grinned. "I already called the station. They can do without you for the rest of the day."

"Thanks. I appreciate that." Blake's tone was even, but he sounded anything but appreciative.

"If you give me the address, maybe I can find it on my own." There was no way she was going to drag him over there against his will.

"Blake doesn't mind. Do you, Blake?"

He gave her a tight smile. "Not at all. We can check on Jed on the way over."

"Great!" Sammi passed an envelope across the countertop. "Call me and let me know what you think."

Well, wasn't this great? Not only had Blake been forced to fly her to Dutch Harbor today, he'd just been volunteered to drag her around half the island. The man had to be thrilled with his lot in life. She was.

Actually, she was. This was her chance to strike out on her own and make her own decisions.

Now, if she could just convince everyone around her to get with the program, she'd be in business.

Jed's place was a wreck.

And from Molly's quick intake of breath, he wasn't the only one who thought so.

Jed, propped on a sofa, his entire leg encased in a cast—no walking boot for a while, according to the orthopedic surgeon—waved them in. "The girls will be sorry they missed you. They only have half a day of school today, so they get out at one. Mark's bringing them home."

Blake glanced at his watch, his muscles relaxing when he noted the time. Eleven-thirty. They'd be gone well before one o'clock.

Molly used her toe to nudge aside a stack of newspapers that had burrowed into the ratty shag carpeting beside the couch before she reached for Jed's wrist and checked her watch. "Do you have someone helping out around here?"

"My sister's bringing in meals, but she's got her own place to take care of." He glanced around, a frown settling between his brows. "And my brother's having to take on extra work over at the dockyard, since I'm out of commission for a while."

Blake could see the wheels spinning in Molly's head as she measured the man's pulse. She was going to spruce up the house. And since he was slated to take her over to the rental property after they left here, he was stuck.

Ah, hell. The last thing Blake wanted to do was stick around and watch his buddy put the moves on Molly. Mark had already mentioned asking her out on more than one occasion, giving Blake a good-natured poke in the ribs as he'd said it. The light-hearted rivalry they'd engaged in as young bachelors no longer seemed all that funny. "Didn't Sammi say someone else was interested in that rental?"

She made a little sound that could be taken as either a yes or a no—depending on one's anxiety level—and began straightening up the end table. He evidently hadn't succeeded in turning this particular plane around.

"I don't have to give them an answer until tomorrow. We have plenty of time," she said.

Plenty of time.

That was exactly what he was afraid of.

CHAPTER SEVEN

SHE'D never seen a man move so fast. Ever.

Even the vacuum cleaner seemed to be huffing and puffing by the time Blake stopped his jerky movements. In less than an hour he'd swept the floors, dusted, straightened the living room and bedroom, and washed a tower of dirty dishes.

Molly looked at what she'd accomplished: making two twin beds and cleaning two bathrooms. She felt like a slug.

He peered around the corner, catching her emptying the trashcan. "Ready?"

That was the third time he'd asked the same question. "What's the big hurry?"

"Just thought you were anxious to see the rental house. At this rate we won't make it before dark."

Her brows went up. "It's not even one yet. Do you have somewhere you need to be?"

He froze, then said, "No. But you can never tell what the weather here is going to do."

"True." She had experienced that firsthand.

Going back into the living room, she checked on Jed. His eyes opened when she touched his forehead, although it was hard to believe he'd been able to sleep with the way Blake had been slinging things around. "Can I fix you a sandwich? I noticed there's some lunchmeat in the fridge."

Blake, who'd followed her into the room, groaned. *Out loud!* She sent him a quick glare. What was wrong with the man?

Her patient shrugged. "My sister should be around pretty soon. She'll slap something together for me."

"Why don't you call and let her know you've already eaten? She could probably use a little down time. I'll leave something in the fridge for the girls as well."

Jed shifted on the couch. "I don't want to put you out, Doc. Blake's right. You've got other things to do."

"That's all right. Blake's going to help me get those sandwiches ready. In the kitchen." She sent him a pointed glance. "We'll be right back."

When it didn't look like he was going to follow her, she grabbed the hem of his shirt and dragged him with her. Once they turned the corner she released her hold and whipped around to face him. "Like I said, if you have somewhere else you need to be, don't let me stop you. I can call a cab and make it to the house on my own."

"I don't have anywhere to be. You heard Sammi. I have the whole day off." He crossed his arms over his chest.

"Then what's with all the little impatient sounds?"

"I haven't been making…"

Her hands went to her hips, cutting off his denial. Dull color crept up his neck.

Molly opened the fridge and pulled out a pack of lunch-meat and cheese. "You want to make some coffee while I do this?"

He paused, then took a step closer, taking the packages out of her hand and placing them on the counter. "I always seem to make a fool of myself when you're around, don't I?"

"Not *always.*" She softened the words with a smile. "My dad said you have to be careful about using absolutes."

And although she held onto the smile, it faded away inside. Her mother had often used those exact things when throwing accusations at him.

You always... You never... Why don't you ever...?

Her father had often caught her mother by the shoulders when she'd been in one of her moods and looked into her face. *Be careful with those absolutes, Hannah.* More often than not, his words had stopped her mother in her tracks. At least until the year before he'd died. Then he'd grown more distant and his absences longer, according to her mother.

"Come again?" Blake's question brought her back.

"Nothing." A warning tingle hovered behind her eyes. *Tears.*

She missed her father terribly all of a sudden. Turning quickly, she made her way over to the breadbox and peered inside, using those precious seconds to will away the moisture.

A hand covered hers, closing the box before tugging her around to face him. His eyes roamed her face, a frown settling between his brows.

"Hey. I didn't mean to upset you."

She shook her head, unable to answer.

Still wrapped around her wrist, his fingers tightened a fraction. He pulled her against his chest just as the first hot tear overflowed her eyelids before being absorbed into his shirt.

"Shh." His hand slid over her back. "I'm sorry, Molly."

She tried to shake her head and let him know this wasn't about him, but he just pressed her closer. Taking a deep shuddering breath, she tilted her head back and glanced up at him. "It's not you. I—I just…" The words wouldn't come. She swallowed and tried again. "I wish he hadn't…"

Comprehension dawned in his eyes. "Your dad?"

She nodded, grateful she didn't need to say anything more.

His index finger teased a strand of hair off her temple before trailing down her cheek. "I know. I miss him too."

Something welled in her chest. The need for the comfort of a fellow human being, surely. Yes, there was that, but something else hummed along beside it as his warm touch moved to her jaw and stroked gently, leaving prickles of sensation in its wake.

"I'm sorry for blubbering all over you."

"It's okay." His fingers slowed as something in his gaze changed, heated. Her breath caught.

The hand at her jaw moved back, curving around her nape, his thumb settling against the underside of her chin. He used it to apply gentle pressure to tilt her head farther back.

His gaze settled on her mouth. Oh, man, was he going to kiss her?

Unable to stop herself, she licked her suddenly parched lips.

"Molly." The word was whispered. A statement, not a question, but she heard the request nonetheless.

She opened her mouth to answer when a voice came from the other room. "You two okay out there?"

Blake stepped back as if shot in the chest, his hand falling away from her face. He looked toward the doorway, clearing his voice. "We're fine. Just getting things together."

It was going to take a few seconds to do just that: get herself together.

What was she thinking? This was crazy. She needed to stop this before it was too late.

Rather than attempt to speak, she gathered the rest of the sandwich makings in silence, not daring to look at him.

He must have been doing the same thing because she

heard the sound of water hitting the bottom of some kind of receptacle. A minute or two later the scent of fresh coffee drifted by her nose as she sliced the roast-beef sandwiches she'd made into diagonal halves.

Rummaging through the refrigerator, she was glad to find a supply of fresh-looking apples in the fruit bin. His sister's work, probably. She took a couple out and cut them into slices, putting some of them on the plate with Jed's sandwich. She tossed the rest of the slices with a bit of lemon water to keep them from turning brown and put the bowl in the refrigerator for the girls. "How do you like your coffee, Jed?" she called.

"Black and strong."

She glanced in Blake's direction and found him looking back at her. He held up a mug, indicating it was ready.

"Let me see if I can find a tray," she said.

Behind the cabinet doors she found nothing but a motley array of dishes, as well as pots and pans.

"I saw a set of TV trays in the front room. If you'll carry his plate and a napkin, I'll take in the mug and the coffeepot."

Once they got to the living room, Molly handed Jed the plate and set a metal tray on its feet in front of the couch. "Do you want me to turn on the news?"

"Thanks." He pulled himself a bit more upright, and she bunched the pillow behind him to support his back while Blake set down coffee.

"Why don't you two at least join me for coffee?"

The same impatient look he'd worn earlier slid across Blake's face, but at least there were no accompanying vocalizations to go along with it.

He doesn't want to stay. But why? Does he have something against Jed?

Or was it because of what had just happened between the two of them in the kitchen?

Whatever the reason, she didn't want to push her luck—or her self-control—any further.

"Coffee sounds great, but Sammi found a rental house I need to look at. I did leave some sandwiches and apple slices in the refrigerator for the girls."

The furrows between Blake's eyes disappeared instantly. So it wasn't her imagination.

Jed's glance went from her to Blake. "Thanks for everything you've done."

"You just work on getting better." Molly forced herself to smile at him, trying to forget that Blake would be the one taking her to see that rental house. Soft wings fluttered across her tummy. She and Blake alone? Without Jed or anyone else to interrupt them?

Oh, Lord, why did that prospect excite her?

Get a grip, Molly. Who said Blake was looking for anything? *She* certainly wasn't. She might have even misread his intentions a few minutes ago.

Jed, totally unaware of the thoughts whirling around her head, picked up the sandwich and took a bite. His eyes shut for a second and he gave a low grunt of approval as he savored the bite. "Roast beef with horseradish sauce. How did you know?"

She laughed, glad to be pulled back to the present. "Easy. No one has a half-empty jar of it in their fridge—especially when the expiration date is still ages away—unless they really like it." She gave him a wink. "I should know. I use the very same brand."

When Blake's glance jerked from the sandwich and landed on her, she cocked her head. "What's wrong, flyboy? You prefer something with a little less kick?"

"If by *kick* you mean having my tonsils shoved through

the back of my throat, the answer is yes." His eyes narrowed in on her mouth. "Other than that, I like plenty of spice."

His words gave that scene in the kitchen a whole new meaning.

She swallowed, trying to bring some moisture to her suddenly dry throat. "If you've got everything you need, Jed, I'm going to take off. You'll be okay?"

Still chewing, and looking as if he could float away at any minute, he gave an I'll-be-fine wave of his hand.

On the way to the door Molly turned toward him one last time. "Don't forget your meds. And I've left my card on the table. Call my cell if you need me."

At his nod she stepped outside, Blake right on her heels.

He glanced at his watch for the umpteenth time just as a car pulled up in the driveway. Molly thought he swore under his breath when the girls piled out of it, rushing toward her, followed by Mark.

She threw him a funny look before the girls reached her, then she knelt down to embrace each of them. "Hi, you guys! How was school?"

"Great. We got out early because the teachers are making plans."

She laughed. "They are, huh?"

The younger one giggled. "Are you coming to visit Daddy?"

"I already did. I left you some lunch in the refrigerator. Sandwiches and apple slices." She glanced up at Mark. "Would you mind getting the food out for them once you go inside?"

"I'd be happy to." He reached down a hand to help her up. "I'm glad you're back," he murmured.

She smiled, removing her hand from his. "It's definitely good to be back on solid ground."

Mark glanced at Blake, who hadn't said a word. "This guy hasn't been trying any funny stuff, has he?"

"Excuse me?" Shock rolled through her. Had he seen something in her face?

"He likes to pretend he's a stunt pilot from time to time, waving his wings and stuff like that."

"O-oh, no. Nothing like that." Along with a sense of relief came surprise. She couldn't imagine Blake, who'd proved himself to be anything but Evel Knievel-like when in the air, pulling anything crazy. Knowing how her father died, maybe he was being extra-careful when she was on the plane. Although he didn't *always* play it safe, according to Mark.

A shiver went over her.

If anything, that should make her more resolute than ever. Stick to being on a professional footing with Blake, both in the air and on the ground.

As if he'd heard her thoughts, Blake finally spoke up. "Don't you need to get inside? I'm sure Jed's wondering where the girls are."

Mark answered with a lift of his brows before shifting his attention back to Molly. "What are your plans for the next couple of days?"

"I don't know. I'm looking at a house to rent this afternoon, then tomorrow I start at the clinic."

"Sammi doesn't waste any time, does she?" There was a slight edge to Mark's voice that he covered with a smile. "In that case, I need to ask while I have the chance. Are you doing anything for dinner, or has this guy monopolized all your free time?" He hooked a thumb in Blake's direction.

She blinked in surprise. Blake had mentioned he might ask her out.

Opening her mouth to refuse, she stopped short. What

better way to get it through her own thick skull that she wasn't interested in a serious relationship?

Mark is kind of a ladies' man. Blake's words came back to her. If that was true, she didn't have to worry about him taking things too seriously. They could go out and have a good time. No strings attached. And Blake would know she wasn't looking to him to entertain her…in any way. "I don't have plans."

Blake shifted beside her, but she didn't look his way. The girls were starting to get impatient as well, grabbing at Mark's hand and trying to pull him toward the front door of the house.

"Great. How about a quick dinner then I can show you what Unalaska has to offer?"

"Sounds good."

"I'll pick you up, say, at seven?" He allowed himself to be dragged away, calling over his shoulder, "Where are you staying?"

"At the UniSea."

"See you there."

With that, the trio disappeared through the door of the house, leaving her alone with Blake. When she finally dared to look his way, his face was blank, not a hint of emotion crossing it. Disappointment filtered through her.

Guess you didn't need to get your point across after all, Molly. The man isn't interested.

"Do you have the address?"

"Somewhere." Molly fished around in her purse, until she found the envelope with the key. The address was typed across the top. "118 North Wharf Drive."

"I know where the street is. It's not too far from here."

Neither one of them mentioned what had happened at

Jed's house or Mark's dinner invitation. Maybe it was better this way.

Heat crawled over her face. And yet if Blake had kissed her back at Jed's she wouldn't have turned away. How could she have faced him after that?

Thank God none of it had happened. And by accepting Mark's invitation, she'd made sure it never would.

"The street should be right around…"

Molly spotted the sign. "There. Off to your right."

"I see it." He made the turn into a modest residential area, the clapboard houses adorned in a wide array of pastel colors. "What was the number again?"

"One-eighteen." Her eyes scoured the buildings. "The even numbers are on the right."

"Three hundred block, so we're close."

"There. The light blue house."

Pulling into the gravel driveway, she noted the "For Rent" sign pushed into grass that was just starting to turn brown. Blake made a strangled sound.

"What's wrong?" Her voice drifted away as she stared at the front of the house. Sammi had said the outside needed a little work, but she didn't notice any of that. She couldn't. Her eyes refused to budge from the words stenciled in bold black letters across the left portion of the building.

SCENTS OF PLEASURE: AROMATHERAPY AND MASSAGE OILS.

CHAPTER EIGHT

"I BET that was really popular with the neighbors."

Molly pulled herself together. "Very funny. Sammi did mention something about a sign needing to be painted over."

"Are you sure you want to do that? You could start a little side business of your own."

She leveled a glare at him. "Did you know this was here?" If so, he could have at least warned her. Maybe that was why he'd acted so funny at Jed's house.

"No, I've never had the pleasu—" He stopped when he saw the look on her face. "No. I had no idea."

He must have realized she wasn't finding any of this amusing, because he squeezed the hand that lay between them on the seat. "I'm sure it's fine. Sammi said the inside was nice, right?"

"I hope so." She pulled the key out of the envelope. "Do you want to stay here while I take a look?" Part of her hoped he would, afraid she might find something other than essential oils and innocent massage items inside.

"This is a nice neighborhood, but I'll go with you, just in case."

They made their way to the door and Molly unlocked it. She then moved aside to let Blake go first, praying he was right and there was nothing kinky inside. A painfully normal foyer met her eyes.

Thank you.

No oils with suggestive names. No "personal" massagers standing at attention.

In fact, the place was nice. Really nice. The living room had creamy white paneling and soft taupe carpet that looked and smelled freshly cleaned. White roman shades were all at half-mast, allowing her to see how bright and airy the place would be during the day.

"This is wonderful. Far better than I imagined."

"Looks like you're hitting a home run at every turn today." The wry tone made her glance up quickly, wondering if he was making a crack about her date with Mark. Nothing in his face seemed to indicate he was making fun of her, though. "It's not always easy to find a decent place to rent. Housing is tight on the islands."

"Oh." She started to move to the next room when a slapping sound came from somewhere in the back of the house. She sucked in a breath, gooseflesh prickling along her arms. "Did you hear that?"

"Stay here." The low words slid past her ear, sending another shiver over her.

Before he could move, a white furry head peered around the corner. Her brain didn't have a chance to process what it was. She automatically cringed sideways, knocking into Blake, who grabbed her to keep her from dragging both of them to the floor.

"Easy, it's just a cat."

A cat. Not a mouse or other creepy-crawly.

She shuddered. "Thank God." Her breath rattled in her chest as she tried to find her composure. Problem was, it was nowhere in sight. Something touched the top of her head, and she realized her side was still pressed tight against Blake's front, his arms wrapped around her, warm breath ruffling her hair—breath that sounded almost as unsteady as her own. The world tilted slightly as he murmured, "You okay?"

She opened her mouth to answer, but nothing came out, her mind zeroing in on each contact point between their bodies and trying to decipher body parts. Chin against top of head. *Check*. Hard chest wall touching right shoulder blade. *Check*. Her right hip against his... *Yikes*.

Clearing her throat and using it as an excuse to pull away, she stuffed her hands in the pockets of her jacket, looking anywhere but at him. "I'm fine. It just startled me."

Blake was right. A cat with dusty white fur and a blue collar inched farther into the room, staring at them with wary eyes. She was surprised the animal hadn't turned around and run away

"Poor thing. I wonder how it got in?" She knelt and called to it softly, holding out her hand.

"I don't know." Blake moved through to the area they'd heard the sound. "There's a pet door back here," he called. He reappeared a minute later.

"Do you think the previous tenant left her behind?" The cat rubbed against her hand, purring softly. "Surely not."

"She knows how to get in." The cat gave a little meow. "She looks well fed, too. Maybe the landlord knows how to contact the people who used to live here."

"I'm supposed to give him an answer tomorrow, but I'm not sure what to do with her until then. I suppose I could keep her as long as the landlord is okay with it. The house doesn't smell bad, so hopefully she's litter trained." She scrubbed under the cat's chin and laughed when the animal tilted its head back a little farther.

The softness of Molly's face as she stroked the cat caused his heart to give a couple of hard thumps in his chest. He stiffened, remembering his lapse a few minutes earlier. When she'd stumbled against him, his instinctual reaction had been to keep her from falling. That primal urge to protect had been short-lived and followed by something else entirely. The scent of her hair had intoxicated him and he hadn't been able to resist leaning closer, his chin coming in for a landing on the top of her head. And those soft curves.

He tried to throw off the sensations, but they hung around the periphery, waiting to pounce on him when he least expected it.

She's going out with Mark. She's made her choice.

As if he were even in the running. No way. He'd taken himself out of that particular race long ago. So why had he allowed himself to get close enough to settle his head against hers? Because it was what he used to do with Sharon? An instinctive reaction?

Maybe, except Molly was a brunette, not a blonde. And her warm scent didn't fill him with memories of shouting matches followed by bitter periods of silence.

Her voice was nothing like Sharon's either. Molly's low, breathy tones turned his gut completely inside out and wiped out any higher cortical activity. Right now, it was brainstem all the way. That made her dangerous. And, oh, so tempting all at the same time.

"She's so sweet." Molly had picked the cat up by this time, holding her in her arms. The cat rubbed the top of her head against Molly's chin. "She's definitely not afraid of me."

Blake, on the other hand, was shaking in his boots. "Maybe we should finish looking at the house." He needed a good reason to get out of this building before he did anything stupid. Like he'd almost done at Jed's. He was a thread away from repeating that mistake, Mark or no Mark.

"Okay." Setting the cat on the floor, they waited to see what she would do. She just stood there twisting her head from side to side as she looked from one to the other. "I guess she's not going anywhere for the moment."

They quickly toured the rest of the house, which Molly liked as much as the living room. "I think I'm going to take it."

"Cat and all?"

"I can't very well kick her out, if she's used to being here. Maybe I can find her owner." She put her hands on her hips. "Or at least a litter box."

She wanted the cat to stay. He could hear it in her voice. Something inside him melted. He clenched his teeth, willing himself not to say the words, but they came out anyway. "I could always put her up at my place until you get your furniture and things settled. At least you'd know she was fed and safe."

"Are you serious?"

What the hell was wrong with him? He should have let Mark offer to take the thing in. He was the one interested in Molly, not him.

Except his friend was allergic to cats…had sneezed every time he'd come face-to-face with his mom's cat when he'd come over to the house. A slow smile came over his face.

"Definitely."

Her hand touched his. "Thank you. Maybe we'll find her owner."

"Maybe. I'll bring a crate over later and take her home and feed her. Once you get settled, you can come by and get her."

Her fingers curled around his. "You won't regret this."

He should regret it. He should make an effort to dredge up some semblance of that elusive emotion. Instead, all he wanted to do was kiss Molly until she couldn't breathe. And that was impossible. Not only because it wasn't a smart thing to do.

But because Mark had already made his move and had, in effect, snatched Molly right out of his hands.

CHAPTER NINE

INSTEAD of heading to the hotel, Molly decided to go back to the clinic to give Sammi the news about the house and see how things had gone with her pregnant patient.

She was also anxious to get to work. While she could make good money in private practice, that wasn't why she'd gone into medicine.

So here were her current challenges: surviving the flights to and from the islands and working hard to prove the government dollars were well spent. If she could do those two things, hopefully the work would continue, even if she couldn't.

"Did you like it?" Sammi tossed her long braid over her shoulder.

"It was beautiful! I'm going to take it."

"What about that sign? Wasn't it a hoot?"

Molly grimaced. "Yeah, especially having a man in the car with me when I got there."

"Hey, you never know. Blake's quite a catch, if you haven't noticed."

She glanced away. "Really? He seems kind of standoffish to me." Picking a chart up from the counter, she flipped it open as if reading it. "Besides, Mark asked me out, and *he* is rather yummy, don't you think?"

A second or two of silence went by and Molly looked

up to find Sammi on the other side of the room, staring out the window. She frowned. "Is everything okay?"

"Yep." The other woman turned around with a smile. "Tell Mark I said hi when you see him. In the meantime, could you give me a hand? I have two patients waiting and the PA is off for the rest of the day."

"Sure." Something about Sammi seemed artificially bright all of a sudden, but she couldn't place exactly what it was that made her think so. So she accepted the file handed to her and went to the exam room the CHA indicated.

A half hour later she swiveled on the stool to face Sarah, her five-year-old patient, gently wrapping an ace bandage around the child's wrist. "It's not broken according to the X-ray, but it still must hurt, huh?"

The little girl's breath hitched as it had several times during the exam, and she clutched her mother's hand. "Uh-huh."

"No more bike riding for the next week or so, okay?"

Sniffling, Sarah leaned against her mother, who stroked her hair and said, "Your arm will be as good as new in no time. You'll see."

Molly nodded. "That's right." She rummaged through a couple of drawers until she found a stash of slings with the clinic's initials inscribed on the outside. Sorting through them, she found one she hoped would fit Sarah's small arm. Maybe the device would also remind the girl why she couldn't ride her bike. She went over to the table and positioned Sarah's limb. "Can you hold your arm here while I put this on?"

The sling went on easily, with no fuss. Afterward, Sarah touched it with her other hand. "It's pink, just like my bike."

"See, isn't that better? You need to wear it until your next appointment." She gave the child's mother a wink and held up crossed fingers, hoping she'd realize the sling was just a prop. Then she helped the child climb off the table.

Sarah's mom mouthed, "Thank you."

"Can I have a lollipop? Sammi always gives me one, 'cause I'm a good girl."

And cheeky, too.

She glanced around the room. "Do you know where she keeps them?"

"She hides them inside there, behind a bunch of junk…" Sarah pointed at one of the upper cabinets "…but all the kids know where they are."

The haughty tilt of her nose said the adults around this place had gravely underestimated their young patients.

The child's mom gave her daughter a warning frown. "Sarah…"

Laughing, Molly went to the cabinet and slid her hand deep into its recesses. Sure enough, toward the back was a large round-bellied Mason jar. When she pulled it forward, a colorful array of treats met her eyes. A big label on the side divided the sweets according to color and what they were intended to reward. Nifty idea.

Red: Valor.

Green: Broken bones.

Yellow: Sunny disposition.

Purple: Vaccinations.

Orange: Courage.

Blue: Stitches.

She pulled it off the shelf and set it on the counter. "Now let's see which one you've earned."

"The blue one stains your tongue."

Molly's brows went up. "It does?" She glanced at the label. "You've had stitches before?"

"No, but sometimes Sammi lets kids choose the color."

The little girl leaned closer, her eyes round. "Even if they cry."

"Does she? Sammi's a very nice lady, to let you do that."

An energetic nod followed.

They'd evidently made their fair share of trips to the clinic. Molly was glad she'd come. Maybe Sammi wouldn't be run as ragged as she'd evidently been the past couple of months.

"So which color do you think you've earned?" She popped open the latch that held the glass lid in place. The scent of sugar wafted up, despite the plastic wrapping around each individual pop.

Sarah studied the label, her lips pursed. "My bone's not broken, right?"

"Right." Molly gave her mother a quick smile. Choosing a sucker was serious business around these parts.

"I was brave, though, wasn't I?"

"Very."

"But the blue..." The child's wistful eyes searched the jar, obviously looking for something.

Molly spun the glass container around. There was only one blue left. That staining feature Sarah had mentioned hadn't made it any less popular. In fact, it appeared to be the most desirable lollipop on the block.

"I think we can make an exception in this case, since you were so brave about letting me X-ray that arm."

"Really?"

"Absolutely." She crooked an arm around the jar and tilted the mouth of it toward the child. "I'll even let you reach in and get it, if you want. It's on the very bottom, though, do you think you can manage it with your left hand?"

"I'm left-handed." The pride in her voice was obvious, bringing another smile to Molly's face.

"Well, there you go."

Tiny fingers wiggled their way through the sea of lollipops until her whole arm was swallowed by the jar's neck. Once she reached the sweet and pulled it out, her mother draped a hand over Sarah's shoulder. "What do you say?"

"Thank you," she said in that cute sing-songy tone children used when responding to a prompt.

"You're very welcome." Molly glanced at her watch. She should probably head back to the hotel. Hopefully Blake had been able to catch the cat. The thought of seeing him again brought a strange little rush of pleasure to her tummy.

Not good.

You've only known the man a little while.

But the fizzy sensation remained, undaunted by the internal reprimand.

Sarah's voice came back through. "Can I eat it now, Mommy?"

"After lunch."

"Can't it be an appet…an apperti…" She searched for the word. "Apperitizer?"

"Appetizer. And, no, it can't. It'll be dessert, which comes *after* we eat."

The girl's lower lip moved back into a threatening position, and her mom gave a little laugh. "Come on, time to go."

Waving as the pair headed out the door, Molly turned back to the room so she could tidy up. She pulled the paper covering the exam table through the feed at the bottom until the surface was covered with a fresh, clean layer, ripping off the used portion and wadding it in a ball. As she turned to toss it into a nearby trashcan, she almost jumped out of her skin when she found Blake standing in the doorway.

"What are you doing here?"

"I wanted to let you know that the cat walked right into the crate as if she'd been in one before. She's already at my house, chowing down on some food. Anyway, Sammi said you had a patient. I didn't want to interrupt you, so I waited." He helped himself to a piece of candy from the jar.

A giddy little laugh came out, and she cleared her throat, trying for a frown instead. She glanced at his hand. "Yellow. Really?"

"Huh?"

She tapped a finger to Sammi's labeling system, hoping to ward off the crazy sensations that were rising in her chest. "Things like that have to be earned."

He squinted at the notations. "Sunny disposition. That describes me to a T."

"Right."

"Besides," he said, "the blue ones appear to be all gone."

She rolled her eyes. "Not you, too."

"Hey, if you can't beat 'em…"

He actually was in kind of a sunny mood. Surprising. What had cheered him up? "So the cat seems to be okay?"

"She's fine. I went ahead and checked with the vet in town. No one seems to be missing her."

He propped a hip against the counter, evidently in no hurry to leave.

As for her, she needed to get back to the hotel and get ready for her date. Anything to avoid standing here staring at Blake.

She opened the chart and began writing up her notes. "I got the rental by the way. I sign the contract in the morning."

"Good to hear. When are you moving in?"

"I'll be at the hotel another couple of days until my things arrive. Probably on Thursday or Friday."

"Hmm."

She snuck a glance at where he was methodically flipping the sucker, catching it by the stick on every second twirl. His biceps—seemingly oblivious to the actual weight of the candy—responded as if it were dealing with a two-ton barbell, tightening into a solid mass of muscle with every toss. Tearing her eyes away took discipline and courage. Two things she lacked right now.

Yeah, she was a professional all right.

"I've still got your things in the back of my car. How do you want to work this?"

Ah, so that's why he was still here. Man, she was dense sometimes.

"I'd totally forgotten about the suitcases. Sorry."

So how *did* she want to handle this? She didn't have a vehicle yet. Maybe Sammi could—

"I could give you a lift to the hotel and drop the stuff off."

Relief swept over her. "That would be great, thanks. I'll see about getting a rental car tomorrow."

She finished jotting her notes, and glanced at the previous ones to see if Sammi had a specific format she wanted followed.

Yep. She'd recorded the color of each sucker for each visit. Curious, she thumbed through the entries. Red. Red. Blue. Yellow. Blue. Blue. Blue.

Molly laughed as she penned blue at the end of her own notes. That made four blues in a row.

"What?"

"Just thinking about how people—even kids—get on a kick and don't want to move away from it."

"Not sure I follow you."

"My patient's favorite lollipop was blue."

"Which means?"

She shrugged. "Even at a young age, we as humans start digging a rut for ourselves and then settling into it. The deeper we dig, the harder it is to climb back out." She reached in the jar and pulled out a lollipop, staring at it for a moment. Holding it upside down, she made a couple of scooping motions. "You can make a shovel out of almost anything if you try hard enough. Even a simple piece of candy."

"I still don't follow."

Maybe that had been part of the reason her parents' marriage had floundered. They'd allowed themselves to settle into an unhealthy routine that had gotten deeper and deeper until they'd been trapped. And her own relationships had followed a similar course. She'd worked harder and harder to please Gary—and her mother—but it had never been enough. She'd just kept digging. Until she'd finally thrown down her shovel and scrambled up out of that hole.

"I was just thinking about my mom and dad, and how they argued about his job. How my mom always tore my dad down. It's hard for people to change when something's become ingrained."

She closed the chart, noting Blake had gone very still. "Something wrong?"

"Just thinking."

She wanted to ask, but it was none of her business, really. To cover up the awkwardness, she worked to put the rest of the room in order. He moved to stand by the wall without needing to be asked when she reached into a cupboard and pulled out a bottle of disinfectant spray. Giving the counter a couple of healthy squirts, she waited a few seconds for the solution to kill any microbes before drying it with a wad of paper towels. Blake remained silent, not even attempting to find a topic of conversation.

Then again, neither did she. She'd evidently said something wrong.

She shut her eyes and realized what it was. He didn't want to hear about her parents' problems. That was something personal, and Molly wasn't even sure why she'd brought the subject up. Blake had worked with her father—had respected him. Why would he want to hear anything that might cast a pall on the man who'd helped train him? Great. Just when she'd thought he was softening, she had to go and mess things up. "I'm almost done."

"No hurry." The words were generous, but the tightness she'd heard at other times was back in his voice. Yep. She'd definitely made some kind of gaffe.

When Sammi poked her head into the room, Molly was grateful for the interruption. "I just finished with my patient. How'd it go with Sarah?"

"Fine. No breaks. Just a bad sprain. I put her arm in a sling and told her to take it easy for a while."

Sammi's eyes went to the candy jar. "I forgot to tell you about the lollipops."

"Don't worry. Sarah let me know." She refastened the lid. "You're out of blue, by the way."

Sammi laughed. "I should have stuck to the chart. But once I let the kids talk me into breaking tradition, there was no stopping them. Blue is all the rage right now. Kind of like a badge of honor for surviving this place. Maybe I should nix that color."

"I wouldn't do that." To her surprise, Blake spoke up, holding up his sucker. "It's not just the kids who are guilty. I play favorites, too."

"So you're a yellow man."

"It would seem that way." His lips gave a wry twist. "Although, according to Molly, a shovel is a shovel, no matter what the color."

CHAPTER TEN

A RUT is a grave with both ends kicked out.

The quote flashed through Blake's head as he rang Molly's doorbell. Holding the pet crate in one hand, he'd shoved his other one into the pocket of his leather jacket, discovering the still wrapped sucker he'd picked up at the clinic two days ago. He closed his fist around it.

What the hell was he doing here? He'd climbed out of one deep rut, was he really stupid enough to start digging another one? He hadn't seen or heard from Mark since that day at Jed's house—when he'd asked Molly out—so he had no idea how their date had gone.

Neither did he care.

His own failed marriage and Wayne's tale of woe had convinced him it took a man with nerves of steel to be both a bush pilot and a husband. Something he evidently didn't have. Which brought him back to the question of what he was doing here. He could have dropped the cat crate off at the clinic this afternoon and let Molly carry it home herself. But he'd been curious about how things were going with her new place. There'd been no real medical emergencies since he'd been back, nothing to keep his mind off things. So here he was. But as soon as she opened the door, he'd hand her the crate and leave.

And he *would* leave.

He might have to work with Molly on medevacs, but following her around the island hadn't been part of that package.

The door opened, and there she stood in a black stretchy top, a hand towel looped over one shoulder. Music with some kind of thumping beat washed through the opening, making him blink, as did the sight of Molly's teeth coming down on her soft lower lip. She glanced back inside the house, the gap in the doorway narrowing.

Was that guilt?

"Um, hi, I wasn't expecting you."

He frowned. Was Mark here or something?

"Sorry for not calling first. Sammi said you'd already left for the day." Actually, he'd been convinced he could talk himself out of coming over here in person, so he hadn't bothered. But here he was…on her doorstep. "Is this a bad time?"

"No. Come on in. My things arrived from the mainland this morning, but I had to leave for work as soon as they unloaded the truck. The place is a wreck."

"That's okay. I can't stay long." He lifted the crate. "I told you I'd bring her by once you moved in."

As if she'd just noticed what he held, Molly knelt and peered inside the box. "Hey, sweetie. You ready to come home?" She glanced back up. "I asked the landlord about the previous renters, but he said they moved off the island and didn't leave a forwarding address. One of the neighbors felt sorry for her, and had been leaving food out, so I guess she's officially mine." She stood aside to let him come in.

The music grew louder and chaos met him as soon as he reached the living room. Half-opened boxes were scattered around the periphery of the space, with similar items grouped together. A laptop computer, perched on top of

one of the boxes belted out a tune from a dance movie, the
screen swirling with patterns that kept time with the beat.
The center of the room was completely clear, as if a centri-
fuge had gone on the fritz and blown everything backward.

It was then he noticed Molly's snug, stretchy top was
joined by a matching pair of Lycra pants. Exercise gear.
And the towel…

She was dancing.

He swallowed. It made sense. The type of music. The
light sheen of perspiration dotting her upper lip…the deep
scoop of her neckline, which had slid off her left shoulder,
revealing a black bra strap.

Realizing he might be staring—*was* staring—and that
his lower jaw was probably located somewhere on the carpet beneath his feet, he cleared his throat. Molly hiked
the renegade sleeve back over her shoulder and turned
the volume down on the music, blushing a deep pink. "I
was just…"

"It's okay. No explanation needed." His imagination
had filled in every possible blank.

"I—I have coffee made. Do you want some?"

Hell, he wanted something, but it wasn't coffee. "Um,
what do you want me to do with…?" He nodded down at
the cat crate.

"Oh, right. Poor thing. I'm a little frazzled."

She wasn't the only one. And the more he pictured her
writhing in time to that wild rhythm she had going, the
warmer he got.

Kneeling in front of him to open the cage, she spoke in
soft tones to the cat, coaxing her from the dark recesses of
the container. She soon had her in her arms. The feline's
head pushed against her chin in greeting. "I've already got
some food and litter for her." She laughed at the way the

cat snuggled against her, front legs dangling over Molly's forearm as if perched on a familiar ledge.

Blake tried not to picture that cat's white fur sticking to Molly's black top, or how she might roll a lint brush over those soft curves later. "There are a couple of toys in the crate."

"You bought her toys?"

The throaty whisper transformed the growing heat in his chest into a small blaze. He shrugged, trying to firm his resolve to clear out at the first opportunity. "Just a few. They were on sale."

There, that should sound tough enough.

She smiled. "Blake Taylor, could you have a soft spot for animals?"

Absolutely not.

Even as the protest bounced through his head, he knew it was a lie. The cat had exited the crate at his house, rubbing against his leg and purring up a storm. The animal had looked up at him. And those eyes…

Luminous green. Changing with her moods. Just like Molly's.

"Come and have some coffee while I show her where her litter box is."

The smart thing to do would be to back out of the room and say a quick goodbye. He followed her instead, watching as Molly set the animal next to a litter box she'd stowed in the laundry area. The cat took one look then turned around and stalked off.

"Pets are kind of permanent. Does this mean you're thinking of staying longer than a year?"

"I don't know. Do you think they'll ever build a bridge from the mainland?"

The smile told him it was a joke, but his chest felt tight

and strange. "I think you're stuck with flying. You'll get used to it."

Standing, she went to the sink and washed her hands, then took two mugs from a nearby box and rinsed them. "Hmm…maybe. I don't think I'll ever really *like* flying, but I've proved to myself I can do it. That's all that matters, right?"

The words were like a boot to the chest, knocking the wind from him.

How could something that was so exhilarating to him— something that gave him a huge jolt of satisfaction every time his plane left the ground—produce the exact opposite reaction in someone else?

Oblivious to his thoughts, she said, "Thank you, Blake. It—it means a lot to me that you watched her and that you cared enough to play with her."

Her gaze met his, and he had to force himself not to look away as thoughts of escape crowded in around him. "She wasn't any trouble."

His hand went back to the sucker, gripping tight. Maybe he'd frame the thing as a reminder: the digging stopped right here. Right now.

Regardless of how his gut twisted at having to keep standing there, he stayed put, even when she took a step closer and touched his arm. He swore he could feel the warmth of her palm, even through his thick leather jacket. "You'll stay and have some coffee? As a small token of my thanks?"

"Yes." The word came out as a croak.

He gulped when her fingers tightened slightly. Pinpoints of heat and cold danced across his body, as if some cosmic disco ball was releasing short bursts of energy as it spun round and round. It blinded him to everything but her touch. "You don't need to thank me. You'd do the same for me."

"Maybe. It depends on what I had to do. Fly a plane, for example? Not much chance of that." Her hand slid a little higher, her thumb sweeping a path across his upper arm.

He sucked down a breath, all thoughts of escape evaporating. Was she aware of what her touch was doing to him? *Talk. Don't think.*

"Don't sell yourself short. You'd do it, if you had to." His voice came out all scratchy and his throat grew tight, along with other key areas of his body.

"As much as I want to believe that, there's not much chance of me ever attempting it. Not unless you passed out in midflight, and even the thought of that happening makes me break out in a cold sweat."

Something niggled at the back of his mind, something other than the wave of lust rushing up his spine demanding to be heard. Even as he fought the urge, he reached toward her, unable to resist touching a lock of that glossy brown hair.

Soft. Silky.

Just as he'd imagined it would be.

When she released a sigh instead of stepping back, he slid his fingers deeper into the shiny strands, letting them sift through his fingertips. No hairspray. Nothing that screamed, *Don't touch.* Just thick, velvety tresses that whispered against his skin.

"I like your hair short like this." Where the words had come from, he had no idea.

"You do?"

His eyes shifted to her lips. Were they as moist and inviting as they looked? He could just lean down and…

Almost before he knew what he was doing, his mouth touched hers. Just for a second. He meant to pull away.

He was certain of it. Then she tilted her head, her hands going to his shoulders as she pressed closer. She had to be on tiptoe to reach him like that.

She wanted his kiss. Liked it.

Damn. His heart and his mind tussled for a second or two before the primal side kicked the rational to the curb, flipping it a bird and sending it scurrying to some dark corner of his mind.

There. That was better.

Molly swayed for a second. To stabilize her—*yeah, that was the reason*—he wrapped one arm around her waist, while the fingers of his other hand remained in her hair, molding themselves to the delicate bones of her skull.

What was he doing?

Something he'd wanted to do from the moment he saw her in the emergency room last year. The day he'd discovered she was Wayne McKinna's daughter. And when he'd juggled his schedule to fly her to the islands.

This moment seemed predestined.

It would have been perfect if not for the flight that exposed the one thing he swore he'd never accept in a woman.

But that didn't stop him from licking his way across those luscious lips with tiny swipes of his tongue, his body flaming when her mouth opened, inviting him inside.

He slid home, the wet heat he found there setting off an explosion that burned away the line he'd drawn in the sand after his divorce—one he'd never cross if he was in his right mind.

But he wasn't, and he had no intention of retreating from this agonizing pleasure any time soon. The luscious friction against his tongue ratcheted up his need, hardening him beyond belief.

She made a tiny sound. Something that straddled the line between a complaint and a contented purr.

Her hands went to the back of his neck, pressing even closer.

Definitely not a complaint, then.

The sound came again.

Molly sucked down an audible breath and stiffened, causing Blake to freeze as well, his tongue still deeply embedded in her warmth.

He pieced together that the noise wasn't coming from her but from somewhere down...

She eased away, her lips sliding slowly over the length of his tongue as they both withdrew. The separation was painful, not only for his mind, but for the area still pressed hard against her belly.

Ah, hell.

"The cat." The low huskiness of her voice scraped along nerve endings that were stretched to breaking point. He wanted nothing more than to lift her onto one of the kitchen counters and see if he could give that Scents of Pleasure sign outside a whole new meaning.

Her hands slid down to his shoulders and pushed slightly, her voice coming again. "The cat wants something."

To hell with the cat.

Then he smiled. Thoughts like that wouldn't endear him to her.

Neither would they solve the problem he was now facing.

He swallowed. What had he just allowed to happen? He was an even bigger idiot than he'd thought. He didn't want to fly her across the ocean, but he sure as hell would let himself get it on with her. And she'd just been out on a date with his best friend two days ago. The fact that Mark didn't play for keeps meant nothing at all.

Releasing her, he stepped back, hoping she wouldn't glance down for a couple of minutes.

Ha! Seeing as the cat was on the floor, there wasn't much chance of her not looking at it.

The floor, that was. Or noticing how she'd affected him in the process.

His eyes went to the source of the noise. Sure enough, the cat—body curved in a half-moon—had wrapped herself around one of Molly's legs. Its tail twitched back and forth as it craned its head up to look at her, the wide-eyed glance both innocent and cunning, the fur beneath its chin as white as newly fallen snow.

"Meooow."

The long drawn-out plea tugged at his heart, despite the lingering irritation at having his prize yanked from his grasp.

Molly gave him a shaky smile. "Well, she's definitely not feral, that's for sure."

The cat might not be, but he was starting to wonder about himself.

Since when had he allowed himself to be ruled by animal instinct?

How about every time he climbed in that cockpit to fly? Or whenever he got within ten feet of Molly McKinna.

How on earth was she able to gather her wits so quickly? He was still trying to figure out how to pull his knuckles off the floor and return to being a biped.

Crouching down, she held her hand out to the cat, who immediately slumped against it. Blake could hear the thing purr even from where he stood.

"What is it, sweetie? I know you have food." The cat trotted to the doorway of the other room, tail held high.

Since Molly was walking right beside her, there was no option but to follow them both. At least Molly's back was

to him, giving him time to haul his body back into submission. A task none too easy since her rounded hips and
the curve of her butt beckoned him closer.

Damn.

The cat glanced back at him and gave a haughty flick
of her tail.

She knew exactly what she was doing. He'd seen his
parents' pug do something similar whenever he'd gone
to Florida to visit them. Jealously guarding its territory.

He doubted that plaintive little cry was anything other
than a ploy to gain Molly's full attention. He'd use the
same tactic if he thought it would work.

The animal went down the hallway and turned a corner, leaping onto the bed it found there.

Molly's bed.

He took a slow, careful breath as she reached out to
the cat, her hand sliding over the animal's fur, her thumb
stroking across its back, just like she'd done with his arm
a few minutes ago. Blake tried not to remember the emotions that light touch had aroused in him, but it was impossible. Every second was permanently seared into his brain.

God, he wanted her. More than he should.

Forbidden fruit. The more dangerous it was, the more
you craved it.

*Eat it and you'll send yourself straight to some pri-
vate hell.*

He almost laughed. Not reaching out and plucking the
apple from the tree was sending him to a hell of a different sort. Was one any better than the other?

Mark had set his sights on her, but was it because he
genuinely liked her or because that was what Mark did? He
saw, he conquered, he moved on to the next woman in line.

If Molly had a choice, who would she choose?

She'd just about kissed him into oblivion, which meant

nothing in and of itself, but since he didn't see her as someone who batted her thick lashes at anyone she passed on
the street...

He stopped himself right there.

Was he any better for her than Mark? He'd been so
busy protecting himself that he'd never stopped to think
about what was good for Molly. He'd warned her off his
friend, but maybe he should have advised her to steer clear
of him as well.

Could he see her without either of them getting hurt?

He didn't think so. The best thing to do would be to
back off and give her some space. Let her get used to the
island and to the work. See how she handled things without someone standing over her and pressuring her.

Could he do it? Could he leave her alone?

Hell, after that kiss, he wasn't sure. But he had to try.
For both their sakes.

Even if it meant handing the winner's cup to his best
friend.

CHAPTER ELEVEN

"WOULD you mind taking some EpiPens over to Akutan? Their clinic is out, and one of the volcano observatory guys has a bee allergy. He left his syringe in Anchorage." Sammi's voice came from the doorway. "I'd do it myself, but Screaming Jimmy is coming in at two."

Molly glanced up from the spider bite she'd been examining on a diabetic patient, a man in his early sixties. "Screaming Jimmy?"

Her patient exchanged a knowing smile with Sammi and said, "Believe me, you don't want to be here when he arrives. *I* don't want to be here…so if you could just give me a tube of antiseptic cream, I'll be on my way."

Okay, that still didn't answer her question. "Is he a kid?"

Sammi laughed. "Oh, he's all man—built like a tank. He just hates needles. He's coming in for a flu shot."

"Jimmy's an embarrassment to his gender," her patient grumbled.

"He literally screams?" Surely not.

"Like a banshee. He's the only guy I know who can shoot off a stream of cuss words all in falsetto." Sammi put two fingers against her open lips and swirled them away as if demonstrating. "He sounds kind of like a crazed opera singer."

Molly finished swabbing the infected bite with cream

and peeled apart a dressing to put over it. "Do you want me to administer the shot?"

"Oh, no. He won't let anyone else do it but me." She grimaced.

"Lucky girl." Molly scribbled a prescription on her pad and spoke to her patient. "Make sure you come back if this starts looking worse. And monitor your sugar."

The man gave a sheepish nod. "I will." He slid from the table. "That it?"

He was in a hurry, either because of Screaming Jimmy's impending visit or because he hadn't been careful about his sugar intake and wanted to avoid a lecture. Either way, she'd better follow up on him.

"Let's see you back next week, just to be sure." She handed him the prescription. "Call me if you have any problems before then."

Once he was gone, Sammi reached into a cabinet and pulled down five EpiPen boxes. "You okay with taking these?"

"Where's Akutan? Is it in one of the neighborhoods?"

"No, it's the next island over."

Molly's stomach pitched. "I have to fly there?"

Her reaction had nothing to do with fear this time, but everything to do with seeing Blake so soon after that disastrous kiss. Three days was definitely not enough time. Maybe a week. Two would be even better. Anything to give her a chance to regain her equilibrium and treat him like a colleague. A vague acquaintance. Especially after her date with Mark, which had been a huge disappointment.

She'd hoped to feel some of the same stirrings with him that she'd had with Blake. But Mark's chaste and polite kiss on the cheek at the door of her hotel room had been nothing compared to the knee-trembling reaction that had shot through her system the second Blake's lips had met hers. She sensed Mark had had the same lukewarm reaction, for which she was relieved.

It also meant she was in big trouble.

Sammi's voice brought her back to reality. "Only if you want to land on top of the volcano." The CHA grinned, straightening the band that held her thick braid in place. "The landing strip's not done yet. But they're working on it… Hey, I'm sure Blake wouldn't mind giving it a try, if you wanted him to…"

"No, that's okay." She could barely stomach landing on Dutch Harbor's runway, much less one that was still under construction. "So, if I don't fly, how exactly do I get there?"

"Boat. It's only about thirty-five miles away. There's a state ferry that travels between the islands every couple of weeks during the summer, but it's not due to dock for several days. The clinic has a boat we use for quick trips." She cocked her head. "You might as well look around while you're there. It's a nice little community. Only two or three cars in the whole place."

All Molly cared about was the word *boat*. That meant no flying. *Yes!* She wouldn't have to face Blake yet. As hard as she might try to stay cool and collected, she knew it was a lost cause. As soon as she saw him, it would all come rushing back. Every fantastic, horrifying second of it.

Had she lost her marbles?

Her experience with Gary should have taught her to keep her personal life and her professional life separate. At least in Anchorage, she and her ex had been in different wings of the hospital. And she had been careful to stick to the emergency room as much as possible.

Even after six months, though, the situation had been awkward, since he'd gone out of his way to run into her. And her mother hadn't helped matters, inviting the man over to dinner from time to time in the hope they might get back together. The encounters had left her drained and exhausted. So much so that the Aleutians job had been a godsend—despite her fear of flying. And yet here she was, locking lips with the first man to cross her path. Worse, a pilot…and a colleague.

Maybe anyone looked good after what she'd left behind. And Blake seemed strong and capable but without the need to control everyone around him, like Gary. But how well did she really know him? He'd been through a painful breakup—he'd been married, for heaven's sake. Who knew what kind of baggage he carried around on those broad shoulders?

She had plenty of her own to lug around.

Getting involved with him was a catastrophe in the making. One she'd come here to avoid. She could and *would* remember that.

At all costs.

Sammi loaded the EpiPens in a little bag. "Just drop these off at the clinic in Akutan and they'll get one of them up to the observatory. Blake's going to meet you at the dock."

Her heart stuttered. "Blake? But I thought you said the airport—"

"I did. But when Blake's not doing medevacs or transporting patients to and from Anchorage, he works with the EMS department here on the island. I thought you knew that."

Emergency Medical Services. Great, that covered just about every job imaginable.

"No, I didn't." *All the more reason to keep your distance.* Yeah, that was going to be kind of hard if the guy did everything from driving ambulances to transporting pharmaceuticals between the islands.

"Here you go." Sammi handed her the bag of epinephrine syringes.

"I think I'd rather take my chances with Screaming Jimmy," she mumbled half under her breath on her way out the door.

Sammi evidently heard her, because she sent her off with a sustained upper-octave shriek—vibrato attached—that any opera singer would be proud to own.

Blake frowned as Molly's car pulled into the lot just as he was making sure the boat was topped up with fuel. He'd understood Sammi to say *she* was taking the medicine to the island, not Molly. If she was pulling a fast one, she was going to get an earful when he got back. He wasn't in the mood for matchmaking games. Not from anyone, even Sammi.

Huffing out a careful breath, he stood a little straighter. No big deal. They were both adults. One kiss was nothing. A fluke. People made mistakes and then moved on.

Just like he was going to do.

But seeing her get out of the car, thin blue sweater topping a casual pair of dark jeans, the raw, wild thrill that had accompanied the press of her lips to his—tongues sliding together—came rushing back. His brain wasn't the only body part that remembered.

He swore under his breath. The best he could hope for was to make this a quick trip. Zip over to Akutan, drop off the medicine, and hurry back to Unalaska. He'd be driving the boat the whole time.

"Sorry, I'm late."

"No problem." He took the bag from Molly and helped her onto the vessel, bracing himself when she brushed against him as she boarded. He released her hand and took a step back.

Keep it under control.

"Sorry." She gripped the chrome handrail that ran along the side as the boat rocked in time with the swells. "I tried to get Sammi to come, but she had a patient to deal with."

"You couldn't handle the patient?" He could have kicked himself the moment the words left his mouth when her face flushed the color of ripe strawberries. The slur was aimed at Sammi, but had hit Molly instead.

"She said she was the only one who could deal with this particular patient. H-he doesn't like shots, evidently."

Blake smiled, relief sweeping over him. Sammi hadn't been meddling, after all. "Jimmy?"

"Yes."

"Half of Jimmy's craziness is due to Sammi herself. He has a crush on her."

"Really? Does she know?"

"It's kind of obvious. Jimmy makes excuses to drop by the clinic every chance he gets. He's obnoxious enough that she has to deal with him personally."

Molly's fingers tightened on the rail, a frown appearing on her brow. "And she just puts up with it?"

"Jimmy's got a thick skull. Besides, he's ten years younger than Sammi, so she figures he'll eventually meet a girl he has more in common with and will leave her alone."

"Well, good luck to her. I hope she finds it easier than…"

He couldn't make out the last couple of words. "I'm sorry?"

"Nothing."

She seemed to be avoiding his glance. Who could blame her? The sooner they got to the island and back the better. "You ready?"

"Yep."

"Look on the bright side. The airport in Akutan is

still under construction, so at least we're not flying in. Although we could probably borrow one of the amphibian planes, if you'd prefer."

"That's quite all right." She finally looked him in the eye with a smile as he turned the key to start the twin outboards. "Lucky for you, I'm not afraid of boats."

"Lucky for you, neither am I."

Her laughter floated on the air, the sound light and carefree, and a day that had been headed straight down suddenly began to look up.

It seemed to take less time than usual to arrive at Akutan. The wind had been chilly once they'd got away from the shelter of Dutch Harbor, so Molly had donned her coat and stayed in the cockpit area with him. Even in the enclosed space, the noise from the engines had made talking at anything less than a shout almost impossible, which was just as well. Blake had wanted to stick with the program this time. As long as he'd been busy manning a set of controls, he hadn't been able to do anything stupid. Besides, she seemed to have already put that kiss out of her mind.

If only he could do the same.

They arrived at the island and dropped the medicine off at the tiny clinic. Molly smiled at the wooden boardwalk system that linked different buildings to each other. "Sammi said there weren't very many cars—I can see why."

"There are a couple used for unloading supplies from the planes. And some of the folks have ATVs. As you can see, it's a pretty tiny place."

Sharon had come here with him once. What should have been a pleasant outing—and a chance to renew a troubled marriage—had turned into yet another war of words. *You actually have to walk everywhere?* They'd stayed a total

of two hours, not even long enough to see the inside of
the tiny inn, then they'd turned around and headed back
to Unalaska. Two weeks later, Blake had returned from
medevacing a critical patient and found Sharon had packed
her bags and caught the ferry to Anchorage. She'd left a
note. Tired and disheartened after losing the patient halfway through the flight, Blake hadn't gone after her. That
had been the end. She'd filed for divorce soon afterward.

"Do you mind if I look around for a few minutes before we head back?"

He blinked. "Of course not."

A few minutes turned into a couple of hours and found
them on the side of the mountain where salmonberry
bushes twisted beside the steep footpath. She fingered
one of the fuzzy leaves.

"A month ago, those would have been loaded with
fruit," Blake said. "We can probably buy some jam made
by the locals, if you want."

"That would be wonderful. Do they have these bushes
in Unalaska as well?"

"Yep. They take vanloads of folks to pick them during
season. It's one of the highlights of the year."

He waited for the scoffing he was so sure would come,
but Molly just nodded, then turned to look out over the
village and the bay down below. She slid out of her jacket
and cinched it around her waist. "It's gorgeous here. The
ocean seems to stretch forever."

There was a second or two in which he was afraid he
wouldn't be able to answer her, and he had to swallow the
lump that formed in his throat. "You're lucky it's a clear
day. You normally can't see this well."

"I'm very lucky." She raked both hands through her
hair and set it loose again, the strands catching the light
as they settled back into place. "I feel free."

Said as if it were something she hadn't been for a very long time. Was that how Sharon had felt when she'd fled their marriage?

Hell. This was something he needed to back away from right now.

"Are you ready? We can pick up that jelly on the way to the boat."

A flicker of something that might have been disappointment went through her eyes. "Sorry, Blake. You probably have plenty of other things to do, and I should get back and see how Sammi fared with Jimmy."

He did have plenty to do, not the least of which was scrubbing the sight of Molly standing on the side of the mountain from his memory. Along with the sudden need to lay her down on the rocky path and kiss her senseless.

Damn.

Time to be proactive.

He started down the path, hoping that if he could move fast enough, he could outrun the longing that threatened to sweep through him.

But even as they boarded the boat for the return trip and Blake throttled up the engines to skim across the water and away from the island, the uneasy sensation followed him, refusing to be left behind no matter how fast he went.

All he could hope was that the two jars of salmonberry jam he'd purchased were the only souvenirs he'd have from this particular trip.

But even as he thought it, a little piece of his heart was already shrugging off that idea as a pipe dream. Because Molly had gotten inside his head. And despite his best efforts, she wasn't going anywhere.

CHAPTER TWELVE

THE champagne fizzed as it hit her skin, icy bubbles bursting as the liquid waterfall cascaded over her collarbone, rushing downward to squeeze through the valley between her breasts. She arched her back, a moan hovering on her lips.

Blake!

Goose bumps formed on her arms, but the chill didn't last long. Warm lips chased after the river, tongue flicking to capture each drop of alcohol before it could escape. She laughed as his mouth came up to meet hers, a dinner bell going off somewhere in the distance.

No food. Not now.

Blake ignored the sound, kissing her long and deep, the taste of the expensive beverage mingling with that of her own skin, the bell going off again. A frown formed on her brow.

Leave us alone!

He raised his head and looked down at her, pupils wide and dark with...

The bell grew more persistent now. Coming closer. Next to her ear.

Her eyes popped open and Blake slid away, disappearing into the shadows. Gasping, she tried to place where she was, who the warm body against her side belonged to. What that sound was.

Bed. Cat. Phone. The words presented themselves, and reality intruded. Molly sat up with a groan.

Lordy, that had been…

Unthinkable!

She grabbed her cellphone from the side table. "Hello?"

"Molly." Blake's voice came over the line, the low growl nothing like the one from her dreams. It was so tempting to just fade away, to feel the… "Molly! Are you there?"

She grabbed a quick breath, trying to banish Dream Blake and replace him with reality. "Yes. I'm here."

"We need you down at the clinic. Now. One of the fishing boats just came in with a crewman with a possible head injury."

The last vestiges of sleep deserted her as she crawled from beneath the covers, trying to avoid the cat, who'd lifted her head to glare at Molly in the dark. "I'll be right there."

She dragged a hanger from the closet which was already loaded with a complete outfit, a habit ingrained from her thirty-hour shifts as an intern—when she could barely think, much less put together a matching set of clothes. Not bothering with the light, she threw her sweats onto the bed in a heap and dressed in the clean clothing.

Head injury. That meant an automatic trip to Anchorage, no questions asked.

Grabbing her keys and coat, she prayed she'd left enough dry food in Samita's—the cat's new name a joke between her and Sammi—bowl to hold her over until she got back. She'd call Sammi, who had a set of keys to Molly's house, and ask her to check later.

She arrived at the clinic in fifteen minutes flat and found the front doors opened. Blake was just inside with

Sammi, the patient already on a stretcher, an emergency services vehicle idling out front.

"Condition?" she asked as she hurried forward.

"Pulse is strong. I've just started an IV…" Sammi looked up "…but his left pupil is blown. A crab pot hit him in the temple."

God.

"Name and age?"

"Peter Laughlin, age nineteen."

So young.

Molly knew from treating other commercial fishermen that empty crab pots were heavy, close to eight hundred pounds each. And in rough seas with fully loaded pots, things turned dangerous really quickly. She glanced at Blake, nothing going through her mind except getting off the ground as fast as possible. "Let's go."

They raced to the airport, getting there within five minutes. Blake had already called ahead, so the plane was standing by, all other air traffic halted until they could get off the ground. While she worked in the back, hooking the patient up to the heart monitor, Blake got them into the air as fast as possible. Molly braced herself during takeoff, no time to worry about anything but her patient. Once airborne, she rerecorded his vitals, relaying every bit of information she could to Alaska Regional. The on-call neurosurgeon had already been contacted and would meet them at the hospital. She glanced at her watch. Three a.m. They should arrive by six.

"Hang in there, Peter," she whispered, squeezing the young man's hand.

A thought crossed her mind. "Blake," she called over the sound of the engines, "has anyone contacted his family?"

"Sammi's working on it now. Mark can fly them in if

they're on one of the islands. I've already called him, he's ready to move."

He had? She wondered if Blake had mentioned their kiss.

Neither the time nor place, Molly.

The aircraft bumped a couple of times, but she stayed in place, her eyes never leaving her patient. "No construction zones today, please."

So many things could go wrong with head injuries—brain bleeds, swelling, pressure that grew to a point that brain cells died.

Molly continued to monitor him throughout the flight, checking Peter's ears and nose for any sign of drainage, which would mean an increase in pressure. Still nothing, so at least brain fluid wasn't leaking from the skull cavity. But that blown pupil worried her. And over the past hour he'd developed telltale signs of raccoon eyes—both orbits turning a deep purple—which pointed to skull fracture, probably at his temple, which was also discolored and swollen.

After what seemed like an eternity Blake said, "We're descending, Molly. Get him ready for transport."

Thank God. "Does the hospital have everything in place?"

"They'll meet us outside. The surgeon is standing by."

Molly had done everything she could. It was time to pass the torch to the next group of caregivers who would work to save the young man's life.

Within fifteen minutes the wheels of the aircraft touched down.

Just another minute or two, Peter.

The plane slowed dramatically, and Molly made sure the patient and the IV bags stayed secure.

"Taxiing over to the hospital area now."

Each tiny bump in the runway seemed magnified as she waited for them to arrive. She took the patient's hand in hers and spoke softly, not knowing whether or not he could hear her but doing anything she could think of to reach inside him and urge him to keep fighting.

The plane pulled to a stop, the propellers slowing down. Blake was at her side in less than a minute, unlocking the wheels to the stretcher and getting the side door open. A group of hospital staff was already waiting outside. Once the patient was on the ground, she ran beside the group, giving them an update and handing over her case notes. Inside the doors they raced down the hallway, one of the emergency room doctors—someone she didn't recognize—glancing at her. "We'll take it from here."

She blinked, still running, before she realized he was telling her not to come any farther. Stopping in her tracks, she watched the stretcher pull out of view, the doctor communicating with the surgeon as he went. "He wants a CAT scan, STAT."

Then they were gone, and the world rushed back into focus. What had been fast-forward action slowed to a crawl. Molly stood in the middle of the hospital hallway, at a loss, her heart still pounding with the rush of adrenaline but with nothing to expend it on any more. This was different from Jed's injury, which hadn't been as serious. She clasped her hands in front of her, trying to figure out what to do. She was used to finishing one case and immediately starting in on the next. And the next.

This was strange. Wrong. There was nothing for her to focus on. Nothing to...

A light touch on the shoulder made her jump. She whirled around.

Blake.

She pulled in a deep breath, her legs shaking. "What

do I do?" The whispered words came from somewhere deep inside.

He squeezed her shoulder. "We go and get some coffee. Come on."

Molly was used to calling the shots, but at the moment she was out of her element, very glad to have someone else to lean on, if only for a few minutes. He didn't take her to the break room but to the deserted cafeteria, which she appreciated. It wasn't open for breakfast yet, but the coffee machine was there.

"How do you like it?" he asked.

"Cream. No sugar."

Blake fixed hers first and went to a nearby table. "Sit. I'll be right back."

She lowered herself into the chair and started shivering. The temperature on the plane had been icy, but she hadn't noticed it until now. Wrapping her hands around her coffee, she tried to absorb the heat into her system.

Blake's coffee was black. Dark. He moved his chair next to hers. "You okay?"

"Wh-why is your plane so damn c-cold?" To her horror, her teeth were chattering.

"You left your coat at the clinic." He wrapped his arm around her and pulled her close, the warmth of his body hitting her. "And handing our patients over to someone else takes some getting used to."

"I've worked in an emergency room for two years. I should already be used to it."

"How did you unwind after shifts?"

She attempted a smile. "I went to bed."

"This is a different world. You go from nothing to a hundred miles an hour in a few seconds, then back down to nothing just as fast. Your body will adjust."

"Did yours?"

He nodded. "I've been doing this for a long time."

She laid her head on Blake's shoulder, knowing it wasn't a smart move, but the continued warmth from his body made her aware she'd only had a little bit of sleep last night. "Sorry. I don't know what's wrong with me." She yawned. "Maybe I'll store an extra coat on the plane."

"Probably not a bad idea." His arm tightened. "Why don't you close your eyes for a few minutes?"

"I should go to my mother's house and get some sleep." She paused. Her mom's was the last place she wanted to go. But Blake had to be exhausted as well. "Do you have anyone you can stay with?"

He didn't answer for a minute, then said, "Not any more."

Before she had a chance to process his words, Doug appeared around the corner, skidding to a stop in front of them.

Molly lifted her head when her friend's brows went up. "I didn't expect to see you here so early."

"It's almost seven. Time for the next shift. I heard you'd brought a patient in." He gave her a pointed look. "And so has Gary. He's on his way."

CHAPTER THIRTEEN

GARY BRANDON, bigshot cardiologist. Well-traveled speaker.
Molly's ex.

Someone Blake would rather not see.

As if on a cord, Molly pushed her chair away from Blake's, the shriek of metal against tile echoing off the walls around them. "Do you mind if we leave? I don't care where we go."

The man who'd warned Molly moved in and squeezed her arm. "I'll try to hold him off for a minute, if you want."

"Thanks, Doug. I'd appreciate it."

Blake got to his feet, not exactly sure what was going on, but Molly obviously didn't want to run into the guy. Why that should make his psyche do a quick slide across the floor he had no idea. "We can go back to the plane. I'm okay to fly, if you want to go home."

Home. Unalaska wasn't Molly's home. At least not yet. But the word had sounded good coming off his tongue.

"Yes. Thanks." She gave her friend a quick hug. "I owe you."

He lifted his brows. "Bet you're glad I made you get on that flight now."

"Get out of here." Molly rolled her eyes, then turned and headed for the nearest exit. "Is the plane still in front of the hospital?"

"They've probably already moved it to the hangar. We can get there through here." He shrugged out of his coat and put it around her shoulders as they made their way to the door.

Molly shoved her arms through the sleeves. "This is getting to be a habit."

One that was going to be hard for him to break.

Sure enough, the plane was no longer on the stretch of tarmac behind the hospital, so they walked toward the terminal. It was chilly outside, but Blake was used to the weather. Besides, he needed to clear his head. Not wanting to see her ex meant nothing. He'd bet Sharon had no desire to run into him any time soon either. Maybe *he* was simply the lesser of two evils in Molly's mind.

"You won't say anything, about my trying to avoid him, will you? I'd rather he not know."

"Gary was the man you dated?" He already knew the answer, but her reaction to Doug's news made him uneasy.

Molly glanced at him. "I guess the hospital grapevine is alive and well."

He nodded, preferring not to tell her he'd seen them together at the hospital or the irritation he'd felt while standing in line at the cafeteria and hearing the man cut Molly off in midsentence when she'd tried to make a point about hospital policy. He might be charming and good at what he did, but the guy was an overbearing jerk. Or was that just his own reaction to seeing Molly with him?

"Anyway," she went on, "things were…awkward at the end."

Realization dawned. "That's why you took the job at the clinic."

"Yes." She paused. "And I'd rather that didn't get out either."

"I told you, I can keep a secret."

She shot him another glance and gave a quick laugh. "You've said that before. You're not with the CIA or anything, right?"

"Not CIA, but I was in the service. Navy."

They reached the hangar, only to find the plane was in the process of being refueled. He opened the door so they'd at least have some shelter from the wind.

"Were you a pilot there as well?"

"Yep."

"Really?" She smiled. "I didn't know the navy recruited stunt pilots."

He didn't return her smile. Just like Molly had wanted to avoid her ex, this was one subject he'd rather steer clear of. So why had he mentioned being in the navy in the first place? Maybe because he wanted to gauge her reaction. He sucked down a deep breath and went for it. "I was a fighter pilot."

A fighter pilot.

Molly's throat tightened. What had started as light teasing on her part turned deadly serious. If he'd wanted an Evel Knievel-style job, a combat pilot was about as close as one could get. So what was he doing, flying shuttle service from Alaska to the Aleutians? "Why'd you get out?"

He paused and leaned against one of the hangar walls. "Just decided it wasn't where I needed to be."

That was a nonanswer if she ever heard one. Time to drop the lid on the curiosity box and lock it tight. If he wanted to tell her more, he would.

Move to a safer subject.

Before she could think of one, he jammed his hands in his pockets and looked away from her. "On the way home from a training mission, a buddy of mine had some trouble with his aircraft. We made it back to the carrier and thought we were home free." Blake stopped for a second. "His timing was off—whether it was due to engine malfunction or pilot error, I'm not sure. Anyway, he overshot the flight deck and his hook missed the wires completely. In trying to pull up to come back around… He didn't make it."

Molly understood almost nothing of what he'd described, but the raw grief in his voice told her everything she needed to know. Blake's friend had died during a flight. Just like her father had. Her heart ached. "I'm sorry."

"It was a long time ago."

"Even so." She wanted to touch him, but his crossed arms and tight jaw warned her not to. "That's why you got out?"

"That and…" he gave a hard laugh "…after the accident, my wife threatened to divorce me if I stayed in after my six years were up."

"Oh." He'd done as his ex-wife had asked, so he must have saved the marriage. At least temporarily. But in the end it hadn't been enough. Who'd initiated that final separation?

None of your business, Molly. Remember that lid you just closed? Keep it shut.

Why would a woman divorce a man like this? What wasn't to like about him?

That flash of straight white teeth and accompanying dimple when he laughed—even in anger—had gone right to her stomach, wiping her mind clear of any rational thought. The long sexy groove in his cheek was like an open invitation, and her eyes wanted nothing more than to stick around and explore further.

The words came out before she could stop them. "Your wife was a fool."

Their eyes met and held. Molly wrapped her arms

around her waist, her mouth going dry. Why had she said that?

She'd never felt this unsteady around a man. Not even Gary.

Fear of flying. It had thrown everything out of whack. Including her emotions.

It made sense. She'd met Blake and almost immediately had received a shot of adrenaline large enough to bring down an elephant. Put her nerves on edge enough times, and her reactions to him were bound to become ingrained, just like Pavlov's dog.

Ding, ding, ding. She could almost hear the little bell that had sent the poor dog's salivary glands into a frenzy.

At least she didn't drool.

Yet.

A man peeked inside the hangar door. "Plane's fueled up and ready to go."

Blake straightened, his gaze slipping away. "Thanks."

Once on the plane, he checked switches and buttons, a dizzying combination she couldn't even begin to grasp. He'd said she could fly if she had to. She didn't see how. Nothing on that panel made any sense to her.

"Buckle in." His voice had gone back to pilot mode—not that the pitch was any lower than it was on the ground. He just infused it with a dose of calm certainty that said all would be well.

Yeah. And her nervous system still wasn't buying it. Not yet, anyway. Fastening her seat belt, she pulled in a deep breath. "You sure you're not too tired to fly back?"

"I'm fine." He glanced to the side. "Do you need to take something?"

"I'll be okay." Sure she would.

All too soon they were speeding down the runway, then into the air. To her surprise, her stomach tagged along for the ride this time. *Yay.* That was a step in the right direction.

"You're clutching again."

"What?"

"Hands."

She glanced down and blew her breath out in frustration. "Sorry." She released her grip.

"I really am a decent pilot."

His tone held not a hint of boasting. He wanted to reassure her. Nothing more.

"I know." She held her arms out straight and wiggled her fingers. "Look…no hands."

He sat up, rolling his shoulders as if relieving an ache. "Do that while landing, and I'll be suitably impressed."

"I bet I can." *Gulp. What?*

But it worked. As they swooped down toward Dutch Harbor with its minuscule landing strip three hours later, she pressed herself deep into her seat, but held her hands up dutifully. They shook harder than the plane had during that first storm, but she kept them where they were. She did close her eyes, however.

They touched down—the lightest of bumps telling her they'd made it back to the island. Still alive. She parted her lids as Blake taxied off the runway, following the guidance of the ground crew. Once there, the engines shut down with a sigh of relief.

"Wow! Did you see that? I did it! No hands." No one was more surprised than she was.

"You certainly did."

He unstrapped his harness and shoved it away before turning toward her. The flare of heat in his gaze made her breath catch in her throat. Her lips parted.

Had she done something wrong?

Without a word he curved his hand around the back of

her neck and hauled her toward him. She barely had time to gasp in a desperate bid to get some air into her lungs before his mouth came down hard on hers.

CHAPTER FOURTEEN

MOLLY gripped his shoulders, frowning when her buckle held her in place, not allowing her to get closer.

Suddenly the strap gave away. Had he undone it?

She didn't care. Her arms went around his neck as his lips continued to move over hers, the hard initial kiss softening into something closer to coaxing.

No need. She was already there. So there.

Fingers delved into her hair and cupped her head, tilting her face to the side just a bit, allowing him to deepen the kiss.

From somewhere within her a moan rose to the surface—just like in her dream earlier. Blake broke contact to look into her eyes. Evidently okay with what he saw, he dipped in for another kiss.

A tattoo rapped against the side of the plane, stopping him.

"Damn."

They both looked toward the sound and saw a couple members of the small airport's ground crew grinning up at them, one backing up with a wrench he'd evidently used to tap on the plane. He made some kind of signal.

Blake swore softly again, his breathing as ragged as hers was. The hand in her hair slid away, and he gave the crew a thumbs-up sign. "They need to secure the plane so they can move on to the next one coming in."

"Oh."

Molly quickly cleaned up the medical area in back, while Blake shut down the controls. They then walked toward the parking lot in relative silence. But the feeling of his lips on hers thrummed through her, refusing to let up no matter how hard she tried to shift her mind to other things. And the look in his eyes...

She shuddered, digging in her purse for her keys, gripping them tightly once she found them. Only her car wasn't here. It was still at the clinic.

"You okay?" He'd come up behind her.

Please don't let that be regret in his voice.

She turned to face him, wishing she had something to lean against for support. "Not really. You?"

He bent close, his warm breath brushing her ear as he murmured, "No. Definitely not. My plane isn't the place I would have chosen for any of this to happen."

Her heart leapt. He had a preferred venue? And just where was that?

"No?"

He brushed a lock of hair behind her ear. "I'm not sure what's going on between us, but am I mistaken in thinking that kiss wasn't completely one-sided?"

A soft laugh broke free. "You aren't mistaken."

Searching her eyes, he said, "I'm trying to do the right thing here, Molly, but I'm having a hell of a time."

"The right thing being?"

"Taking you back to the clinic and letting you drive away."

She swallowed hard, the chill of the air seeping through Blake's coat. "Is that what you want?"

"I don't know what I want."

"Would it help if I said I didn't want to drive away? If I asked you to take me back to your place instead of the clinic?"

Did you just proposition the man? Heat washed over her face.

He went very still. "If we go back there, it won't be to sleep."

"I know."

"And you still want to?"

She nodded, afraid to let her tongue loose again. Who knew what it might come up with next?

He took her keys from her hand and pocketed them as if afraid she might change her mind and make a run for it. How? Her car was nowhere around.

"You can take me to pick up my car later this morning."

"I don't think so." He took her hand and backed her toward his own car. "If you come home with me, you're mine until this afternoon. No one expects us back before then."

The sensual promise behind those words kicked her heart into gear, just like when he throttled up the engines of the plane as he prepared to take off. She should be afraid of the dark gleam in his eyes. But she wasn't. She felt nothing but elation. Wonder. The gorgeous pilot who'd taken none of the women from the hospital to bed was taking her home with him.

Thinking about the "whys" would do her no good. Better to just sit back and enjoy their time together, no matter how brief. They reached the passenger door of his red Mustang. He didn't open it, evidently waiting for a response to his declaration.

"Okay. This afternoon, then." She hesitated. "I do need to show up at the clinic after that."

"I know." A slight frown appeared between his brows

before the muscles released, and he opened the door, allowing her to slide inside.

He went around to his side of the car and climbed in, slamming the door behind him. He gripped the steering wheel for a moment before shoving the keys into the ignition. She waited for him to turn the engine over, but he just sat there.

Second thoughts? "Are you sure you want to do this?"

"Yes." He swiveled toward her and brushed his knuckles across her cheek. "Just trying to remember something."

She was pretty sure he wasn't trying to remember how to actually *do* it. It had to be like riding a bike. Once you took the training wheels off, you never forgot how to pedal. Ever. Especially someone like him.

Leaning over, he closed in for a brief kiss. "I don't think I have anything at the house."

"Anything?" The last thing she wanted to think about was eating. "If you're talking about food, I'm not really hungry."

A low chuckle broke free. "Not food. Definitely not food. But I do need to stop at the store."

"Oh." She realized what he meant. *"Oh!"*

His fingers drifted down her cheek to her throat, pausing at the spot where her pulse was beating up a storm. "I wish I didn't live so damned far away."

"Is anything far on this island?"

She understood what he meant, though. She wanted his lips back on hers. Didn't want to stop at any stupid drug store, but for once she wasn't being the sensible one. Ever since she'd agreed to take this job, it seemed her ability to stop and make rational decisions had been tossed into the nearest medical waste receptacle. But taking her hands off the seat of that plane and holding them up for him to see had given her a rush like none she'd ever felt. Was this what her father had experienced on every flight? If so, she could understand his fascination with his job.

His fingers curved around her nape like they had on the plane, his thumb still strumming the side of her throat. The heat his touch generated had nothing to do with the cool fall temperatures and everything to do with warming her from within. She could barely believe she'd soon be burrowing deep under the covers with this man.

Hurry!

Maybe something in her eyes gave her away, because he leaned in for another soft kiss before starting the car and backing out of the parking space. Once headed away from the airport, he located a store in short order. "I'll be right back."

"Okay."

Was she doing the right thing here? She'd been dead set against getting involved with another colleague. Almost seeing Gary at the hospital should have knocked some sense into her.

On the other hand, by spending this time with Blake, maybe she could funnel away some of the growing tension between them and life could return to normal. She could look on it as a quick fling—plenty of her peers indulged in brief affairs after all. Otherwise, if she took this too seriously and something went wrong—she bit her lip—things could get ugly really fast.

Blake was back within five minutes, toting a small plastic bag. See-through. Heavens. Nothing like advertising what they were about to do to the world. The whole island would probably know in short order.

He climbed inside and tossed the bag into the backseat. "Do you want to take a nap?"

"Can't."

Switching the heater vents on, he pulled out of the lot. "I hope there's a good reason for that."

"Definitely." Against her better judgment, she gave voice to something she'd thought of earlier. "You never considered dating anyone at the hospital?"

"No."

A one-word answer. Okay, so this was something he wasn't anxious to discuss. And he was obviously smarter than she was in that regard.

What did it matter? Neither of them was looking for anything permanent.

He surprised her by expanding on his answer. "As you've guessed, my marriage wasn't exactly a happy one once I took this job."

She took a second to digest his words. He'd said his wife had threatened to divorce him if he didn't stop flying fighter jets. He'd done as she asked, and she still hadn't been happy? "She didn't want you to fly at all?"

"Oh, she was fine with my flying. Just not as a military pilot. And certainly not as a bush pilot. And she wanted nothing to do with Unalaska. She wanted to me to change over to commercial passenger jets. Go back to living in Anchorage, or move to another—bigger—city. I tried, but I hated it. And she hated that I hated it." His jaw tightened. "Sorry. I don't know why I brought that up."

A subtle warning, maybe? A declaration that he'd choose his job over any relationship?

"My fault. I asked about your personal life." She was going to ruin everything, if she wasn't careful. "Can we rewind?"

He paused. "To how far back?"

"To before." Maybe he'd changed his mind after all? "Do you still want to go through with this?"

"Do you?"

She blinked at him. "Yes. Definitely."

His slow smile drew her to him, along with that damned crease in his cheek. "Good answer."

"It *was* good, wasn't it?" She forced some bravado into her voice. Actually, the courage came from knowing he still wanted her.

His hand slid over hers. "Yes, but it's about to get a whole lot better."

First the silky scarf around her neck, then those small pink buttons on the sweater that lay just beneath the jacket. One button at a time.

Maybe it wasn't the coolest move to plan exactly which pieces of clothing would be the first to go, but the pressure was building. Not just behind his zipper but in his head and in his chest. He wasn't sure if it was pleasure or desperation. Maybe a mixture of the two.

A wave of need had washed over him as soon as she'd unclenched her hands from the seat. Yes, she'd been scared, but that fear had changed to elation once they'd landed. He'd seen it in her face. And there'd been no hint that she wanted to stay in Anchorage. In fact, she'd been anxious to get back to the island. Yes, it had been because of her ex, but he sensed she liked it here.

He drove the streets by rote, clicking his blinker on and off at the appropriate times. When he finally reached his driveway, he pulled into it, seeing the place through critical eyes as he shut off the engine. Unimaginative white paint coated everything in sight. Empty flower beds. Lawn in need of a good cut.

He hadn't taken very good care of his parents' home.

Because it wasn't a home. Not any more. It was a place

to sleep and not much else. The last woman he'd brought here had been his wife.

No one else. Until Molly.

He swallowed. It didn't mean anything. His career kept him busy.

"Aren't you going to invite me in?" Molly's low voice came from beside him, a hint of uncertainty coloring the words.

Damn.

"Yeah, I was just noticing what sorry shape the place is in."

"It's fine, Blake." She hesitated. "Or would you rather go back to my place?"

"Too far away." Leaning across the seat, he kissed her, preferring actions to pretty words. He'd learned during his marriage that he didn't always know what to say to a woman.

And she tasted wonderful. This was so much better than talking anyway. He raised his head. "Ready to go in?"

Her tongue scooped across her lower lip. "In a minute. After you do that again."

"Gladly." He smiled and drew her close, the heady feel of her open mouth calling him home. Unable to resist, he slid inside, taking time to explore the textures and softness he found there. His body responded, knowing that as good as this felt—and damn if it didn't feel good—there were other things that were going to set his furnace burning on high. So many things he wanted to do to her…for her.

Molly's fingers slid into his hair, her thumbs following the shape of his ears and stroking along them. His whole scalp turned warm. That heat traveling down his jaw and centering on their joined mouths. Her tongue slid along his, the exact way he imagined her bare calf would float along the back of his thigh as he entered her. Slowly, drawing out each ounce of sensation.

He needed to get her into the house, but he couldn't seem to move from this spot. Couldn't stop kissing her.

Who needed to breathe? All he wanted—needed—was this woman and the crazy mix of emotions she pulled from him.

The sound of a car slowly traveling down the street made him pull back.

Neighborhood watch.

The two elderly gentlemen heading up the program wouldn't hesitate to stop and put their hands to the sides of his tinted windows to see what was going on inside the vehicle. The last thing he wanted was for them to find him making out with the island's new doctor.

He glanced at her, taking in her flushed cheeks, the plump red lips that looked totally ravished. "Let's go inside."

"Okay."

Oh, yeah. That husky word sent any number of sensual thoughts roaring through his skull.

He opened his door and got out, moving around to open Molly's door. He found her reaching into the backseat, straining to get something.

Of course, the condom package. He'd completely forgotten. Not good.

She exited with the plastic bag and handed it to him with a sly smile. Being a doctor, protection was probably something she stressed time and time again to her patients. He should be glad she was so careful, but at the moment he felt clumsy and unsure.

How long had it been again?

Too long.

He glanced at the street, but the car had disappeared.

No way of telling if it really had been the neighborhood patrol guys or not. But he didn't want to wait around for them to come cruising back, in case it had been.

Molly wrapped her hands around his arm and snuggled close as he flipped his key ring around his index finger until it landed on his house key. "If a car drives by, don't make eye contact with whoever's inside."

"What?"

He rolled his eyes. Why had he said that? "I have some nosy neighbors."

"Is it a problem that I'm here?"

This was why he should stick to kissing and leave the talking to men who did it better than he did. Like Mark.

His jaw tightened. Molly was here with *him*, not with Mark. "No, it's not a problem. They'll just talk your ear off if you let them." He pulled her closer. "And talking's the last thing I want to do right now."

And that, my dear Sherlock, was the truth.

As soon as they walked through the door, he threw the keys and the little bag on the table in the entryway and drew her against him. "Do you want something to drink?"

"No."

"Eat?"

"It depends. Is it something interesting?" She sent him another knowing smile that had his mind off and running in all directions.

Exactly how did you answer a question like that? "Depends on what you find interesting."

"You."

"That's what I was hoping you'd say."

Blake's mouth was on hers in an instant, all the hunger he'd shoved to the side washing over him in a flood that threatened to swamp his senses. Her hands gripped his shirt, whether to pull him closer or to keep from being shoved backward by the force of his kiss, he had no idea. But whatever the reason, he liked it. Liked that she seemed just as eager for him as he was for her.

With one hand on the small of her back and the other cupping her head, he eased her backward step by step, never taking his lips from hers.

How many times had he come home late at night so exhausted he'd found his way to the bedroom in the dark? Lots. He could do this with both hands tied behind his back. Or better yet, with Molly's hands tied behind her back.

Before they'd covered five steps, she tugged her mouth from his, bringing a frown to his face. "Bag," she muttered.

"Your purse?" *Stop talking and keep kissing, woman.*

"Condoms."

"Right." He let go of her for the two seconds it took him to cross the hall and retrieve the bag. That was the second time he'd almost forgotten them and the second time she'd remembered. Was he really that messed up over the thought of having her at last?

Oh, yeah.

Condom package in hand, he moved toward her, only to find she was already in the living room, her head tilted as she studied something on the wall. Reaching up, she touched a framed snapshot, her head swiveling toward him. The question was there in her eyes, even before her mouth formed the words.

"Blake, where did you get this?"

CHAPTER FIFTEEN

"Your father gave it to me."

Molly's breathing thickened as she stared at the picture of her dad beside an airplane very much like the one Blake now piloted. A smile wreathed his face, while one hand rested on the aircraft beside him. She could almost imagine him caressing the metal framework in pride. She hadn't seen her father this happy in a long time. "When was it taken?"

"Does it matter?" He moved to stand beside her, draping one arm around her waist, making no move to take up where they'd left off.

Her fingers touched the face in the photograph, remembering patting it as a child. He'd smiled back then, too. Big beaming smiles that had made her heart swell with love. "He looks happy."

"Yes."

"Did you take the picture?"

He nodded. "I had it framed for his birthday." He paused, a muscle working in his jaw. "He gave it back to me a couple of weeks before his plane went down. Said it was a graduation present for completing my training."

His fingers tightened on her waist. "He was a good friend."

"I'm glad." Her brain struggled to work through seeing her father through someone else's lens. "I miss him."

"I know."

She believed he really did know. "I never really saw this part of my dad's life. My mom tried to protect me. Probably too much. She ended up resenting my father for keeping his job; she said it meant more to him than we did. She always badgered him to…" a sudden thought came to her "…quit. To become a commercial pilot. Like your wife wanted you to be. That's strange. Did you guys ever talk about it? Did you know about my mom?"

The arm behind her back stiffened. "We talked about a lot of things."

They had talked about it. Something about that hurt. Like a stranger peering into her bedroom window and seeing all her secrets.

Well, Blake hadn't been a stranger to her dad, but he'd been an unknown to her at the time.

"I see."

Blake turned her to face her. "He loved you very much, Molly. He was so proud of your accomplishments, that you were making great grades in med school."

Her vision went misty, and she blinked a couple of times. Blake came back into view.

Strong. Stable.

A man her father had been able to count on as a confidant. Someone with whom he had shared his deepest, darkest secrets, and never worried about them getting out. The way Blake had promised to keep hers.

In that moment, her heart expanded with an emotion she couldn't quite identify. An amalgamation of grief, wonder, and something else. Something she refused to put a name to. Instead, she took Blake's hands, the plastic bag he held crackling as she did.

"Take me to bed."

His Adam's apple dipped as he stared into her face. "You sure?"

"Never more sure of anything in my life."

Before she could say another word, he scooped her into his arms and carried her down the hall—her father's picture receding from her sight, his bright smile burned into her memory. She snuggled closer, lifting her head to plant several kisses along the underside of Blake's jaw. She wanted this man. A man her father had cared about. Maybe it was one more step toward finding peace with his memory.

That was what that wave of emotion had been about. It had to be.

Would Blake care that she was using him to exorcize this particular demon?

No, because he was using her to gain a little satisfaction of his own, so they could call it even, after tonight.

They entered a darkened room. She couldn't see, but Blake moved surely toward the center of the space and set her down. Her back met the softness of a coverlet and she sank into the welcoming warmth.

"Lights on or off?" He leaned down to kiss her, smoothing her hair away from her face as he did.

"Don't leave me." The words had nothing to do with the lights, and everything to do with being as close to this man as she could get.

"I won't." He settled next to her, resting on his elbow. All she could see was the glittering of his eyes as he looked down at her.

"Kiss me." She wanted to lose herself in him. Or was it to find herself? Everything inside her twisted and turned, nothing seeming to make sense any more.

Nothing.

Except Blake.

He did as she asked, kissing her softly. Too softly. She wanted more. Asked for it, her tongue sliding along the seam of his lips and pushing inside.

A groan rose from his throat as she delved deeper. The sound intoxicated her, made her think of all the ways she could make him growl with pleasure. She wanted to do each and every one of them before the night was over. And more. So much more.

Needing to keep him close, she reached up to hold him in place, the warm texture of his neck drawing her attention. She tested it, the tiny hairs at his nape tickling her fingertips.

While she explored the small amount of exposed skin, Blake curved a hand around her rib cage, the splayed fingertips spanning half her width.

Big. Everything about him was solid, making her feel… what? Weak.

No, not weak.

Cherished. That was it.

Her hands moved down his back, bunching his shirt and tugging it from his waistband. More skin. Warm. Inviting. Her half-closed lids melted against each other, fusing shut.

That silky first touch of skin deceived, though. Because beneath that softness lay ridges of muscle that were firm. Strong. She pressed her fingertips against them experimentally.

He raised his head to look at her. "You okay?"

"Yes. Except for this." She tugged harder on his shirt, using her actions to ask him for help.

In a second he'd shrugged out of it, casting it to the side.

She sat up as well, running her fingers over his chest, the lightest smattering of crisp hair meeting her touch. It was too dark to see the color, but she imagined it dark brown. She followed the trail down, loving the way his abs shuddered beneath her hands as she slowly skimmed over them. The band of hair narrowed below his belly button where the waistband of his trousers halted her progress. But not for long.

"Wait." The graveled command stopped her in her tracks.

Surely he wasn't about to back out. Was he?

Oh, please. Don't.

"I'm not sure I unders—"

"It's…" He cupped her face and kissed her. "It's been a long time."

She saw. Smiled. "It's okay. It's been a while for me, too."

As if she'd just released a spring that had been holding him back, his next kiss was anything but tender. Devouring her in the way she'd craved from the moment he'd carried her through that doorway.

Her shirt came off, his fingers tracing down her spine until he came to the catch on her bra. Hardly slowing him down, he unlatched it as he continued on his way. His tongue pushed into her mouth, sending a shot of heat rushing down her stomach and pooling between her legs. She shifted closer, wishing she'd remained on the bed instead of sitting up. Body parts didn't match up this way.

She shimmied out of her bra and let it fall between them, pressing against him the best she could, the heat of his body hardening her nipples in an instant. He released a shuddery breath, his hands moving from her back to her sides, skating over the farthest edges of her breasts. She leaned back again, hoping he'd take the hint.

He did.

Warm hands covered her, his palms creating gentle friction as he squeezed.

Oh, yes. Just like that.

His mouth soon followed, one hand curving around her right breast as his tongue lapped against the peak with slow wet strokes.

She wanted him down on the bed, but when she tried to urge him in that direction, he stayed right where he was, suckling her until she thought she would explode from that alone.

"Blake, please." The words came at the end of a long moan.

Her fingers went to his buckle, and this time he didn't try to stop her. She threaded the end backward until it released. Pushing it aside, she found the button on his khakis and fiddled with it, finally getting it through the hole. *Almost there.* He kissed his way to her other breast. Applied gentle suction. A wave of pleasure swept over her, and her hands went slack under the onslaught, all rational thought fleeing. It took several seconds to find her place and the tab of his zipper.

Zip!

The sound pulled Blake up short, and he looked into her eyes. "Last chance to back out."

Was he serious?

"That chance came and went a long time ago."

He chuckled, but it sounded strained. "Good, I'm glad you said that."

Easing her down onto the bed—something she'd tried to get him to do a few minutes ago with no success—he undid her slacks in record time, skimming them and her panties over her legs and letting them drop to the floor.

She flung out a hand, searching for the clear plastic bag.

"I have it," he murmured, standing and divesting himself of the rest of his clothing. When he came back down, he was already covered. A flicker of disappointment went over her when her hand closed around him. She'd wanted to feel every silky hard inch of him with no barriers between them. At least with her hand, if nothing else.

Next time. He'd promised her until this afternoon.

His palm brushed over her stomach in light gentle strokes, moving closer inch by inch. Her hips pushed up, needing something he seemed determined to withhold. She tightened her hand around him and the hissing sound of his indrawn breath made her smile. Two could play at this game.

Then he touched her, and all bets were off. His fingers drew something wild up from the pit of her stomach, but before she had time to put a name to it, he'd parted her legs and thrust into her.

Hard. Before she'd had time to think, to prepare…to hold off.

Her breath exploded from her lungs as a torrent of sensation ripped through her, her fingers digging into his back as she clenched around him again and again. He buried his face in her neck and groaned out her name, the sound agonized as he rode with her up the crest…followed her over the edge.

The weight of his body was the only thing anchoring her to the bed, to the earth—and she clung to him for all she was worth, waiting for her frantic heartbeats to slow. Blake's lips touched her neck in light, brushing kisses that worked magic on her soul.

"Sorry," he murmured, his breath warm against her skin.

She turned her head so her chin rested on his cheek. "For what?"

"I meant that to last a lot longer."

"Yeah. Me, too." She couldn't hold back the laugh, so glad he hadn't apologized for making love to her. Or for anything else. A quick arrival she could handle. Regret she couldn't.

She slid her hands down his back, his skin moist even though the room was cool.

Rolling to the side, he took her with him, dragging the bedspread over both of them.

A huge yawn rolled through her despite her best efforts to hold it at bay, drawing a chuckle from him. Between flying to Anchorage and back and caring for a critical patient, she was suddenly exhausted.

He smoothed her hair back, and something about the gesture touched her, just as it had the other times he'd done it. "Sleep," he said.

If she did, this day would end far too soon. But her eyelids were heavy. Already drifting shut. "Wake me later?" she whispered on a sigh.

"You can count on it."

"Don't tell anyone at the clinic about this, okay?"

He smiled. How many things had she asked him to keep to himself so far? Three? Four? The list was growing fast. And heaven help him, if he didn't want it to keep on growing.

Blake gave her a quick kiss as he cleared away the dishes from a very late lunch. "It'll be our secret."

"That's right, Mister Fighter Pilot, you said you were good at those." Propping her elbows on the counter, the motion of her hips twisted the barstool back and forth, the tails of his dress shirt parting to reveal a tantalizing length of leg. He'd handed her the garment after she'd got up, so she'd have something to wear while her other clothes went through the washer and dryer.

Damn.

Three times, and he still wanted her. How could that

be? A twinge of apprehension came over him. Some things should definitely be kept to himself.

"Secrets and I are like this." He crossed his fingers, using the symbol to reassure himself as well as her.

Being with a woman couldn't be this simple. Not for him. He was the master of jumping into things with both eyes shut and then coming to rue them in the cold light of day.

Like Molly?

His teeth ground together. He hoped not. This was one night he didn't want to look back on with regret.

She hopped off her barstool. "I'll help clean up."

"When do you want to get back?"

"Soon." She wrinkled her nose. "I probably should head over to the house and put on a different set of clothes."

"I'll take you." Glancing at his watch, he found himself glad to put a little space between them. He couldn't think with her swiveling back and forth on that stool, because it brought up thoughts of her swiveling back and forth on him. Something they didn't have time for. "Do you want to shower here, or wait until you get home?"

"Here." She sent him a smile. "Want to join me?"

He gave a rough laugh that he hoped sounded pained. "I never thought I'd say this, but I think you've worn me out."

It was a lie, and he knew it. His body was ready to take her again and a shower sounded…

Dangerous. Far too intimate. To be standing under the hot pounding spray with nothing between them but soapy lather, and slick needy bodies…

Hell, what was wrong with him?

It was too soon. He'd jumped the gun. Again. He should have waited until he knew for sure she was going to stay, because if she suddenly balked—suddenly decided she couldn't handle flying any more—he was screwed. Or if she decided she wanted to go back to Anchorage, it would be even worse.

Unaware of his thoughts, she pulled the shirt a little lower over her thighs. "Your loss." Walking toward the bathroom, the saucy twitch of her hips was full of invitation. "If you change your mind, you know where I'll be."

As soon as she was out of sight—the door to the bathroom clicking shut—he threw the dishrag on the counter and dragged a hand through his hair. His body was an inferno of need, his chest aching with something he dared not define.

She was brave, resourceful, willing to face her fears—so far.

Was she out of that shirt yet?

The sound of the shower turning on confirmed she was. He grew harder.

Time to recite all the reasons he shouldn't go in there.

He stood in the center of his kitchen, not a single thought coming to mind. He tried. Really he did.

You shouldn't go in there because...

Ah, hell. He left the dishes on the bar and headed for the bathroom. If he was going to screw up his life, he might as well finish the job.

CHAPTER SIXTEEN

"Hey, is this hard?" Molly picked up a video game case that was lying on a bookshelf as she waited for him to get dressed. Her legs were having a dickens of a time holding her up, and she'd been forced to walk around, trying to convince her muscles to do their job.

He peered around the corner of his closet door and gave her a smile. "Not yet. But it could be."

She lobbed a pillow at him. "I meant this."

Crossing over to her, he glanced at the cover. "A flight simulator?"

"You got me thinking." She turned the cover over and read the description. "I said I couldn't fly even if you were passed out at the wheel. I was joking at the time, but what if it really happened? Or what if you were incapacitated?"

His brows lifted. "You mean like now?"

"I'm serious." A laugh came out and belied the words.

He took the case from her hands and stared at the cover. "We can try it out if you want, but I thought you weren't interested in flying. That you were going to tolerate it for the sake of your job."

Yes, she'd meant those words at the time, but a subtle shift had taken place. Not only had her father loved flying but it was Blake's life. And because of that...

No, don't go there. Not yet.

But even as the thought whispered through her mind, she was already searching for an excuse to see him again. To not walk away and forget this morning ever happened.

But why? They'd still be working together, so they'd have to see each other.

But it wouldn't be the same. She'd lose something special once she left this house. They might have known each other for a few short weeks, but if Blake considered their time together a one-night stand...

Surely not. She'd sensed something desperate in his lovemaking that last time in the shower, as if he was fighting something inside himself. Whatever it was, it hadn't stopped him from bracing his hands against the tile and bringing their time together to a shattering conclusion.

One that had left her limp and shaking.

He'd had to wrap his arms around her to keep from sliding to the floor in a heap. In the harsh light of day, the memory sent a shiver of fear through her. She'd never experienced goodbye sex before, but it was probably pretty similar to what they'd done.

Hello and goodbye all in the space of twelve hours. Maybe he was the smart one.

"When are you off next?" he asked.

"Not until Saturday." Almost a week away.

"I could come over and install the game on your computer, if you'd like. Show you how to work it. Then you could try it out at your leisure."

She paused. "I could make us lunch."

"Will it involve horseradish?"

Molly laughed again, remembering his reaction to Jed's sandwich. "You'll have to wait and see. Think of it as expanding your horizons." She tapped the game he held in his hand. "Something we should both consider doing."

* * *

The week crawled by, and Blake didn't appear at the clinic once. Neither did he call. By Friday morning her mood had slid downhill, landing at the bottom with a splat.

She met Sammi outside the exam room with a scowl. "Nail guns should not be sold without a permit."

The CHA held out the set of pliers Molly had asked her to hunt down. "Hey, *I* have a nail gun at home."

"Yeah, but you didn't use it to fasten your hand to a crate on one of the fishing boats." She rolled her eyes. "How is it that a man who can open a beer bottle with his teeth can't stand the thought of pulling a nail out of his own hand?"

Sammi winced. "Sounds like someone I know could use some chocolate. Mark hasn't called?"

"What?"

"You said you went out with him a couple of weeks ago." The other woman studied the bright yellow polish on her nails.

It took Molly a minute to even remember the date. "We did, but I think we're destined to be friends. Nothing more." All she could hope was that Sammi hadn't heard about her spending a large chunk of time at Blake's house.

No one knew. And he'd sworn he'd never tell.

Although why it was okay for Sammi to pair her up with Mark and not Blake she had no idea. Maybe because she was still smarting from needing to be with him more than he evidently wanted to be with her.

Hurt swept through her.

Sammi touched her shoulder, bringing her back to the present. "You okay?"

"Fine." She sighed. "The clinic's just been busy this week."

"I heard the head injury patient is going to recover. The

blown pupil was from a previous eye injury. I thought it was from being hit by the crab pot."

"Me, too." She squeezed the other woman's arm. "Hey, listen. I'm sorry for being such a grouch."

"Don't worry about it. It happens." Sammi shrugged. "What are you doing this weekend?"

She wasn't sure. Blake had said he'd come over on Saturday and install the flight simulator on her computer, but she had no idea if that was still on or not. "Samita and I are going to lounge around the house and be lazy."

"If you get bored, call and we can do something."

"Thanks, Sammi, I will." Being with her new friend would definitely be better than moping around all day. "I need to get back to my patient."

Fifteen minutes of wrestling and her patient's hand was free of the board and the nail. She examined the wound again. The metal had shot into the space between the second and third metacarpals. No actual bone involvement, just skin. A stitch or two, a tetanus shot, and some antibiotics, and he'd be as good as new.

"I'd like you to give this hand a break for a few days," she said as she sutured both the entry and exit wounds.

"My captain's already threatened to kick my butt if I touch that gun again. He lost almost a whole day bringing me back in to have it looked at." He checked out the repair and closed his hand into an experimental fist. "Doesn't hurt at all."

Molly dropped the needle and tweezers back onto the tray to be sterilized and stood, patting his shoulder. "Wait until the lidocaine wears off. You're going to want to take some ibuprofen before that happens—six hundred milligrams worth—in about an hour." She smiled. "But at least you won't be carrying a board around with you any more."

He glanced at the instrument tray. "Uh…Doc. You don't

suppose I could have that nail you plucked from me, do you? I want to show it to my boys."

Her brows went up. "On one condition."

"Yeah, what's that?"

"That you promise to teach them about tool safety and practice it yourself from here on out."

The burly fisherman gave her a sheepish grin. "It's a deal."

Rinsing off the offending nail and then dropping it into his hand, they both stood. Her patient slid the sharp object into the front pocket of his worn jeans, causing her to cringe. Hopefully he would remember it was there before getting into his car to drive away. She really, *really* didn't want to have to pull it out of him again—especially not from that region. "Take care, okay?"

"Will do."

Pushing through the room's heavy door, Molly watched him walk toward the reception area.

A few strands of hair fell over her forehead, and she shoved them back, the locks feeling as lank and lifeless as she did. She moved into the hallway and turned right, heading in the same direction her patient had.

"You busy?"

The familiar voice caused her heart to skip a beat. She stopped in her tracks, then spun around, finding Blake standing behind her, arms folded across his chest. "You scared me. Where did you come from?"

"Sammi said you had a patient, so I thought I'd wait for you in the hall. Anything serious?"

"Nothing a two by four to the head wouldn't cure."

On second thought, maybe she could use one of those herself, judging from the way her heart was still ricocheting around in her chest at the sight of him.

"Ouch. Bad day?"

"About normal for a Friday." She could be distant, too. Really she could.

He nodded, studying her face for a moment. "Are we still on for tomorrow?"

It took her a minute to realize he was talking about coming over to her house for lunch. Somehow it really miffed her that he hadn't offered any explanation for his absence, or even tried to see her. "Sure. If you're still up for it."

"I am." He paused as if trying to come up with the right words. "Listen, sorry I haven't been around. I don't want you to think…"

Everything inside her clenched. Was he about to give her the we've-had-some-fun-but-let's-just-be-friends speech?

Holding up a hand, she tried to head him off. "Don't worry about it."

A small frown appeared between his brows, and he lowered his voice. "I started to come by the clinic a couple of times, but I remembered what you said about keeping our time together a secret. I didn't think you'd want me hanging around."

I didn't think you'd want me hanging around. Those words made her tummy do a back flip. So that was why he'd stayed away.

She did want him to hang around. Very much.

She gave him a smile. "I thought you were going to say… Never mind."

"Then I had to go to Fairbanks on Wednesday and Thursday."

"A patient?" Surely she would have heard or been asked to go along.

"No. I had some property that's been up for sale for a while. The Realtor finally found a buyer, and I had to meet my ex-wife to sign the papers."

Relief turned to dismay. He'd met his ex-wife and stayed for two days? How long did it take to sign a piece of paper?

You're being unreasonable, Molly. He just said he was thinking about coming by the clinic.

"That's okay. Did the sale go through?"

He glanced down the hallway, then tugged a lock of her hair, letting it fall back in place. "It did. I'm glad that's over."

If he was glad, she was glad. Except he'd made no move to kiss her.

Why would he? She'd asked him to keep things quiet. Besides, no sense in either of them getting too serious. They were colleagues. That was one strike. A second strike was that the hospital might not even renew her contract at the clinic after the year was up. Which meant she'd end up...not in Anchorage, where she might still see Blake from time to time, but in some other city. Probably in the lower forty-eight.

Where she'd never see him again.

Her heart tumbled even as she smiled and said she'd see him tomorrow.

Two strikes. One more and Molly would be forced to call it a day.

She needed to pray that she could pull herself back together if that happened.

CHAPTER SEVENTEEN

BLAKE used his elbow to ring the bell, his hands full of flight-simulator equipment.

The door opened a few seconds later, and Molly, dressed in snug jeans and a green silky top with some kind of fluttery sleeves, smiled in welcome, Samita by her side. Her feet were bare, soft pink polish on her toenails.

No music came from inside today, which was a good thing. Although those dainty toes…

He swallowed. Maybe this wasn't such a good idea after all.

"Come in."

Too late to run now. He'd gone out last night for some liquid courage, hoping to get up the nerve to call her and say he'd had second thoughts. He'd run into Mark at the bar and immediately tensed, but his buddy had surprised him by clapping him on the back and wishing him luck.

"With what?" he'd asked.

Mark had responded with raised eyebrows, slugging back his first shot of whiskey and then asking for another.

His friend knew.

The serial dater of Dutch Harbor was actually stepping aside instead of pursuing a woman who'd caught his interest. The agreement passed between the two old friends without a word being said. Blake used to think Mark and

Sammi had something special going on, but after Mark had come home from the military something changed between them. The two barely spoke any more.

He came back to the present with a bump, realizing Molly was still waiting for him to enter the house. She took some of the items from his hands as he moved past her. "The computer's in the living room."

The scent of some kind of grilled meat permeated the air, making his mouth water. "Whatever you're making smells delicious."

"Pork chops. They should be ready in a few minutes."

Leading him to an oak, slant-front desk with delicate curved legs, she folded down the front panel, revealing a laptop computer inside. "I hope this is okay."

"It's fine."

She paused for a second, and an awkward silence ensued. "Do you think you could set it up while I finish lunch?"

"Not a problem."

He pulled the computer forward onto the desktop, and waited for it to boot up. Glancing around the room, he noted everything was neatly put away—no more boxes lining the walls. She didn't have a lot of furniture, but what she did have looked comfortable.

A beige leather sofa, paired with a rustic plank coffee table, sat under the picture window, its sleek lines adding a modern touch to the traditional space. On top of the coffee table a trio of chunky candles had been arranged on a silver tray, a manila folder resting beside them. A small flatscreened television perched on a narrow table against an adjacent wall.

He smiled. The TV looked like a miniature version of his own. Men and women seemed to have different priorities in life. He couldn't imagine watching the Super Bowl on a screen that size. The players would look like ants.

He turned back to the computer, finding it ready to use. He first installed the program and then set up the yoke and pedals just as Molly walked into the dining area, carrying a platter. "Are you ready to eat?"

"Yep. Can I help?"

"The salad is on the counter in the kitchen. Would you mind bringing it in?"

Blake found a crystal bowl housing an assortment of greens and tomatoes. His stomach growled at the sight. He hadn't realized how hungry he was.

"It's just down-home cooking, hope that's all right," Molly said as he joined her.

"I can't think of anything better."

A line of plump pork chops—a sauce of some kind drizzled down the center of the tray—fired up his salivary glands. Along the outside of the chops lay new potatoes, a sliver of skin peeled away from each one.

It had been ages since he'd had a meal like this one. He normally subsisted on sandwiches or prepackaged meals. Seeing Molly standing there, her hands twisting together in uncertainty, made his chest ache with a strange sense of longing.

"Do you want wine? Or would you rather have iced tea?"

Neither. He wanted her.

But no way was he going to say that. He'd already decided he needed to hang back for a while and see how things went. His jump-in-with-both-feet tendencies were officially on vacation. "Wine would be great."

She handed him a glass, and they sat at the table. The meal was delicious, but his eyes were on Molly as she talked about her week at the clinic and asked about his work. She leaned forward, focusing intently on him as if she really cared what his boring day-to-day routine involved.

Enough about him.

"So how are you finding the islands so far?"

She sat back, sipping her wine. "They're different than I expected." She must have seen his frown, because she quickly added, "In a good way. I love Sammi and working at the clinic. The pace is just slower than what I'm used to."

"Unless we have an emergency." He remembered how lost she'd seemed at the hospital after they'd delivered their head-injury patient into the hands of other doctors. "Then it can be crazy for a while."

"Definitely." She paused, before setting her glass down. "Listen, about the way I ran out of the hospital the other day, I know I must have seemed totally off my rocker, but Gary, my ex, is persistent. We stopped seeing each other six months ago, but between him and my mother...well, let's just say I was happy when this job opened up."

"You don't have to explain." But it did answer a question that had lingered in his mind. She'd said she wanted to make peace with what her father had done, but he hadn't been able figure out why she'd waited until four years after his death to do that.

She shrugged. "Just thought you should know, in case it happens again. I'm sure we'll have more patients to transport."

"Is he harassing you?"

"No, he's not calling me any more, if that's what you mean. He just makes it a point to run into me at work." Her laugh was pained. "And my mom likes him—always has. Besides, he's firmly planted in Anchorage. It would take a natural disaster to uproot him."

"So *you* left instead."

"That pretty much sums it up." She cleared her throat. "So, moving on to another subject. What did you think of the sauce?"

Blake put his napkin on the table. "I think my empty plate speaks for itself."

"It had horseradish in it."

"You're kidding." The sauce had been mild and creamy with the barest hint of tang. Nothing like the molten lava he remembered his mom serving with roast beef.

"Nope." She smiled and sipped at her wine. "Like I said, maybe you should expand your horizons."

"Maybe I should." His eyes met hers and held, as they'd done several times during the meal.

She cleared her throat. "Well, if you're ready, we can take our drinks into the living room and you can show me how to work the game. I know you said you weren't interested in helping me through a twelve-step program, so I won't make you sit there and watch me."

"It's okay. We can just look at it as fun, with a little therapy thrown in for free."

They carried their wine into the living room. Samita, who'd been lounging on the coffee table, her front feet on the manila folder, glanced up at them and yawned.

"What if I crash?" she asked.

"We'll take some easy routes with nice long runways and work our way up to the challenging stuff."

Her brows went up, and she took another sip of wine. "We can accomplish that all in one day?"

"No, but we could work on it a little at a time."

Now that he'd said it, he realized what a royally stupid idea it was. He took a hefty swig of his wine. Why subject himself to the torture of sitting shoulder to shoulder with her, helping her handle the flight stick, when it was already putting all kinds of thoughts in his mind?

"Sounds like twelve steps to me," she muttered.

"Maybe it'll be a shorter version. Two or three steps." He set his glass down and started the program.

Molly dragged a chair from the dining room and sat next to him. Her scent surrounded him, bringing back memories of tangled limbs and the desperate kisses they'd shared a week ago.

Hell.

He should have taken her to a public place like a video arcade, but since he already had the game this had seemed like a good idea.

Yeah. A great one.

Kind of like the decision he'd made to put his arm around her and comfort her when she'd found the picture of her father on his wall.

Comfort her. What a crock.

A quick fling had seemed easy and painless when his lips had been welded to hers. But it hadn't been. He'd realized that the second they'd pulled away from each other.

"This was really nice of you, Blake."

"You might not think so after an hour or two."

He positioned the chair to have access to the rudder pedals he'd placed on the floor beneath their impromptu work area.

"Okay, you can sit here in front of the computer."

She licked her lips. "Could you do the takeoff, and I'll just fly it for a minute or two—under optimal conditions?"

"Sure." A sick feeling worked its way through his chest. One screw-up on his part, and he could make everything worse—could make her more afraid than ever. What had started out as a game suddenly seemed deadly serious.

He selected the absolute easiest program on the list. Molly leaned closer, the warmth and the scent of her shampoo flowed through him, lingering in places it didn't belong. It took everything he had not to lean closer and draw it deep into his lungs. "You can help me throttle up, how's that?"

As long as he didn't allow *himself* to get any more throttled up than he already was.

The screen flickered and showed a Cessna sitting on a long stretch of runway. "Do you want the view from inside the cockpit or outside?"

"You choose."

"Inside. It'll seem more realistic."

Her nose crinkled. "Great."

He couldn't hold back a smile. "It won't be as bad as you think."

"I'll hold you to that."

Switching the view, he tapped the throttle controls. "This is where much of your engine power comes from." He showed her how to increase and decrease the prop speed until she was able to hear the high-pitched whine that signaled they had enough power. "Ready?"

"I hope so."

"We're going to taxi into position." He used the foot pedals to turn the plane on the screen. Once he was lined up with the centerline of the runway, he took her hand and placed it on the throttle along with his, the coolness of her fingers in direct contrast to his overheated senses.

"We're going to take off. Push the throttle in, slowly. That's it." The speed increased, the plane moving forward. "Once we reach around sixty miles per hour, I'll pull back on the yoke to get the nose into the air."

The virtual plane moved faster and faster. Long runways like this one bored him under normal circumstances, but something in him felt energized today. Molly would experience a little of the thrill that he did on each takeoff. He couldn't look into her face to see if she was enjoying the experience or terrified as the wheels left the ground. "Now I'll straighten out a little bit, climbing slowly." He readjusted the throttle then let go of her hand to tap the altimeter on the screen. "When this reads six thousand five hundred feet, we'll start leveling off by pushing the yoke forward until the plane is flying straight. We can go as high as twelve thousand feet, but we won't today."

"My heart is in my throat right now, and I'm not even doing the flying. Is that normal?"

"There is no normal. Every flight is different."

It was true of flying. Maybe it was true of relationships as well.

Once they were at cruising altitude, he switched places with her. "All you'll need to do is keep it in the air. We'll do some easy turns. You don't have to worry about other planes. It's just you and me. With the sky all to ourselves."

Her head swiveled to glance at him for a second, her pupils widening before she turned back to the screen.

Okay, so the *sky to ourselves* narrative could have been stated a little differently. His attraction was already outside the boundaries he'd established for himself, and growing fast. And seeing her behind the controls of the plane only made it worse—played a mind game on him that could easily send everything spinning out of control.

He cleared his throat. "Let's start banking to the right."

"What?"

"We're going to make a turn. You'll steer like you would a car, but do it gradually. Nothing fast. You want the wing on the right side to dip slightly, then we'll raise it back up when we're ready to fly straight again."

Her teeth dug into her lip as she concentrated. "At least there are no road bumps when fake flying."

He grinned. "We can vary the weather conditions, if you'd like."

"No!" She glanced back at him, then saw he was joking. "Don't even say that. I don't want to crash my first time out."

Neither did he. Only his crashing had nothing to do with flying and everything to do with the woman seated next to him. "You're doing great. Now straighten back out."

She turned too fast and the right wing bumped up, then went about twenty degrees above the horizon. A tiny yelp came from her throat as she realized what she'd done. He laid a hand on one of hers and helped her bring the plane back under control.

A half hour later, when she seemed a little more relaxed, he decided to end on a good note. "First step accomplished. You flew a plane. Are you ready to head back to the airport so we can land this thing?"

"Only if you're the one in control."

His body leapt for a second, and he had to remind himself they were talking about landing. Nothing else.

He directed her to do another wide swinging turn—which she aced this time. He upped the cruising speed so the return flight would take less time. "See? You're getting it."

Her mouth quirked to the left. "Yeah. I'm a regular stunt pilot."

He laughed. "Not quite. But could you have pictured yourself doing this a couple of weeks ago?"

"No." She shrugged. "But then again, I couldn't imagine myself ever wanting to take this job a month ago. And it took a dare for me to actually get on the plane."

"A dare?"

She nodded. "When we got to the airport that first morning I chickened out, said I couldn't go through with it. My friend Doug had to double-dare me to get on the plane." She must have noticed his confusion because she continued, "We've been friends a long time. He knows how to push my buttons."

Friendships could turn into something else. Once the thought went through his head, he grimaced. What was with him?

"What?" Molly stared at him.

"Nothing."

"You rolled your eyes." Her lips tightened. "Sorry if that seems a little childish to you, but it did get me on the plane."

If he told her what he was really disgusted at, she'd be out of there faster than you could say *Assume crash positions*—something he wasn't quite ready to do.

He slid his hand across the one gripping the wheel, covering it and holding the plane in position. "Molly, look at me."

When she did, he mustered up all the sincerity he could and let it shine through his gaze. "I promise, I wasn't making fun of you. I think you've done an awesome job today. You proved you could do something you never dreamed possible."

She looked back at him for a few seconds, then the fingers beneath his parted, allowing his fingers to drop between hers. The plane on the screen jiggled for a second at the change in pressure. Unaware of what had happened, she squeezed his hand. "Thank you."

His breath stalled for a second. Did she realize they were almost holding hands? He didn't want to move. Let their little plane run out of gas and plow into the ground for all he cared.

None of this was real. Nothing but the touch of her skin against his. The pressing of flesh to flesh.

He forced himself to ease his fingers from hers. "We should be almost to the airport."

"Okay, tell me what to do." Her eyes went back to the screen.

He saw the runway in the distance. "You're going to overshoot the airport on this pass, so we'll have time to switch places." He glanced at her. "Unless you want to attempt the landing yourself?"

"No. Just…no."

Scooting the foot pedals back under the table, he got ready for the change of positions. He put his hand back on the yoke, well away from where her fingers were this time. "Okay, I've got the wheel. Go ahead and move to your left. I'll take it from here."

She got up, and he changed seats with her, rearranging things and banking into the turn. As he pulled back around, he lined the plane up with the runway, explaining what he was doing, just like he'd done during their takeoff. He made a smooth descent, landing the plane with a minimal flickering of the screen.

"There, all safe and sound." He taxied off the runway, then powered down the plane. Swiveling in his chair, he found her staring at him.

A soft flush had stolen across her cheeks, and her lips were stained a deep pink, either from gnawing on them during the flight or from some other reason. He didn't much care which at the moment. All he knew was that the woman was gorgeous.

She took his breath away, like no other woman ever had.

"You okay?" he asked, half afraid of the answer.

"I think so…" She ran a hand through her short locks, the motion pulling the green shirt taut against her breasts.

His mouth went dry as she met his gaze and slowly lowered her hand. "Do you know what this means?"

Yes, and he could kick himself for bringing her here,

where all he wanted to do was take her to bed and kiss her senseless. He needed to say something, but what?

"No, what does it mean?"

Her eyes glittered, and he prayed those weren't tears of fear. Or anger.

"Blake...I can fly."

CHAPTER EIGHTEEN

HE CUPPED her face with gentle hands. "You can fly."

The memory of those hands running over her body as they'd made love last week rose up in her chest…along with all the other emotions he'd dragged from deep inside her.

This was a man who was fearless, unafraid to pitch in where he was needed, even on Jed's gruesome injury. And of all the daredevil professions he could have chosen—skydiver, deep-sea fisherman, ski instructor—he'd chosen one that not only thrilled him but saved lives. That seemed to go along with being a rescue pilot, his EMS work, and even his combat training. All designed to serve and protect others.

A lump clogged her throat. This man was…

Oh, Lord, was it possible to fall in love this fast?

Her stomach turned over in a way that had nothing to do with the meal she'd just eaten.

It wasn't love. It couldn't be.

It had to be their shared experiences: the danger of Jed's rescue; the trip to Akutan; his patience in showing her how to use the flight program.

The knot in her throat tightened. She needed to give herself a little space to think. Make that a lot of space.

Hard to do with him looking at her like he wanted to devour her.

As if he sensed the tangle of emotions he'd generated inside her, he murmured, "I know we kind of did this backward, and I wouldn't blame you if you decided you wanted no part of any of this. But…"

She bit her lip. "But?"

Letting go of her, he rubbed the back of his hand along his jaw. "If I asked you out, on a date, would you say yes?"

Of all the things he could have said, this was the last thing she'd expected. "*If* you asked me out? Are you?"

"Only if you're planning to say yes."

Her heart lightened, and a shaft of joy went through her. "What happened to that daredevil blood you claimed to have? The stuff that tells you to take a chance?"

"It sometimes deserts me at the worst possible time."

She smiled. "Okay, so ask me and see what happens."

"I know things have been a little awkward ever since… well…last week. But would you go out with me tomorrow? If you're not working, that is."

"I'm not."

"In that case, I'd like to take you to dinner. I know a good place."

"That's because there's *only* one place."

His face changed, going very serious. "Is that a problem?"

"No. I happen to love that particular restaurant."

"I'm glad." He took a deep breath and then got to his feet. "I think I'd better go. If I don't I'm going to ruin all my good intentions."

"What about your flight program?"

He stroked his fingers down her cheek sending a shiver over her. "Don't worry, Molly. I know where you live."

* * *

She stared in the mirror over her dresser, trying to decide if she looked lightly made up or like some sort of freakish clown. She fluffed her hair one last time, then sighed. There was nothing else she could do but wait for Blake and hope for the best.

Hope for the best.

Did she dare? She'd never thought she'd ever date another colleague. Or a pilot. And Blake was both.

Anticipation built slowly within her chest. He'd asked her out. Something that had taken her by surprise.

You know you wanted him to, Molly. Stop trying to fool yourself.

Now, if she could just go slowly, like he seemed to want. Because all *she* wanted to do was rip the man's clothes off and take him right there on her bed.

But she wouldn't. For a daredevil, he sure had a lot of common sense when it came to the important stuff. She needed to trust him.

Samita leapt on top of the dresser, head butting her chin when Molly bent down to her level.

"Silly girl." She hugged the animal close. "You are cute, though."

Setting the cat on the floor, she headed into the living room and sat on the couch, staring at the manila folder that was still on the coffee table. Within it lay her future. Something she didn't want to think about right now.

It was getting dark outside, so she went over to pull down the shades, seeing Blake's car pull into the driveway as she did. Her heart stumbled for a step or two, before taking off at a run. She gave a little wave and slid the shade the rest of the way down, before moving to open the door.

When he came up the walkway, damp hair slicked back from his face and a bouquet of flowers clutched in his right hand, he took her breath away. Why did he have to be so gorgeous? Even his civilized khakis and polo did nothing to detract from the image of raw masculinity. This was a man who could ride out the apocalypse and come through unscathed on the other side.

"Thank you." She somehow managed to get the words out as she took the flowers—a mixture of Gerber daisies and tiny pink roses. They were already arranged in a vase, which was a good thing, since she didn't remember packing one. Hers was probably still at her mother's house, boxed up with the remainder of her things. "Come in while I get my jacket and purse."

Samita trotted into the room and rubbed against his leg, drawing a laugh from Molly. "You do have a way with women."

He bent down to pet the animal, and she finally noticed he hadn't said a word. If anything, his solemnity was a bit unnerving. Maybe he was as jittery as she was.

And she was a mess.

"Are you all right?" she asked, setting the flowers on the coffee table.

"Fine." He stood, his eyes finally meeting hers, sliding over her beige cashmere sweater and chocolate-colored slacks. "You look lovely."

The way he said it put her on alert. "Thank you. You don't look too shabby yourself."

He cupped her face, thumbs sliding along her cheekbones as he'd done when she'd successfully conquered the flight simulator. The intensity in his touch made something flip in her chest. Before she could react, he leaned in, pressing his cheek to hers and inhaling deeply.

Her hands automatically cupped his nape and held him to her.

"You're a special woman." His breath warmed her ear

sending a shiver through her. "You deserve so much out
of life. So much more than I…"

The half-finished phrase and his obvious struggle to
get the words out made her knees quake. Was he getting
ready to drop the ax on whatever had begun between them?

Oh, God.

"If you're having second thoughts, I understand."

He drew a shuddery breath, then his lips trailed along
her jaw. "No second thoughts."

Relief swamped her, changing quickly to need. Drugged
by his touch, she shifted to intercept his mouth as it continued on its path. It worked. His lips slid over hers, and
electricity shot through her, burning from her lips to her
very core. She wanted him. Needed to hold him to her so
he wouldn't drift away. It wasn't rational, but the sudden
press of fear didn't allow for coherent thought.

Her fingers burrowed deeper into his hair, while she
pressed her body to his. The heat coming off him was incredible and every hard inch of him felt ready for business.

Yes, that was more like it.

He pulled back slightly. "Dinner, remember?"

Her lips ached where he'd kissed her, and her heart beat
a wild rhythm inside her chest. "How hungry are you?"

"Very." The passion in his eyes testified to a very different kind of hunger.

The strong pulse of a vein in his neck drew her, and
she lifted on tiptoe to slide her tongue along it, relishing
the clean taste of his skin, the steady beat matching that
of his heart. Reaching the top of his jaw, she nibbled it.
"Let's eat in."

His fingers tangled in her hair, drawing her mouth away
from him. "Hell, woman, I can't think while you're doing
that."

"Mmm. That's the whole idea."

Was she crazy? Maybe. But kissing him was addictive. And like any addict, she craved more.

He held her there, his lips inches away. "If we stay here any longer, you're going to miss a meal. Maybe several."

The slightly threatening edge to his voice made her legs go wobbly and left her eager to see exactly where that warning might lead.

"I'm willing to risk it."

"Molly, hell, I… You're so beautiful." His throat worked as he swallowed. "I want you like I've never wanted any other woman."

Not even his ex-wife. The words hung between them for several seconds before her eyes misted. She needed to affirm the sentiment. "Me, too."

The next several seconds were a blur, and Molly wasn't sure who moved first, but suddenly they were in each other's arms, mouth on mouth, hands searching, exploring. Heartbeats collided as Molly struggled to stay afloat in the onslaught.

"Bed," she managed between breaths.

"Shh."

In the end she needn't have worried. Blake stripped her of her clothes piece by piece, kissing each exposed area as it appeared. Then, holding her hands, he drew her into the bedroom, pushing the door shut to hold the cat at bay. He released her just long enough to shrug out of his own clothes before sitting on the edge of the bed. His rigid flesh was right there. Bare. She wanted to feel it beneath her hand, in her.

Unable to resist, she stroked him, reveling in the strength that lay beneath that velvety soft layer of skin, in the low sound he made in his throat as she slowly tightened her grip. But when she went to kneel before him, he wrapped his hands around her upper arms, stopping her.

"Not this time." His voice came out as a low growl. "I want you up here. With me."

At his urging, she straddled him, taking the package he held in his hand and sheathing him, making sure she drew out the process until he groaned out a protest between clenched teeth.

Still holding him, she lowered onto him until all she felt was him filling her, his hands on her breasts, kneading, coaxing, using them to guide the speed and depth at which she took him in. She was on top, and yet Blake controlled her every move. Her every sensation.

And when she couldn't stand it any longer, she threw her head back and let go, releasing on a long keening note as his hands urged her to take him deeper, harder until, with a muttered oath, he thrust into her one last time, tumbling after her into oblivion.

Molly awoke to find herself sprawled across Blake's chest—still on her bed, his hand at her back holding her to him. Her arm dangled off the side, and when she moved, she was startled to find they hadn't uncoupled.

She gulped. And he was still hard. How long had she been asleep? Turning her head, she found him very much awake, his crooked smile tugging at her heart.

"I wouldn't wiggle around, if I were you."

Her hips gave an experimental pump, the sensation bringing a gasp from her lips. And a low curse from his.

"You mean like this?" she whispered.

He gripped her hips, holding her still while his teeth dug into her shoulder, his tongue lapping over the spot. This time her gasp morphed into a moan.

"That's what you get."

"Do it again."

Blake repeated the action a little to the right, his bite a little rougher this time before suckling the spot. Molly's senses blanked out for a second before roaring back to life.

Maybe there was something to those vampire books after all.

Would a doctor with a dozen hickeys really inspire confidence?

Oh, hell, she thought as he moved to the top of her left breast. *Did she really care?*

Something to the right of Blake's head churned to life, a familiar tune causing them both to freeze. He turned to look as her cellphone burst into song.

"Really?" Blake's brows went up.

"I have to get this, but..." she wiggled her hips again "...hold that thought."

She answered the phone, half laughing as his hands splayed across her bottom, cupping it as he grew even firmer inside her. "H-hello?"

"Dr. McKinna? This is Greta Benson, Darrin's wife."

Her mind drew a blank. Of course, it could be due to the warm tongue lapping along the joint of her shoulder.

The woman's voice came back through. "My husband came in with a spider bite a couple of weeks ago?"

"Oh, oh, yes." She held up a finger to Blake, asking him to give her a minute. She pulled away, gritting her teeth at the sense of emptiness the move brought about. Her robe was thrown across a nearby chair, and she pulled it on. "How can I help you?"

"Well, he hasn't checked his sugar today, and I need you to fuss at him."

Molly rolled her eyes. Oh, the joys of living in a small community. "Okay, put him on." She noted Blake had gotten out of bed and was pulling on his clothes.

Damn.

They hadn't had dinner yet. Maybe he was hungry.

She shook off her irritation at the interruption and focused on her patient.

Blake went into the living room to give Molly some privacy. He wandered around aimlessly for a minute or two before sitting on the sofa and picking up the remote. He'd come over here with a determination he hadn't felt in a long time. He wanted to give this thing with Molly a shot.

She wasn't Sharon. The more he was around her the more he realized she was cut out of very different cloth. She loved the islands, was coming to grips with going up in a plane. They could make this into an actual partnership.

At least he hoped that might be an option. He wanted to do more than just take her on a quick spin around the block—wanted much more than just two nights in her arms.

And damn if that didn't scare him at least as much as flying scared Molly.

He glanced at the remote in his hand, but before he could click the power button, Samita came running from somewhere in the kitchen, leaping toward the coffee table while still several yards away. Instead of landing squarely on the wooden surface, however, her paws hit the manila folder that was lying there, sending them both skidding off the edge.

Blake grinned when the cat made an irritated yowl in the back of her throat and glared at him as if he'd been personally responsible for the mishap, before stalking away with all the dignity she could muster. Papers had slid out of the folder and were strewn halfway across the room. He knelt and began gathering them, the letterhead on the top sheet drawing his attention.

Cleveland Clinic.

His eyes scanned the sheet for a second before realizing it was a letter responding to a request for information.

Dear Dr. McKinna,

Thank you for your interest in Cleveland Clinic. As a facility which offers world-class care, our physicians have access to cutting-edge research and...

He frowned and looked at the next letter in the stack—Duke University Medical Center.

There must be twenty letters from hospitals in major cities all over the United States. The one he was staring at was dated just a week ago. Right around the time they'd slept together for the first time.

Dread rose in his throat.

She was leaving. And she'd never said a word.

A sound made him look up. Molly stood in the doorway, a white terrycloth robe cinched tightly around her waist, her face almost as pale as the garment.

He stood, still holding the letters in his hand. "What are these?"

CHAPTER NINETEEN

SHE'D meant to put the folder away before he arrived, but had forgotten. She looked at his face, but saw nothing there, just a tight jaw and empty eyes.

"My contract with the clinic is only for a year. You knew that."

"If they don't extend it, I assumed you'd return to Alaska Regional—"

"No. I won't go back there." Not with the relationship with her mother the way it was. Not with Gary being there. She'd wanted a clean break, and she'd gotten it—loved the feeling of being her own person at last. If this job fell through, she'd be forced to move somewhere else. Even though everything she'd come to love was here in Unalaska.

Everything she loved…

An ache settled in her chest.

Blake dropped the papers onto the coffee table, not seeming to notice that the top sheet slid back onto the floor.

He moved to stand in front of her, not touching her. "What if I asked you to stay?"

The breath she'd been releasing caught in her throat and guilt flooded her. She couldn't think of an answer that would make sense to herself, much less to him. "I'm a doctor, Blake. What would I do here if I didn't practice medicine?"

"Maybe the clinic could hire you outright."

"They barely have enough funds to cover their month-to-month expenses. I can't justify asking them to pay me on top of that. Sammi is living on a pittance as it is." She stared at him, trying to come up with a solution, but her mind didn't seem to be functioning. She touched his face instead. "We still have almost eleven months, Blake."

"And after that?"

She dropped her hand. "I don't know." She studied the growing anger in his eyes and said quietly, "What if I asked you to give up your job? Give up what you love doing?"

"You wouldn't be the first one." The bitterness in his voice came through.

"Exactly. I don't *want* to be that person. Do you?"

He dragged a hand through his hair and turned away, swearing. He stood there, hands propped on his hips for a long time, ignoring Samita when she rubbed against his leg. When he finally turned back round, the anger was gone. In its place was a sense of quiet resignation. "No. I don't."

The second he stroked the back of his fingers across her jawline, the touch as soft as silk, she knew how this was going to end.

No. Don't do this!

"Goodbye, Molly."

The front door clicked shut behind him as he let himself out. Molly pressed both hands against her mouth to hold back the scream that bubbled up in her throat, the words whispering through her skull instead. *Please don't go*.

Blake leaned against his plane for what seemed like ages. He'd gone to the bar and sat there with two shots of whiskey lined up in front of him. But if he drank, he couldn't fly. And that was what he needed to do right now, fly as far away from Dutch Harbor as he could.

What the hell had he been thinking?

He'd been a fool. Thought he could have the rosy image of love—sitting on a mountainside, watching the sunset day after day.

But he wasn't his parents. There was no happy ending in sight. No retirements in Florida, no growing old together.

He should have learned his lesson the first time around.

Damn if Mark wasn't a whole lot smarter than he was. His friend didn't get involved, didn't hang around long enough to get hurt.

On some level he knew that wasn't exactly true, but his buddy had figured out a system that seemed to work. That was what Blake needed to do as well. Work out a system all of his own. He gave a hard laugh. Until then, flying off into the sunset was the best he could do.

Reaching into the pocket of his jacket, he found the lollipop he'd put there days ago. Looked like he wouldn't need to frame this thing after all. He'd finally learned his lesson. Had finally stopped digging.

Blake walked over to the trashcan and dropped the piece of candy inside. Then he turned toward his plane, climbed inside the cockpit and started his preflight check.

"Molly, slow down. I can barely keep up with you."

Resetting the length of her strides, she wound back her speed until she was jogging beside Sammi again. "Sorry. Where are all those endorphins you promised I'd start feeling?"

In reality, Molly didn't feel anything. A numbness had settled over her when Blake had walked out of her house three weeks ago that nothing had been able to penetrate.

"They…take time to kick in." Sammi's voice sounded strained. Molly had a feeling it was from more than just the running they'd been doing.

"Really? How long?"

The other woman laughed. "I don't know. I haven't actually experienced them myself either."

Molly stopped in her tracks. "Why the hell are we running, then? I could have been sleeping instead." She'd been doing a whole lot of that lately. Sleeping. The one place the numbness didn't matter. Molly knew it wasn't healthy, knew she was wading dangerously close to the line between a normal dose of grief following the end of a relationship and something more serious.

"Because it's good for us? That's what we tell all our patients, anyway." Sammi put her hands on her knees, trying to catch her breath.

Molly hadn't seen Blake since he'd left. Hadn't even tried to. And Sammi, sensing something was seriously wrong, had taken up the slack, going to the EMS department herself whenever they needed something. Blake must have felt the same, because the one medevac she'd done in the interim had been with another pilot. Someone named Ronny. She'd told herself it was for the best, that the frisson of disappointment that had gone through her was normal.

Normal.

Yeah. If she said the word enough times, that had to make it true.

She walked alongside her friend to cool down, hands on her hips. It was still early, and a thick fog had descended during the night. She knew the ocean was to her left, but she couldn't see it. She just heard the crashing of the waves as they beat against the rocks. "Can I ask you something?"

"Mmm."

"What would you do if the clinic closed?"

There was a minute or two of silence, then Sammi stopped and looked at her, water droplets from the mist clinging to her dark hair. "I don't know. Why?"

"Blake asked me to stay. Even if my contract isn't renewed."

The other woman's eyes widened. "He did? What did you say?"

"I told him I couldn't."

"So that's why…"

Molly eyed her. "Why what?"

She shook her head. "Nothing."

"Do you think I did the right thing?"

"I'm sorry, Molly, but I'm the last person you want to take advice from." She pulled her braid over her shoulder, wrapping it around her hand a couple of times. "I will say this, though. The one time I didn't listen to my heart, I made the biggest mistake of my life."

Listen to her heart.

What was it telling her to do?

She had no idea. It was numb like the rest of her. Molly looked deeper, the beating in her chest growing stronger, rising within her. No, it wasn't numb. She'd just tuned out its cries. It was telling her to do something that filled her with fear…and a strange sense of hope.

"I have to go to the EMS station."

Sammi blinked. "Why?"

"I have to tell Blake I'll stay. Somehow. I'll find a way."

"Oh, honey." Her friend's teeth came down on her lip. "I thought you knew."

"Knew what?"

"Blake's not at the department."

The tiny spark of hope sputtered. "What do you mean? Where is he?"

"He flew to Anchorage three weeks ago. No one's heard from him since."

What?

It was unfathomable that he would go away—leave the island. He loved it here. Loved his job.

And now he'd left it all behind.

Because of her.

Oh, God.

Her jaw firmed. No. No more crying. She had to make this right. She *would* make this right.

Somehow.

"Can you watch Samita for a day or two?"

"Sure, but what—?"

Molly turned around and started jogging back the way they'd come. "I have to go to Anchorage."

She'd only made it a few yards when Sammi's voice came through the fog behind her. "Call Mark. He'll take you."

CHAPTER TWENTY

BLAKE pressed "end" on his cellphone and scratched a line through another name on his list. Four down, sixteen or so left to go.

He'd been to hell and back during the three weeks he'd been away from Unalaska, but he'd also done a lot of thinking. He'd been selfish—and foolish—to expect Molly to change her whole life to accommodate his wants and needs.

This morning he'd come to a decision. Yes, he'd given up things for a woman before, but he'd resented each and every instance. Whenever Sharon asked for something more, his root of bitterness had dug in a little deeper. And although he'd appeared to give in to her, he'd always held back part of himself. Not consciously, maybe, but he'd done it just the same. It was possible Sharon had sensed that. Maybe that was why she'd never been satisfied with what he'd offered her.

He swallowed. Molly, on the other hand, hadn't asked him for a damn thing.

And that was exactly what he'd given her. Nothing.

He'd expected her to change her whole life for him. And when she'd blinked, what had he done? He'd stormed out of there without giving her a chance to think, without giving them a chance to come up with a solution.

But that was about to change.

If she'd have him back.

He loved her, dammit. If she felt the same way, they *could* work something out.

He knocked the back of his head against his plane's fuselage a couple of times. If he hadn't already screwed this up completely, that was. His eyes searched out the next number on his list and flipped open his cellphone, turning to face the plane for privacy. The dial tone gave way to ringing once he finished punching in the buttons. He waited a second or two.

"You promised to teach me to fly."

"Hello?" His mind went deadly still when he realized the voice hadn't come from his phone, but from somewhere behind him. He shook the instrument just to make sure, then put it back to his ear. Still ringing.

"Blake."

He knew that voice. Clicking the phone shut, he turned around slowly, expecting to see empty space. Instead, his gaze fell on the person who'd driven him to call every major hospital in the United States looking for another Care Flight job.

Molly. Green eyes shining, something gripped between her fingertips. The apparition took a step forward.

"I'm sorry?" He had to be sure he wasn't trapped in some kind of stress-generated delusion.

"I said, you promised to teach me to fly." Her hand came up, holding a small plastic case. He recognized his computer simulation game. "I should buy my own copy, though, so I don't have to keep borrowing yours."

"You want me to teach you to fly?" He drew a careful breath. "Why?"

She licked her lips, a hint of hesitancy behind her eyes now. "I've decided to stay on the island. Or go back to

Alaska Regional if my contract isn't renewed. Either way, I'll be doing a lot of flying back and forth."

"What about Gary? You said you couldn't go back because of him."

"I know, but I've spent my whole life trying to avoid conflict, trying to keep the peace. First between my parents as I was growing up, then in my relationships as an adult. When I couldn't avoid conflict, I backed away from it. I've never run *toward* anything in my life." She looked at him. "Until now."

A rush of moisture gathered behind his eyes, and he tried to force it back. "Are you sure this is what you want?"

"It is. I love you. I want to be wherever you are, or as close as I can get." A frown appeared. "Unless you don't feel the same?"

"I do." He held up his list with a laugh. "I've racked my brain trying to remember all the hospitals you had in that folder of yours, and I've been calling every single one of them, looking for a job."

"You have? That's just…" She closed the space between them. "I'm sorry, Blake. I should have told you about the letters. It just seemed so far off at the time. And I didn't want to make waves."

"It's okay. All I want to know is one thing. Did you mean what you said?"

"About staying on the island?"

"No. The other thing."

"Yes. I meant it." The merest trace of a pause. "I love you."

"Thank God." He hauled her against him and kissed her with everything he had in him.

When they finally broke apart, she pulled in a couple of quick breaths. "Does that mean what I think it does?"

"Yes, I love you, too."

She leaned against him, her arms going around his waist.

Everything in his world righted itself at her touch.

Unable to resist, he bent down to kiss her again, a melding of mouths and spirits that held the promise of a bright future. "Can you handle living on an island and being involved with a pilot? If not, I can change. Do anything you want me to do."

"All I want you to do is come back to Unalaska with me." She paused, tightening her arms. "When Sammi told me you'd left, I panicked. Wondered if I'd ever see you again."

"Mark knew where I was."

She smiled. "I know. He's the one who helped me find you."

"Remind me to thank him." This time there was no jealousy involved. Only a grateful heart. Maybe there was hope for his friend after all.

"I will, once we get back." She pressed a kiss to the underside of his jaw.

"Sure you don't want to stay here for a few days?"

"I'm sure. I just want to go home."

He stroked his fingers down the side of her face. "Even though it means we have to fly?"

"That's why I brought the program with me." She let go of him long enough to glance at the case she still held in her hand. "I know how much you love your job. I want to be a part of it. That means facing my fears instead of running from them."

His heart threatened to burst out of his chest. "We'll work on it. Whether it takes twelve steps or two thousand, I'll be there."

"That's good, because you never know. If something happens, I might just need to find us a safe place to land."

He smoothed her hair back from her cheeks and leaned in for another kiss. "I think we're already there."

* * * * *

A sneaky peek at next month...

Medical Romance

CAPTIVATING MEDICAL DRAMA—WITH HEART

My wish list for next month's titles...

In stores from 6th July 2012:

❑ Sydney Harbour Hospital: Marco's Temptation
   — Fiona McArthur

& Waking Up With His Runaway Bride — Louisa George

❑ The Legendary Playboy Surgeon

& Falling for Her Impossible Boss — Alison Roberts

❑ Letting Go With Dr Rodriguez — Fiona Lowe

& Dr Tall, Dark...and Dangerous? — Lynne Marshall

Available at WHSmith, Tesco, Asda, Eason, Amazon and Apple

Just can't wait?

Visit us Online

You can buy our books online a month before they hit the shops! **www.millsandboon.co.uk**

0612/03

Special Offers

Every month we put together collections and longer reads written by your favourite authors.

Here are some of next month's highlights— and don't miss our fabulous discount online!

On sale 15th June

On sale 15th June

On sale 6th July

Find out more at
www.millsandboon.co.uk/specialreleases

Visit us Online

0712/ST/MB377

Have Your Say

You've just finished your book. So what did you think?

We'd love to hear your thoughts on our 'Have your say' online panel
www.millsandboon.co.uk/haveyoursay

- 🌹 Easy to use
- 🌹 Short questionnaire
- 🌹 Chance to win Mills & Boon® goodies

Visit us Online

Tell us what you thought of this book now at
www.millsandboon.co.uk/haveyoursay

YOUR_SAY